Nina D'Aleo wrote her first book at age seven (a fantasy adventure about a girl named Tina and her flying horse). Due to most of the book being written with a feather dipped in water, no one else has ever read 'Tina and White Beauty'. Many more dream worlds and illegible books followed. Nina blames early exposure to Middle-earth and Narnia for her general inability to stick to reality. She also blames her parents. And her brother.

Nina has completed degrees in creative writing and psychology. She currently lives in Brisbane, Australia, with her husband, George, their two sons, Josef and Daniel, and two cats Mr Foofy and Gypsy. She spends most of her days playing with toys, saying things like 'share', 'play gentle', and 'let's eat our veggies' and hearing things like 'no', 'no way' and 'NEVER!'. She is also working on more books – including the next book in the Last City series.

Nina's website is www.ninadaleo.com and you can also find her on Twitter and Facebook.

The Last City

Nina D'Aleo

MOMENTUM

First published by Momentum in 2012

This edition published in 2012 by Momentum

Pan Macmillan Australia Pty Ltd

1 Market Street, Sydney 2000

A CIP record for this book is available at the National Library of Australia

The Last City

EPUB format: 9781743340493

Mobi format: 9781743340646

Print on Demand format: 9781743340653

Cover design by Patrick Naoum

Editing by Alexandra Nahlous

Copyediting by Sarah Hazelton

Proofreading by Glenda Downing

To report a typographical error, please email errors@momentumbooks.com.au

Visit www.momentumbooks.com.au to read more about all our books and to buy books online. You will also find features, author interviews and news of any author events.

For Mum,
my inspiration

Though they go mad they shall be sane,
Though they sink through the sea they shall rise again;
Though lovers be lost love shall not;
And death shall have no dominion.

— Dylan Thomas

Part One

1

Aquais, Scorpia City

The last living city

Uneasy forms, made faceless by shadows and nameless by circumstance, drifted through the infinite blackness of Scorpia's underside to Mortimer Road Marketplace, where clusters of dim street lamps lifted the dark to gloom. Silho pushed through the crowds, moving as fast as she could without running, alert to the danger of showing fear in Moris-Isles. She eyed the people around her, but at this hour they were mainly refugees, keeping their heads down and mouths shut, hoping, as she was, to blend with the walls and vanish.

A tremor shook the ground beneath her boots and she stumbled back as a clutch of hefty Tangelan Burrowers, subterraneans from the fallen city Mayhem, broke out through the concrete footpath with giant razor-clawed hands. They went to gather with others of their kind, passing time by betting on gutter-rat races and visiting the communities of shabby prostitute tents. The women for sale loitered around their territories, sizing up passers-by with eyes intent on picking flesh. The winding whistle of a gypsy busker's flute drowned the sounds of unsavoury purchase. The spiralling tunes sent an enchanted stick puppet jigging in circles around market stalls where rainbow-skinned Ohini Fen morphed inanimate junk into useable wares. The Fen auctioned each piece, haggling with irascible, giant-fanged Twitchbaks, snarl-barking in the language of the sabre-breeds.

The musky scents of magics lingered everywhere. Silho checked the crowds for reptilian-faced palace enforcers but saw no red uniforms. In the years since the last purge of dark magics observation of the city's lower levels had become lax, and the fear had faded enough for many people with natural skills to start using them again in public. Yet some still kept to the shadows.

Silho clenched her gloved hands to stop their trembling. A group of pale Androts, machine-breeds born, not made like their lesser robot relatives, brushed past her. Their black barcodes stood out bold on their necks. Silho watched them vanish into the marketplace, intent on doing their masters' bidding and getting out before darkfall. She drew a shaky breath and forced herself to follow, navigating through the maze of stalls and barrage of sellers and beggars, finally breaking out on the other side, on the corner of Whitter Avenue, where a set of stairs disappeared into the black depth of a basement living block.

Pausing on the top step Silho re-checked the paper marked with her scrawled handwriting – *8 Whitter Ave – 6 dead*. Sweat crawled over her skin and she felt eyes on her back. She glanced behind her, but saw only shuttered windows and barred doors. Her boots slid off the first step to the second and then the third onwards until, halfway down, a putrescent stink, unmistakably of death, knocked her back. Swallowing down her fear Silho kept going until she arrived at a corridor drowned in utter darkness. Eyes that gleamed with a nocturnal sheen turned her way and a growling voice spoke in the shared language of Urigin. 'Go back! This is a state crime scene.'

'I'm an Investigator.' Silho fumbled with her ID and dropped it on the ground. She bent to pick it up, and when she straightened the eyes were right in front of her, the heat of the guardian's breath hot on her cheek.

She held up the folder and the man gave a grunt of surprise. 'Oscuri Tracker . . . I haven't seen you before.'

'This is my first day,' Silho admitted.

'Ill-starred,' he growled. 'Follow me.'

The eyes vanished as the guardian turned away from her. Silho blinked into light-form vision and saw the man's body-lights, weakest at the back of his neck, retreating down the corridor. She hurried after him until a glowing sliver appeared up ahead. She blinked back to normal sights. Her guide, a human-breed with the bloodline marks of bear and wolf curling up his arms, stood in front of a partially open door. He nodded and Silho slipped into the room.

A single pale globe, hanging from the ceiling, cast shadow-riddled light over a chaos of objects and flesh. The concrete walls told a horror story in splotches and streaks of blood dried black, a handprint here, a claw mark further up, drag lines and red stains saturating the ground where six corpses lay in varying states of mutilation. Silho noticed the person-sized cage in the shadows of one corner and a chill prickled her skin. A hologramographer stood beside the door capturing images of the scene, and clusters of investigators in grey uniforms took notes and murmured among themselves. Two Oscuri Trackers, with weapon belts like Silho's around their waists, stood over the bodies in the centre of the room. One tracker was an Ohini Fen with golden star bloodline marks, and the other a silver-skinned Ar Antarian, wearing night-vision glasses. His arms and legs up to the elbow and knee were mixed-metal prosthetics and an arachnid-shaped robot perched on his shoulder.

The Fen spoke with a musical Ohini accent. 'Cadavers are at a similar stage of bloating and putrefaction, but the infestation differs. The two in the centre haven't been touched, whereas the others are crawling. It doesn't make sense.'

'And look at the way the stomach wounds of these two seem almost cauterised,' the Ar Antarian pointed out, 'as though the skin was burned to seal the haemorrhaging. With injuries like this, why would anyone bother?'

He looked upwards and Silho followed his line of sight to someone crouching upside down on the roof examining a blood-spatter pattern. After a moment, the man twisted around and dropped down. Silho stared, recognising him from holograms as the notorious Commander Copernicus Kane, a tall human-breed of viperous blood heritage, his eyes midnight black and deeply disturbed, scars marking his face in flowing lines of symmetry and shape like a life story written in his skin. He turned towards Silho and she froze, drawn into the darkness of his stare. After hearing other female soldiers talk about him and seeing his pictures for herself, she was aware her new boss was attractive, but she was completely unprepared for the surge of feelings that rushed through her at the sight of him. She'd never felt anything like it and couldn't look away. Their eyes stayed locked until Silho finally realised that he was actually waiting for her to identify herself. With embarrassment burning her face, she hurried forward and held up her ID, but his eyes didn't shift from her face.

'I'm —' she began.

'Barely out of military school,' the commander said. His voice gave away no thought or emotion, but his eyes said everything. He stepped past her and crouched down beside one of the corpses.

A sickness spiralled from Silho's stomach to her knees, leaving them weak. The Academy Placement Officer had explained to her that Commander Kane had not requested any new recruits. He never did. He had only ever selected his own people from the highly experienced and elite. However, due to the growing number of unsolved homicides and abductions, the United Regiment had assigned her without his consent to the Oscuri Trackers, a special operations unit with the primary purpose of hunting the most dangerous serial killers. She hadn't expected a friendly welcome, given her inexperience and age. At twenty-one she was the youngest of the trackers by several year cycles and younger than the commander by almost ten; still, she felt his animosity like a punch. Silho blinked stinging eyes and tried to focus on the other two trackers standing in front of her. The Ar Antarian shifted uncomfortably and cleared his throat, and she realised she was still holding up her ID. Sinking into humiliation, she lowered it.

The Ohini Fen smirked, contempt in her eyes. She pushed a bag of empty capped test tubes into Silho's hands and said, 'We need fluid samples – bagged, tagged and in your possession until we get back to Headquarters. Think you can handle it?'

Silho nodded.

'Let's hope so.' The Fen shoved past her and began to speak with the hologramographer.

Silho immediately searched her weapon belt for any type of swab or scraping tool, but found nothing. Her face burned. 'I didn't know trackers took samples. I didn't bring any instruments,' she tried to explain to the Ar Antarian, who stood watching her from behind his night-vision glasses. The grey tint disguised the colour of his eyes.

'Don't worry,' he said, an educated, upper-level accent edging his softly spoken words. He took a scalpel from his belt and handed it to her. 'You're right, we're not supposed to collect evidence, but . . .' he glanced over at the commander, engaged in a controlled argument with one of the forensic specialists, 'the commander likes to run his own tests. He has his own way of doing things – everything – as you've no doubt heard.'

'Yes,' Silho said. The commander was a man with a million rumours chasing his name.

'You're Silho, right?' the Ar Antarian asked. 'I'm Jude. The Fen is Diega and this is SevenM.' He pointed to the arachnid robot on his shoulder. Red lights gleamed behind his many mirrored eyes. 'It's good to have you on board. Let us know if you need a hand.' He gave her a quick smile and walked across the room to join the commander.

Silho moved from one corpse to another taking samples and silently noting the condition of the bodies. Four were marked with signs of torture, hands bound behind their backs, with ropes cutting into the flesh. The other two in the centre were completely hollowed out, their insides missing. After collecting the final sample, Silho crouched in one corner, pretending to be organising the vials while trying to clear her mind and slow her heartbeat. During childhood and military training she had seen many dead bodies, but none so gruesome. She could almost hear the echo of their screams.

A powerful craving to touch the closest wall hit unexpectedly and threatened to overwhelm her. She closed her eyes and tried to fight it.

She couldn't believe this was happening – she'd taken her medication that morning. Yet the pull was relentless and she was helpless to stop it. Silho watched on, detached, as she flipped back the cap of one of her gloves and pressed a finger to the wall. Instantly, she felt a sensation of slipping underwater.

Through a mind not quite asleep, yet not awake, pictures, memories, flirted with focus, clear/unclear, teasing the senses. In this disquieting state of lukewarm awareness, the walls, darkened with shifting dusk-light shadows, became blending shapes, indistinct, unstable. They stirred, whispered, hesitant to show the secrets they stored behind thin paper faces. An image came clear. A concrete room, four people tied to chairs, two standing over them, the scream of the word 'Morsmalus'. Time flickered into explosions of red and objects whirring around the room. Six lay dead and two gruesome creatures with sunken, baleful eyes fled the room, leaving a tall spectral-breed standing alone with blood on her hands. The grey figure staggered and fell to her knees, her hand coming down on something. She picked up the object and looked at it under the light – a ring. The sound of voices startled her and she dropped it. The golden band rolled into a fissure in the wall and the spectral contorted her body to vanish into the floor.

Silho resurfaced from the trance and felt immediately ill. She stared at the wall in front of her, terrified to turn around. She was sure everyone would have seen what she just did, that they'd be watching her, condemning her as unnatural. Bracing herself, she glanced over her shoulder. All the investigators were busy with their own work and Copernicus Kane and the two trackers stood on the other side of the room with their backs to her. Her eyes shifted from them to the place where the ring had rolled into the wall. Silho stood, leaving the bag of vials on the ground, and made a casual path towards it. Once there she crouched down and used the scalpel Jude had given her to drag out the band. It was a man's ring inscribed with a horned Galley rhinoceros – the family crest of Christy Shawe, the human-breed King of the Gangland.

A shadow fell over her and Silho looked up into the commander's face. His eyes were fixed on the ring. Before she could say anything he took it from her and examined it. Jude and Diega, standing beside him, exchanged a glance.

'Where did you find this?' the commander demanded, turning the metal band over in his hands.

'In the wall,' Silho responded, her voice barely a whisper.

'How did you know it was there?' Copernicus' stare lifted from the object and locked onto Silho's eyes.

She searched for something to say, but her thoughts stalled and blanked out. If the rumours were true, he always knew when someone was lying.

'Caught the light, maybe?' Jude suggested. The Ar Antarian checked his chronograph and said, 'Almost darkfall in the upper levels . . .'

'Shawe will be at the breakwall,' Diega finished for him. The massive wall dividing the gangland from the rest of the city was a known hangout of the gangster king.

Copernicus slipped the ring into his pocket and moved with silent, seamless steps to the door. The other trackers hurried to follow. They grabbed up their equipment and left the room without a backward glance. Silho headed after them, but paused in the doorway to follow her training and take a final overall look at the scene. Before she could, a face with haunted grey eyes pressed out of the far wall – the spectral-breed from her vision. The second it appeared, it vanished. Silho stared, her nerves buzzing.

'See something?' a voice spoke beside her ear. She looked up into the yellow eyes of the hologramographer. After a moment, she shook her head. 'No, nothing.'

Silho backed out and hurried through the corridor, past the gleaming gaze of the guardian and up the stairs. She came out onto the street as Diega took a silver coin from her pocket and threw it upwards. The Fen called the word *xpel* and the coin morphed, stretching wider and wider, shaping into an open-topped transflyer – the *Ory-4*. Diega climbed into the pilot's seat, the commander beside her and Jude in the back. Silho slipped in with the Ar Antarian, noticing the engine bay at the rear of the craft was empty. Jude saw her expression and a faint smile touched his lips. He nodded to Diega and said wryly, 'She's an electrosmith of rare and frightening talent. Better strap yourself in.'

During training, Silho had learnt about the exceptionally skilled individuals that could channel power from the planet's magnetic field through receptors in their hair and use it to animate anything electrical, but she'd never actually met one.

Using only this skill to control the craft, Diega tilted the flyer almost vertical and hurtled them upwards at an impossible speed.

2

The Matadori Desert was a graveyard, a place of silenced screams and unburied dead consumed by the carnivorous suns. Only the insane or outcast kept company with the corpses; all others fled the predatory shadows and the slimy sweat of their own fear. For Ev'r Keets, the Matadori was her homecoming. Here she was born, here she would die. In walking her life-path, she had ended up in the same place where she had begun and now could only conclude that she had been lost all along. Yet this was no surprise. She had learnt long ago that control was nothing but fool's gold, life nothing but a blink away from death.

Sand-spiked wind dragged at her cloak, stinging her skin. Her eyes wept and the desert howled, a soulless, wild keening, begging her to stop, begging her to listen. Ev'r fought against it, leaning into the fury until she finally smashed through to the quiet eye of the storm. Here she knelt and slid the rucksack off her back, but left it fastened. She didn't need her equipment to know that she had arrived – returned, though she had once sworn never to set foot in this place again. The light of day had begun to grey as the darkness started to rise. A stirring in the distance warned that the desert freaks had picked up her scent – warm flesh for the eating.

'Not tonight,' she murmured.

Ev'r slid her machete from its sheath – the black blade by the name of Morsus Ictus. Though it was forged an eternity ago, the handle fit her hand perfectly, as though made just for her. Ev'r ran her fingertips along the metal, over familiar notches and etchings. The weapon hummed, alive to her touch. How long would it be before she had to turn the blade on herself? Was it too much to hope for to just lie down in the midnight desert and die while she slept? Perhaps so. She wanted to live too much to go quietly.

Ev'r reached into her pocket and dragged out the vial of green antidote – liquid time machine. For a while, the shaman-made medicine had been worth its immense cost and turned back her body's changes, but now, just like all the others before it, its potency was fading. The slight relief it gave her from her affliction no longer justified enduring its side effects. There was no cure for a Ravien bite, and this antidote was the absolute last type of restorative potion produced by any physician or shaman in Aquais. It was only a matter of time now before the changes took over. It was this knowledge that had driven her here, to the edge of desperation, throwing off her fear like unwanted baggage in a final attempt to survive, though she knew that there was no hope. She was the walking dead.

Ev'r clenched the vial in one hand, toying with the idea of hurling it into the desert. Just one day without vomiting, without itching and blistering, without earth-shivering dizziness and sweating rivers. Just one day, before the final day. The decision tore her one way and then the other, to the point where her hand raised, ready to throw, but then it dropped. She couldn't bring herself to give it up. Instead she tipped the antidote down her throat. Instantly she coughed and gagged. Burning pins and needles spread out from her stomach and a tidal wave of sickness broke over her, making her collapse to one side and vomit until there was nothing left inside her. Ev'r rolled onto her back and the earth rocked around her like a storm-struck ship. Grabbing handfuls of cooling sand, she let the grains slip gradually between her fingers until the sickness lessened and she could sit up.

Ev'r dragged her bag in front of her and unzipped it, laying flat the tools of her trade – electrifier, blades, nuclear grenade, light-blaster, hackaxe, rope – all equally useless against the magics she'd have to confront beneath the sand. A strangled, disbelieving laugh escaped her, and for a moment her courage faltered in a way it hadn't since she was a child, lost and alone in this desolation: an outcast, torn apart by desert freaks. That day, the devil had been her saviour.

The Mocking Witch of O'Tenery Asylum had taken her in, along with the other throwaways, runaways and screeching crazies. She saw herself in her mind, walking silent as a shadow through the asylum building, the labyrinth of rooms haunted and lurking in a permanent state of semi-darkness. Low ceilings pressed lower and constricting walls crept closer until she felt as though she was sliding on her belly, suffocating in the rancid air of rotting waste and a thousand unwashed bodies. Eyes peered at her from behind rusted bars that were now no more than grisly reminders. Scorpia's government, the Standard, had long since abandoned the derelict building and its broken wards. Now only their minds kept them prisoner, and Ev'r knew the truth better than anyone: there was no escaping yourself, no matter how far or fast you ran.

As she walked through the building, she passed many rooms and places where the Mocking Witch had shown her terrors that had aged her mind ten years for every day, and taught her with a cruel sort of kindness to live a life in opposition to domination, caged in body but never in mind. She'd taught her to fly. It was the second biggest mistake the witch ever made. Ev'r's mind dragged her through the hallways of her memories to the great black stone door engraved with the runes of Ignatius, translating to 'Thou Shalt Not Enter'. It was the witch's quarters. Shadows shuffled beneath the door. Ev'r's thoughts ventured towards them, then scurried back in terror at what they saw.

Ev'r jolted into the present. She was so distant from that girl of the past that she barely recognised her or her pain and fear. That person, that child, was dead. She had died in a cave in the Lava Diavol Mountains, leaving just a stone other, with a heart too hard to break. Ev'r gathered up her weapons and stowed them in her bag, all except her electrifier and the Morsus Ictus, which she slid into sheaths at her hip. Drops of acid rain sizzled into her skin, but she ignored the ravenous downpour, shutting her eyes and preparing her mind to sink into the Murk, the grey drift behind the mask of reality. Here, in the birthplace of magics, time, space and distance held no power and physics and chemistry were forgotten. Ev'r pulled her scarf up over her nose, her night-vision glasses down over her face and hauled her bag onto her shoulders. She released one long breath with whispered words embedded in the rise and fall of the life-air. Then she was slipping backward, falling in slow motion, but she didn't fight it. The darkness around her greyed and the land and sky lost their definition, distorting and bending, blending together. Her body became a flowing mist; once the sensations stopped she prepared herself to travel down deep into the sand, where the asylum now lay buried – some would say buried alive.

Before she could begin sinking through the sand, a sound echoed out into the Murk, a word that froze her limbs and stopped her heart. Ev'r sucked in a breath and held it, waiting. *Couldn't be – surely not.* The word sounded again and Ev'r bit her lip. Instead of travelling down, she flew out, moving through the Murk towards the sound. She glided across the Matadori Desert with incredible speed, shrinking distance in her stride, until movement ahead halted her flow. Forms shifted the greyness ahead of her. It wasn't unusual for others with learnt skill to use the Murk, but the shapes Ev'r saw, drifting in and out of focus, made her body tremble with a primal terror that she couldn't hold back. What she saw was impossible, but undeniable.

They had risen.

A face with terrible, sunken eyes blurred by the mist turned her way. A mouth opened and she smelt a burning stench. Gasping, Ev'r pushed away with all her strength, hurtling backward through the Murk, just barely avoiding the death-curse that was thrown at her by the creature. She tumbled out of control and heard herself shouting the words of release. They catapulted her into reality and she skimmed along the ground like a skipping stone before smashing against something solid that brought her to a dead stop. She struggled to breathe, her dazed mind spinning madly. After a moment's recovery, panic pushed her to move. With her stomach churning, Ev'r dragged herself to her feet.

A voice called out of the darkness in front of her, 'United Regiment – identify yourself.'

Ev'r's head snapped up and she saw the form of a soldier. She grabbed for her electrifier holstered at her side, but before her fingers found the weapon, the soldier drew his stunner and fired. Ev'r had a second to marvel at the speed of his hands, a moment to feel the sting of rage and horror at capture – and then she was thrown backwards into darkness.

3

Copernicus Kane stood at the top of the Greenway breakwall, the immense structure of fortified stone that quartered off the gangland from the rest of Scorpia. Gangster-built over generations, it crept upwards from the age-blackened rock of its first foundations to the newest-laid bricks that were red and fresh and reached all the way through 512 of the 997 living levels of Scorpia. In real terms, the gangster nation laid claim to a very small part of the city, yet their push to expand outwards and upwards was relentless and bloody.

Copernicus crossed the viewing platform built above the breakwall. He looked out, following the line of the wall as it intersected the 512th level, Ayar, and continued on and down as far as he could see. The levels of the city had been constructed to step out from each other like a mammoth staircase, all the way down to Rim, where the sunlit levels ended and the perennial darkness of the subterranean levels began. In the underside, it was disturbingly easy to forget the existence of the suns, but here in the upper levels, Copernicus could feel the memory of the day's heat radiating from the rock wall below. In the open sky above, the last of the sunset's peach-and-wine red was fading to darkness, turning the towering structures of the upper levels into a galaxy of lights, glittering like neon stars. At this time of year, known as noctus-renium, the hours of night doubled those of day, and the nocturnal breeds celebrated with extended festivals. Copernicus breathed in, sensing the people moving in the streets around them. He memorised the identity of each by the vibration of their footfalls, their body-heat signature, the shape of their thoughts. He widened the scope of his mind outwards to the crafts and smaller domestic transflyers speeding everywhere, across, over, up and down the buildings in buzzing lines of light. Public transporters circled the perimeter of the city, bypassing the outer-Rim towns full of Blue-Ten addicts, scullion-gypsy outlaws and masses of renegade Androts, rejects from an already outcast race. Where the last wasteland shanty ended, the Matadori Desert began. Copernicus watched the darkness spreading across this dead land, where the suns did not fall, the night rose and smothered them – starless, freezing and silent, but for the lunatic howls of the cannibal masses and slither of Skithers swimming through the sand. Beyond the Matadori, the Boundary Wall separated civilisation from the unknown Brine, a place of damaged evolution, where logic was meaningless and hope absurd. Of those who had ventured beyond the boundary, none had ever returned. This night, a fury of storm clouds lurked behind the night darkness, and the air bit with the chemical tinge of acid rain – and with something deeply wrong.

Copernicus turned the ring from the crime scene over in his pocket, his thoughts crowded by dead faces. In the past few months the city had seen an overwhelming increase of unexplainable murders and vanishings, bringing disorganisation and unpredictability to a world he usually found highly predictable. Christy Shawe had been his prime suspect, but this was the first and only piece of evidence linking the so-called King of the Gangland to the crimes. This ring had belonged to Christy's father, Hamish 'Ironfist' Shawe, and been passed down to Christy when he died. Knowing Shawe the way he did, Copernicus understood that surprise confrontation was the best chance of getting the gangster to slip up. So now they had to wait.

The commander straightened his back, more scar than skin, and glanced at the new recruit Headquarters had sent him. Silho Brabel stood motionless, facing the darkness, looking upon it without expression, though her eyes held the searching, injured stare of a person who has seen horrors young.

From some angles she appeared familiar to him, though he couldn't place why. An intricate pattern spread across half her neck and chest. To Copernicus it was strangely incomplete, as though someone had started to paint a thousand tiny pictures on her skin and stopped suddenly, leaving her forever unfinished. Bandages wrapped around her arms, concealing her bloodline marks and genetic heritage. This kind of concealment was not uncommon for military personnel in dangerous positions wanting to maintain some level of anonymity.

According to Silho's military file, her parents, now deceased, had been human-breeds of mixed descent, part-Ivory Condor, part-Nightcat. Both had been middle-class, with normative academic and social achievements and no criminal records. Yet something about Silho denied such an average background. In her military exams, she had scored far higher than any other new recruit he'd ever heard of, even smashing Jude's records. Brilliance in training, however, did not always equate to brilliance in the field. Other factors always came into play, such as personality. This was why Copernicus had always recruited his own soldiers. Brabel's nervousness and social ill-ease had hindered her significantly at the crime scene, and cast doubt on the actual depth of her knowledge and skills. It troubled him that Silho may not be psychologically ready for this level of work, but it troubled him even more that his actual sense of her from her body-heat and thought patterns had been extremely mixed. He found most people straightforward to read, but she was a maze of complex lines and conflicting flares. This suggested deception, though not necessarily criminal, perhaps just personal. In any case it was abundantly clear to him that Silho was uncommon, an unknown island in a sea of sameness, her surface just a suggestion of what lay hidden underneath. And he intended to find out whatever she was hiding.

'He's coming.' Jude's voice broke into Copernicus' thoughts.

'How close?' the commander asked.

Jude blinked, seeing through the eyes of his arachnid robot, SevenM, whom he had sent out to search for Shawe.

'Two flights down and climbing, with a company of three.'

As expected, Shawe and his companions were using the steps, carved in the gangland side of the breakwall, to access the platform.

'Let them come up all the way, then put them down. I'll deal with Shawe,' Copernicus instructed Diega and Jude, then looked at Silho. 'You just stand back there and observe.' He indicated a building behind the platform. She nodded and backed up.

'One flight and they're here,' Jude said. He and Diega moved to separate spots out of sight of the top of the steps. Copernicus sank back into the shadows.

Slurred voices, heavy with the Greenway accent, grew louder, until Christy Shawe appeared at the top of the wall. The musclebound fighter stomped across the platform to survey his kingdom as he always did at nightfall. No traces of anxiety or uncertainty pinched Shawe's scarred face, dominated by a large, repeatedly broken nose. His knuckles were white and thick with scars, and his red hair shaved down to skin too tough for blades to pierce. Shawe was a walking armoured tank. A stink emitted from the gangster that Copernicus could only describe as pub stench – unwashed armpits and old alcohol.

As Shawe's companions moved to follow their boss, Jude and Diega leapt out, threw them down and drew weapons on them. Copernicus lashed out with viperous stealth and grabbed Shawe's arm, twisting it behind his back. The gangster yelled and bucked with enormous strength. They struggled for a moment before Copernicus slammed him into the wall close to where Silho stood. Instead of leaping aside, she got in the way. Shawe threw a punch with his free arm and clipped the side of her head, knocking her to the ground. He shook off Copernicus and spun around with his fists up – to stare down the barrel of Copernicus' electrifier.

Shawe lowered his hands and cursed. 'What the trutt do you want, you podsucking gadfly?'

Copernicus replied with quiet control, 'Just a word.'

'Didn't know the carnival was in town,' one of Shawe's men sneered. Diega booted him in the gut and he doubled over, cursing her.

'A word about what?' Shawe spat, red-faced and staggering drunk.

Taking the ring out of his pocket Copernicus held it up in front of Shawe's eyes. To his disappointment, he didn't see the realisation and guilt he was hoping to find in the gangster's expression, just confusion.

'Where did you get that?' Shawe asked, a sober change in his tone.

'Crime scene in Moris-Isles. Six tortured and killed. Two of them gangsters from Kelly's Crew – rivals of yours.'

'They're rivals alright,' Shawe admitted, 'but I haven't set foot in that hole in five year-cycles at least. Why would I?'

'If you weren't involved, then how did this get there?' Copernicus turned the ring over in his hand.

Shawe said nothing. The commander realised it was because he didn't know, and that the gangster was feeling something else, something foreign to him that he hated – worry.

Copernicus pushed the ring back into his pocket and Shawe's eyes darted up to his.

'Give that here,' he demanded and held out his hand. He was wearing, on his middle finger, an identical ring to the one they had found.

'This is evidence,' Copernicus said, hiding his confusion. During his time in the gangs, he had only ever seen one ring of this type in Ironfist Shawe's possession. He'd believed it was unique, but obviously not. He gestured with his electrifier. 'Get lost – for now.'

Shawe stared at him, lips snarling. He stepped forward and purposely pressed his chest against the tip of the electrifier. He spoke so only Copernicus could hear. 'I was the one who broke you out of your grave and I'm going to be the one who puts you back under – I swear it.'

The threat, well worn over the years, barely caused a ripple in Copernicus' flowing stream of thought. If Shawe had his ring then whose was this one? He gestured to his trackers to release Shawe's men. They immediately started to retaliate, but the gangster king barked, 'Leave it!' He spat at Copernicus' feet then hurried back to the steps with a speed that suggested an agenda, his men close behind.

The shadows shifted and Jude's robot, SevenM, scurried out from its hiding place and up the soldier's body to perch on his shoulder. Copernicus disarmed his electrifier and pushed it back into its holster. He walked with the others to where Silho was sitting holding her head.

'A piece of advice,' Diega snapped at the new recruit. 'Next time someone tries to hit you – move.'

'He wasn't trying to hit me.' Silho spoke with restraint, but Copernicus could see the angry flares of her body-heat. 'He was trying to hit Commander Kane.'

'And you thought you could – what? – save him?' Diega sneered.

'I thought I could assist my commanding officer.'

Diega gave a nasty laugh, 'Well done.'

'Go easy. It's her first day.' Jude intervened in the escalating dispute. He offered Silho his hand and helped her stand. She swayed unsteadily on her feet and almost fell. Red blood trickled down the side of her face.

'I don't believe this!' Diega snarled. 'Look at her! She can't even follow the simplest instructions and now she can hardly stand. She's a liability.'

'Are you fit for duty?' Copernicus asked her, interested if she would tell him the truth.

She nodded and he saw the lie, though it was well hidden.

'She's fine,' Jude said. 'I'll patch her up. She'll be okay.'

Diega gave him a bad look and Copernicus sensed her body-heat flare with jealousy. Frustration twisted inside him. A fractured team was the last thing he needed right now.

His communicator buzzed and he lifted it from his belt and read the message from Headquarters: *Big news, big catch, first name starts with E, second name starts with K. No kidding – Eli.*

The commander re-read the message and a rare smile touched his lips.

4

Eli opened the bathroom door the slightest fraction and peeked out. Across and down the corridor, United Regiment soldiers of all ranks and races massed outside the locked door of the interrogation rooms, where he had, approximately a quarter of an hour ago, placed his prisoner – or more accurately, secured his prisoner with several spans of the anti-dissipation, anti-telekinesis, anti-contortionist, anti-camouflage, anti-just-about-everything chains, which he had designed and produced some months earlier. He had secured the prisoner, double-checked the securing, triple- and quadruple-checked the securing, then walked with a nonchalant swagger out into the corridor, where already his colleagues were gathering. He'd locked the door behind him. He'd brushed away questions with a casual wave of his hand and a *tut-tut, you know better, I have to wait for the boss, if you'll excuse me*, walked with the same swagger to the men's bathroom, entered, closed the door with a smile and wave at the crowd – then dashed to the toilet and lost his dinner and, quite possibly, everything he'd ever eaten, including the entire set of playing cards he'd downed on a dare on his first day of school.

Eli swallowed and winced as foul, acidic bile burned his throat. Sweat boiled on his upper lip and dribbled in tickling streams down both sides of his body and down his back, making his unhappily bound, cramped wings damp and sticky. Shrugging his shoulders back several times, he blinked away the dizzy specks of light dancing across his eyes. The crowd outside the interrogation area was

21

growing by the second. Commanders, guardians and new recruits alike jostled each other for a place in front of the small, circular, frosted-glass window of the door to the interrogation rooms. It seemed everyone in Headquarters was desperate for a glance, however brief and frosty, at the military's newest prisoner. Eli had left the thoroughly bound figure lying face down and unmoving, making it impossible for anyone to tell if the rumours, spreading like a virus, were true – if this really was the legendary treasure hunter, Ev'r Keets, risen from the dead.

He had captured Keets in a moment of pure luck when the fugitive had literally fallen at his feet while he was installing some equipment in an outpost in the Matadori – equipment with the express purpose of tracking Keets. Now he found himself teetering somewhere between shock and horror that he, Eli Anklebiter, had not only managed to survive the encounter, but had also brought Keets in – all by himself. He couldn't decide whether to laugh or cry and found himself doing both, giggling hysterically with tears running down his face. Feeling a faint coming on he applied the usual remedy for his condition, counting back from forty-six, forty-five, forty-three, forty-two, forty-one, forty . . . His pet otter, Nelly, squirmed in his pocket and he said, 'I know. We have to go back. We can't put it off.'

His gran'ma had always said, 'Don't put off to tomorrow what you can do today', yet the grandness of her philosophy was some-what spoiled by her diet and exercise plan to lose substantial girth, which was always going to start tomorrow.

His nerves jolted as his communicator buzzed at his hip. He grabbed it up to his ear.

'Yes, boss.'

The commander's voice, precise like a razor cut, demanded, 'Where is she?'

'Interrogation cells. I bound her with the new chains. So far so good – I'm assuming.'

'You're assuming?' the commander asked. 'Where are you?'

'Ah . . .' Eli glanced around at the dingy Headquarters' bathroom. 'I'm . . . preparing her file.' A loud and unmistakable toilet flush resounded from one of the cubicles. Eli coughed, hoping the commander hadn't heard, but knowing well that he had. The commander didn't miss anything.

'Are you near?' Eli asked.

'Just landed. See you in a minute. End.' The line went dead.

Eli burst out giggling and slapped a hand over his mouth. He spoke sternly to himself. 'Get control, don't embarrass yourself. Just be normal – *be normal*. Okay, I'm ready, we're ready – brace yourself, girl.' He tapped the otter in his pocket. 'Let's go on one, two and three.'

Sucking in a deep breath, he shoved open the bathroom door and stepped into the corridor. He managed to make it halfway to the crowd before being spotted. Then people descended on him from all angles.

'Anklebiter!' A sub-commander named Lucian from the Narcotics Squad grabbed him around the shoulders and squeezed him close with considerable enthusiasm. Eli's neck squelched against the man's very damp armpit. 'Is it her? Is it Keets?'

Mo Modalias (Mo-Mo) from the Transflyer and Traffics unit snatched him away and said, 'Eli, buddy, what's the word? We're dying here.'

Kev T-bor from Public Nuisance was next in line, grabbing him by the shirt and huffing disastrous moonshine halitosis into his face. 'Little Kelli saw you bring her in!'

'Eli!' Tye and Tie McManus, the Siamese twins from Forgery, locked onto either side of his trousers and in their eagerness lifted him right off the ground. He winced as his underwear pulled uncomfortably upwards. Spittle sprayed his face from left and right. He gritted his teeth and endured, silently cursing his God, who had blessed him with an impossibly fast intellect only to turn around and leave him with the muscles and body span of an underdeveloped imp-breed girl, along with elephantine ears, episodic blackouts and a voice just slightly too high to ever command any respect. That was the imp-breed God – big on humility and ironic humour. A real prick, though he wasn't entirely to blame.

Eli was keeping his mouth shut, not just because he couldn't comment until the commander arrived, but because these situations of mass attention, or any kind of nervousness, usually brought out the worst in him – the worst being the profusion of speech, sound and movement defects for which he could thank his parents. Years of corrective therapy, while equipping him with skills to communicate and act almost normally, had never changed the fact that he was the by-product of an illegal love breed between a Golgi Glee and a Bracken Greer – both imp-breeds, but of non-compatible blood types. In short, he was a chromosomal cocktail for uncontrollable misbehaviour.

His parents, the geniuses that they were, had decided to defy both law and science. They got together, then fell apart and proceeded to dump him – illegitimate and a compulsive liar and kleptomaniac – on his grandmother's front steps. There was a reason they hadn't waited for her to open the door after they rang the bell, the same reason why the word *smother* primarily consists of the word *mother*. His gran'ma was big, loud, interfering and mean in the nicest possible grandmotherly way. Being weird with a crazy gran'ma at his side day in and day out had not made his childhood and adolescence any easier, to say the least.

Eli finally made it through the crowd. He brushed his hand over the sensor on the doors and they opened from the centre. From the doorway, he turned to face his gabbling audience. They strained to see around him into the room. Someone at the back was even jumping up and down trying to get a look.

'Thank you, thank you,' Eli said. 'Anyone else wanting to touch my perfectly sculpted body can make an appointment.'

The crowd laughed the way people always did at all his comments, no matter how unfunny they were. He guessed it was a perception thing – he looked funny, he talked funny, so he must be funny. He gave them a final wave and stepped backwards into the interrogation office. The soundproof panels closed shut behind him. He dropped his arms, straightened his shirt, checked Nelly was alright and exhaled.

'Tough crowd out there,' a gravelly voice sniggered.

He turned to the two guardians on watch duty in the interrogation room entrance. The guardian who had spoken was a Twitchbak, a sabre-breed with long yellow fangs and spiky dark hair that ran in a long strip over his head and down the length of his back. His name was Renoir Snaggles and he smelt so strongly canine that Eli's eyes watered every time he talked to him. Renoir had the usual cutting humour of a Twitchbak, which was often mistaken as sarcastic spite, but he was really a friendly guy and, above all, staunchly dedicated to the Regiment and his job. The other guardian, Renoir's partner, was Charles 'Tiny' Twigs, an immensely tall and wide soldier, part human-breed, part gargantuan-breed. He stood, huge, dumb and gentle, blinking at Eli with three childlike eyes. Eli could not imagine, even with his untameable mind, what feats of acrobatic daring and sheer stupidity Tiny's human-breed father must have performed to impregnate the surly, huge and hideous gargantuan-breed woman whom Tiny called mother.

'*Lai Lai*, boys,' Eli responded with the imp-breed version of the Urigin phrase 'Come on now'. 'You try being funny with your underpants riding halfway up to your neck.'

'I don't wear underpants,' the Twitchbak confessed and Eli shuddered.

'That's truly disturbing.'

Renoir gave a fangy grin and, after several moments of computing, Tiny boomed with laughter.

Eli glanced up from them to the holo-screen showing images of the interrogation cells, which were further down the corridor behind where the two guardians stood. His smile disappeared and something flip-flopped inside his gut. Ev'r Keets was well and truly up, standing – vicious, striking and perpetually unimpressed – in one corner of her cell. She was staring straight into the robotic spyer monitoring her – straight into Eli's eyes. Being a one-way-spyer, the theory was he could see her and she couldn't see him, but he was pretty sure the theory didn't apply to Keets. Not many did. She was, to utilise a word used many times to describe him, *weird*, but she was also, to his immense relief, still definitely chained up.

'She tried to bribe *us*,' Renoir told him. 'Said if we let her go, she'd give us the gold on her arms.'

Eli studied the bands of gold the fugitive wore up and down both her arms. From his study of ancient history, he guessed they were from the Forego Era and worth more than he could say without stuttering. They wholly concealed Keets' bloodline marks – the twisted mass of dagger-like shapes of the Ohavor, the Blackwater Wolf family. During their many year-cycles hunting the fugitive, the commander had discovered that Ev'r Keets had been born Zingara Ohavor into a filthy poor scullion-gypsy family in the outcast village of Ont. Her tribe was large, violent, dirty and generally criminal.

'We told her what she can do with her blood money,' Renoir snarled.

'We told her,' Tiny echoed in his deep tones. 'It's blood money, that.'

Eli stared at the image of the prisoner and saw her full pale lips form one word. Eli gulped. He didn't need his lip-reading skills to know what she had said – *Snack-size*. Keets had given him this unfortunate nickname the third time the commander had arrested her, only for her to be released by the courts on insufficient evidence. Eli had ridden along in the transflyer transporting Keets to the courthouse, and she'd spoken to him of a time in history when just giants, imps and human-breeds had existed on Aquais. She had said the humans were a meal to the giants, but the imps were only snack-size. The trackers had continued to arrest Keets with the same outcome until finally, the last time they'd brought her in, during the year-cycle of the Frost, a judge too old to be scared of death, too cunning to be charmed and too rich to be bought, had decided to make the charges stick. Keets had escaped just after being sentenced to death. It had been widely believed that she had been killed in the ensuing high-speed chase into the desert. The commander had never bought it and Eli hadn't either.

The secondary entrance to the interrogation area slid open. The commander stood in the doorway, with Diega and Jude behind him. The guardians snapped to attention and each slapped an arm across his chest to salute their superior officer.

The commander entered the room, his steps soundless on the stone floor. He acknowledged Eli with a nod, then spoke to the guardians.

'Stand down,' he ordered, adding for Tiny's benefit, 'leave.'

Both guardians jumped to obey. They exited the room as Diega and Jude entered. Diega flashed Eli a beautiful smile that made her eyes shimmer like the stars of her bloodline marks. She went to stand beside the commander, both of them staring up at the screen monitoring Keets.

Jude came to Eli's side. 'Well done, my friend.' He extended his hand and Eli clasped it, the metal cold against his skin. 'Have I told you lately that you're a genius?'

'About an hour ago,' Eli replied, grinning at his Ar Antarian friend and the spider robot sitting on his shoulder.

'Well, I feel like I need to say it again,' Jude said.

'If you must.'

'You're a genius.'

'Thank you. So are you.'

'Well, birds of a feather . . .' Jude shrugged and SevenM bobbed up and down.

'Eli,' the commander cut in. 'Turn this off.' He gestured to the monitor.

Eli went to the control panel in the wall and disconnected the signal. Keets' image faltered and vanished.

'Where did you apprehend her?' Copernicus asked.

'I don't know,' Eli said before he could stop the lie.

The commander watched him with infinite patience and waited for him to get it right.

'I mean . . .' Eli took a deep breath and Jude gave him an encouraging slap on the shoulder. 'I do know . . . it was between the towns of Scudera and Fletchy, just beside Outpost 43.'

'What happened?'

'I was there installing the spyers to monitor if she was using the outpost as a hideout. I heard a loud thump against the outpost wall. I went outside and saw someone getting up off the ground. I told them to identify themselves. They went for their weapon, so I stunned them. When I went to cuff them, I saw it was Ev'r Keets.'

'And she let you bring her in?' Jude asked.

'Well, she didn't actually regain consciousness until I got her here,' Eli confessed.

Jude's eyebrows shot up and Diega said, 'She must be playing at something. No way could a stunner knock her out.'

Eli hadn't thought about it until then, but he realised Diega was right. Previously, virtually nothing could keep Keets down. She was highly resilient and resistive.

'You've searched her?' the commander asked.

'Yes, boss,' Eli said quickly. 'I put everything in her bag.'

He moved to the far wall and swiped his hand over a sensor. A hidden drawer shot out from the stone. He dragged out Keets' bag, the weight of it almost pulling him to the ground. The commander took the strap from him and easily lifted the bag onto the table in the centre of the room.

'No triggers?' The commander eyed the zippers.

'None,' Eli confirmed.

'That's not like her either,' Jude commented, crossing his metal arms over his chest. Keets was notorious, among many other things, for the violent traps and triggers that protected her belongings.

'She's playing,' Diega echoed her previous thoughts. 'Must be.'

The commander unzipped the bag. All Keets' equipment was there, including her infamous knife – the Morsus Ictus. Copernicus pulled on the gloves from his weapon belt then picked up the black blade, examining it. He placed it back into the bag and lifted out a bottle of green potion. He swished it around, studying the contents.

'Run a full analysis on this and all other liquids in here,' he said to Eli.

'Now, boss?'

The commander shook his head. 'After we talk to her.'

'You want me to talk to her?' Eli squeaked and his heart thudded faster.

A smile stirred the darkness of the commander's eyes. 'No, Eli. I will talk. But I want you to observe.'

Eli nodded, relieved. Observing he could do. Interrogating a super-intelligent psycho like Ev'r Keets was more the commander's realm of expertise.

The commander left the bag and started down the corridor towards the cells. He paused and turned back. 'Eli.'

'Yes, boss?'

'Well done.'

'Thank you, boss.' Eli managed to keep a straight face, but on the inside he did a jump for joy. The commander's praise was, to him, like a rare, rare gold.

The commander continued to walk, Diega at his side. Eli waited a moment to bask in his own newly acquired glory. He lifted up and down on the balls of his feet, feeling like bursting into flight. Jude chuckled beside him and Eli grinned at him, only then noticing another person in the room, standing in the shadows of a corner. The person was a lovely-looking girl with an impressive lump and mean bruise on one side of her head, making her no less lovely.

'This is our new tracker,' Jude told him. 'Silho Brabel.'

Eli's grin stretched wider. The new recruit they'd been expecting for several weeks returned a small and uncertain smile.

'I'm Eli,' he said and went towards her. His legs got tangled in each other and he fell at her feet.

'Careful, buddy.' Jude picked him up with embarrassing ease. 'You'll do yourself an injury.'

'Sorry,' Eli said to Silho. 'I'm sorry. I'm clumsy. I . . . ah . . . have problems with walking sometimes.' He cringed at what he had just said, and yet still found himself saying, 'And with talking too . . . and with just about everything actually.' Eli noticed, though she was obviously a human-breed, she also resembled a pixie with an uptilt to her eyes and long lashes. From this close he could see from the grey tinge to her skin that she was unwell.

'We'd better catch up.' Jude nodded towards the corridor where the commander and Diega had disappeared. 'Silho, follow us.'

Eli entered the interrogation cell last. The cell's walls, floor and ceiling were all made from reinforced grey-rock – the most effective substance for muffling screams. In the centre of the room a table and two chairs stood bolted to the ground. They were made of steel and slightly reflective so, as Diega said, prisoners could see a distorted twin of themselves – and kiss it goodbye. The tang of disinfectant, washed over urine and blood, tainted the air. Eli pushed his hands into his pockets and clung to the warm comfort of his pet otter, Nelly. She slept on, oblivious to the fact that she was in the presence of one of the most feared criminals of all time.

The commander and Diega fearlessly moved within striking distance of where Keets stood facing the wall. Staying as far from Keets as possible, Eli studied her back. What he could see of it, between the wraps of chains binding her arms, was a collage of mismatched skin grafts stitched roughly together, forming jagged scars, criss-crossing over faded and broken tattoos and symbols. Ev'r's head hung low; her white-blonde hair, shaved short at the back and left long at the front, fell in her eyes.

'I knew you weren't dead.' Diega was the first to break the cold, dragging silence.

'Good for you,' Ev'r responded, her voice emotionless.

'You know how I knew you weren't dead?' Diega asked. 'Because only the good die young.'

'Like Fen children – right, fairy-girl?' Ev'r shot back.

Eli cringed. The rainbow colours of Diega's skin flared vibrant.

'Or like gypsy girls, *Zingara*,' Diega said.

Ev'r's back arched in a predatory way at the sound of her real scullion-gypsy name. She turned to face them. Her gaze flickered over Diega and locked onto Jude. Her eyebrows lifted and an unpleasant smile curled her lips. 'You.' She made the word sound simultaneously like a question and a threat.

Jude crossed his metal arms over his chest and met her stare from behind his tinted glasses. Eli felt a definite struggle of energy between the criminal and the tracker, and he noticed Copernicus looking from one to the other, studying their expressions.

'Didn't you die?' Ev'r finally asked Jude.

Diega stepped across, blocking the fugitive's view of the Ar Antarian. 'You don't get to ask questions,' she spat.

Ev'r glared at Diega, but spoke to Copernicus. 'Call off your yapping little girlfriend, Kane, before I break her trutting neck.'

Diega laughed. 'It's your neck you should be worried about,

Zingara. The guilogutter that silenced Englan Chrisholm is still assembled. I'm sure the king would happily roll it out again for you.'

Ev'r cursed at Diega and the force of the dark-words stung Eli's eyes and tugged at the protective amulet he wore on a chain around his neck.

'Enough.' The commander's voice rose, echoing around the walls. 'You won't use the cursed magics in my presence.' Lightning flashed in the darkness of his eyes.

Ev'r gave a derisive snort. 'Why not, Kane? Hits too close to home, does it? Reminds you too much of Daddy? Well *too bad*!' she yelled and Eli shrank back. 'You can't command me! I'm not your soldier or your servant or your whore-like fairy-girl here.' She turned to Diega. 'I know about you two. I know about what you did together – what he did to you.' She gave a spiteful laugh. 'Your family must be so disappointed. I bet they wish you had died – instead of your sister.'

Diega sprang forward and shoved Ev'r against the wall. The fugitive pushed off it with her bound body and knocked Diega back, landing on top of her on the ground. Diega flung her off and Ev'r rolled, her chains clanking, across the ground towards Eli and Silho. Eli dodged her with a flying leap, informed by the years of dance training his gran'ma had forced him to attend, but Silho stayed frozen where she was. Ev'r crashed into the wall beside the new recruit and leapt straight onto her feet, whipping around to face Silho. The others were all behind Ev'r, making Eli the only one to see the immediate, drastic and momentary shift of Ev'r's features – from bloodthirsty hatred, to sheer shock, shadowed by sadness so extreme it could be mistaken for pain. As soon as it appeared, it passed into a neutral stare.

Jude launched himself at Ev'r. He grabbed her and, with the strength of his metal arms and legs, dragged her back to the table and slammed her into one of the chairs. She tried to rise to her feet, but Jude forced her back down. Diega came at the prisoner, her fists clenched, but Copernicus stepped between the two of them and said, 'That'll do.'

After a moment Diega shrank back, glaring hatred at Ev'r. Eli exhaled, his heart thudding fast. Despite years as a tracker, violence still appalled him to the same degree it had on his first day. He had only pursued a military career to follow Copernicus, his best friend for most of their younger life.

The commander spoke to Ev'r. 'You know what you've done. You know why you're here. You know what's going to happen. You've been marked as a state traitor. You won't get a trial – just death by whatever means the magistrate decides, and you know it won't be quick. I can influence that decision if, and only if, you co-operate.'

Ev'r watched Copernicus with eyes that were dead calm. Their colour reminded Eli of the dangerous green of a storm rising.

'What do you know about the recent murders and disappearances?' the commander asked.

'Nothing,' Ev'r replied.

'Is it gang-related? Is Christy Shawe involved?'

'No idea.'

'What can you tell me about this ring?' The commander took a gold ring out of his pocket and held it up in front of Ev'r's eyes.

'Nothing.'

'Why is your body-heat signature altered? What's happened to you?'

The abrupt change in questioning made the corners of Ev'r's mouth jerk and the skin beneath one eye twitch. Ev'r swallowed slowly and held the commander's stare. 'I don't know what you're talking about.'

The commander nodded. 'You know, Keets, before they execute you, I can have your mind purged. I will see everything you know, everything you've seen, one way or another. I can hold you here for seven day-cycles with an Assistant to Investigation order, after which time, if you don't give us anything to present to the courts, palace enforcers will come for you – and then it will be too late.'

'It's already too late.' Ev'r finally spoke. 'For everyone.'

She turned her face away from the commander and he said, 'Think, Keets. You of all people should know there are bad ways to die and there are tolerable ways. Your crimes have brought you to this place where you have no control over the time, but you can

32

choose the way. It could be painless. That's more than most people get. Think about it. We'll be back.'

*****

Eli deactivated his security system and waved the others into his office laboratory. A vast organised jumble of machinery bits and pieces, computer parts and partially made inventions shared space with countless collections of odds and ends, anything Eli could lay his hands on. In one corner, behind glass, he kept his antique paper books, his written word – almost-extinct relics from an era long past. Each book was well used, well loved and holographically stored in his memory. Sensing she was back in her own territory, Nelly shot out of his pocket, up his body, and jumped onto one of his long workbenches. She raced up and down, dodging piles of objects, chiding Eli in a high chattering voice. The sound of her scurrying claws syncopated with the clicks, ticks and taps of his equipment and inventions. Eli noticed Nelly instinctively avoided the area where his latest weaponry advance sat in a transparent box. It was skunk bombs, made from the excretions of skunk-heritage human-breeds. His donors had been very happy that their socially offensive spray could now be put to a good use. Nelly bounded from the bench onto her table, where she snatched a pinkfin fish from her dish and, snapping it down, dived into her pool.

The commander offloaded Keets' bag onto the table beside Eli. He noticed Copernicus was keeping his eyes down, not wanting to view the mess Eli called home. He didn't feel offended. He held the belief *each to their own.* The boss liked extreme organisation; he liked productive chaos.

'I'll set the liquids to analyse now,' Eli told him. He reached into Keets' bag and withdrew the vial of green potion and anything else liquid he could find. The bottle and vials clanked in his hands as he hurried to the far end of his office and put them into his compound-assessor. He shut the glass door and pressed the setting he desired – stage 7, deep and thorough analysis. He knew it would take that level of analysis to ascertain the ingredients of

Keets' concoctions. She was known to use products from places most people would never dare to tread in a billion years.

Opening the cooler beside the compound-assessor, Eli searched for some ice for Silho's head. He thought it would be a nice gesture, but all he had was a bag of raw bones he was storing to give to the Headquarters' guard dogs later that night. He abandoned the search and turned back to the others.

Diega was pacing, swearing about Ev'r Keets, while Jude sat on one of Eli's patched and mismatched lounges. The chair creaked unhappily under his bulk. He sighed and massaged his neck and Eli sensed his friend's unease. Silho stayed near the door, watching the ground.

The commander was talking on his communicator to the Custody Superior with instructions on how to house and contain Keets for the next week. Observing the commander reminded Eli that the upgraded communicator system he'd been working on was now complete and ready to go active. He trotted around the office, rounding up the various parts. As he worked, he heard Copernicus give a direct command to the Custody Superior that no information on Ev'r Keets was to be given to the media. He also wanted a blanket ban on any United Regiment personnel discussing the fugitive with anyone outside of the force. Eli thought this was a good move, but also knew without a doubt that tonight, with or without the ban, every single soldier would tell their family about the capture of Keets, and then their family members would tell their friends and their friends would tell their families and so on. He gave it a day and a night maximum for the streets in front of Headquarters to be overcrowded with people either protesting or supporting the death penalty, or just there for a good old look. Copernicus, obviously thinking the same thing, began giving the Custody Superior instructions to reinforce security at all entrances and exits of Headquarters.

As soon as he ended the conversation, Diega burst out, 'She knows something for sure. She's playing us. We have to go back and make her talk. We can drug her, mesmerise her – whatever. It's not like we have to stick to protocol with her. She's as good as dead.'

Copernicus shook his head. 'Nothing will work on her. We'll have to have her brain purged before her execution.'

'There's no guarantee the courts will allow that,' Diega argued.

'I'll have a psychic analyst evaluate her and rule her as withholding information. Under the present conditions in the city, the courts will grab at anything to stop the deaths.' The commander rubbed a hand over his forehead in an uncharacteristic display of stress.

Jude shifted uncomfortably on the couch and said, 'I'm sorry, Commander, but how could Keets have anything to do with what's going on? She hasn't been anywhere near Scorpia in year-cycles, before I even joined the Regiment, and besides, aren't Keets and Christy Shawe enemies?'

'So?' Diega asked.

'So if he's the instigator, he wouldn't have recruited her, would he? What's the point of purging her mind if she doesn't know anything?' Jude said.

'She knows everything,' Diega insisted. 'This is Ev'r Keets we're talking about. And since when have you been against purging?'

'What do you mean since when have I been against purging?' Jude demanded, sitting forward in his chair. 'You know very well how I feel about that sort of thing.' SevenM moved restlessly on his shoulder.

Diega shook her head. 'You're against the death penalty, you don't agree with imprisonment, you don't like purging. Are you sure you're in the right profession, Jude?'

The Ar Antarian's face flushed deep grey. 'I'm in the profession of saving lives, Diega. What's your vocation?'

Diega laughed. 'My vocation? You know what Jude, come back and talk to me after you've been a tracker for a few more year-cycles, because you obviously haven't been on the job for long enough.'

'Long enough for what?' Jude raised his voice. 'To become so desensitised and cold that I stop feeling anything at all?'

Diega snorted and Copernicus stepped in. 'Jude, Keets has been marked as a traitor by the king himself. He will want to make an example of her. Keets won't be shown any kind of leniency.'

'And neither should she,' Diega added. 'She is a murderer. She took life, she deserves for her life to be taken, and before she does, we'll split open her mind and expose her thoughts. She will be of use to us whether she agrees to it or not.'

'Commander,' Jude said. 'Maybe if we just reasoned with her —'

'Did you not see what happened back there?' Diega talked over him.

Jude ignored her and spoke again to the commander. 'Just keep talking to her. Maybe she will give us something.'

'Why would you even care what happens to Keets?' Diega demanded.

'I understand how you feel,' the commander replied to Jude. 'But Keets won't give us anything. I know her. She's a scullion. She will never talk. She will never change. There is no way to reach her. There's nothing I can do. End of story.'

Eli thought of the way Ev'r Keets had looked at Silho and wondered if this was completely true. It had definitely appeared as though she had recognised the new recruit. Eli glanced at Silho. She was keeping silent so he decided not to mention what he'd seen in front of everyone. He would talk to Copernicus when they were alone. In the meantime, there was an unveiling to be done.

'Okay,' Eli jumped in at the pause in conversation. He dumped an armful of equipment onto the table in front of the others. 'As promised – the new and improved tracker communicators.' No one responded, deep in their own thoughts. It wasn't the level of excitement Eli had hoped for, but he ploughed on regardless. 'New functions of the Communicator 8020 include holo-speak, multi-talk and multi-message, which means I could call everyone on the team at once and either have a conference call, with or without image display, or leave a group message, which you could all access. Additionally, it has an automatic message function, so if the connection doesn't go through or the machine is switched off, you can still leave a message, which will sit in the lines until the other system can receive it. As well as that, it has improved sound quality, range and speed of connection. It works underwater, underground and at high velocity, and it also has the highly

36

anticipated detachable locator function, so we can check our systems and see exactly where everyone is at all times.'

'Great,' Diega said, her tone flat. 'Exactly what I needed – minus zero privacy in my life.'

'You've done well, Eli, as always,' Jude said. He sat forward and took one of the new communicators. SevenM scurried down his arm and patted at the locator screen with one metal limb.

'See,' Eli leaned in and pointed to the screen, 'we're all a different-coloured marker. I'm yellow, Diega is pink, Silho is green, the commander is black and you and SevenM are blue. And the whole system is fingerprint operated, so if anyone else grabs your communicator it will immediately shut down, and if someone tries to access the internals without a security pass the communicator will explode. I've already programmed them to override the old system, so all we need to do is activate them and you can hand in your old machines.'

'I don't want to be pink,' Diega complained.

'You're pink. Deal with it,' the commander said. He leaned over and took one of the communicators. He powered it on and pressed the locator screen to activate the machine. As he did, the communicator emitted a deafening high-pitched squeal. Eli hurriedly fiddled with the settings and managed to stop the sound.

'It may take a bit of time to iron out all the glitches.' He gave a nervous giggle.

The commander's new communicator buzzed with an incoming call and Copernicus answered.

'Yes.' He paused. 'Yes.' He moved away from the group to talk.

The others handed in their old systems and activated their new machines. Eli noticed Silho didn't have to take off her gloves to activate her system. She just flipped up the capped end of one of the fingertips. He found himself staring. She really was unusually stunning.

His stomach rumbled, gurgled and gave a flatulent squeak. Diega looked at him and raised an eyebrow. 'Hungry?'

'I was up before dawn this morning and early rising gives me gas,' he explained.

'That and everything else,' the Fen teased.

'Not everything,' Eli said. 'Just silence, emotional speeches, running, sudden bouts of laughter, baked beans, lentils, cabbage . . . Please, like I'm the only one.' He grinned. Nelly sprang off the edge of the bench and landed back in Eli's pocket. She curled up and fell asleep.

'What's that?' Diega asked, pointing to something on Eli's workbench.

'This,' Eli said grandly, picking up the object, 'is my latest design in shielding technology.' He showed them the large mirror-faced shield. 'It's made of smash-proof, lightweight sagittarian glass, resistant to extreme heat or cold, with the unique radiating protection designed to completely shield the holder, even the parts of the body not covered.'

'*Dimenef reflets*,' Diega said. The shield shivered and shrank down to a compact palm-sized mirror. She gave a teasing grin.

'It's a work in progress,' Eli said, mentally kicking himself for not taking morphing skill into consideration when he was designing it. 'Here.' he handed it to Silho, 'a welcome to the team gift from me!'

The new recruit spoke a soft thankyou and took the mirror.

Copernicus rejoined them. 'There's been another attack – another hollow body.'

Diega cursed. 'Where?'

'Fortitude Hill. Eli, I want you on site for this one. I want you to evaluate the injury and tell me what kind of weapon could have made it.'

'Yes, boss.'

'And try not to upchuck this time,' Diega poked Eli in the ribs as she got to her feet.

'I have everything under control,' Eli said, his voice projecting far more confidence than he felt.

5

The suburbs of Moris-Isles and Fortitude Hill were 640 levels and an entire universe apart. Somewhere between the two, desperate, dirt-dredging, seven-families-to-one-room poverty had given way to pristine, sculpted gardens, highly polished transflyers and seventeen-rooms-to-one-man mansions. Here, under the eternal blazing stare of high-powered laser-globes, the feeble lantern-lights of the city slums and the shadow people who subsisted beneath them faded to a half-forgotten dream. Silho stood on the corner of Saint Wickham and Berry Streets, surveying the neighbourhood through the underwater waver of a concussion. Her head throbbed in a remorseless pounding rhythm and a migraine pain ached behind her eyes, but she fought not to show it. Not today – the first day of really living after a lifetime of dreaming.

In this neighbourhood, only the snip-snip of water sprinklers and the gurgle of fountains broke the silence of night. Scents of freshly cut lawn and citrus leaves perfumed the air. Silho glanced around at the others climbing out of the transflyer. Their movements were shaky. Diega had put them through a punishing trip of speeding swoops and swerves and very near misses. Silho hadn't needed to be an empathetic sensor to feel the Ohini Fen's undercurrent of frustration sparking into anger. Ev'r Keets had got to her badly, though in exactly which way Silho didn't know, and, in truth, didn't care to know. Diega's nasty attitude was getting old fast, and Silho's dislike for the Fen, though she hid it behind a well-practised mask, was growing by the second. As for Ev'r Keets . . . Silho's chest constricted painfully and her throat tightened as the memory of what had happened in the interrogation cell replayed again behind her eyes. During her military training, she had never connected the renegade Keets with the scullion-gypsy girl Zingara Ohavor – someone she remembered as a friend, someone she had looked up to, had wanted to be, if only because she reminded Silho of her mother. What she felt seeing Zingara after so long, in such a way, could only be described as heartbreak – if what was already broken could be re-broken – because it meant only one thing. Ismail had died and taken to his grave every grain of hope and goodness Zingara had tried to hold on to, and she had tried, leaving behind the shell – Ev'r Keets.

Silho blinked away the empty sadness misting her eyes. She forced it back into a dark corner of her mind, to stay until she was alone, in her own room, where she could press her face into her pillow and cry as loudly as she needed to.

'Silho.'

A voice jolted her out of her reverie and she turned to the imp-breed tracker, Eli Anklebiter, standing beside her.

'Sorry, I meant to startle you – I mean, I did *not* mean to startle you . . .' He tripped over his words and angry red splotches broke out all over his neck.

Silho considered him. He was short and slight with a shaved head and protuberant ears. His large, dark eyes sparkled and a mischievous smile played constantly at the corners of his mouth. His bloodline marks were a harlequin colour struggle between the blue stripes of a Glee and the purple dots of a Greer. That explained a lot.

'How . . . how are you holding up?' he asked.

Silho opened her mouth to reply, but was interrupted by Diega calling out beside them,

'*Eizenef aregz'amon.*' With an unnecessarily loud crack of Fen magics, she morphed the tracker's transflyer, the *Ory-4*, into a silver coin and then pushed it into her pocket.

The commander spoke to the group. 'Number 201 Berry. Move out.' He stepped out into the street and everyone fell in silently behind him. They walked along the avenue lined with identical straight-trunk trees pruned to a tedium of perfection. Tall street lamps, placed at exact and equal intervals behind the trees, blazed above their branches. Silho kept a vigilant watch on her surroundings as much as she could with the sick haze veiling her sights. She looked up into the lights and saw that no bugs swarmed the glowing globes.

Eli, trotting at her side, noticed her looking and said, 'It's because of the nets, super-fine Wraith-woven silks, encircling the entire suburb. They keep everything out.'

'Look at this trutting place.' Diega sneered at the angular mansions completely encircled by front, side and sky gates like big cages. Silho stared at all the darkened windows, searching for some light.

'Not a soul in sight,' Eli commented.

'Murder tends to scare away the well-to-do,' Diega said nastily. 'In case they get blood on their fine linen and manicured hands.'

Silho noticed Jude grit his teeth. SevenM, riding on his shoulder, stroked the side of the Ar Antarian's face with one multi-jointed leg in a soothing motion. She'd been too stressed to really think about it when they'd first met, but it now occurred to Silho how strange it actually was for an Ar Antarian to be a tracker – or any kind of active soldier for that matter. Ar Antarians, the upper-level racial group to which the king of Scorpia, Miron U, belonged, usually held positions of power and left the grunt work for everyone else. Jude was obviously an exception – and obviously not afraid of murder.

As they neared the end of the street, Silho registered a shift of shadows up ahead. She blinked into light-form vision and saw a glowing figure standing beside an open gate in front of one of the houses. The person saw them as well and drew back. Silho hesitated, but when the others didn't pause or draw their weapons, she continued on as well. They took several more steps before she placed the shape and size of the form as belonging to a machine-breed. When they came within talking distance, the Androt stepped out into a pool of light and Silho changed back to normal sight.

The Androt woman wore a white uniform with a blue servant's apron. Her dark hair was pulled severely back into a low bun, exposing the barcode numbers on her neck – 363430. She wrung her hands like a wet cloth.

Copernicus spoke to her. 'United Regiment Oscuri Trackers.' He held up his identification, but the Androt didn't look at it, gazing instead at their faces, studying their facial features and movements with expert, robotic precision.

'You called about a suspected murder.' Copernicus pocketed his ID.

'Yes, sir.' She spoke with a lowered voice. 'If you wish, I'll show you in.'

'Show us,' Copernicus consented.

The Androt led them up the path, towards the mansion house. She glanced back several times with nervous eyes. Silho noted the distinct lack of light in the yard compared with the other houses. Garden sculptures crouched in the shadows like stalking beasts. The Androt showed them up a set of stairs and through open double doors into the lobby of the mansion. Silho noticed two things immediately: the biting cold and the smell of blood. Her eyes followed two grand staircases leading up from either side of the lobby into a second storey. A chandelier twinkled above them. Works of art hung on the lobby walls, mostly portraits of sad-looking girls, barely dressed and strewn over lounges. Silho avoided staring too long at the pictures. She looked instead at Copernicus Kane and saw, by the rapid movement of his eyes, that he was taking in the surroundings – not just looking *at* but *beyond* and *through*. He felt her stare and turned towards her, studying her with the same deep scrutiny. She quickly lowered her eyes, nerves buzzing inside her.

The Androt maid closed the door behind them and said, 'If you wish, please follow me.'

Copernicus nodded and she led them again, through the lobby and into a corridor dimly lit by overhead globes. They passed many rooms big enough to swallow Silho's apartment whole and headed towards the end of the corridor where a light shone brighter. They reached the doorway and the Androt stepped aside. She gestured for them to go in and bowed her head. Copernicus and Diega entered first; Jude said a quiet thankyou to the Androt and followed them.

Eli went after him, tripping and almost falling on the carpet. Silho grabbed his arm to steady him. He gave a nervous giggle and whispered, '*Oops*'. They entered together and Silho heard the maid's footsteps retreating back down the hallway.

The room was a parlour with tasteful tapestries lining the walls, delicate china displayed in glass cabinets, a large fireplace with various sculptures posed above it, and, on the ground in front of the fireplace, a hollowed-out corpse lying in the centre of a shaggy rug. A dark red stain had spread out around the body of the middle-aged woman.

Silho's eyes were drawn to the corpse's glassy dead stare, then down to the terrible gaping wound in her stomach and chest. The wound looked as though it had been cauterised, like the two other hollowed-out victims at the Moris-Isles crime scene. Silho noted no signs of torture apparent at first glance, but the bruising on the corpse's legs and arms, and the overturned and smashed objects and drag marks all over the carpet suggested a violent struggle. Silho immediately noticed an inconsistency. The corpse was a human-breed with red blood, but the rug and walls were also splattered with white machine-breed blood, so much of it that she doubted even a fast-healing Androt could survive the loss.

So there had to be a second body somewhere.

The sound of the commander's voice broke Silho's concentration. 'Mrs Parkingham,' Copernicus greeted a short woman, wearing a lavender satin dressing gown. She stood beside the fireplace staring at the blood-stained walls. Two Androt maids flanked her.

The woman jolted and turned. She was a human-breed with the petite, pinched features of rabbit heritage. She stared at the commander with bloodshot eyes streaming tears behind thick glasses and held a scrunched handkerchief close to her nose. It gave an occasional twitch.

'I'm Commander Copernicus Kane of the Oscuri Trackers.' He gestured behind him. 'My team.'

Silho noticed everyone else had dispersed around the room, as though by silent command, to do their own tasks. Jude and SevenM were examining the shattered window of the sitting parlour, a possible entry or exit route for the murderer. Diega and Eli knelt on either side of the corpse. Silho didn't know what she should be doing, so she stepped back to stand beside Jude and continued to observe the commander speaking with the woman.

'Mrs Parkingham, I need to ask you a few questions.'

The woman dabbed her nose with the handkerchief and her maids helped her to sit on one of the couches. Copernicus sat opposite her, leaning forward.

'You are the owner of this house?' he asked.

Mrs Parkingham nodded.

'Did you discover the deceased?'

She nodded again and said in an accent that swapped between commoner lower-level Urigin to uptight upper-level Urigin, betraying her newly rich status, 'I heard a sound. I came downstairs and . . . and . . .'

'And what did you see?'

'This room – like this . . .' She gestured around.

'You didn't see anyone exiting the room?'

She shook her head.

'Do you know the deceased?'

'Which one?' The woman's lip quivered.

The commander gave her a look that prompted her to explain. 'Well, look,' she squeaked, pointing to the walls. 'How can he still be alive? Tell me how. Our poor Kry!' She covered her face and dissolved into sobs. The Androt maids also began to cry. Copernicus turned to them.

'Who is Kry?'

They glanced at each other and one answered hesitantly, 'Mrs Parkingham's gardener.'

'Kry is an Androt?' the commander clarified.

They nodded. Silho felt a tug of surprise – most Androt owners called their servants by their numbers, not their names.

Mrs Parkingham spoke again, her voice choked and wet. 'This *person*,' she gestured to the body, 'must have broken in with someone else. Kry heard them and tried to save me. It would be like him to do that. He managed to stop this one, but the other one must have injured or killed him and taken away his body. We've searched all the house and garden and there is no sign. Maybe he could still be alive somewhere. What are you going to do about finding him?' she demanded.

'Everything we can,' Copernicus assured her.

'What do you care?' Jude spoke abruptly from where he stood at the window. He stared at Mrs Parkingham with open hostility. His silver face had flushed to dark grey. 'Are you concerned your garden will fall into disarray without your slave to tend to it?' SevenM stood to his full height on Jude's shoulder, also glaring at the woman. There was a moment of silence broken by the parlour chronograph ticking over and chiming two hour cycles past darkfall, with a long night still ahead. The commander lifted an eyebrow at Jude in silent question. Diega and Eli sat staring in suspended motion beside the corpse, Eli's mouth making an O.

Mrs Parkingham stammered, 'I'm concerned for him. For his . . . his wellbeing . . .'

'I can imagine,' Jude replied, his upper-level Ar Antarian accent pronounced in his anger. 'It must be expensive to buy good slaves, especially ones willing to risk their lives for your silverware.'

'How dare you!' Mrs Parkingham said. 'I have never —'

'Jude, Brabel,' Copernicus interrupted, 'go into the next room. Run a body-heat scan.' When neither moved, he gestured with his head, 'Now!'

For a moment Jude didn't budge, then he turned and barged out of the room. Silho hurried to follow. She closed the door on the sound of the commander explaining that Jude was still learning his role in the trackers.

Jude stood beside the window, looking out into the unlit garden. The many red lights of SevenM's eyes reflected in the glass.

Silho approached the Ar Antarian carefully. 'Are you alright?' she asked.

He shook his head. 'I'm fine. I shouldn't have said anything.' But it didn't sound to Silho as though he meant it.

'You said what you felt.'

'Exactly,' he replied, his words heavy with bitterness.

'You don't like the way Androts are treated?' Silho said.

'You could say that,' he replied.

'Neither do I,' she admitted. She glanced around the room for signs of hidden spyers recording their conversation. 'Never have. I hope it changes.'

Jude exhaled and his rigidly held shoulders sagged. 'Nothing changes without action,' he said. 'Action by braver men than me.' He lowered his head and his tinted glasses slipped a little down his nose, showing a hint of electric blue – the eye colour of an Ar Antarian noble. Silho couldn't help but stare. Jude was not just one of the upper-level Ar Antarians, but had obviously come from one of the few noble-blood families. It was difficult even to imagine why someone like him would want to go from being nobility to military – especially considering the two groups were mutually exclusive. Jude must have left everything behind to become a soldier. Silho was lost for words and desperately searched for a different topic.

'I've never seen an Ar Antarian with a companion robot before,' she said. 'Did you . . . did you make him?'

After a moment Jude replied with a more composed tone, 'I found him.'

'Really? Where?'

The spider robot shone his gaze down on her, his eyes moving over her face.

'Sirenseron,' Jude said.

Silho raised her eyebrows. She didn't personally know anyone who had been inside the king's palace – or even anywhere near the fortified grounds on the very top level of the city.

Jude noticed her surprise. 'I worked there – before I joined the Regiment. SevenM was a serving robot in the kitchen. He malfunctioned and they dropped him down the rubbish chute to be compressed.'

'You felt sorry for him.'

Jude nodded. 'I went to find him and remade him. We became friends. People laugh at that, a man making friends with a machine.'

'I don't think it's funny,' Silho said.

'You're different,' Jude said. He looked deeply into her eyes. 'I can see that.'

Silho swallowed and dropped her gaze to the ground, avoiding the intensity of his stare. 'You seem very close . . . like brothers,' she said in an attempt to divert his attention.

Jude didn't reply for so long Silho began to wonder if he'd actually heard. She glanced up to find he was still looking at her. His expression had shifted slightly. There was clarity in his gaze.

'Silho, you're right,' he said softly. 'We are brothers. I take care of him and protect him from being enslaved by people like that woman out there. He takes care of me and gives me the gift of seeing through his eyes. I see the world as he sees it. It is a beautiful world, but it's also twisted and cruel.'

'Yes,' Silho agreed with more feeling than she had intended. Jude's sincerity and warmth invited her trust, but she knew that confiding in anyone about her past was a mistake that could see her dead. So, as always, she held her silence. She looked out into the night and sensed Jude still studying her.

'You're beautiful, you know,' he said unexpectedly.

She froze, his words sending her mind spinning. No one had called her beautiful before and she had no idea how to respond. *Thank you* sounded vain, *No I'm not* seemed desperate and saying nothing at all might come across as cold. An embarrassed heat seared her face as the silence stretched out between them. She felt so awkward that she couldn't even raise her eyes. Thankfully the moment broke as the door handle rattled and the door slid open, scuffing over the thick carpet. Eli popped his head around the corner and said, 'Forensics are here. B.L. is baying for us to leave and the commander is ready to fly. See you guys outside.' He grinned and vanished.

Jude smiled and spoke to Silho, his tone back to conversational. 'B.L. Jenkins is the lead forensic investigator and he hates the commander – a lot. We'd better get out of here before he comes in and accuses us of compromising his scene.' He brushed a hand over her back as he left the room.

Silho stayed where she was, looking out the window, trying to gain some control over her thoughts. Her gaze zoomed in on a white smudge on the windowsill, partially hidden by the curtain. It looked like a fingerprint of Androt blood. As she examined it, she caught a flash of something darting among the sculptures in the darkened garden. She stared, hoping to catch another movement, but everything remained still.

Her hands twitched, wanting to touch the walls, to delve into the memories of the house and extract the truth of this terrible night. The craving flared unbearably and she flipped back the cap of one of her gloves and reached out. A sudden feeling of being watched stopped her. Through the window, she saw that the trackers had gathered beside the front gate and the commander was looking in directly at her. Silho swallowed, shaken by the second close call that night.

She hurried for the door and pushed out of the room into the parlour, now crowded with grey-uniformed forensic investigators. They swarmed around the body. A short, round man she took to be B.L. Jenkins stood barking orders. Mrs Parkingham and the Androt maids were gone, possibly taken by guardians to another room to give their statements. Silho reached the door as the yellow-eyed hologramographer was arriving. They brushed past each other muttering hello and goodbye. As she stepped out into the night's warmer air, she also saw the human-breed guardian from the first scene standing by the door. They nodded at each other and she hurried back along the path towards her team. She glanced into the darkness of the garden, feeling eyes watching her.

She reached the others as Jude was finishing a long-range body-heat sweep.

'Nothing unusual,' he said. 'No one injured.'

Silho forced herself to speak up. 'There was a spot of, I think, blood on the windowsill in there.'

'This?' Jude asked, as SevenM brought up a hologram he'd taken of the window and the smudged Androt blood.

Silho nodded, surprised that she hadn't noticed him taking the shot earlier.

'We have actually done this once or twice before,' Diega smirked. 'Unlike you.'

'Actually, Diega, this scene is Silho's second scene – so that's twice. Why don't you give it a rest, or people will start to think you're jealous,' Jude challenged.

Diega's eyes widened with shock and anger.

'Alright, let's move to a clearing and take off,' the commander intervened. He stepped down onto the road and headed back the way they'd come.

Silho and Eli both hurried after him, leaving Jude and Diega to follow. Even with distance between the two groups, the tension between the pair was palpable. Silho felt grateful to Jude for standing up for her, but couldn't help but wonder why. Was it just because he was a nice guy or did he want more from her? During the year-cycles of military training, she'd managed to keep to herself, but with the tracker team being so small and tight-knit it would be difficult to remain distant. She had to talk to them and let them into her life to a certain extent, otherwise they might become suspicious, but she could never let them get too close. The fact that Jude seemed so genuine and caring wouldn't make keeping him away any easier. And then there was the commander. How was she going to keep up her front when he left her permanently stammering and blushing, torn between hoping he was looking at her and desperately trying to avoid those eyes? The pounding in her head intensified, and she only just stopped herself from grabbing at the pain.

Fortunately, Eli again provided a distraction. He took a frame from his pocket and activated the holo-screen inside it. It displayed a still hologram of four Androts. Three of them Silho recognised as the maids from the house, the one that had showed them in and the two from the parlour; the fourth was an unknown machine-breed man.

'Ada, Joy, Zoe and Kry,' Eli read from the near-invisible tag on the side of the hologram. 'I swiped this from the room.'

The commander took it from him and held it up to his face.

'The missing Androt's barcode is 939993,' he said, sounding as though he were committing it to memory. He handed the picture back to Eli. 'Run a face and barcode search on it when we get back to Headquarters,' he instructed. 'See if we get any hits on this Kry.'

Eli's stomach gurgled and growled. 'I suppose there's no chance of a break?' He looked up hopefully at Copernicus. 'The brain does function better with regular rests.'

The commander considered it then conceded, 'A short break.'

Eli grinned and skipped. Silho looked back over her shoulder. Diega and Jude were still trailing behind exchanging brief, angry words. Behind them the shadows of the trees stretched across the streets and, within their twisted darkness, a silhouetted form stood watching. Silho's senses jolted. For a moment she thought it was a Midnight Man, one of the most dangerous types of spectral-breed, but when she blinked, the form vanished. Unable to trust her own eyes, she turned away and said nothing.

6

Everything about this man disturbed her. His bleached white shirt and off-centre bow tie, clean hands with dirty nails, encouraging smile, uninterested eyes. How could she trust a walking contradiction?

'What are your thoughts, Ms Keets?' The man leaned back in his chair, his hands clasped in front of him. Ev'r studied his pose, weighed and judged the alignment of his limbs and found it counterfeit – not a true gesture of professional concern, but an imitation of learned behaviour. *This is how you act when you're a doctor.*

'On what?' Ev'r replied. The chains constricting her body were attached to the magnetised table, holding her prisoner in her chair.

'On what we were just discussing.' The psychic analyst spoke with a surface tone of utmost patience and an undercurrent of antagonism. She wasn't playing by his rules. This was where she was supposed to break down and tell him what was wrong with her, diagnose herself and make his job easier, but, in truth, even if she had wanted to speak, she wouldn't have known what to say. What she felt had no description anymore. It was a formless misery, a shape-shifting apparition of feelings, an illusive suggestion of thought – intangible, untraceable, incurable – unless, of course, it became possible to raise the dead.

'That folder,' she said, looking at the portfolio lying on the desk beside the doctor's outstretched hand. 'Looks like dragon hide. It must have cost you a fair coin.'

'It did,' he conceded with a dip of his head.

'And yet you've spilt food on it.'

A vein twitched in the doctor's neck. Four hours into the session, four minutes to mid-dark, and she hadn't given him an inch. He leaned forward over the metal table.

'Ms Keets, I don't think we're making any progress.'

'I agree,' she replied.

'Then what do you propose we do about it?'

'You're the doctor – you tell me.'

His right hand involuntarily clenched into a fist. 'I cannot help you if you are not willing to help yourself.'

'Then you can't help me,' Ev'r said with finality. The fluoro light above them had begun to hurt her eyes.

'If you cooperate with the state and give indication of knowledge, things will be better for you,' he continued.

Ev'r retreated into a dark and silent room in her mind. *Things* – he meant death. At least Copernicus Kane, though she hated him with all her being, had the backbone to say it. It was a choice between death and death more appalling, but what they didn't know, even though Kane had detected a change in her internal body structure, was that long before the state would have the chance to take her life, she would become a Ravien and they would be forced to exterminate her by the quickest means possible. Her last dose of antidote had completely worn off and the nausea was gone, but now she felt the beast she was becoming pulsing in her chest. A blackness was spreading out from under her fingernails, and a meaty stench polluted her senses. It wouldn't be long now.

Ev'r stared at the chains binding her arms to her sides. The imp-breed soldier, Snack-size, had tied her securely but not cruelly, and the chains didn't feel so foreign against her skin. Captivity wasn't a stranger. It had long been an enemy, but she'd grown to understand that the captivity she hated had defined her. It had given her a purpose, a goal to reach, enemies to hate. It had destroyed and re-formed her so many times that she was little more than a composite of the scars it had given her, painful truths it had taught her and years lived one day at a time, second by second. Inside captivity, she had known who she was and what she wanted – only to be free. Yet once free, she had lost herself, known nothing. She was no one. Her thoughts crept back to the asylum, where she had left her memory-self cowering outside the black door with the inscription, 'Thou Shalt Not Enter', scratched across it. She had ignored the warning back then and she decided to ignore the warning now. There was nothing left to lose.

Ev'r's memory-self pushed her weight against the doors of the witch's quarters and they opened inward, slow and heavy. She stood on the threshold of a room. It smelt strongly of urine. Its many barred and grimy windows looked out across the desert to the immense Boundary Wall in the far distance. Rays of sunlight lay ragged on the floor. Ev'r cried out; it felt as though it had been year-cycles since she'd seen the suns. She started forward then stopped abruptly. A tall man stood by one of the windows, looking out through a patch of glass wiped clear. The mark on the back of his neck displayed his high military rank and the dark line crossed over it exposed his dishonourable discharge. She studied his broad back and powerful arms, large rough hands held at his sides. His wrists were scarred and he was swaying slightly. He sensed her presence and turned. Recognition rushed through her and she inhaled sharply as it twisted a knife in her gut.

'Ismail?'

The man narrowed his dark eyes.

Ev'r studied the face she'd seen every day growing up and found only traces of the boy he'd been. Pain and anger had carved his features into sharp relief, though his lips still curved in the way she remembered. She stepped forward slowly. There was something bestial in his expression that said to move quickly would be a mistake.

'Ismail, it's me – Zingara.'

He blinked, his stare drug-heavy and full of torment. He turned fully around and the aggressive lines of his face began to smooth out. Her eyes passed over the thick scar across his neck. It looked like a failed beheading. Around the scar were red marks like love bites, and down his chest, in the line of his unbuttoned shirt, she saw the burns of electrodes, tracks of needle-stabs and weeping sores of symbols re-carved in his flesh day after day. These were signs of experiment-ation and torture. Anger choked her. Who had done this?

She held out her hand, but he just stared at it. So she reached for him and took him in her arms. The touch of him and smell of his skin was so familiar it burned inside her. When she pressed her face against his chest, his heartbeats sounded faint and uneven. He kept his arms at his sides, unresponsive. Ev'r mumbled some words, a mind-clearing enchant the Mocking Witch had taught her. Ismail's body jerked. She pulled away and looked into his face, where com-prehension struggled through the haze.

'Zara?' he whispered, his words still slurred. 'Is it you? Are you real?'

Tears overflowed from her eyes. Ismail had been the only one who cared for her, the only one she'd loved. They had planned to escape together. She'd waited at the place they'd decided on – waited and waited and waited. He'd never shown.

'Where were you? Why did you leave without me? You prom-ised,' she sobbed.

Ismail shook his head. 'Your father had me arrested. I couldn't get back. I tried – I swear I tried so hard.' His dark eyes misted over and they clung to each other, rocking, trying to find some comfort in this nightmare.

'Where am I?' he finally whispered.

'O'Tenery Asylum,' she told him.

'Asylum?' His eyes widened.

Sounds of nearing footsteps echoed in the corridor outside the forbidden door.

'The witch!' Ev'r gasped and turned towards the door.

'No!' Ismail grabbed her arm in his cold hands, terror stretched over his face. 'Don't go! Don't leave me!'

'I won't. I'll hide.' Ev'r's eyes darted around the room and she saw an ornate wardrobe in one corner. She ran to it and threw herself inside, closing the door behind her and peering through the keyhole, just as the Mocking Witch appeared in the doorway. The hag's eyes roved suspiciously around the room.

'Why was this open?' she demanded of Ismail.

He wisely stood unmoving and silent, staring back out the window as though nothing had happened.

Ev'r's chest heaved, her heart crashing, as she watched the witch close the door and move in on Ismail. The woman reached up to his shoulder and turned him to face her. He kept a neutral expression, though his dark eyes lifted for a second to the wardrobe where Ev'r hid. Ev'r held her hand over her mouth to stop its trembling. The witch stood gazing at Ismail and a lascivious smile spread over her vile face. Her eyes glowed with lust and she dragged his face towards her, her lips quivering with the anticipation of pleasure. Ismail closed his eyes. Ev'r stared, boiling with an emotion so mixed it was unnameable. Ismail was her childhood love. They had kissed under bridges, under tables, under beds and under everything two kids could hide under, until they and their love were too big to hide anymore. And here he was, drugged and helpless, abused and tortured – by the witch. Ev'r had confided in the witch about Ismail – described him. This evil woman knew exactly what she was doing, and exactly to whom she was doing it.

Before the Mocking Witch could kiss Ismail, Ev'r kicked out the wardrobe door. It snapped off its hinges and flew halfway across the room. She stepped out as the witch spun towards her.

'Zingara!' The hag emitted a horrible shrill cry of shock. 'Get out!'

Ev'r stood her ground and stared the witch straight in the eyes.

The witch curled her lips in a sneer. 'You wouldn't dare.'

Ev'r raised her hands and released a curse with so much fury and force that it blew out the entire wall and sent the witch plummeting to the desert far below. Ev'r jumped after her, riding the wind to where the witch had landed on her feet. The witch screamed excuses at her, screamed that she had saved Ev'r's life.

'You saved my body and killed my soul!' Ev'r spat.

They attacked each other with raw and snarling hatred. Ev'r remembered little of the battle that followed, just that she knew she would never stop until either she or the witch was dead, and as they fought the asylum sank slowly into the ground behind them, the force of their magics cracking the earth. Ev'r recalled only in snapshots of motion, grabbing the witch by the chain around her neck, where she kept a vial of cure-all. The witch had told her of the meetings between the dark sects, all the witches and sorcerers so untrustworthy and murderous that before every sip of drink anyone had taken, they had each poured their own elixir into their cup to save themselves from sure poisoning. Ev'r had twisted the witch's chain tighter and tighter around her neck until she felt the woman's strength ebbing under her grasp. Finally she had flung her lifeless body to the ground, the vial of liquid thudding against the witch's chest. Broken from the spell of hate, she'd turned towards the sinking asylum to see people scrambling out to escape. Ismail was among them. They'd run to each other, into each other's arms, together at last.

A cruel blast of sound dragged Ev'r out of Ismail's grasp into reality, where she lay on a piss-dank floor convulsing and frothing at the mouth, staring up at a weasel-blood human-breed shouting her name.

'Keets!' the psychic analyst bellowed again, slamming his palm down on the panic button on the table.

Four guardians burst into the room – one Twitchbak, one giant and two human-breeds.

'She just collapsed. I didn't do anything!' the analyst told them.

The guardians closed in on her, and Ev'r stared up at their faces. Horror shivered through her. Beneath the faces of the two human-breed soldiers, she recognised the same evil she had seen in the desert just before her capture – Skreaf demons. They were already here in the city. They had infiltrated the United Regiment, which meant something big must be about to happen – maybe even sooner than the Ravien change would take her. Death was one thing, but dark magics . . . some things were worse than death. She needed to get out – now – and as she saw it, the Ar Antarian soldier whom Kane had called Jude was the key. This man had another name. He had a terrible secret. The only thing left to find out was: how far would he go to save himself? Who would he betray?

7

Copernicus pushed open the door of Winston Dunn's diner on Upper Kettle Street, several blocks from Headquarters. The diner was, as always, overcrowded with military personnel, uniformed and plain-clothed, off and on duty. A discordant chorus of sounds assailed Copernicus' senses, gabbling conversations, clink-clanking glasses, the sizzle and spit of grilling meat, and yells from the crowd watching a pedal-ball match on the holo-screen projected above the bar.

He entered, triggering the buzzer above the door. Numerous people turned towards him then quickly away, their eyes shifting nervously, their body-heat flaring. The lower-ranking soldiers on duty saluted him. The crowd parted to make a path for him and a murmur followed his back. He headed to the booth where the trackers always sat. It was occupied by two young soldiers sharing fried thistle stalks, talking with their heads close together. Copernicus looked at them without saying a word. They quickly picked up their plates and shifted to another spot. The commander sat down and used a napkin to brush their crumbs off the table surface. Silho slid into the seat opposite him.

He could feel her watching him, studying what he was doing. He looked up – she looked down. He looked down – she looked up. To outsiders, it might have appeared to be a dinner date – she a little nervous, never quite meeting his eyes, he leaning forward, perhaps on the edge of conversation. It might have appeared like that, but anyone worth the air they breathed knew appearances were deceiving. This was, he thought, especially true for Brabel. She presented as meek and submissive, but her eyes spoke another story, and though she attempted to keep herself hidden, she obviously didn't understand that what she didn't do told him as much about her as what she did do. He had begun to piece her together like a puzzle that would eventually show the true picture of who she really was. Already he knew her tolerance for pain was far above and beyond the norm. He could see her body-heat throbbing, flaring like flames around her neck and head. She was in significant distress from her injury on the breakwall yet her face betrayed nothing – and that said something. Again he thought that her features were familiar.

Eli's laughter burst out repeatedly from somewhere in the midst of the bar crowd, which had consumed him on his way to get their drinks. He finally emerged, red-faced, ruffled and grinning, juggling an oversized plate of fried potatoes, a shot of mossink for Copernicus, water for Silho and a strawberry and ketchup milkshake with extra ice-cream for himself. He made it to the table and plonked down beside the commander. He slid in so close that their sides were touching. Copernicus tolerated this otherwise unacceptable proximity because it was Eli and all imp-breeds struggled with the concept of personal space. Eli dispensed the drinks with a rapid whirr of his hands. In the same movement, he grabbed up all four bottles of various sauces from the back of their table and used them to drown the fried potatoes. When they had well and truly vanished, he squirted more sauce into his milkshake then started in on the food – licking his fingers, crunching and slurping, slopping sauce everywhere. Imp-breeds were notoriously messy eaters, banned from many restaurants, especially anywhere near the upper levels. Copernicus could see Eli squishing potato in one hand, barely managing to keep himself from throwing it at someone . . . but barely controlled was far better than he'd been when they had first met each other in late childhood, a time when Eli was virtually unintelligible and stole anything within his grasp. He had, through intensive personal effort, progressed a long way since then.

Eli nudged the commander in the ribs and offered him some food. Copernicus shook his head. A sharp pain stabbed in his chest and he felt short of breath. He touched his lower right ribs and the pain intensified. Most likely, he thought, he'd broken a rib or two during the scuffle with Christy Shawe. His mind returned to the case, to the two rings, the crime scenes they had attended that night, the hollowed-out bodies and missing Androt, Ev'r Keets . . . Somehow it was all connected – but how?

Eli nudged him again in the exact same place and Copernicus bit back a groan as pain lanced his body.

'Mechanical issues, hey,' Eli said, referring to Diega, who had asked Jude to wait back with her and check a mechanical issue she was having with the transflyer.

'Apparently,' Copernicus replied, his tone dry.

'That's funny because the *Ory-4* sounded fine to me. How about you?' He took a slurp of his drink.

'Perfect.'

'Must have been their relationship that needed the repairs then.' Eli grinned. 'Oops, I forgot, we're not supposed to know. I keep forgetting that. Must be because it's so obvious.' He reached into his pocket and scooped out his pet otter, placing it on the table. The furry creature stood up on its hind legs and lapped at Eli's milkshake, its little pink tongue darting in and out.

'And I wonder what got to Jude at the crime scene? He kind of lost it. It's not like him,' Eli continued. He blew bubbles in the drink and the otter sneezed.

Copernicus nodded. Jude *had* kind of lost it, and he was quite sure this had something to do with the Ar Antarian's encounter with Ev'r Keets. He hadn't missed their silent exchange in the cell. He'd recruited Jude after Ev'r's last arrest and alleged death, so that meeting was supposed to be their first, but it had definitely felt as though they already knew each other – or, at least, knew *of* each other. Jude had read Ev'r Keets' in-depth profile as part of his training, so that was where his knowledge could have originated, but how did Keets know Jude? Copernicus remembered the way the fugitive had used the word *you* – and she had been momentarily surprised. She'd said, *Didn't you die?*

Copernicus knew Jude had been born to a noble family, but was disowned after he'd decided to join the military, which explained why there was no trace of him in the city records. Being disowned by the upper levels meant being erased.

Facts aside, the question stuck – where in his privileged and exclusive upbringing had Jude encountered Ev'r Keets and why would she think he was supposed to be dead? The commander had always suspected there were things about Jude's past that he kept secret, though Copernicus had never directly interrogated him. He felt they shared an unspoken understanding that some things were better left unsaid and some scars better left unexamined. As far as Copernicus was concerned, full disclosure of childhood was not necessary for a soldier to be trustworthy, but concealment of a criminal history – that was another matter completely. He resolved to talk to Jude about it the next opportunity he had – the kind of talk that received answers whether the other person wanted to give them or not.

He tipped back his glass of mossink and downed the black liquor in one go. It settled warm in his stomach as he considered another factor that might have contributed to Jude's loss of control at the second scene. Ev'r Keets had revealed that he, Copernicus, and Diega had a history, which, considering Jude and Diega's current relationship, might have made Jude feel jealous. If Copernicus hadn't already felt uneasy about Jude's situation, he would have told the Ar Antarian that he had nothing to worry about. He didn't want Diega. He didn't want a girlfriend at all. He loathed stumbling first meetings, despised the back and forth – *Oh, you like that? I like that too, we're so much alike.* He was done with it. All he wanted was a willing partner for the exact time it took to satisfy his primal needs and not for a second longer. For the rest of the time, he wanted to be alone.

The door buzzed and Jude and Diega entered, looking, if not happier, at least more controlled. Jude, with SevenM riding on his shoulder, came straight to the table and sat down beside Silho. SevenM's head swivelled towards the new recruit, and the robot reached out a leg and lightly brushed her cheek. Copernicus narrowed his eyes, watching the interaction carefully. Obviously the two of them had developed a rapid connection. And what was it that attracted people – likeness? She was hiding something – was Jude as well? Copernicus found himself studying Jude more closely than he ever had since he'd recruited him. Jude glanced up and Copernicus looked away to the bar where Diega stood, talking to several of her buddies and watching the game. Without a doubt she'd have money riding on it. Ohini Fen loved to gamble, but hated to lose – especially Diega.

'All good?' Eli asked Jude.

The Ar Antarian sighed, absently rubbing a hand over his neck, the way he always did when he was stressed. 'Yes, just tired.' He activated the menu function on the table and a hologram of the day's specials appeared in the air before him.

'I know,' Eli said, 'nothing like turning night into day, is there?' He stretched and yawned and his otter yawned straight after him. Copernicus stifled his own echo of the motion. Out of everyone, he should have been feeling the most tired. Fens didn't sleep at all, imp-breeds took only minimal rest, and Ar Antarians needed probably half that of human-breeds, who needed sleep the most. Diega finished up with her friends and joined them, sitting down beside Jude, but not too close. She had bought a drink for herself, but nothing for Jude. Copernicus saw Jude glance from the drink to Diega and back and read a slight annoyance. The Fen was oblivious. She glanced over at the menu, then noticed Eli studying a processor part he'd taken from his pocket. A smile tugged at her mouth. With a whisper of Fen magics, she morphed the metal part into a big phallic sculpture. Eli gaped at it for a moment then realised what she'd done and retaliated, throwing the piece of squished potato he had been playing with directly at her. It splattered on the seat behind her head. She peeled it off and threw it back. He snatched it out of midair with a snap of his hand and grinned wickedly.

'Eli, enough,' Copernicus said, knowing he had to intervene before it became an all-out food fight and they were banned from yet another diner. It wasn't because he liked socialising with his colleagues that they chose to come to this particular diner. It was for the lack of other options. Eli dropped the food, looking shamefaced.

61

'And Diega,' the commander said to the Fen, 'no one needs to see what's on your mind.'

Diega gave him a dirty look and said, '*Xpel.*'

The suggestive sculpture changed back to the processor part just as a tall Ohini Fen guardian passed the table. He called back to Diega. 'Hey, Dee – see you tomorrow night. And come wary. I feel lucky.'

'You keep saying that, Antonius, but you've never won once!' Diega called back with a laugh.

'What's happening tomorrow night?' Eli asked.

'Card game,' the Fen replied.

'Just you and the boys again,' Eli said. 'You know you could at least make *some* female friends for my sake.'

'Still no girlfriend?' Diega asked.

'Nope,' Eli replied. He blew more bubbles in his milkshake. 'But you never know.' He looked around the bar with so much innocent hope that Copernicus felt a rare stirring of pity. Eli was one of those poor unfortunates who women loved to hang around with, loved to have as friends, but had absolutely no romantic interest in, and the girls he always fell madly in love with were bossy and controlling – like Diega and his grandmother – and they ran straight over him.

'You're too nice,' Diega said. 'That's your problem.'

Jude snorted. 'What does that even mean? How can someone be too nice?'

Diega ignored him. She nodded to a very short girl in very tall heels standing by the bar. 'What about her? She looks about your size.'

'Hestia Ingrahm,' Eli said. 'She works reception at Headquarters and she is a *very* nice girl who likes a *very* nice boy called Kinnon West from Narcotics. He's big, built and handsome. Girls like big, built and handsome, not,' he glanced down at himself, 'small, weedy and questionably attractive. Gran'ma always told me it was what was inside that mattered. What a load that was.'

'How is Nanna?' Diega gestured to the bar for another drink.

Eli sighed.

A waitress came and gave Diega her drink, then activated the touch screen on the tabletop. She smiled widely at Copernicus, flashing a jaw full of crowded shark-like teeth. The front teeth were smeared with red lipstick and Copernicus felt, as Eli would say, that he was being sized up for the kill. He looked away. Diega had told him, on many occasions, that he was paranoid when it came to women, that he always had a negative first reaction to any woman that approached him. While that was not necessarily untrue, she didn't know his reasons.

'What can I get you?' the waitress asked them.

They ordered their usual meals: the charcoaled steak for Copernicus, sickly rich Fen cakes for Diega, ice-cream and raw eggs swimming in ketchup for Eli, and Jude, after his typical long search through the menu for anything better, took the soup. Silho echoed his order, and as she did, Copernicus noticed her eyes roll back slightly as her pain started to get the better of her. He watched her for a moment, then the subject of food took his mind to another issue he was dealing with that none of the others knew about – a personal problem for which he had, so far, failed to find a solution. He glanced at his chronograph. He needed to come up with something and soon. It wouldn't be long before Luther reappeared, needing his help. He thought he might have even sensed him for a moment at the Fortitude Hill crime scene, and that was a bad sign. It meant he was getting desperate.

'Alrighty,' the waitress said as she finished registering their orders. 'Won't be long. Can I get you more drinks?'

'A cask of water,' Jude said.

'And a milkshake, please, Fatima,' Eli added. 'And can this one be banana and ketchup, with . . .'

'Extra ice-cream?' she said with a smile. 'For you, Eli, anything.'

Diega downed the last of her beer and held up the glass. 'Same again.'

Fatima took the glass and walked back to the bar, swaying her hips.

'What about her?' Diega asked. 'She looks like she'd feed you well.'

'Already married,' Eli said. 'And she feeds her nine children, all of them already taller than me, very well.'

'What about a Fen?' Jude muttered. 'You'll never have to think for yourself again.'

'No thanks,' Eli said. 'Not much into fairy-breeds.'

'You used to like me,' Diega smiled at him, fluttering her purple eyelashes.

'Yes, but that was before I knew you,' Eli said.

Diega laughed.

'It's just this problem I have,' Eli said.

'Which one?' Diega teased.

'The talking thing. When I'm with you – my friends – I'm fine, but when I'm with a girl, suddenly I'm back to square one, talking gibberish or saying the opposite of what I mean. And I'll usually end up stealing something from her,' he said.

'Well, we might as well just take you out the back and shoot you – you're no good to any of us,' Diega said. She stood, too impatient to wait for the drink to be brought to her. Another Ohini Fen soldier bumped into her and greeted her in Fenlen.

'*Dazzl.*' He offered her his drink as a sign of friendship.

'Commander Santana.' She saluted him, then took the drink.

The Fen soldier, Santana, glanced down at their table and, unlike most people, deliberately met Copernicus' eyes. There was no nervousness in his steady stare; instead Copernicus saw the complex, multifaceted emotion commonly given the entirely uncomplicated title of *respect*.

'Commander Kane.' Santana saluted him in full view of everyone even though they were equally ranked.

Copernicus responded with a nod.

'Hi,' Eli piped in.

Santana's eyes shifted down to the imp-breed. 'Hello,' he replied.

'I'm Eli Anklebiter,' Eli said and extended his hand.

'Santana.' The Fen slapped his hand in the Ohini way. He leaned down and said, 'Eli, your commander there,' he looked again into Copernicus' eyes, 'is a great man.'

'Thank you.' Eli took it as a personal compliment.

Santana nodded. He straightened up, spoke to Diega again briefly about how much she had riding on the game, then left.

'He seems nice,' Eli said.

Diega sat down with her drink and said, 'He's not *nice*, he's a sniper and he was team leader on my first job, which was also the first time I worked with our *great* commander.' Diega locked eyes with Copernicus and the corners of her lips quirked upwards. 'You remember, right?' she said, speaking to him as though he was the only one in the room.

Copernicus nodded. He didn't forget anything, but if he did, this wouldn't be something that would slip away so easily. It was year-cycles before he'd made commander, while he was still pushing his way up in Homicide. He had been hunting the same serial killer for months and finally tracked him to his hideout. He'd gone in and done what was usual for him – find the victims or their corpses and apprehend the perpetrator, or make *him* a corpse. Santana wasn't working the case, but he was personally attached to it. One of the abducted women was his wife. Copernicus had uncovered the hideout and stormed it just before the perpetrator had ended her. The superiors had ordered him to wait for backup. He had not waited. So, in Santana's eyes, he was a great man, but to others he was a freak and a liability. Either way he was unfazed. He was who he was and opinions were like mouths – everybody had one.

His mind skipped from history to present, back to the case they were now working. He met Diega's gaze again and he saw she was thinking about the same thing. Like him, Diega lived to work; their life-paths demanded it. He tuned out of his thoughts and into a conversation between Jude and Eli on how to fix the busted lock of Jude's front door in his apartment at Headquarters.

'Hey, turn that up!' someone yelled from the bar.

The pedal-ball game had paused for half-time and the holo-screen was broadcasting a news update. Complete silence engulfed the diner, save for the food sizzling and the wail of music from the back-room. A full-size hologram of former Oscuri Tracker Commander Oren Harvey stepped out of the screen and stood in midair while the newsreader spoke.

'*Tomorrow marks the fifteen year-cycle anniversary of the disappearance of Commander Oren Harvey, hailed as our era's greatest soldier. Her countless acts of service to the state and people of Scorpia have directly and indirectly saved billions of lives and continue to do so to the present day. Harvey's final act as Commander of the Oscuri Trackers was the capture and arrest of the city's most evil serial killer, Englan Chrisholm.*'

An image flashed up of Chrisholm's ordinary, even pleasant, face and the crowd erupted into a storm of booing and hissing. A general shushing overcame the sound as the newsreader continued to talk. '*In the year-cycle of the Everdark, Chrisholm, a famous artist, was convicted of the savage torture and murder of over ninety children.*'

The air around the holo-screen filled with holograms of children's smiling faces. '*Chrisholm was executed for his crimes, survived by his daughter, Enie, who, weeks after his arrest, died in a fire at the custody house where she was being held, despite Commander Harvey's efforts to save the child.*' An image flashed up of paramedics stretchering out a body covered by a white sheet.

'Burn baby burn!' One soldier yelled out to cheers and applause before there was more shushing.

'*Soon after this event, Commander Harvey was seen leaving Scorpia, never to return. So the question remains – what was the fate of the soldier, the commander, the hero Oren Harvey? Tune into* Newsdirect *tomorrow night for a full exploration of the life and deeds of Oren Harvey. In other news . . .*'

Copernicus glanced at Diega. She was still staring at the screen, her jaw clenched, skin flashing vivid colours. General babble resumed to full volume and the waitress returned with their food. Eli jumped into his with both hands. Jude tasted the soup and grimaced and Diega slid her meal around her plate, but didn't touch it. Copernicus inspected his and saw a distinct line of prickle-like boar hairs all along one side of the steak. He shook his head in disgust, but wasn't overly surprised.

He considered offering the slab of meat to the others, but Eli seemed to be the only one with an appetite, and as he'd told

Copernicus the first time they'd met, Eli never ate anything that once had a face and feelings. He pushed the plate away and waited.

As soon as Eli finished his meal, Copernicus threw the coin on the table and they left the diner.

Outside, the street swarmed with people, mainly military personnel on their way to and from work. Copernicus stood surveying the passers-by, locking on to various familiar body-heat signatures then skipping to the next. He saw a group of scullion-gypsy women and girls standing on a corner of the street, begging for money. Copernicus watched them for a moment as they played out their show, their faces and bodies pushed into practised poses of neediness and desperation. Memories of what the carnival scullions had done to him when he was a child threatened to replay in his mind but he blocked them out.

On the other side of the road a band of Androts and smaller machine-breed robots worked to repair a long strip of street that had collapsed down into parts of an underground passageway dug in the early history of Scorpia to allow the then emperor to travel unseen between Palace Sirenseron and the stadium to witness the gladiator fights. Watching the machine-breeds work reminded Copernicus of something he needed to ask Jude. He turned to find the Ar Antarian standing close by, also watching the Androts, his expression troubled.

'Jude.' Copernicus spoke with a lowered voice so that only he would hear. 'I need you to send SevenM to track Christy Shawe. I need a location on him.'

With no perceptible communication between the Ar Antarian and his robot, SevenM dropped from Jude's shoulder, landed on the ground with a click of its eight dextrous legs and scuttled away into an alley. Copernicus nodded thanks, but Jude didn't see. His eyes were fixed on something over the commander's shoulder. Copernicus turned. Silho stood on the footpath, swaying on the edge of collapse. He moved swiftly to her and grabbed her arm before she fell. She instinctively pulled back, but he held her firmly. Her arm was very hot under the bandage, a heat unusual for her Nightcat and Ivory Condor bloodlines.

Jude and Eli rushed over as well.

'Are you okay?' Eli asked her.

Silho nodded, but Copernicus shook his head.

'Brabel, that's enough,' he ordered. 'You're no good to me with concussion. You should have admitted your state of injury the first time I asked you. It's unprofessional and I'm not impressed. You're dismissed from this shift and the next. I'll evaluate you when you come in on the third.' He released her arm and Silho stepped back, pain clouding her eyes.

Diega came to join them. 'Did you give Eli the fluid samples from the first crime scene?' she asked.

Silho looked up with dismay.

'Where are they?' Diega demanded.

'I must have left them there,' Silho admitted.

'I don't believe this!' Diega didn't bother to hide her anger and disgust.

'I'll go and get them,' Silho offered in desperation. She staggered and almost fell again, making her new communicator slip out of her pocket and clatter to the ground. Eli grabbed up the machine for her and clipped it onto her belt. He stood by her side, looking up at her with concern.

'No point,' Copernicus said. 'The forensics would have taken them. We'll have to wait for their report.'

'*Kitcher,*' Diega swore in Fenlen.

'I'm sorry,' Silho whispered.

'She's sorry,' Diega mocked her.

'Eli, take her home,' Copernicus said.

Silho lowered her eyes to the ground, and Jude said, 'You did really well tonight, Silho, and tomorrow's a new day.'

Diega laughed unpleasantly.

Eli took Silho's arm and led her away. Copernicus watched them move towards Headquarters where Eli's transflyer was parked.

'I don't like her,' Diega said beside him, echoing her previous sentiments. 'She's incompetent.'

'She's new,' Jude argued. 'She's nervous.'

'Don't defend her!' Diega snarled. 'We're talking about people's lives here! There's something seriously wrong with that girl – I'm telling you.'

Copernicus looked back to the disappearing figures and narrowed his eyes. He didn't need Diega to tell him there was something wrong with Brabel; he already knew that. The question was – what was it?

8

Eli led Silho across the rooftop parking lot of Headquarters. They passed a member of the Dog Squad and his canine partner conducting a random search around the crafts.

'Hello, Bill, hello, KC,' Eli greeted the human-breed soldier and his dog.

Bill, struck mute by a blow to his head during his time as a lower ranking guardian, nodded in greeting. His dog, KC, tilted his head to one side and watched Eli with sharp, yellow eyes. He licked his lips. Eli often snuck food down to the soldier dogs while they were on duty at Headquarters. He knew he shouldn't, but he couldn't help himself. They always gave him *that look* and he couldn't resist. Since childhood, he'd wanted a pet dog, but first his gran'ma hadn't allowed it, and now his otter, Nelly, was completely against the idea. The little creature glared at him from inside his pocket.

They reached his transflyer, an antique exo-craft named *Summer Holiday*. He had restored the flyer's shell, ripped out its existing mechanics and replaced it with a hybrid engine he had designed using what he considered the best parts from a variety of transflyer makes and models. The result was a craft that everyone expected someone's hard-of-seeing grandmother to be driving, with the kick and thrust of an elite racer. He enjoyed it when arrogant or stupid pilots gave him a hard time for flying slowly. Then he could take off and leave them shocked and rocking in his jet stream. He'd added on a variety of mods, some of them useful, like the chameleon wash-over that gave him camouflage mode, some of them not so useful, like the back massager that tickled and made him laugh so much he couldn't see through his tears.

Eli slid the starter flash from his pocket and unlocked the craft, then hurried to the passenger side and pulled open the door for Silho. A million chocolate wrappers and tech parts avalanched out onto the ground.

'Sorry about this.' He grabbed them up in armfuls and dumped them into the back. He shoved everything else off the passenger seat and dusted off the fabric. Nelly darted out of his pocket onto the seat. When he tried to lift her away, she nipped him.

'Sorry, she gets very jealous of other girls,' he tried to explain to Silho as he wrestled with the furry otter.

Silho held onto the side of the transflyer to keep herself upright, and Eli gave her full credit for the fact that even though she'd been embarrassingly dismissed early from her first shift, she was still trying to pay attention to what he was saying instead of slipping into a trance of self-pity and ignoring him. Eli managed to grasp Nelly and stuffed her into her safety carriage at the back of the craft. She sat clinging to the bars, puffing out her fuzzy cheeks and chattering furiously.

'If you please,' Eli made a sweeping gesture for Silho to enter and smacked his hand on the transflyer door.

She murmured her thanks and ducked down into the craft.

Eli ran around the back, cursing and shaking his stinging knuckles. He jumped into the pilot's seat and wrinkled his nose. The craft smelt like someone had passed a lot of gas, leapt out and shut the stench inside.

'Wet carpet,' he tried to explain. He gave a nervous giggle and hurried to turn on the air. The engine ignited and the motor purred into life. The craft lifted up until it was hovering higher than the other parked transflyers, then Eli extended the flight wings. He restrained himself from explaining to Silho all the small details of his creation. If she was like most of the girls he knew, such information would cause her to lapse into a coma of boredom within seconds. He swooped the craft upwards and away from Headquarters to where a line of transflyers waited to merge onto the main skyway of the level.

'You live on Level 502 – Angelstown, right?' he asked Silho.

She nodded. 'Forty-five Hall Drive. Thank you for taking me home.'

Eli smiled at her, and his eyes were drawn to the tiny pictures partially covering her neck and chest. They were separate but joined. They were like something he'd seen before, but he couldn't place where.

Eli swerved out and joined the flow of transflyers, masses of people hurrying to get home, or at least as far away from work as possible. Though Eli loved his job, that was one of the downsides of being a tracker – home was at work and work never ended. He glanced at the glowing chronograph embedded in the dashboard of his craft. It was only mid-dark – still half the night to go. He veered off the main skyway into pipeway seven which ran from Level 150, where Headquarters was located, all the way to the murky places of Level 840. He had never personally been below Level 700 and had no desire to. People had a way of vanishing without a trace in the places with no natural light.

Once inside the pipeway, he punched the engine up to hyper-speed and they shot straight downward, the tunnel lights flashing by on either side. Eli looked over at Silho.

'In three months you'll be off probation. You can live at Headquarters then if you want to. I do. Jude and the commander do as well. Diega lives offsite with other Fen soldiers. She says we're too boring for her.'

Silho nodded, barely lifting her eyes, and Eli felt a stab of pity for her.

'Don't worry, today was disastrous – I mean, it *was not* disastrous. You didn't do well – I mean you *did* well.' He cleared his throat, silently cursing himself, and changed the subject. 'Your bloodline.' He nodded to her bandaged arms. 'Ivory Condor and Nightcat? I read your personnel file. I hope you mind – *don't* mind,' he corrected himself.

'I don't mind,' Silho replied, and Eli liked how her soft voice caressed his ears.

'You're an interesting mix . . . the birds and the cats usually don't intermarry,' he continued.

'My parents . . .' She began to explain but then stalled, and Eli quickly rushed in, 'Don't worry, I understand – mine too. Glee and Greer – there's a reason it's illegal.' He snorted. 'Actually, I don't know whether you've heard about this yet, but the Standard and the independent governing councils are discussing implementing more serious penalties for people who participate in illegal breeds. It just produces children with too many problems – like me. It's not just the talking and stealing thing, I'm actually also allergic to my own saliva. I have to wear this,' he indicated to the cap on one of his pointed teeth that gradually dispersed medicine into his system, 'so that my body doesn't swell up like a balloon and burst.'

Alarm registered in Silho's eyes and he hurried to reassure her, 'Don't worry it's secure – I hope – just kidding.' He giggled, but Silho was still looking decidedly uneasy, so he hurried on.

'But you know,' he steered the craft out of pipeway seven and onto a shorter westward-bound tunnel, 'some of the greatest warriors and minds of all time have been illegal cross-breeds. Sometimes an unusual mix can create unusually strong and unique skills and strengths. Of course the downside is that the person is also usually completely insane – but elite nonetheless. There's just a fine line, I guess, between trying to prevent birth defects and impeding the natural freedom of the different races. I mean, look at what already happened to the Midnight Men.'

Not so long ago the Standard, on behalf of the king, had given an extermination order against any person who was a crossbreed between a Midnight Man and any other race. The Midnight Men were a largely unknown kind of spectral-breed – their title given to them in the absence of anyone knowing their true name and because they only usually appeared at mid-dark. They were thought to feed on the essence of death and were also called 'Scorpia's Vultures' as they tended to stalk people whom they sensed were about to be injured or killed. When the person went down, either dead or close to it, they would attack, finish the job if necessary and then eat their flesh and drink their blood. As a result there hadn't really been that many cross-breed Midnight Men, due to the fact they tended to rip apart anyone who got near them, but there had been a strange few mixed with other kinds of spectral-breeds, many completely harmless, who had been rounded up and executed. The Standard and its governmentals had feared what would happen if the Midnight Man gene started dispersing more widely into other races. Eli understood their fear, but their methods had been brutal, and he couldn't help but feel sadness for the slaughtered Midnight Men, and worried that one day the state might also decide all imp-blood cross-breeds were dangerous and have them exterminated as well.

'Your parents – are they still together?' Silho asked him.

Eli laughed. 'I'm not sure they ever were. They both took off a long time ago – left me with Gran'ma and Grampy. They raised me.'

'Did you like living with them?' Silho asked a question that, for Eli, had no simple answer.

'Grampy was a very kind man,' he said in reply. 'But he died quite young. He left me an absurdly enormous collection of hats. One night during a storm, a streak of electricity hit the building where I was living and knocked all the hats off the rotating hinge system I'd hooked up to display them. I was sleeping in bed at the time and became buried under this mountain of hats. I almost died – death by hats – unpleasant to say the least.'

'I . . .' Silho started and Eli saw she was really struggling for a response, the look in her eyes somewhere between amusement and horror. He made a mental note to try to dull down his weirdness.

He said, 'I ended up putting them in storage. I couldn't bring myself to throw them away. They were his life's work. You know what I mean?'

She nodded and he got the feeling she really did understand, that she was someone who had lived a lot longer than her years.

'But honestly,' he continued. 'No one is pure-blood anymore – probably not even the king, and every breed has its own violent past, even the human-breeds. Have you studied their history?'

'Not so much,' Silho replied softly. 'I haven't really had the chance.'

'Well then, here's a million years in a minute,' Eli said. 'In the Devil's age, humans were almost extinct, so to survive they mixed

magics and genetics and bred out into non-verbal animal bloodlines, which resulted in their being outcast for several thousand
generations.'

He went over an air bump and the green Khaiti diamond pendant
hanging on a chain around his rear-vision mirror clinked. The sound
drew Silho's eyes to it. Eli glanced at her, checking her reaction.
His religion was a somewhat archaic one and not always accepted.
His gran'ma was a staunch believer and had brought him up to
strictly follow the laws of the temple. Once living independently,
he'd thrown it all away. Then, some year-cycles later, he'd gathered
the fragments of his beliefs back together, rearranged them to his
own understanding and logic and had held them close ever since. In
a way, rediscovering his belief had felt like coming home, though he
would still be considered an outsider by other Khaiti followers as his
thoughts didn't exactly line up with their ideology – but that was the
strength of them. He had taken the ideas and made them his own,
so they were unshakeable by outside forces. Diega had often teased
him for his diamonds, but it had no effect on him. He wasn't alone
in his belief of Paradise waiting. Many others, of all different races,
believed in variations of the same.

Silho's expression was neither mocking nor openly interested.
Instead she said, 'I read that green diamonds have the power to drive
away creatures with dark intentions.'

Eli nodded. 'Once a Midnight Man tried to attack me – I held up
this diamond . . .'

'He fled?' Silho said.

'Yes, but only after I threw it at his head.'

Silho's lips curved upwards and Eli saw she was like Diega:
beautiful when she was serious and stunning when she smiled. He
grinned back, delighted to be finally getting a positive response.

'Can I ask you a question?' he said. 'Today with Ev'r Keets . . .'
Silho's smile vanished and he could see her retreating back into herself. He quickly diverted his words. 'I just . . . I just thought it was
strange. Keets literally burst out of the Murk and crash-landed into
territory she knew we'd be monitoring. That's not like her. I mean,
she's been travelling in the Murk since she was young. She knows

what she's doing and she's powerful, but this time – she seems different, weaker. I mean, the commander even said that her body-heat signature has changed. I wonder what that means. Maybe she's sick. Maybe I should go and see her and offer medical help. The commander wouldn't like it, but I don't think anyone should suffer.'

Silho gave a slight nod and turned to look out the window.

Eli spotted the exit to Level 502 coming quickly up ahead and veered the craft into the merging lane. They burst out of the tunnel into suburban airspace and Eli dropped the craft back to normal velocity. He joined a northbound line of traffic heading towards the suburb of Angelstown. Trying to lift the uneasy silence, he said, 'If you look down you'll see the Ohini Fen boroughs of Estabana and Loquitas. Diega grew up in Estabana.'

He triggered one of the transflyer's mods and the entire base of the craft became transparent so it felt as though they were riding on air. Below them stretched a rainbow ocean of Ohini Fen and other types of Fens partying long into the night, celebrating the noctus-renium. They weren't actually nocturnals, but since they never slept, they considered themselves worthy to join in the festivities. In truth, Fens didn't need an excuse to party.

Silho stared down at the Fen streets, a dark expression on her face. Diega was obviously not her new best friend. It was true, Diega was as tactful as a blunt axe, but she could also be kind and funny. There was another side to her and Eli felt he had to explain this to Silho.

'She's a bit tough,' he began. 'She means harm – I mean, she *doesn't* mean any harm . . . really . . .'

Silho looked up at him with doubtful eyes.

'She's not always had things good, if you know what I mean,' he continued. 'I'll tell you this, but you have to keep it to yourself. She'd kill me if she knew I was telling you. When she was twelve year-cycles old, her little sister was abducted and killed by Englan Chrisholm. She was one of the kids we saw today on the news. What was the media saying at the time? *Alive no more but forever young.*'

A shadow passed over Silho's face but she said nothing.

'So, I mean, she's never said this, and Diega never would, but I'm sure it affected her badly. I know she ran away from home soon after and ended up in the gangland. And now she never visits her parents, which is sad, especially considering most Fens live for their family and community. She must feel very alone sometimes . . . But speaking of Englan Chrisholm . . .' He swooped down low over the suburb of Sunnyside. 'There's Englan Chrisholm's house, where they found all his victims' corpses.'

Eli looked down at the wrecked and desecrated house. Silho touched her head and closed her eyes, grimacing as though the pain was worsening.

'Sorry, probably not the best time for the Scorpia's-most-notorious tour. We'll be at your place in a flash. Is there someone there who can take care of you?' Eli asked, accelerating.

Silho shook her head.

'Your parents?'

'They passed away when I was young.'

'I'm sorry.' He knew he shouldn't push for more information, but curiosity had always been one of his issues. 'So who raised you?'

'A friend of the family.'

'Did you live close to here?'

'In the outskirts mainly.' Silho said. 'The man I lived with was a salt-panner in the Matadori.'

'Really? Is that where you met Ev'r Keets?' Eli said before thinking.

Silho looked him squarely in the eyes and said, 'I don't know Ev'r Keets.'

He saw she wasn't lying. Everyone knew Copernicus could see a lie, but few knew Eli also had the skill. There was a saying among the imp-breeds – *you can't lie to a liar.*

'So no husband, then?' he asked.

'I'm not married,' Silho replied.

'Boyfriend?'

'No.'

'Why not?' Eli asked and Silho squirmed uncomfortably.

'I'm sorry,' he said, realising he was being invasive, the way his kind usually were. 'It's none of my business, but if you're looking, I'm available.' He grinned again but Silho didn't see. She held one hand over her eyes, obviously not doing so well.

Before Eli could voice his concern, the navigation system beeped to signal that they were almost over the target destination.

'Here we are,' he said and swooped down low, landing outside number 45 Hall Drive. The building was a huge government-funded high-rise for low-income earners. Most of the lights were out, only nocturnals or night-shift workers still awake at this hour.

'I'll walk you up,' he offered.

'Thank you, but I'm fine,' Silho said in a tight voice that told him she was definitely not fine.

'I insist.' Eli leapt out of the transflyer and ran around to open Silho's door. She let him help her out of the craft and he walked with her to the front door of the building. Silho scanned her hand over the sensor and the doors swung open. The lobby light switched on. The elevator was out of order so they took the stairs to the fourteenth floor, where Silho led Eli along a corridor with tattered carpet and flickering overhead lights to her apartment – number 1464.

After opening the door, she turned in the doorway to face him. He peeked around her into her living space, tidy and sparsely furnished with well-worn furniture. A big pod-shaped plant sitting in a pot on the windowsill caught his eye. Plant study was one of his favourite pastimes.

'Pinkface Lily,' he identified it. 'That's not a common bulb.'

'True,' Silho said with an edge to her voice that said she was impressed. 'I bought it at a flea market – the seller had no idea,'

'Did you know that the sap of a relative of that lily – the Venus Lily – has the strongest medicinal qualities of all known plants?' Eli asked.

'As long as it's prepared right, otherwise it's fatal,' Silho added.

It was Eli's turn to be impressed. His pitch rose in excitement. 'True – too bad they're impossible to breed and beyond impossible to find,' he said. In truth, there was actually believed to be a bountiful supply of Venus Lilies in the city, on the very lowest level – Level 997 – known as Venus, alleged to be overrun by dangerous and violent plant life. No one but Oren Harvey had ever ventured down there. She had returned with the Venus Lily, but had been seriously injured and had never spoken of her journey except to say there were many more where it had come from, but that she strongly advised against trying to retrieve them. He would have loved to inspect the plant closer, but he could sense Silho's fatigue deepening.

'Okay,' he said. 'Call me if you need anything.'

'Thank you – goodnight,' she said.

'No problems at all,' Eli responded. 'And I think it's more like good morning,' he added with a laugh as she closed the door. It clicked shut and the lock shunted into place.

Eli stood looking at the door. He recognised loneliness in Silho. He himself had been very lonely for a very long time, yet he was also sure, even though they were both lonely, that he would never have a chance with her. They were too different. He was too different from everyone. People said there would be someone out there for him, who would love him and whom he could love, but he was starting to think this might not be the case. Even imp-breed women thought he was too short. Turning away from the door, he headed back down the corridor, only to pause in mid-stride as a ripple in the wallpaper seized his attention. Frowning, he reached out a hand and touched the place where he had seen the movement. But the wall was solid, with not even a scratch on it. Eli guessed it was probably just a spectral-breed, a Wraith or a Ghost of some sort. Shrugging off his unease, he glanced one final time at Silho's door then hurried away. His wings were cramped and chafed and he couldn't wait to go home and stretch them.

9

Silho stood in the centre of her lounge room, present in body, but gone in mind. Alone in the sanctuary of her own square of the city, she dissected the day, her every utterance, her every step. Every raw and ugly detail magnified and processed with the harshest of scrutiny. Hours passed in seconds, and when she emerged into the present, blinking in time with the dripping kitchen tap, her stomach muscles ached and her jaw was throbbing. She unclenched her teeth, released her fisted fingers and drew in several deep breaths, blowing out each one slowly to regain equilibrium.

Today she had failed, but it wasn't the first time and it wasn't the end of time, so tomorrow she would try again. This was the way she did things. This was the way she survived. Take it in, let it out, keep moving. Hammersmith had taught her that. He had never tried to replace her father, but he'd always treated her like his own child, and made her work so hard she'd screamed her hatred at him and learnt day by day that wherever her limitations lay, she hadn't yet reached them. This knowing fed her strength, but at the same time, Silho understood she was unwell. She could see that she was living a life of contradiction, spending her days half-asleep and her nights fighting to stay awake. When she spoke, she lied, and when she lied, she was trying to speak a truth so horrendous there were no words for it, just images seared into eternal remembrance.

Today, she'd taken all the hits everyone had aimed at her, and had, as always, bitten back her violent words and swallowed her anger. It tasted of bleach and burned her black from the inside out. It wasn't that she was faking, it was that she was fractured, both full of courage and fear, full of doubt and certainty, so anchored to her purpose and so lost inside it. She knew this conflict within her was responsible for her nightmares, where her parents lived grotesque half-lives in the witching hours between mid-dark and dawn, but she didn't know how to reconcile herself. Only that she had to keep going. She had to find the truth within the twisted lies. That was why she had enslaved herself to her study and training, day and night, for three year-cycles without a break, without a life, to become a tracker. She'd risked everything – always half a step from being discovered.

Silho moved on automatic, looking up to the ceiling, searching for I-eyes and spyers. She blinked into light-form vision and searched the apartment for traces of any body-light. When she saw none, she physically checked under every surface and behind every door. Once the task was complete, she did it again, prisoner to a mind that always doubted and second-guessed itself. When she was sure she was alone, unwatched and unrecorded, she unclipped her weapon belt and shed her gloves. Flexing her fingers, she allowed herself to stretch out and touch one of the apartment walls. Her hands sank into the plaster and images flashed through her mind – hazy pictures of what had happened in her apartment while she was away. The hands of the chronograph on the wall spun through time. Outside her windows daylight faded to nightlight and the shadows of the stray cats she fed brushed against the pane of glass. Her Pinkface Lily yawned and idly snapped at a passing mosquito. Her door opened. She saw herself saying goodbye to Eli . . .

Silho pulled back from the wall, satisfied, only to gasp in agony as the pain from her injury lanced through her skull with renewed force. Using the wall as support, sparking images with her bare finger-tips, she staggered towards her bedroom. Christy Shawe's fist had actually barely skimmed her skin and yet still had felt like a sledge-hammer blow. It was almost unimaginable how destructive the full force of the gangster king's strength would be – *enough to punch through a man's stomach?* Scenes from the breakwall replayed in her mind, causing her to inwardly shudder – *Why didn't I move?* She had been too focused on the commander. Seeing him fighting with Shawe, seeing the cold rage in his dark eyes, had both repelled and mesmerised her. Silho wasn't sure why, but wasn't surprised that she was so conflicted.

She made it to her bedroom, but left the light off, seeing well enough by the street lamps outside. Their glow called to her and she moved to the window and peered out behind the edge of the curtain, looking into the apartment block beside hers. There was something comforting about seeing other people living their lives and knowing she wasn't alone. In one apartment, a couple lay in bed kissing passionately. Their flimsy curtain, fluttering in the breeze, gave them little privacy. They didn't notice or maybe didn't care. Silho looked away, embarrassed to be watching, but her eyes were drawn back. She wanted that closeness with someone, to be unafraid and unashamed, and held skin to skin, but she couldn't imagine that ever happening. Her thoughts hovered momentarily over images of Copernicus before she blocked them out. It could never happen.

In an apartment several storeys above the couple, a man struggled to hang a large painting by himself. Silho glanced at the canvas then immediately turned away, but as she did, vibrant colours appeared on the white wash of her deliberately blank walls, dazzling blues and pale pinks, oranges and yellows. They spread, twisted with each other, becoming new colours, which further fused to create more. The picture evolved before her eyes, faces, bodies, landscape and sky. She couldn't just see the colour – she could taste it. Black was aniseed, pink musk, blue blueberry – sweet and sour tingled on her tongue. This wasn't just a painting – it was alive, and it called to Silho to create it, to buy paints and let other people see what her mind made from blankness, but she couldn't. So she squeezed her eyes shut, and when they reopened, the colours had disappeared and her mouth was dry.

She took one of the half-empty glasses of water that sat on every surface of the room. This hoarding was a peculiarity she'd developed after growing up in the desert where there was never enough water. Her guardian, Hammersmith, had believed in the character-building effects of deprivation. Big and bearded, with a booming voice, people had been terrified of him, until they got to know him. Zingara Ohavor, now Ev'r Keets, had said he must have had some giant in him. Silho clearly recalled the slight gypsy girl facing off with the huge hulking form of Hammersmith. Ev'r had stolen from their food stash and, being an ex-Oscuri Tracker, Hammersmith had hunted her down easily and demanded it back. He believed in discipline and getting things the hard but honest way. Zingara believed in every man and woman for themselves – except when it came to Ismail.

Silho remembered him. She remembered him sitting with her and listening quietly as she'd gabbled on about nothing important, overwhelmed to see other people after only having Hammersmith for company for so long. Though she'd been much younger than them, she'd recognised the deep love in their eyes when they looked at each other. She'd also seen, in light-form vision, the darkness closing in around Ismail's glow – and understood what that meant. When she'd started crying, he'd taken her hands in his own much larger ones, scarred rough from years of military duty. He had spoken softly to her. He'd told her it was okay, that he wasn't afraid. Paradise was waiting for him. Zingara didn't know and Silho didn't tell her because something in the darkness of Ismail's storm-black eyes had begged her not to. Zingara and Ismail had left together, hand in hand, walking through the desert towards the setting northern sun.

Hammersmith had said to let them go. Silho was sure he knew. He had a certain unusual sense of things. He used to look into the night sky and tell her stories about other worlds. It was his one and only dream to fly into space and find these worlds hidden among the stars. When Hammersmith had passed away she'd buried him in the sand and left immediately for Scorpia City, her steps driven by the need to prove her father's innocence.

Silho looked back out of the window and down to the street below. A small group of Androts had gathered in an alley beside the neighbouring apartment block and stood talking. Being out at this hour, they were breaking machine-breed curfew. This was something she had been seeing with increasing regularity – something that never used to happen. Things were changing, she could feel it.

83

The pain in her head forced Silho away from the comfort of the window. She went to the bathroom, where she turned on the light and looked into the mirror. A shiver ran along her back. When had she fallen asleep and woken up as her mother? Her thoughts flickered back to the night in the Matadori Desert – the last time she had seen her mother, Commander Oren Harvey. Silho spoke to her silently in her mind, as she stared at her own reflection,

The last time I saw you, you were kneeling in the sand, you said to recognise this deadland for what it was – a pilgrim's rest, away from walls and thoughts and a million pleading voices, a place to right my mind and soul before the final battle. You said that here the circular, binary universe of iniquities revisited and patterns repeated started to make sense to you – where your fight ended and mine began, where the future became the present and the present the past. The past where Silho's father, the paintsmith Englan Chrisholm, had been condemned and executed by the state. They took blood for blood – leaving only the fractured reconstructions of the man resurrected every night in her dreams. His truth according to her mind's eye. And this truth screamed his innocence. Englan Chrisholm had not tortured and murdered all those children. There had been forbidden places in their house, rooms with locks, cupboards with chains, but he'd stored his important art there, not the twisted pieces of flesh that the soldiers had dragged out on the day of his arrest. In the aftermath of his arrest and her incarnation, Silho had begun to hear the walls speak and knew she was either insane or gifted – and since she was sane enough to consider insanity, she decided she was gifted, but horribly so. She was someone whose very life was heresy. Imprisoned by palace enforcers, her mother had been her saviour. Oren had freed her and taken her to Hammersmith for a new identity, a new life, but too injured from the battle, Oren had been unable to save herself. Tears misted Silho's eyes and she didn't look like Oren anymore. It was said that her mother had never been afraid of anything. *I'm just the ghost of your shadow,* she told her.

Silho took a bottle from the sink and shook out two black pills into her hand – black pills to blacken the past. As she swallowed them down, a sense of calm settled over her.

She stripped off her clothes and the bandages binding her arms and stepped under the shower. The warm water streamed over her bloodline marks, the orange flame of her Pyron mother and the fire-bird dragon of her father. She ran her hands over the colours and up to the picture on her neck and chest. They had first appeared in the desert without explanation or possible cause.

When the aching of her head had eased and the water was completely cold, she grabbed a towel and went back out to her room to sit at her desk.

'Activate,' she told her computer system.

The last image she had been looking at before she'd shut down the system earlier that day came up on her holo-screen. It was a hologram of Copernicus Kane. As she stared at the picture, the pills she'd taken numbing her emotions, dulling her pain, a thought came into her mind. *Why not go back to Moris-Isles and search for the samples, just for yourself? Just so you know you can do it, so you know that they are wrong and you are right.*

Blood trickled down the side of Silho's face. The wound had reopened in the shower, despite the stitches. They *were* wrong that she was incapable and she *would* prove it to herself. The next thing she registered, she was already dressed, her arms rebound and weapon belt clipped around her waist. Silho left her apartment without looking back, not thinking for a second that she'd never walk through that door again.

10

'**D**iurnal eyes in eternal darkness hold no use, but when the eyes cannot see the mind imagines . . .'

The echoing slither-snap of a lash and a close-by agonised scream silenced the man. He retreated into the shadows of his cage as far back as the shackles would allow. He'd worn the bindings for so long that skin and steel had fused into one. The torch flames, chained to the cave walls, quivered and flapped.

'Show me what is to come.' Ev'r Keets stood before him, not as herself, but as her ancestor, a dark-faced woman with glowing yellow-wolverine eyes and sharp carnivore teeth. She felt the child kicking inside her and she remembered her own baby's kick, before the desert freaks had ripped the half-formed child from her body. The man extended a shaking chain-hand from the shadows and pointed behind Ev'r's head. He whispered, 'Imagine.'

Ev'r turned. The cave walls were no more. In their place stretched a land of darkness, of pitch-black silence, where nothing moved and nothing spoke. Where nothing lived. All was dust. Aquais was a corpse land battered by a howling wind. It swept along a symphony of screams, a chorus of cries from beneath the ground, from the pits of hell, where the chanting of demons trembled the foundations of earth itself. The sound was the monotone drone of the most accursed and powerful of dark magics – the Skreaf magics. Ev'r sank into the Murk and sped through its mist, until she saw ahead a well stretching down into the depths of the ground. She paused above the well and looked into it. Her sight sped down and down and down until it found the tortured hordes of prisoner slaves. Skreaf demons stood guard over them, ruled by the most horrendous of all the devils. In this monster's eyes, rage coupled with utter despair showed the wager of his choices. This being had lost his grip on truth and set himself adrift in the desert of his mind, with death behind him, death in front of him, death everywhere he looked. He was the Morsmalus.

Ev'r gasped and jolted upright. Her chest heaved as these memories that weren't her own, but passed down through her blood, echoed in her mind. The people of her bloodline were natural seers. Those strongest skilled, as she was, were able to travel far into the past and several steps into the future. Ev'r had denied the skill, as she had denied her heritage, but seeing the Skreaf demons hiding behind the skin of the human-breed soldiers, evil dressed in flesh, had triggered it without her consent.

Drawing her legs closer to herself, she rested her head on her knees. Saliva pooled in her mouth. The changes of her jaw and teeth were making it difficult to swallow. The Ravien could snap bones with one bite. An image, the same image she'd been seeing for hours now with increasing regularity, blared into full and horrible colour before her eyes – Silho Brabel screaming, gurgling, drowning in her own blood.

Ev'r shivered. This vision of Brabel was an adult version of the girl she had met deep in the desert after fleeing the wreckage of O'Tenery with Ismail. Brabel was in trouble – or going to be in trouble of the worst kind. That was clear. Ev'r was trying not to care. Why should she care about someone she had met only briefly a whole lifetime ago, someone who was now one of Copernicus Kane's minions? Ev'r asked and answered the question. It was because of Brabel's eyes – what they had reflected – what they'd said to her in their moment of re-meeting. They had said *I remember him.*

Ev'r sensed the main door of the interrogation area opening. She looked up into the spyer trained on her, expecting to see the witches. They were alternating with the other two guardians and she felt they were keeping a close eye on her. It was no coincidence that Skreaf were stationed in the interrogation area. They must have seen her in the desert – seeing them – and now they were waiting for the right moment to silence her. She felt their intentions like a spreading shadow, but instead of the witches she saw the soldier she called Snack-size entering the area. He was carrying a tray of food. A growl, alien to her ears, rumbled deep in her throat. The magnetic forces of the table zapped to life and dragged her across the room, slamming her down into the metal chair. The door to her cell slid open and the puny soldier stood timid in the doorway.

'I didn't bring you food – I mean, I *brought* you food,' he said shrilly. 'You'll be able to eat it without your hands, if you lean forward.'

'Trutt off,' she snarled. 'You think I'm going to eat like an animal?'

He shrugged. 'I would. I'm going to put it on the table and then you can eat it or leave it – it's up to you. I just didn't want you to go hungry.'

'How kind of you,' she sneered.

He took small steps across the cell and gingerly slid the tray onto the table. The steel of the tray melted into the steel of the table, removing any chance of her using it as a weapon. The food sat on the table surface. Her stomach gurgled and she felt another growl starting in her throat. Scrunching her eyes shut, she managed to control it. Her eyelids blinked open. Snack-size was still standing beside the table, studying her with innocent curiosity shining in his big dark eyes.

'What do you want?' she demanded.

He stepped back at the force in her voice. 'You seem well, I mean, you seem sick.'

'So?'

'I thought maybe there was something I could do.'

Ev'r narrowed her eyes. 'I'm about to be executed and you're concerned about my health?'

His eyes swivelled as his brain computed what she'd said. He responded in a small voice, 'I can't do anything about your sentence, but I can help you in the short term. I don't want you to suffer.'

'Trutt off,' Ev'r repeated clearly and slowly. 'I don't need your pathetic pity. You don't know anything about me.'

'I know you can travel in the Murk. I know you're strong. I know you never give up and never give in. I know you know more about ancient architecture, civilisations, customs and people than all of the scholars put together. I know you're gifted with chemicals and sub-stances and I know you're very rich, but you don't think much of money. I know your favourite colour is brown and I know you're not well because your bag was full of regenerative potions. I tested them and found they were made from a wide variety of ingredients from all over Aquais. You must have travelled long and far to gather them all. You must have gone —'

'Alright,' Ev'r cut in.

She eyed the short soldier. Obviously he was intelligent and a tal-ented inventor – no one before him had ever made chains that could hold her – but she saw he was also soft, very soft, and possibly easy to manipulate. If her efforts to sway the Ar Antarian, Jude, failed, he could be her Plan B, a second chance to get out and get back to the Matadori before she changed. If she could do that and get what she needed from the asylum, she might still be able to outrun the Skreaf scourge about to envelop the city, and cross over the Boundary Wall into the Brine as she had planned to do.

Most people believed that the land beyond the boundary was uninhabited, poisonous and corrupted into something evil, but she had once found an ancient written word book that described the Brine as a place governed by strange, indefinable magics that made it impossible to navigate or map, lands existing within lands with hidden doorways to other realms and planets and places inescapable. It was true no one who had crossed the wall had ever returned to tell what lay on the other side, but she wasn't just any fool crossing over on a whim, dream or dare. Where others would die, she could survive – that was the legacy of a lifetime of struggle.

'I have a growth in my stomach that keeps getting bigger,' she lied. 'I need something to slow my body.'

'Okay.' She could hear his brain ticking fast. 'Then you'll need something with a sapphire base.' He pulled a black bag seemingly out of midair and clanked around in it for several minutes. He emerged with a syringe full of red liquid.

He hesitated, then darted in, injected her, and darted out so quickly she probably wouldn't have been able to stop him even if she'd tried.

Ev'r didn't feel the changes in her mouth and jaw reversing as they had with the antidotes, but she did sense a stopping of their progression, and a slowing of her system. It calmed her.

Footsteps shuffled at the door and Ev'r looked up to see the two non-Skreaf guardians, the giant and his sneaky-eyed, sabre-toothed pal, standing in the doorway watching.

'You right, Eli?' the sabre-tooth asked, his voice husky and slurred around his fangs.

'I'm fine,' Eli held up one hand. Ev'r saw it was trembling.

'We're just here,' the soldier said, 'if you need us.'

'Right here,' the giant echoed.

They stepped back only one or two paces and stood there waiting. Ev'r knew if she wanted to bend Snack-size to her needs she'd have to start working on him now, while he was separated from Copernicus Kane.

'Eli? Is that your name?'

He nodded.

'Listen, Eli . . .' But before she could continue, images of Silho Brabel screaming intersected her mind. She gasped, straining forward against the pull of the magnetised chains. This time she could feel Silho's pain, feel the fear choking her. Ev'r gagged in response as though it were her own neck being squeezed.

Eli rushed towards her and grabbed her shoulders, screaming at the guardians, 'Cut the magnets! Cut the magnets!'

The guardians reappeared instantly, but neither moved to obey. They eyed Ev'r with distrust.

'What are you doing?' Eli yelled at them. 'She needs help. Cut the magnets!'

'You come out first and then we'll cut them,' the Twitchbak said.

'But she needs my help!'

'We don't care,' he said. 'Come out!'

'Silho . . .' Ev'r managed to say with a choked gurgle.

'Silho?' Eli leaned in, watching her mouth.

'Something's wrong,' Ev'r rasped.

'With Silho?' Eli grabbed the communicator off his belt and checked a small locator screen. 'She's at home, where I left her.'

'Eli!' The sabre-tooth Twitchbak stepped into the cell with his electrifier drawn. 'Come out! She's dangerous.'

'One second,' Eli called. 'Are you okay?' he asked Ev'r when she seemed to stop choking.

She nodded. The vision had faded and her body was stabilising. With effort, she managed to sit up straight.

Eli spoke softly to her. 'I'll keep an eye on Silho and I'll keep an eye on you.' He pressed a camouflaged spyer under the metal table. 'When you need more medication signal me. I'll see you. I'll come.'

He gave her a small sharp-toothed smile, then walked to where the guardians stood and left the room.

The Twitchbak growled at Ev'r and slammed the door shut. The magnetic pull of the chains against the steel table released. Ev'r groaned and lowered her head. Momentarily, she lost sight of time and it skimmed past her. When the chains again snapped rigid against the table, she jolted into clarity. She raised her eyes and saw the Ar Antarian soldier, Jude, standing inside the cell staring at her. She felt no surprise. She looked him over from head to toe. Of course he was the epitome of high nobility – powerful blue eyes, perfectly aligned features, metal limbs. The steel parts made all Ar Antarians smell like piss – including him.

'Speak of the devil,' Ev'r greeted.

'How did you know?' He didn't waste words.

Ev'r smiled. Her foresight had already shown her this scene, when this man – the Crown Prince Isaiah U whom the entire city believed had been dead for almost a decade – stood in front of her and asked her that exact question. And it was a good question considering he didn't know her. She had never met him as the prince, and even if she had, he would have been veiled from head to foot.

'Does it matter?' She played with him.

'What do you want?' he asked.

'What do you think?' she replied.

His eyes flicked over her chains. 'I can't do that. The commander would know I helped you. I can't lie to him.'

'Obviously you already have,' Ev'r said.

'No.' He shook his head. 'I have told the truth – just not the whole truth.'

'Whatever,' she said. 'I don't care. I want out or I'll tell Kane everything.'

'Ev'r, what would you gain from that?' She could see from the look in his eyes, a patient kind of searching for understanding, that he was going to try to reason with her – to appeal to her better nature. She couldn't help but laugh.

'Are you going to get me out or what?'

'I told you,' he said. 'I can't. The commander would have to arrest anyone who helped you.'

'Then get rid of him.'

'What do you mean?'

Ev'r looked up at him from beneath her eyelids. She didn't need to say the words.

'No. No way. Never.'

She nodded and let the silence settle around them for a moment before saying, 'What do you think your commander is going to do once he finds out you've been lying to him for all these year-cycles? You must already know that Kane doesn't like liars and he doesn't like being made a fool. And then there's your little girlfriend. What do you think she will say? Do you really think they'll forgive you, accept you? Kane will have you discharged, and then where will you go? When they purge my mind everyone will know what you are. You wouldn't be able to hide and who will protect you? The military won't back you. You've lied to your friends. You'll have no one. You'll be outcast . . . hunted . . .'

The prince sighed and lowered his head. He held the sides of his neck with both hands. She could see he was trembling.

'But if you get me out of here, I can help you. I'll hide you.'

The Ar Antarian raised his eyes to hers and said firmly, 'I told you, I can't.'

'Then I have no choice,' Ev'r said.

'There is always a choice,' he countered.

'Poignant,' she smirked. 'But wasted.'

The prince studied her for a moment longer, an edge of sadness in his blue eyes. 'Much like this whole conversation,' he said before turning and leaving the room.

The magnetic stranglehold cut off and Ev'r slumped back in the seat. She stretched her neck one way and then the other. The conversation had not gone the way she'd expected it to. Every high noble she had encountered to this point had been piss-weak and utterly self-centred, but this Jude . . . It was just her luck to get the one royal in all of history to have a spine. Regardless, next time Copernicus Kane came to her cell, she'd have something very interesting to share with him. The thought brought a smile to her lips.

11

It was always the same. Passing through the doors of the All Hallows Corridor and seeing the entrance to his residence up ahead felt, for Copernicus, like a long-distance runner with the finish line in sight or sometimes, when he'd spent too long in the company of others, more like a drowning man dragging himself closer and closer to the surface. Of the years he had lived in the Commander's Quarters, he had never once paused in the corridor to study the portraits lining the walls, of soldiers who had owned the title of Oscuri Tracker Commander before him. When he was leaving his apartment, it was with a purpose, and when he was heading home, his adrenalin kicked in, his throat tightened and all he could see was solitude. While Diega's happiness was fed by the company of others, he needed to be alone to regenerate for a time, before facing the world again.

The eyes of the fallen commanders followed him as he moved with stealth along the marble corridor.

'Open,' he commanded.

The security system responded, 'Immediately, Commander Kane.'

Laser lines scanned across his face and torso, checking his retinas and fingerprints, his bloodline marks and body-heat signature, a security measure Eli had designed and implemented for him. Eli had also designed much of Headquarters' new system. Satisfied he was the true Kane, the doors to his apartment parted from the centre and he stepped through. The doors slid shut and locked behind him. He breathed out and his shoulders relaxed, the heat of the air warming his skin. He massaged a hand over the back of his neck and took stock of his apartment. It was as he had left it – dark, silent and spotless.

On moving into the quarters, a need for open space had prompted him to smash down all but a few of the dividing walls, leaving one expansive main room. Along three of the high walls his weapon collection hung from floor to ceiling. He owned numerous antiques with years of history etched into their surfaces; many others were unique, designed by him and custom-made by Eli. Each had their own space on the wall and special place in his collection, but by far his favourite was the short blade named Solace – owned by the former commander Oren Harvey. It was designed never to lose its edge and he was sure it had hidden powers he hadn't yet figured out how to access, but he would.

Copernicus took his ID from his pocket, slipped the chain with its protective talisman from around his neck and placed them both on the glass table beside the door. He took off his jacket and unclipped his weapon belt, hanging them on hooks above the table. He left his second blade strapped to his ankle and moved across the polished marble floor to his kitchen. He'd blacked out the wall of the window inside the kitchen. It had given spectacular views across the entire city, but a view was low on his priority list when compared with privacy. His automated bar system poured him a drink, half-guinapple juice, half-Araki, the potent human-breed spirit. He took the drink and sat down at his desk. It was one of his favourite possessions. Diega had given it to him when he'd made Commander, even though he knew she was secretly upset it hadn't been her.

'Boot up.' He voice-activated his computer system. A holo-image of Eli's face appeared above his desk and grinned at him. He shifted uncomfortably. He had tried to change this default image after Eli had installed it, but had, so far, been unsuccessful, and he couldn't bring himself to ask Eli to do it. It would hurt his feelings too much. If it had been anyone else he wouldn't have cared about how they felt, but Eli had been a friend to him through too much to disregard him, and the imp-breed was far more sensitive than most people knew. He joked about himself, he put up a good front, but he had a soft heart, too soft for his own good. He put the needs of others far above his own and felt driven to help people even when it put him at a disadvantage. Copernicus saw in his friend so much potential as a soldier and as a person, but Eli didn't have any confidence in himself and he was too swayed by his pity for others.

'You have three new messages, Commander Kane. Would you like to hear them now or later?' holo-Eli asked.

'Now.' He took a mouthful of drink.

'Message one playing now.'

'Kane,' High Commander Levis Kline coughed his name and glared through the holo as if it were a window. Copernicus couldn't help but snarl in disgust. Levis was high ranking and highly annoying. He was part of the upper echelon of the United Regiment made up of ancient has-beens who refused to die, gaining their high status only through a process of elimination. He was so old his skin looked like it was melting off his face.

The holo of Levis continued, 'Kane, this week alone I've had twenty-four more complaints about the conduct of your trackers – twenty specifically about you. I'm getting fed up with your antics and disrespect. Reel yourself in, or you'll be disciplined – again!'

The message ended and Eli's holo-face re-appeared. He started to ask, 'Would you like to —'

'Delete,' Copernicus said before the options could be given. He gritted his teeth – *disciplined again.* How could it be *again* when it hadn't ever happened? They kept threatening him, but no one was really going to touch him. They needed him too much. After Oren Harvey had vanished, city conditions had deteriorated badly and though the soldier who had replaced her as commander, a human-breed called Sammael Sy, had tried, he had been largely ineffectual in policing the city. Once in power, Copernicus had lifted the standard again – until now, anyway. He tipped back the glass and drank some more of the Araki mix.

Holo-Eli said, 'Message two playing now.'

An aging woman with masses of dark curls and blood-red lipstick popped up on the screen. She spoke with a breathy voice. 'Hello,

Commander. It's Madame V from Club Fantasia. We haven't seen you in a while. We miss you. Call me.'

Copernicus snorted. 'You miss my money . . . delete.'

The holo-Eli's face reappeared, a grin quirked his lips as though he'd actually heard what Copernicus had said. 'Message three playing now.'

The real Eli flashed up on the holo-screen. 'Hey, boss, it's me, Eli, as you can see,' he giggled, then gulped it down. 'I'm in the *Summer Holiday*. And I'm heading back to Headquarters now. Silho's home safe and beautiful . . . I mean *sound* . . . so I'm just heading back now, as I said. Okay, I'll see you soon. Talk to you then . . . bye-bye.'

Copernicus checked his chronograph and compared the time with when the message had been sent. Eli would have arrived back a while ago.

'Return call,' Copernicus said.

He heard the static whirr of his system reaching out to Eli's. The systems connected and he heard Eli's recorded voice, 'Sorry, I'm not available, please leave a message.'

'Eli, call me when you get this. End,' Copernicus said.

'End of new messages,' the holo-Eli told him. 'Would you like the news headlines now or later?'

'Later,' Copernicus said. He exhaled and massaged his forehead. First he had to do something he hated doing.

'Call Forensics,' Copernicus said to his system. It reached out and linked with the Forensics branch.

'Yes, Commander Kane. How may I help you?' The lead forensic investigator's assistant, a human-breed man with a skinny pinhead, possibly of mantis-blood heritage, answered. His prim and patronising cheeriness always irritated Copernicus to the extreme.

'I need the fluid results from today's Moris-Isles murder scene,' Copernicus said.

'Why of course, Commander. Just one moment please while I check the files . . . Ah yes, we will have them ready for you in . . . three day-cycles.'

Copernicus inwardly cursed. 'Can they be ready any sooner?'

'Ah, no, sorry, we have a backlog. How about I have them delivered to you just as soon as we have them?'

'End,' Copernicus said curtly and the connection hung on just long enough for him to see the assistant purse his lips with indignation.

Brabel's mistake had cost them time, and two of the things he hated most in the world were waiting and wasting time. His thoughts focused in on the new recruit. Diega disliked her, but Diega disliked virtually everyone who wasn't either male or Ohini Fen. Jude liked her, but Jude thought everyone deserved a chance – even murderers. Eli also liked her, but attractiveness dazzled Eli like staring into the suns. The impartial judgement would have to be his.

'I want you to run a face match on new recruit Silho Brabel. Match six points or more,' he told his system.

It retrieved her file and projected her image. It was a bad picture, not capturing the unusual depth of her eyes. The computer system mapped her features and started the search, flicking through millions of faces a minute, of both the living and dead, looking for facial points in common. He'd set it high at first and would work down from there.

Copernicus leaned back in his chair. He took the ring out of his pocket and examined it again. Ev'r Keets would have known immediately who had made the band and from what, but as he had told the others, Keets would never help them. Scullions never changed.

His chronograph alarm sounded, signalling it was time for his scheduled training. He placed the ring back in his pocket and went to the training area of his apartment. Panels of wall pressed back and the floor lifted up to reveal mirrors and his well-worn equipment. He bent down, took his secondary blade from his ankle holster and spun the weapon, twisting it around and over his fingers. He glanced into the mirror and, before his eyes, the steel of the blade blended in with the black, purple and blue of his viper bloodline marks and vanished. Copernicus jolted back, shaking his hand and dropping the knife. This was happening more than it used to. Like the unstoppable release of anger when pent up for too long, his skills were releasing themselves even though he wanted nothing to do with them. He cursed himself for his weak reaction and snatched up the blade. The movement sent pain stabbing through his chest. Gritting his teeth, he gripped his ribs until the ache lessened. He put his blade down on a side table and unbuttoned his shirt, slipping it off his shoulders. Blue and black bruises spread out over the entire right side of his chest. Copernicus cursed again, thinking of Christy Shawe, once his best friend, now his worst enemy – a grand title considering the number of people he arrested or aggravated on a daily basis.

He abandoned his training and, turning to the wall beside him, punched a code into the security panel. A hidden door, the entrance to his diagnostic chamber, slid open. He unbuttoned his trousers, dropped them and entered the chamber naked. The chamber's holo-screen activated, thankfully not in the shape of Eli's face in this area of the apartment.

'Body scan in process,' the system told him, and he felt the heat of lasers crossing his body, analysing his condition. After a few mo-ments the system spoke again. 'You have a visitor.'

'Show me,' he instructed and the holo-screen displayed an image of Diega standing outside the door of the All Hallows Corridor, repeatedly ringing the bell-alert with one hand and holding a black case in the other. She had the look of grim determination on her face that she always wore when she felt the need to force him into conversation about personal matters. He seriously considered telling her to come back later, but decided against it. Putting her off just made things worse. Besides, he needed to see the file he'd asked her to compile from the data they'd gathered at both crime scenes.

'Unlock for Sergeant Diega Bluejay,' he ordered his system.

Diega walked up the corridor and entered through his front door. He sensed the vibration of her footfalls as she approached the chamber until she appeared in the doorway, holding the black hardcopy case notes. He didn't bother to turn around or try to hide his nakedness. She'd already seen everything he had. Ev'r Keets had spoken correctly. They'd had a brief relationship, and he called it that only because Diega objected to him saying 'sexual encounter'.

She'd come up to him after attending one of his lectures on serial killers at the United Regiment training facility. She'd asked if he wanted to get a drink. He had said no, so she'd asked if he wanted to go back to her place. To that he had agreed. He'd actually known her as an acquaintance many year-cycles before that when they'd both lived in the gangland, but he'd never been with her then. She had been only thirteen at the time, three year-cycles younger than him, and too young for his taste.

Diega looked him up and down then set her lips together and crossed her arms. He'd been right, she wanted to talk or, as the Fens said, *endai sefrents seres* – discuss at loud volumes. The conversation was inevitable.

'So, you and Jude, then,' he said.

Diega tilted her head to one side and her hair slipped down over one eye. 'How long have you known?'

Copernicus sighed. It never failed to amaze him when the people closest to him forgot he could see body-heat. 'I knew before you did.'

She shook her head. 'And you're the one who's always complaining about having no privacy. We can't even like each other without you *reading* us.'

Copernicus laughed. 'If I could turn it off I would. I don't know why you'd even bother being secretive. I don't care if you're together as long as it doesn't affect your work.'

Diega picked up his knife from the table beside the wall and ran a finger down the flat of the blade. Her eyes lifted to his, her expression subtly changed. She looked more deeply at him, into his eyes, and he understood from that look, the flare of her body-heat and the shape of her thoughts, why she hadn't announced her and Jude's relationship to everyone.

'We have no chance,' he said bluntly. 'You're my soldier, my friend – that's it.'

Diega's colours flared, and she looked for a moment as though she was going to throw the blade at him. 'What are you talking about? I can't believe how conceited you are! Why would I want someone who treats me like leftovers when I could have someone like Jude?'

'Are you asking me or yourself?' Copernicus said.

'*Kitcher*,' she swore at him in Fenlen. 'So you've known about us all along – good for you. Go buy yourself a prize or something.'

The laser scanners paused. The system informed him of his fractured ribs and asked if he'd like treatment now or later.

'Now,' Copernicus told it. Several mechanical arms extended from the walls of the chamber and clamped onto his skin. He felt intense heat around his injury.

'I don't want to argue with you,' he told Diega. 'You like Jude, that's good. Just make sure there're no repeats of today.'

'Meaning what?'

'Meaning you were more focused on your arguments with him than on the job and —'

'That's not true,' she cut in. 'And you know it.'

'I know what I see. I know what I sense.'

'You know what you *think* you see, you know what you *think* you sense. It's your subjective view, Copernicus, and I know you think you're always right – but you're not.'

'Okay, Diega,' Copernicus said, wanting to end the discussion.

'Regeneration complete,' the system said and the machines retracted. Steam puffed out to clean the site of the wound. Copernicus stepped out of the chamber and inspected the injury in the mirror. The bruising had faded to yellow and the skin was no longer tender. He swung his right arm around several times to test for pain. Diega watched him and he felt her eyes moving over his body like fingertips brushing over his skin, touching him in sensitive places. He quickly stepped back into his trousers and pulled them up. Fens were good lovers, probably the best, but he couldn't. Diega had feelings for him, which meant it had gone way past the point of being able to call anything that happened casual.

He held out his hand for her to give him his blade and the hardcopy file. She pushed the black case into his grasp, but as she was handing over the weapon, she spoke words and morphed his knife into a bracelet.

'Change it back, Diega,' he ordered.

She shook her head.

'Fine.' He stepped around her and went to his desk to load the file.

Diega followed him. She took his glass and drained the rest of the Araki and juice. He gave her a look and she said, 'What? It's like four thousand degrees in here. Why do you have to have it so hot all the time?'

'Because that's the way I like it.'

'It puts people off visiting you.'

'Even better.'

Her eyes focused on Silho's image on the holo-screen and her face darkened.

'It's disgusting,' she started in. 'That the superiors would try and push *that girl* onto us. You and I both had years of military service before we became trackers. Eli had been contracting technology to the United Regiment almost all his life and even Jude had been learning martial arts, weaponry and strategy since he was a child. As far as I've been able to find out, this girl just blew in from the desert, enlisted and five seconds later, we're babysitting her. It's a trutting joke,' Diega fumed.

Copernicus tried to speak, but she cut in over him. 'The only logical explanation I can come up with is that either she's an Internal Affairs spy sent in to investigate us, or she's playing lover to one of the superiors and got preferential treatment. How can you stand by and let them get away with this? It makes a mockery of our work. It —'

'Diega.' Copernicus raised his voice. 'You know I didn't request Brabel, and I could have her transferred out, but I've chosen to give her a chance. She's not a spy or anyone's lover. She was posted to the trackers because she scored exceptionally on all facets of her training.'

'Exceptionally!' Diega laughed. 'True – she's exceptional at leaving evidence at the crime scene, getting in the way, staying on duty when she should have retired herself, not having a clue what to do.'

Copernicus sighed, tiring quickly of her yelling. It was one of the reasons he could never be with Diega. They were alike enough to be close friends, but opposite enough to make it impossible to stay in a relationship.

'End of the day,' he cut in again, 'if I decide she should go, then she will. But if I think she should stay then *she will*, and you will have to accept that. End of discussion.'

Diega rolled her eyes again and the computer continued to flick through faces searching for a match for Silho Brabel. Copernicus' communicator buzzed and he picked up.

'Yes?'

Eli's voice came through the receiver. 'Hi, boss, it's me.'

'Eli, I need to talk to you about something. Meet me on the roof and leave your otter at home.'

'I'll be there in a flash,' Eli said.

'End.' Copernicus stood up, deactivated his desk and activated his wardrobe. It dropped down from the ceiling.

'You're going back out?' Diega eyed him. He knew she considered herself to be second in charge and hated being left out of anything.

'Yes – privately.' He selected a black shirt and dressed, then pulled on his socks and boots and swallowed a deodorising capsule.

'Are you seeing someone?' A possessiveness flared Diega's body-heat.

'Yes, I'm seeing Eli. Do I have your permission?' He jabbed impatiently at his touch screen, uploading the case files to his transflyer and to Eli's system.

'If that's the way you like it.' She turned and headed for the front door. 'You know,' she looked back at him, 'not all women are your enemies – *xpel.*' She morphed the bracelet on his desk back to his blade.

'I could say the same to you,' he muttered at her disappearing back. He strapped the blade onto his ankle. 'Call Jude,' he said to his system as he dragged on his jacket and secured his weapon belt around his waist.

'Commander.' Jude's face appeared on the holo-screen. He was sweating and his training equipment sat in the background.

'Do you have the coordinates for Christy Shawe?' Copernicus asked him.

'Right here.' Jude leaned forward and grabbed something off-screen. 'Twenty-three twenty – Greentown. SevenM is still there on surveillance.'

'Anything interesting?'

Jude blinked, changing his vision to see through the robot's eyes. 'No, just a lot of drinking, smoking and gangsters doing the jig to terrible Galley music.'

Copernicus snorted. 'Keep me updated and don't tell Diega. She'll want in.'

Someone knocked at Jude's door and Copernicus saw from the nervous swivel of the Ar Antarian's eyes that it was Diega.

'And Jude, I know . . .'

The Ar Antarian's face tensed.

'. . . about you and her,' Copernicus finished the sentence. 'And she knows I know.'

Jude's features relaxed and he said, 'Good. I knew you would. Don't know why she wanted to keep it a secret.'

'Who knows,' Copernicus said, feeling a slight unease. 'End.'

12

The commander's transflyer, the *Ebony Rain*, was a jet-black speed machine with a full jacket and windows tinted to the darkest dark. Eli had created the custom weaponry hidden both inside and outside the flyer. Copernicus brought the *Rain* down onto the rooftop. The passenger side door lifted upwards and Eli hurried forward. He slid into the moulded seat and greeted the commander with a smile.

'Boss.'

Copernicus nodded. 'Alright?'

'Ready to roll.'

The door lowered, sealing them in. Unlike his own craft, the interior of the *Ebony Rain* always smelt and looked brand new. Eli ran his hands over the supple fabric of the seat. Copernicus steered the craft up and swung it sideways, directly into the flow of traffic. He punched the jets and the flyer zoomed forward, leaving everyone else behind. Some kind of rhythmic bassline pounded through the speakers of the craft. It was the kind of music Diega liked to dance to. Sweat slicked Eli's skin, not because of the commander's driving – he drove like he walked, fast and smooth – but because the temperature inside the flyer must have been somewhere just over boiling. Being cold-blooded, Copernicus' sense of heat was unusual.

Copernicus glanced over at him. 'Too hot?'

'No, it's good,' Eli lied.

Copernicus raised an eyebrow. He killed the heater and opened a window, letting in a rush of cool night air. Lights buzzed by all around them.

Eli sighed in relief and checked the navigator on the dashboard. The coordinates read 20–3–20. Eli's eyebrows shot up.

'Greenway Central?' he asked. It was one thing to go to the break-wall on the very border of Galley territory – that was usually safe during daylight hours – but entering inner Greenway at any time was like straying into a war zone.

The commander nodded slowly. 'Christy Shawe is behind all the recent killings – I know he is. Something big is going down in the Gangland and the only way we're going to get a lead is to target the source.'

'The superiors will never sanction a raid without strong evidence of wrongdoing,' Eli reminded him. 'They don't want anyone interfering with the Gang Squad's work.'

'The Gang Squad,' Copernicus repeated with disdain. 'What have they ever done that's been of any use? It doesn't matter, though, we're not entering Greenway officially; we're going in on our own time, just to observe Shawe's movements.'

Eli nodded and gulped. The first time he had met Christy Shawe was back in the days when, as kids, Copernicus had run with Shawe and the Galleys. The commander had befriended Eli, intrigued by all his inventions and ideas, but Shawe had given him significant grief, only tolerating him at all because of Copernicus. Eli had been scared to death of Shawe then, and he was equally, if not more, scared of him now. Once Shawe had yelled at him so loudly that he had almost peed his pants and, in fact, he felt like peeing them again just thinking about it. He rubbed his sweaty palms along his jeans and bit his lip.

'Don't worry,' Copernicus said. 'No contact, just surveillance.'

'I'm not worried,' Eli said with a trembling voice.

Copernicus closed the craft window and turned the music off. 'Have a look at the crime file I uploaded to your system and tell me what you think.'

Eli activated his holo-screen and found the file. He flicked through the crime scene information, studying the pictures taken by SevenM of the victims and the surroundings.

'Well, I can say that it looks like four of the six victims at the first scene died from injuries inflicted during torture, and that the other three hollowed-out victims, the two at the first scene and the one at the second, appear to have been killed by the same person, or at least by the same weapon, but I've never seen injuries like these before. It looks to me,' he squinted at the images, 'as though something has come *out* of their bodies and not *in*. I mean, look at the way the skin is ripped.'

Copernicus glanced at it and nodded. 'What sort of weapon could create that wound? Something swallowed then expanded inside their stomachs?'

'I'm not sure.' Eli's mind sped through possibilities. 'But from my viewing of the second body, I don't think so. It wasn't just an explosive puncture wound, like an implanted or swallowed weapon would cause. It looked more like something had entered the body and consumed or overtaken it, then broken out. I mean, the body was little more than just skin, and that's consistent with . . . well . . .' He hesitated to say it.

Copernicus did it for him. 'Demonic possession. Exactly what I didn't want to hear.'

'I'm sorry,' Eli said.

The commander shook his head. 'We have to find out if Shawe has made a deal with any of the dark-magics sects still in operation and, if so, which one.'

Eli nodded. He scrolled further into the information. 'Diega ran a blood match for the missing Androt – Kry 939993 – but he has no priors and no record. Mrs Parkingham said she thought the Androt had surprised burglars, attacked and killed one of them and then been killed or injured himself and taken away.'

'Not likely,' Copernicus said. 'If Kry killed the invader, it means that he was also the killer at the first crime scene. You said the wounds are identical. More likely the invaders broke in for another purpose, he got in the way, injured one of them, and then the other invaders finished the injured one off for whatever reason and —'

'Took him,' Eli said.

Copernicus' eyebrows drew together in thought. 'A dead or unconscious Androt weighs a ton – it would be very difficult for most people to lift him without magics.'

'Well, I didn't see any dark symbols there,' Eli said. 'Doesn't mean there weren't any though, I guess. You know, even if we find out it is something to do with a dark sect, we can't present the evidence anyway. I get the feeling the palace enforcers are waiting for any excuse to lock you up. At the first mention of dark magics they'll be dragging us in.' Eli shivered at the thought of the big lizard-breed guards.

'I'm not concerned about the enforcers,' Copernicus said. 'The only important thing is to find out what's happening and to stop it. What are your thoughts on this?' He took an object out of his pocket and handed it to Eli.

It was the ring the commander had shown to Ev'r Keets. It sat heavy in his palm. 'Ironfist Shawe's ring,' Eli said with a stirring of trepidation. Ironfist Shawe, Christy's father, had been a bushy-faced barbarian who drank so much he must have had alcohol instead of blood running through his veins. He'd lived hard and taken anything he wanted from anyone. He earned a fearsome reputation for his violence, but never the title of King of the Gangland that his son now owned. Ironfist had died in a blazing shootout with the United Regiment. Even the memory of the fierce gangster was enough to make Eli tremble.

'Brabel found it at the first crime scene,' the commander told him. 'But when we went to question Shawe about it, he was wearing the same ring. I only remember one ring from that time, though. What about you?'

'I only remember the one as well, but maybe Christy had a replica made so that the real one wouldn't be stolen or damaged. Maybe Christy dropped the replica at the crime scene and put on the real one to cover it up,' Eli suggested.

Copernicus considered this, his eyes moving left to right. 'Yes, maybe, but it wouldn't be like Shawe to worry about things getting stolen or damaged.'

'I guess not,' Eli said. He lifted the ring closer to the lights. 'It's not gold or silver or a gold blend. I'm not sure what it is. I have a friend, Solvang Steel. He's an expert in metals and works for the Counterfeiting Squad. I can scan the ring and send the report to him. He'll be able to tell me what it is and it might give us a lead on where and when it was made.'

'Good,' Copernicus agreed.

Eli took his scanner from his weapon belt and ran the light over the ring. He wrote a brief message to Solvang and sent it, before handing the ring back to Copernicus.

As he did, the commander said, 'Eli, I need to ask you a favour.'

Eli felt a glow inside himself. He'd never heard Copernicus asking anyone for assistance, ever.

'Yes, boss,' he said eagerly.

The commander paused to choose his words carefully. He glanced in the rear-vision mirror. 'I need a blood and flesh substitute that owns all the properties of actual blood and flesh – real and fresh.'

'Like for an injury graft?' Eli asked.

'No,' the commander replied.

Eli's mind wrestled with understanding. 'Okay, can I ask what it's for?'

'No,' the commander repeated. 'It's unofficial. Very unofficial.'

Eli nodded. Unofficial meant illegal.

'So unofficial that I don't even want you to work on it. I just want you to tell me what to do and I'll do the work. It's for a friend – an old friend – who needs my help. It's urgent.'

'Well, I'm sure we can come up with something,' Eli said. 'I'll need a bit of time in my lab.'

'Fine, but don't keep any records,' Copernicus said.

'Only in here.' Eli tapped the side of his head.

The commander's new communicator made a sudden choking sound and emitted a high-pitched squeal the way it had in Eli's office. Copernicus unclipped it from his belt and handed it to Eli. He worked quickly and killed the sound.

'I'm going to have to do some extra work on this one,' he said. 'I think it may be reacting with your body system. You can take my com into Greenway and I'll pick up the signal on the craft's system.'

'I'm not going into Greenway,' Copernicus told him.

'But . . .'

'*You* are going into Greenway.'

Eli stared at him.

'I set foot in there and I'm dead,' the commander continued. 'You know the streets as well as I do and you can fly. You can keep to the rooftops and shadows – blend in. An informant told me there's a big meeting tonight between all the gangs. That's never happened before. SevenM is tracking Shawe. So all you have to do is use your system to track SevenM and he'll lead you there.'

'I don't know, boss, I really don't know. What if I get caught?' Eli asked, his fear written on his face.

'You won't,' the commander said. 'I have every confidence in you. You need to learn to trust yourself. You should unbind your wings now, we're almost there.'

Eli gulped and reached behind himself to untie the bindings that kept his wings under control while he was in company. Copernicus steered the transflyer in for a landing. He brought the craft down on a quiet side street in Hackside, the suburb backing Greenway, the towering breakwall separating the two.

The commander turned to him. 'I'll wait here. Remember, we need to know if Shawe's made a deal with a dark sect and, if so, which one.'

'I'll do my best,' Eli whispered. The passenger side door lifted up and Eli forced himself to slide out.

*****

Eli fluttered on lithe, semi-translucent wings across the Greenway rooftops towards SevenM's signal. Shouting voices, blaring Galley fiddle music and zaps and bangs of electrifiers resounded through the air all around him. A stream of electricity carved up the darkness right ahead of him and Eli dropped down onto a roof for a moment's rest and a chance to control his tremors. He leaned against a chimney pipe, panting.

'Hey, you!' a gruff voice with a Greenway accent yelled behind him. 'What do you think you're doing up here?'

Eli turned slowly towards the man, while counting silently back from forty-six to stop himself from passing out. He didn't dare to breathe or raise his head.

'I said, what are you doing up here?' the man repeated. Sour smoke from his cigar tickled Eli's nose. The man stepped closer and Eli, half-hidden by shadows, murmured something, imitating the cadence of the Greenway accent as best he could.

'Well, get down then!' the man said. 'No Spats allowed up here. Don't make me tell you twice.'

Eli sprang to the fire escape ladder, not daring to fly in front of the man. He hurried down the metal stairs, silently repeating *thank you thank you thank you* to the Khaiti God who had given him a body that was easily mistaken for that of a Spat, the child gangsters too young to be fully initiated into any gang and too old to be with their mothers. They ran feral for a while before they were accepted into one of the gangs.

He landed in the side street with a thud that jarred his feet and took off running through cluttered alleys, through shadows with faces, his heartbeat hammering and breath coming in ragged gasps. A cardboard box tripped him and he fell, sprawling onto the concrete. The contents of his pockets spilled out around him. Ignoring the sting of his grazed hands, he began to frantically grab up his belongings. As he snatched his remote systems machine, he accidentally activated its holo-screen and the last image of the first crime scene he'd been studying flashed up. He quickly deactivated it, but before he did, he noticed something he had previously missed – the face of a Wraith was looking out from one of the walls at the scene. The image vanished and he scrambled to his feet. He checked the locator and saw the dot representing SevenM drifting across the screen. Obviously Christy Shawe was on the move, on his way to the meeting that the commander had spoken about. They were coming closer towards him.

Eli followed the signal, moving out of Greenway, where the Galley's horn-and-fist symbol was painted over every wall, into neutral territory. It was in the centre of the Gangland, but no gang owned it. SevenM's location spot paused again and Eli managed to catch up with it. He followed it to the base of a building and, checking left to right to make sure no one was watching, whirred his wings and flew up to the flat roof. As he landed, he saw a momentary blink of red lights – SevenM beckoning him. He ran, bent double, to where the spider robot was crouched in the shadows, his eyelights turned off. SevenM nodded to him and Eli looked into his eyes and gave a shaky thumbs-up to Jude, who would be watching through the robot.

A babble of voices broke out in the distance and Eli followed SevenM as the robot climbed over several more rooftops towards the source of the sound. They reached the final building, which had a skylight cut into its flat-topped roof.

Eli crawled to the edge of the building and looked down over the famous Whitlow Square. It had once been the stage of so many gang rumbles and deaths that it became known as *the battlefield*, but was later agreed to be neutral territory. Crowds of gangsters were filling the square. The centre of Whitlow was dominated by the gang second in rank to the Greenway Galleys – the Crook'd Town Pride. The mass of hyped and boisterous Pride members had geared up in their best gold and purple dress. They, like all the other gangsters, were infected with a delirium-like excitement, a dangerous invincibility. It rippled the air electric like a new summer wind. The Pride members paced and stalked, greeting each other loudly with the gang's call of *Prey together, stay together*, and flashing the Pride sign. The Pride girls, known as Esses, wore short skirts and shorter tops and flirted with the men.

Eli saw a definite hierarchy in the massing Pride. Dukes, generals and foot soldiers kept to one side, while the princes and family girls, those Pride by blood as opposed to those traded in from other gangs, stood on the other. In a circle around the Pride, the gang's lions and other great felines sat with calculated patience, eyes of infinite understanding and sorrow fixed into the distance as they waited for Caesar, their leader, to appear. They sensed his presence in the absence of light.

The other gangs spread out around the Pride as they arrived in basic order of Gangland hierarchy. The whip cries of Kelly's Crew rivalled the maniac yells of the Northside Chaos – the third and fourth ranked gangs. After them, was the Eastern Rim Mafia, standing silently, all dressed in black, with black bowler hats and their gang beasts, the Jada – part-avian, part-puma – crouching beside each man. The Western Rim Taipans, ranked next, were wearing copper-coloured clothing with the gang symbol of the snake on their backs. Each member had a deadly adder draped around his shoulders, to which the West Rim had natural immunity. Following them was the League, ruled by a tech-head called Minimum Maximum. They stood on hover-bikes and speed-drift platforms, a small but wealthy gang due to the technology they created and peddled.

Following the League in rank were LD's Troopers, all dressed in camouflage, majestic golden eagles riding on their shoulders. On the tail of the Troopers the Tribal Boys galloped in on their spotted and striped horses. They'd painted their faces with the gang symbol and held spears in one hand, raising them up and giving long high-pitched cries. These calls were soon replaced by the howl of the Hound Boys and their dogs, the big pack renowned for its ability to track food. One of the hounds just barely missed the snapping jaws of a blue-belly alligator as the Bay Boys arrived. The ragtag H-Town Mob followed them into the square together with the Penny Little Alliance (a union between two small gangs, Penny Place and Littletown). The Peacetown Pack was second last, along with the Bell-Tower Bulls, with horned helmets and rings through their noses. Finally the Wolf-Tower Weres and their wolves slunk into the square. The scruffy, bearded gangsters snarled with sharpened canines and were avoided by all. They were known as the scavengers of the Gangland, violent and unpredictable, half-crazed from drinking weir water. The final and only unofficial gang appeared on the tops of the buildings on the opposite side of the square. They were the Rooftoppers, or as the other gangs called them, the Gone Girls. They were the only all-female gang and had not been accepted by their male counterparts. All the gangsters kept to their own, while standing uneasily close to bitter rivals – everyone right on the edge of an all-out Gangland war.

At the sound of nearby footsteps, Eli and SevenM flattened themselves into the shadows of the rooftop ledge. The door to the roof swung open and Caesar K-Ruz, Pride leader, and Smudge K-Ruz, Caesar's first cousin and leading Pride girl, stepped out under the lantern light. Eli remembered them both well from his time around the gangs. Caesar was very big and muscular with pure black hair and lion eyes that, like the commander's, could see beneath the skin. Smudge was a stunning beauty, her gang name originating from the brown birthmarks all over her face and body.

The mighty gangster boss moved to the edge of the roof and looked down over the square, while his shadow, in the form of a giant lion, stayed guarding the door. Eli held his breath hoping the shadow would not sense him. Smudge moved to Caesar's side, her big black cat, Inski, slinking around her legs.

'No sign of the Galleys,' Smudge said. 'Looks like Christy Shawe's going to be a monkey's arse about this.'

'Goes without saying,' Caesar replied, his voice deep and rich. 'But he'll show.'

'It's not too late to cancel this,' she told him.

'And put what in its place?' he asked.

Smudge shrugged. 'Breakfast.'

A weary smile touched the edges of Caesar's mouth.

'I am serious, Caesar. You don't have to go through with this,' she told him. 'You don't have to do what Shawe says. He's nothing compared to you.'

'As much as I despise Shawe, what he's saying is right. Life in the Gangland is not sustainable anymore.' He sighed. 'There's no going back now.'

He turned away from her, and the look Eli saw in Smudge's eyes, directed at Caesar, made him feel guilty that he was watching and fascinated at the same time. Truth was, ever since Eli had known her, Smudge had suffered from a degenerative, incurable disease – love – and not just any kind of love, the worst love a person could have: forbidden love that could never be returned. Eli had no doubt that Caesar knew how she felt for him, and she probably knew that he knew, and he knew that she knew that he knew, yet everything was left unspoken, unfixable, unchangeable.

'The Galleys are coming,' Caesar said, though Eli heard no sound.

The gangster boss moved out of the shadows and stood up on the ledge of the roof. In the square below, all eyes turned his way and every conversation, even between rivals of the Pride, ended immediately. All the gathered Pride members fell to their knees, their heads bowed. After a moment's quiet appraisal, Caesar lifted his hand and the masses burst onto their feet releasing wild, deafening roars, making the Pride sign high in the air. Caesar's great felines paced and stalked, silently pawing the air, eyes fixed on their leader. Caesar leapt off the roof and landed lightly on his feet some four storeys below. He waded out into the crowd greeting his Pride brothers and sisters, speaking to each by name.

'No turning back,' Smudge whispered to herself. She crossed herself, and she and Inski jumped off the roof after Caesar. They went to join their family girls, each with the sleek physique of hunting cats.

The distant sounding of a horn jarred Eli's nerves and silence fell again over the crowd, but this time not out of respect for Caesar. This silence was the disquieting still before the storm. The blast sounded again.

'Can you smell cabbage?' Eli quipped to SevenM. It was a joke between him and Jude about the Galleys, known for their violent brawls, potent brews and foul cabbage soup.

The horn sounded a third time very close and the Greenway Galleys turned the corner. The leading gangsters held up banners decorated with their gang symbols, the horn and the fist, and each wore a cap tilted to the left towards Greenway. Some had even dyed their entire skin green for the occasion, patriotic to the extreme. This top-ranking gang was not *blood in blood out* like the other gangs. To really be a Galley, you had to be born a Galley. As they neared the crowd, the arriving gangsters flashed the Galley symbol, both thumbs crooked and pointed out like the horns of the gang beast – the Galley rhinoceros. These hulking and ill-tempered giants lumbered in the midst of the men, some permitting riders, others given a wide berth. Every Galley member was armed with a thick sword, fashioned after the horn of the great rhinoceros, displaying their collective cynicism that this would be a peaceful meeting.

115

At the head of the gang strode the Galley boss and King of the Gangland, the fierce and ugly Christy Shawe. He was wearing his lucky dragon-skin jacket. Eli pressed further into the shadows. He hadn't quite remembered exactly how huge and how ugly Shawe was. He led his gang up Baxter Street and they poured into the square, assembling opposite the Pride. For a few long moments the rival gangs stood in utter silence staring each other down – then Caesar snarled, Christy Shawe gave him the middle-finger salute and all hell broke loose.

From their opposing sides of Whitlow Square, the Crook'd Town Pride and the Greenway Galleys fought to out-shout, out-stomp and out-curse each other. Their deafening sounds shook the ground. Eli's skin prickled at the terrifying and awesome display. Swears hurtled back and forth and both sides made insults of their rivals' gang signs, but no one threw any objects. No one dared to violate the neutral ground treaty. All the other gangs stood on the periphery of the square, no one stupid enough to get between the superpowers. Christy Shawe laughed and jeered with his gang-mates, but Caesar K-Ruz stood silently taking everything in. The essence of the long-standing rivalry between the two men spoke in the pauses between the sounds. Neither side backed down and nothing changed until a Pride prince made the distinct mistake of questioning the Galleys' manhood. In response, Christy Shawe grinned savagely, his teeth yellow and chipped, and immediately whipped down his trousers and waved his genitalia in the prince's general direction, to the out-rage of the Pride. Eli tried to look away, but the sight was somewhat mesmerising. To say Shawe had been blessed with more than his share of manhood was an understatement.

'You've seen mine,' Shawe yelled at Caesar. 'Let's have a look at yours then, or are you scared?' Shawe staggered, even more drunk than usual, and that was really saying something, but it was also strange behaviour considering the importance of this gathering. Shawe liked to party and get completely smashed, but he was also a sharp and gifted leader who would have never, as far as Eli knew him, turned up pissed to an event as significant as the first ever combined Gangland meeting. Something was obviously seriously wrong.

116

Caesar spoke, his voice ringing loud and clear around the square. 'I didn't come here for a pissing competition. I came here to talk strategy.'

'Yeah, Shawe, we're not here to watch the grass grow,' Jimmy Hatfield, boss of Kelly's Crew, shouted.

To the relief of all there, Christy Shawe finally pulled up his trousers and said to them, 'It's not the grass growing that's the problem, it's our ranks. We have no more space. So either we start killing each other or we start expanding into other areas of the city.'

'Which means killing off civilians,' Jimmy Hatfield said, pointing in the general direction of the rest of Scorpia. 'I don't like it, Shawe. Every time we directly attack the Regiment, we end up losing people and getting punished. It's never worked before.'

'If you're scared, Jimmy, stay back with the women,' Shawe mocked him.

'Typical Galley – all balls, no brains,' Maximum, boss of the League, said. 'Hatfield is right. Unless we have a clear and workable plan there's no point.'

'And there is also no point if we don't work together. This has been our mistake in the past; we attacked separately, not as a whole.' Caesar said. 'Why don't we discuss this further inside?' He gestured to the bar behind him.

'Great,' Shawe mocked. 'Then we can all join hands and sing "She'll be Coming Home at Noon". Discussing won't change anything. Only war will.'

'You just don't get it, do you, Shawe.' Maximum stepped off his hover-bike and, with two of his high-ranking men, walked towards the building below where Eli sat. They entered and all the other bosses silently followed their lead, with Shawe being the grudging last. He took a swig from a flask and stomped through the door, slamming it shut behind him.

Eli crawled as silently as possible to the skylight and lay on his belly peeking into the building. He couldn't hear anything, but could see the gathering of bosses, Christy Shawe in the centre, pacing, smoking, drinking, stopping to yell at one person and then at another. Caesar's lion shadow moved up and down the wall, twitching the tip of its tail. Soon things became heated between Shawe and Jimmy Hatfield, and Shawe's two men had to intervene. They escorted Shawe out a side door into the alley beside the building for some air. Eli scurried to the side of the roof to listen to them speak. He peeped over, only able to see the outline of their shadows cast on the opposite wall to where they stood.

'Christy, mate you need to calm down,' the man, whom Eli recognised as Malcolm, one of Shawe's cousins, said. 'We need to get everyone on side with this, otherwise the plan will be blown.'

Eli strained up on his tiptoes, listening carefully for any mention of dark sects.

'Trutt the plan!' Shawe cursed. 'I don't give a rat's arse about it anymore! I just want to find him.'

'We will, Christy, we will. Like I said, I bet you anything he's just holed up somewhere with a few girls and some flagons of Araki and he's lost track of time. We did the same thing when we were young like him. He'll show up when he's ready.'

'No, Mal!' Shawe yelled. 'Stace would never do that – never. I know him. Something happened to him and I know Kane's behind it. I told you. He has Stacy's ring, for trutt's sake. Said he found it at a crime scene, but I know he's lying. Kane has him. He has my brother. He's messing with me. Trutt! I'm going to kill him this time, I swear. I'm going to rip his head off and piss in his trutting skull.'

Eli's foot slipped and he fell on the roof with a thud. The talking below him stopped abruptly and he could feel the strained silence of listening.

'Oi!' He heard Malcolm calling back into the building. 'Check the roof! Now!'

They were made.

SevenM instantly fled, scurrying into the darkness. Eli buzzed his wings and took off fast, not looking back, expecting the zap of an electrifier to fry him any second. He zipped around corners and through open windows and out the other side, gradually losing the shouting voices behind him. He slowed to gain his bearings and eventually found his way back to Hackside. He paused in the air above the *Ebony Rain* where the commander stood a few paces from the craft, talking with someone half-hidden by shadows. Eli knew it was impossible, but the other person looked like a Midnight Man. Eli flew down and landed. Sensing his presence, the commander turned. The shadows shifted and the shape was gone, but Eli could still feel eyes watching them from the darkness. He moved swiftly to the craft. The commander jumped in on the other side and they took off, not talking until they had put some distance behind them.

'Anything?' Copernicus finally asked.

'In short,' Eli said, 'Christy Shawe is trying to get the gangs together for the first ever combined uprising. Only Shawe's losing it, because his brother, Stacy, is missing. The ring we found – it belongs to Stacy. Please never ask me to do that again.'

'Stacy?' Copernicus said. 'He was so young when I left the Gangland, I didn't even think of him. So he gave the actual ring, or at least a replica, to Stacy – that's why there are two?'

Eli nodded. 'Must have, but Shawe is blaming you for Stacy. He's seriously crazy-angry and he's coming after you.'

Copernicus gave no sign of concern. 'Any mention of dark sects?'

Eli shook his head. 'Honestly, I don't think Shawe is involved in the crimes. I think his brother may have even become a victim of whatever's going on.'

The commander considered this in silence.

'Who were you talking to back there?' Eli asked.

Copernicus glanced at him. 'An old friend.' He said no more.

13

Eli hurried along the white corridors of Headquarters, his boots squeaking on the shiny surface of the floor. He saw a group of colleagues turn the corner up ahead and darted through one of the many hidden shortcuts he'd discovered in the walls. At the present moment, he didn't have time to be the centre of entertainment or be embroiled in a long and pointless conversation about someone's boyfriend. Right now he needed to talk to Jude. He was worried that the commander was in real danger from Christy Shawe and that he wasn't taking the threat seriously. Eli wasn't sure what could be more serious than someone wanting to rip off your head and piss in your skull, but the commander was disturbingly unaffected by the notion.

Racing up the flights of stairs, Eli bypassed several floors and came out on the residential level where Jude's apartment was situated. He found Jude's door unlocked and slightly ajar and remembered the Ar Antarian saying his apartment security needed to be fixed. He was in the part of the building still functioning on the old system, which Eli hadn't designed. Eli opened the door and padded in.

Jude's apartment was neat but functional. He liked neutral tones and had very expensive tastes in everything. His training equipment took up the bulk of the main living area. A can of Androt fuel stood beside the equipment; Eli guessed it was to grease up the working parts of the training gear or for SevenM to drink. Eli headed towards Jude's study, where his friend could often be found, but slowed at the sound of voices. He came to the end of the corridor and saw a light on in Jude's bedroom. The door stood open just enough for him to see in. Jude and Diega were in there together. She got out of bed, naked, and started to gather her clothes. They had obviously been making up for a night of arguments and tension. Eli froze, stuck in the moment, not knowing whether to try to leave quietly and maybe get caught, or announce himself and have the embarrassment of explanations of what he had and hadn't seen.

Jude sat up in the bed, staring at the bedside table where his tinted glasses lay. His eyes were distant in thought. He spoke, his upper-level accent stronger now that he was off duty and in his own place. 'I'm not saying he should be given a medal of honour or anything, I'm just saying that Christy Shawe is far more intelligent than people give him credit for. If he is orchestrating these murders and abductions, I'm sure he'll have no loose ends for us to follow back to him.'

'What are you talking about?' Diega laughed, pulling up her trousers. 'What about him leaving his ring at the crime scene? Shawe is as dumb as an iron pole. He's just got a lot of protection around him. But it's only a matter of time before he slips up bad and then we'll have him. Why are you always trying to see more in people than there actually is?'

'I'm trying to see the truth. Not everything in this life is as black and white as it seems. Sometimes people have no choice but to act in a certain way – do you understand what I mean?'

'Jude, there aren't different shades to Christy Shawe, just facts. He's a gangster and a criminal and he's Copernicus' enemy, so he's my enemy as well, nothing further needed.'

'That's a simplistic view of things,' Jude said.

'Well I'm sorry we can't all be educated geniuses like you, with a perfect balance of logic and reason,' Diega retorted, dragging on her shirt.

Jude leaned out of the bed and caught Diega around the waist. He pulled her down onto his lap and said, 'And we can't all be beautiful like you, but somehow we survive.'

Diega smiled and the frustration melted from her expression. She kissed him and he lifted off her shirt. Eli backed away as metal arms and rainbow skin blurred before him. He made it back to the front door without being detected and stepped out into the corridor. He sighed.

'Eli,' Copernicus said, right beside him.

Eli jumped and babbled, 'Hello. I was just visiting Jude, just to talk about stuff, a few random things, nothing important really. What about you?'

'Visiting Jude,' the commander said.

'Great minds think alike, hey,' Eli giggled.

Copernicus gave him a look that said he knew exactly why he was there then lifted a hand to the door. It swung open.

Eli swallowed and said, 'Ah, boss, I'd probably knock first.'

The commander stood in the doorway and called out, 'Jude, Diega – you're needed!'

Within seconds Diega emerged from the hallway, clipping on her weapon belt. Her hair was ruffled. She looked at Copernicus and a silent undercurrent of something Eli couldn't quite place flowed between them.

'Jude's on the toilet,' she said bluntly.

'There have been more incidents,' the commander said. 'Another hollowed-out body in Moris-Isles, and a large-scale attack on the Galleria Majora – at least twelve dead.'

Diega cursed and Copernicus continued, 'I'll send Jude to Moris-Isles and we'll cover the Galleria.'

'What about Keets?' Diega asked. 'What if she gets out of hand here? I don't trust anyone else to know what to do.'

'Oh . . . I forgot,' Eli piped up. 'I hid a spyer under the table in her cell, so we could keep an eye on her.' He lifted up his communicator and a small hologram of Ev'r Keets' cell opened above the machine.

'I've been recording her for several hours now,' he said, skipping through the stored footage.

'Stop!' Copernicus commanded.

Eli stabbed at the pause button and the image scrambled then re-settled on a picture of Jude entering the cell. Diega leaned in closer, staring at the hologram. Her forehead creased.

'Is that Jude?' she asked.

'Play it,' the commander said.

Eli hit play and they watched Jude and Ev'r Keets talking. When the conversation ended, no one said anything. Eli, feeling as though his hands were working without his direction, shut down the hologram image and clipped the communicator back on his belt. He shifted uncomfortably, not daring to look up at the commander or Diega. Keets hadn't said what she would tell the commander if Jude didn't cooperate, but it was obviously something significant. The silence stretched on and a bad feeling gurgled inside Eli's stomach.

Jude appeared at the end of the corridor dressed and belted up. 'Commander.' He nodded to Copernicus. 'Hi, Eli.'

His friend gave him a warm smile and Eli winced. He felt so bad. He wished he could shrink to microscopic size and scuttle away.

'There have been more attacks,' Copernicus said, his voice controlled. 'We'll have to separate, but first we're all going to talk to Ev'r Keets. She's left a message with the guardians watching her that she has something important to tell me. Are you ready, Jude?'

The warmth left Jude's eyes and he swallowed. He spoke with difficulty.

'No, Commander, I'm not ready.' He cleared his throat. 'There's something I have to tell you first . . .'

'So tell us,' Diega demanded. Her skin was vibrant and her stare hard.

Jude wrung his metal hands together. 'I think I know what Keets is going to say. You . . . you already know I come from a noble family . . .'

Eli found himself nodding.

'Well I do, and more . . .' He paused.

'Yes?' the commander prompted, his voice dangerously soft.

'I come from the royal family,' Jude confessed. 'I am . . . I am Crown Prince Isaiah U.'

Eli giggled hysterically before he could stop himself, then slapped a hand over his mouth. He glanced at Diega and Copernicus. The Fen looked confused and angry. The commander's face was completely blank. Jude swayed where he stood, emotion threatening his composure. Eli pitied him. He wanted to say something, but didn't trust himself to open his mouth.

'The Crown Prince is dead,' the commander finally said.

Jude shook his head. 'When I was thirteen year-cycles my uncle, the Vice-Standard U, tried to have me assassinated. I escaped, so he knows I'm not dead, but not where I am. I didn't know who to trust. Please understand that I didn't mean to lie to you.'

'You didn't know who to trust?' Diega repeated. Eli could feel the angry heat rolling off her skin.

'Why did the Vice-Standard want you dead?' Copernicus asked.

Jude looked up at the ceiling. He said, 'Our views clashed.'

'What views?' Copernicus pushed.

'Why didn't you tell me?' Diega demanded.

Jude looked from the commander to the Fen and back. 'Just . . . views about people . . . about races. I didn't think the way they wanted me to think. I wanted people to have equality,' he tried to explain. 'And I didn't tell you because I haven't told anyone. I wanted . . .'

'What?' Diega said.

'I wanted to forget, to leave it behind. I'm sorry. I'm so sorry.' Jude moved forward and held out his hand to her.

She stepped back and kept her arms at her sides.

'I've told you things about myself that I haven't told anyone,' Diega said. 'And you've been lying to my face.'

'I haven't lied,' Jude insisted.

'You're the Crown Prince!' Diega yelled. 'I don't remember that coming up in any conversations!'

'Diega, it's me. I'm the same person,' Jude implored.

He tried to reach out to her again and she yelled, 'Stay away!'

Jude stopped. He lowered his head. Tears welled in Eli's eyes.

The commander took control and said, 'Jude, you and I will need to discuss this further, but first we need to investigate these attacks. Are you fit for duty?'

After a moment, Jude nodded.

Diega shook her head and mumbled something.

'Then go to Moris-Isles, 9 Delta Street. Diega, you come with me to the Galleria. Eli, stay here, work on analysis of the data we already have. Find us some leads, and lean on Forensics to release the fluid results from the first scene. We need to know exactly who the victims were and exactly what killed them.'

'Yes, boss,' Eli said.

The commander's communicator jolted on his belt and started whistling again. Copernicus thumped his fist into it and Eli flinched at the thought of the extremely delicate components within.

The whistling stopped.

Diega turned her back on Jude and spoke to Eli, her voice flat. 'Mine's not working either. I can't hear my messages. There's too much static.'

'I'll have to work on them more when you get back,' Eli said. 'I'll fix them.'

Diega muttered, 'Whatever,' and stalked out the door. Copernicus gave Jude another look and then followed. Jude watched them leave, sorrow clouding his eyes.

'Don't worry,' Eli managed to say. 'It'll be okay.'

The Ar Antarian shook his head.

'I don't have to start calling you *Your Majesty,* do I?' Eli heard himself add and cringed, but it brought a smile to Jude's face and tears to his eyes.

'No, Eli. I'd really prefer that you didn't.'

'Don't say that or I won't be able to help myself,' Eli said. 'You know I can't shut up.'

'And I can't talk. We're a good pair,' Jude said sadly.

'Speaking of which, has SevenM returned from the Gangland?' Eli asked him, searching to change the topic, scrambling back to familiar ground where they could stand and talk as friends as they always had.

Jude blinked to see where his robot was. 'He's still making his way out. Taking his time so he doesn't get any unwanted attention.' He blinked back. 'He'll be fine.'

'I would have carried him, but I'm not strong enough,' Eli said.

'I think you're stronger than you know,' Jude said quietly. 'I'd better get going.'

Eli nodded. They walked out into the corridor in uneasy silence and Jude shut the door behind them. He turned to head away and Eli remembered why he had come to the apartment in the first place.

'Jude, I wanted to talk to you,' Eli called him back. 'I don't know whether this is the right time —' he suspected it was most definitely not '— but you heard what Shawe said in the Gangland. I don't think the commander's taking it seriously.'

'The way I hear it, they've been warring for a long time,' Jude replied.

'They have, but this is different. Shawe thinks the commander has taken his brother. Who knows what he'll do to get the boy back.'

'I agree, but I don't think I'm in any position to be advising the commander,' Jude said. 'He'll probably end up discharging me – at the least.'

'Don't think like that,' Eli said. 'You know the boss makes up his own rules and his own mind. You're a good person – better than all of us. He can see that.'

Jude gave a small smile. 'Thank you, Eli.'

He turned and walked away and Eli watched him go. 'Be careful,' he called out as the Ar Antarian turned the corner.

Jude didn't hear. He vanished.

*****

Eli sat hunched in front of his workbench. He blinked, his sights pixelated from staring at holo-images for so long. His stomach growled and gnawed at itself from hunger, and Nelly sat on the hard-copy data file he needed, refusing to budge until due attention was given to her. She was still angry at him for leaving her behind when he went to Greenway.

'You wouldn't have wanted to go,' Eli tried to reason with her. 'A very scary man lives there.' He gently slid her aside and she berated him in a high chattering voice, her fuzzy cheeks puffed with outrage.

'I know, I know, but I need to keep working. We're in a crisis here. Go have a swim. Or eat some fish – look, nice fishies over there.' He pointed to her dish.

She gave a final disgruntled huff and slunk away.

Eli rubbed his eyes and stared around at all the holo-screens full of information surrounding him. He had so much to do that he didn't know where to start. There was everything from the crime scenes, the disturbing possibility of a gang uprising, the unofficial flesh and blood project the commander had asked him to think about for his 'old friend', and he was also waiting on a reply from the metal specialist.

Eli turned to one of the holo-screens and flicked through the crime-scene images. The image that he had accidentally opened in Greenway flashed up and he saw the spectral-breed's face pressing out of the wall. He cursed himself for forgetting about it and not telling the commander. On closer inspection, Eli was pretty sure it was a Skilsy Wraith. Several year-cycles ago he'd conducted a study into the different spectral-breed subtypes to add to the combined knowledge of the trackers, but his findings had been limited by the spectrals' suspicion of anyone outside of their society. The racial group, made up of Wraiths, Phantoms, Midnight Men, Living Ghosts, Deaths and various others, were an extremely secretive people ruled by their own councils and courts. They very rarely communicated with anyone outside their own kind. Some types of spectrals, like Midnight Men, couldn't even talk. Skilsy Wraiths could, though, and they were also a unique type of spectral, in that each Wraith was born both male and female in one body and could switch between the sexes until they were separated into two different bodies. Eli hadn't been able to discover when or how this happened. He considered how easy it would be for the Wraiths. They never had to look for a partner because they were born with their very own soulmate attached.

He continued to study the Wraith's face. Why would a Wraith be at the crime scene? They weren't a curious type of spectral and they weren't blood-fascinated. Maybe it had just stepped through the wrong wall or the wrong floor and stumbled there by accident? He'd run it by Copernicus when he got back.

Eli glanced at the holo-screen showing the footage of Ev'r Keets' cell through the spyer he had planted under the table. The fugitive was crouched unmoving in one corner. Eli thought about Jude and his confession for probably the billionth time that hour. He shook his head in disbelief. Ev'r shivered and Eli remembered something else that Jude's announcement had blotted from his mind – he remembered Ev'r's warning about Silho. Grabbing the communicator off his weapon belt, he checked the locator screen. The green spot representing Silho was not at her home where it should have been, but in Moris-Isles. Uneasiness wrung Eli's gut.

'*Lai Lai*, Silho, what are you doing there?' he said to himself, then instructed his system, 'Call Brabel.'

14

Droplets of blood shimmered ruby in the lantern light as they dripped from Silho's head to her trousers, blossoming crimson flowers on the grey dullness of the fabric. She pressed her hands into her face, aware of the other passengers. They looked, but didn't really see, all eyes focused inward.

A tinny voice erupted over the intercom, 'Next stop Eastend Station, Moris-Isles.'

Silho dragged herself to her feet and went to stand in front of the door. She looked into the darkened glass and met her reflection's stare. A sickness spiralled inside her. Oren Harvey's eyes stared out from under her hood. They looked inside her heart and they mocked what they saw. What did she think she was doing going back to the crime scene? What would disobeying orders accomplish, other than getting herself discharged from the team or even killed, or worse? Why was she trying to retrace footsteps made by shoes she could never fill? *I'm just the ghost of your shadow* . . . Silho took the bottle from her pocket, shook out two more pills and swallowed them down. Synthetic serenity silenced her fear. And distorted her judgement.

The public transporter swooped to a halt at Eastend Station and the doors slid open. A hot gust of Moris-Isles air, stinking like an abattoir, rushed into the carriage. Some passengers covered their noses, others averted their eyes. Silho left them to their silence and stepped out onto the platform underneath a jittering fluoro light swarming with kamikaze moths. The doors closed behind her and the transporter zoomed away.

The neon lights of Eastend, Moris-Isles, gleamed in the distance and a booming bassline thudded in time with Silho's heart. Bottles smashed, voices yelled and cursed. Someone screamed. Silho took in the barren platform littered with cigarette butts and rubbish. Anything once there, both freestanding and bolted down, had long since been broken or stolen, and graffiti marked every inch of space. Below Silho's boots the words RIP Dupuesta, Weldido, Brahe sprawled across the concrete – the names of the first gangsters, the originals. Silho crossed the platform towards the top of the stairs, where a group of gang members dressed in the yellow leather of the Penny Little Alliance were loitering. As Silho neared, one of them, a human-breed of leopard blood, stepped out to her.

'What you looking at, gadfly?' he spat.

Show no fear, Silho told herself. She drew her military standard electrifier and pointed it at him. His self-assurance drained and he said nothing more as she passed.

Silho picked her way down towards the street. The steps, termite-eroded and precarious, without a railing to hold, blurred under her feet and she fought to focus around the pulsating of her head. Blood seeped from the wound. Afraid the smell would attract the Midnight Men, she pulled her hood further over her face, then jolted at the sudden buzz of her communicator. She snatched it off her belt, cursing herself for not leaving it at home. Her first instinct was to not answer, but then the team might think she was in trouble and come looking. But what if it was the commander and he sensed she was lying? With shaking hands, she pressed the receive call button.

'Silho.'

She breathed relief to hear Eli's voice. 'Yes.'

'My locator says you're in Moris-Isles. Is that right or is my system glitching?'

'No, your system is right. I'm just – visiting a friend,' Silho tried to sound casual.

'In the Isles?' Eli seemed unconvinced.

'She lives here. She asked me to come over.'

'At three hours to dawn?'

'She's nocturnal . . .' Silho winced as she said it.

'But you should be at home. You should be resting. The commander ordered it,' Eli reminded her.

Silho swore again silently and replied, fighting to keep her voice calm, 'I know. I just – she had an emergency, an emotional emergency. Women's business. Can you just keep this between us?'

Eli paused. His voice dragged with reluctance and uncertainty. 'I suppose so, but I really think you should head home.'

'I will,' Silho lied. 'Thanks, Eli.' She pressed the end transmission button, then found the communicator's power switch and shut it down. She knew it would look suspicious, but she couldn't have him seeing her return to the same street as the crime scene. The friend story wouldn't be enough to cover that.

She came to the last stair and moved out into the street, but her steps faltered as roaring snarls sounded close by. Two packs of Stogs, troll-breeds, turned the corners either side of where she stood. They were wielding spiky mallet-like weapons known as thupclubs and stretching wide, gooey maws full of blade-like teeth. Looking from one pack to the other, she realised she was in the centre of an imminent Stog turf war. She ran, ducking into a transflyer parking lot, which led away from the station district, and into the backstreets of night-time Moris-Isles. Silho's heart thundered, throat too dry to swallow, but she moved quickly and purposefully, keeping a fearless front and her electrifier drawn.

The brothel district was still in full chorus of squeaky bedsprings, moans and screams when Silho hit the main stretch. As she passed under the windows of one grindhouse, a tall figure stepped out of the doorway and started following her. With her electrifier armed, she turned to face him. He hissed and evaporated – Midnight Man. Silho shivered and pressed onward until she finally reached Whitter Avenue and stopped at the top of the stairs leading to the crime scene. The boards that the guardians had nailed across the doorway to stop people entering had been ripped away. With nerves prickling, she tightened her grip on her electrifier, blinked into light-form vision and moved down the stairs.

A red light shone from the crime scene. Silho crept along the corridor towards the room and stopped beside the doorway. She swapped back to normal sight and peered in. The coroners had cleared away the corpses, but blood still stained the floor and walls. A vulture-faced woman, dressed in a long dark blue cloak, paced the room. Silho's senses flared in warning. This woman reminded her of one of her early training missions to the cursed city of Glargsh, where the dead had scrambled from their graves and walked out to meet them. They'd been as this woman was, shrivelled and hollow-eyed with gnarled claw-like fingers, their bodies wafting of rot. Silho moved closer and saw the woman pause at a makeshift bench where someone lay squirming slowly, groggy. The cloaked woman arranged small pots around the bench and dipped a fingertip into each. She drew on the prone person's face in blood red – a triangle within a triangle, within a square. From inside her cloak, the woman took a severed arm and cut flesh from it, dropping pieces into each pot. They began to boil and rattle as her voice uncoiled from the darkness shrouding her face.

'Power of Morsmalus, accept this flesh offering, accept this blood offering and grant your humble servant guidance to the key. Light the way to its resting place.' She made some guttural sounds and the chamber shook. The shadows swirled around the walls. Silho stared in disbelief. The woman had used dark-words, curses, forbidden and punishable by immediate death without trial. They smelt of burning tar and stung Silho's eyes.

The witch untied the cord from around her neck and let the cloak drop to the ground. She stood, naked and hideous, her scabby skin mutilated with symbol scars. A creature was moving inside her, pushing hands and a demon face against her back. Silho's shock deepened. This wasn't just a dark witch, this was a Skreaf – the worst of the demon cults. Silho recalled from her training that the Skreaf craft had once been, along with Cos, nature's voice, the most widely used of the magics, but that the demons had been wiped out long ago in the purges during the reign of King Miron V. The Skreaf literature had been destroyed and little passed on about them, except that their members, born largely unskilled, paid for their power with flesh and soul.

The witch lifted something above her head and Silho saw the shimmer of a blade. The Skreaf plunged it down towards the trapped figure's face. Silho's instincts kicked in, overriding her shock. She aimed her electrifier at the Skreaf's awful, writhing back and sent a massive surge of electricity into her. For a second the witch was trapped in a circle of light, then thrown forward, smashing into the wall. She lay crumpled on the ground, smoke rising from her skin.

Keeping the electrifier trained on the Skreaf, Silho moved swiftly to the trapped person. A spectral-breed, the Wraith whom she had seen earlier in her vision and in the wall, stared up at her with haunted grey eyes. There was nothing visible binding the Wraith to the bench, but her movements were sluggish, eyelids heavy – cursed.

'Come on!' Silho tried to help the grey-skinned spectral to sit up.

The Skreaf stirred and Silho sent another blast of electricity into her. The witch palmed away the beam of power and rose to her feet. With a flick of her hand, she melted Silho's electrifier into a boiling mess. Silho threw it down and the witch started towards her, but then stopped, her eyes widening.

'You?'

Looking at the Skreaf closer, Silho saw a vague likeness to someone she had known as a child – a woman named Bellum, curator of the Galleria Majora. She used to come to their house and talk to her artist father. Silho remembered Bellum had a cold, clinical stare even when her lips had twitched into the semblance of a smile and when she'd called Silho 'my dear'.

'Ms Bellum?' Silho asked.

The Skreaf released a terrible high-pitched shriek. She lunged at Silho and grabbed her neck, strangling with impossibly strong, vile-smelling hands. The shadows in the room swirled. They formed shapes that stepped out of the walls and came towards them.

Silho gasped and shifted to light-form vision. She saw the writhing demon creature living inside the Skreaf's skin. She drew power from the demon's body-lights into her gloved hands, but had only taken a small amount before she felt a terrible burning, as though her skin was being set alight. Forced to break the connection, she used the power already gathered to shove her attacker away. As the witch flew back her fingernails scratched across Silho's neck. Silho thought she saw a fleeting emotion in the witch's eyes of something like surprise at the strength of Silho's retaliation, but it was quickly glazed over by rage. The shadow figures caught the Skreaf, Bellum, before she hit the wall and she slunk back towards Silho, sinking low to the ground, her hair becoming snakes, her face a terrible sunken skull with blood-red eyes. She opened a foul, rotting mouth and spoke dark-words against Silho. Silho collapsed to the ground, agonised, as though stabbed by a thousand needles. She convulsed, unable to control her body. Her head and feet smashed against the floor again and again.

Behind Silho a voice hissed a Cos enchant, '*Indigo.*'

It caught the Skreaf by surprise, throwing the witch and her shadow army backward to the wall, which swallowed them up, trapping them inside the concrete. They stretched the rock like plastic trying to get free.

Silho rolled onto her stomach and warm blood spilled from her nose and ears. Her heartbeats sounded loud and detached. A figure appeared beside her and she stared up at the skeletal spectral-breed, wrapped in a giant moth-wing cloak. The recovered Wraith stood perfectly still, more like a sculpture than a real being. An image born out of a troubled mind, blending with the shadows, beautifully grotesque. Blood gurgled in Silho's throat. The Wraith bent down and touched her face with velveteen fingertips. Silho struggled, unable to breathe, her vision blurring. She coughed and sparks flew from her mouth, burning her lips. A red glow ignited behind the Wraith's eyes, and it lifted Silho to her feet with a strength belied by sickly thin limbs. It whispered a word: *Omarian.* Silho's senses regathered around her and she saw the wall holding the witch starting to shake and crumble.

'Run!' she yelled at the Wraith and they both bolted for the exit. The spectral-breed passed through the wall, Silho through the doorway. She crashed along the pitch-black corridor and up the stairs. She didn't stop at the top, but kept running, losing track of the Wraith and all sense of direction, not caring now who saw that she was afraid. Buildings blurred on either side of her and she hurtled over holes in the road made by the Burrowers. A terrible presence followed her, gathering, gaining. Silho grabbed at her weapon belt, her fingers finding her communicator. She ripped the device up to her mouth, grappling to turn it on as she raced forward. It buzzed to life.

'Call Eli!' she shouted.

The machine whined and whispered and found Eli's system.

He answered. 'Silho. Why did you —'

'Eli!' she screamed into the communicator. 'Help me!'

'What's wrong?' Eli yelled back, his voice rising several octaves. 'What's happening?'

'A witch is chasing me! She's behind me!' Her feet pounded on the concrete and she gasped for air. A stitch ripped along one side of her body and blood streamed from her nose over her lips and chin. She glanced behind her at the shadows swelling like a storm. Another voice murmured behind the static of the communicator, but Eli's reply blurred it out.

'Keep running! I'm calling the commander.' Silho heard sounds of Eli crashing around, then his frantic calls, 'Boss! Boss! Come in – are you there? Diega – are you there?' He spoke again to Silho. 'Their machines are off, but I'm coming for you right now. I'll find you! I'll . . . Oh no!' Silho heard a clunk and Eli's voice dissolved into static.

'Eli!' Silho struggled to breathe. 'Eli, answer!'

'Silho!' Jude's clear, deep voice cut in through her machine. 'I'm here, not far from you. I'm under attack as well. Look at your locator. Can you see me?' She heard the zapping sound of Jude firing his electrifier and something screamed horribly. Silho lifted the machine to her eyes, the dots blurry through her watering eyes, but she made out the blue spot that was Jude. He was close.

'I see you!' she said.

'Keep running towards me,' Jude yelled over the noise of weapon fire. She heard him groan. Silho took a sharp turn down an alley and a stranger lunged at her and grabbed her by the shoulders. With the entire force of her terror behind her, Silho punched him in the face and smashed him out of the way. He screamed abuse after her, but his voice was cut to a bloody gurgle by whatever was chasing her. Silho didn't look back. She was almost to Jude – two more corners. One more corner.

She flung herself over another hole in the street and stumbled into an alley, only to skid to a halt and freeze in terror. Skreaf witches and sorcerers crowded the backstreet. They had surrounded Jude. He was lying unmoving on the ground, covered in white Androt blood. Other people, chained to each other, stood shaking and crying nearby. The forms of some of the Skreaf were dissolving into mist and wrapping around the prisoners. One was a teenage boy with fire-red hair and Galley bloodline marks.

All the Skreaf's eyes suddenly snapped Silho's way and locked onto her. They started to speak curses. Silho stumbled back, trying to escape them. A hand shot up from the Burrower hole behind her. Silky-soft fingers clamped hard around her ankle and yanked her downwards. The Wraith dragged Silho through the tunnel so quickly she couldn't get a grip on the gravel and she couldn't catch her breath. Abruptly, the ground vanished from beneath her and she dropped, deeper, down and down until she crashed to the ground and was buried by an avalanche of dirt and rocks. That was when blackness took her.

15

Ev'r had realised the extent of Ismail's sickness when he'd tried to tell her how much she meant to him, that she was the only one he had ever loved, that they were soulmates – that even though this life had ripped them apart, they would be together again in Paradise. Together forever. The Mocking Witch had been keeping him prisoner, and keeping him alive with the elixir she hung around her neck at all times. It was a cure-all of unfathomable power, enough to prevent Ismail's heart, pierced through the centre by a blade, from splitting in two. But the potion had worn off by all but the last drop, and their time together, brief and perfect, was over. Ev'r had half-lifted, half-dragged him into a cave in the Lava Diavol Mountains. She'd sat beside him, held his hand and watched helplessly as he'd struggled for his last moments of life. Afterwards she'd looked into his dulled eyes and understood that everything that had been her soulmate was now gone and that for all she'd loved him, she could never bring him back. Nothing ever could. That was death – and there was no Paradise at the end of it. There was nothing.

Ev'r crouched in one corner of the silent prison room, under the ventilator gushing freezing air. It chilled the twists of chains pinning her arms firmly to her sides. The cold metal burned her skin, and her leg muscles ached under the weight of her body. Still she held her position, refusing to allow herself to move, knowing the cold would slow the changes of her system. Memories came to her mind of a person she hadn't thought about forever – her mother. It was a word to describe the woman, but it held no meaning for her. Though the woman had been dead in her mind from the moment she'd left her sight, Ev'r saw her with absolute clarity – cringing, crying, weak in her husband's shadow. What he said she did, and she rushed to please him even when he hurt her children. Ev'r didn't believe in reliving the past through pitiful self-reflection, but now that she felt her time running low, she thought about her childhood and she understood that everything in her life up until this point had been built around trying to be as far opposite to that woman – *mother* – as she could be.

An image blurred by years of focused forgetting came to her. A straggly girl lay struggling on the ground, her face pressed into the dirt by a boy. He was nondescript. He had no identity, just the same ugly, snivelling face as every other scullion-born son of filth. Her father had promised her to this boy, this no one. He had grown impatient and without Ismail to protect her; he'd taken what wasn't his.

Torn and dirty, she'd stumbled home. She hadn't gone to her mother then; it wasn't until she'd felt the baby growing inside her that she had made that mistake. It was a moment of blind desperation, where she forgot all reason and truth. Maybe she had hoped, however stupidly, that the woman who birthed her might stand up and protect her when it really mattered. She hadn't. Ev'r was blamed for what was not her fault. Her father and the other men of her family tribe kicked her out. They'd pelted her with rocks to drive her away, while her mother stood by and watched and wept, but they were selfish tears. They meant nothing.

After this, part of her had sung with freedom from the drudgery of scullion existence, but another part had screamed to go back. Her home town was built from filth and garbage, but it was the only home she had known. Alone and pregnant, she'd faced the freezing desert nights and boiling desert days. She'd scavenged, she'd starved, she'd done everything she could to stay alive, until the day she was ambushed by desert freaks. They'd destroyed her child before it took its first breath, and though she had never wanted it, she was devastated to see it dead. Before they'd been able to finish her off, the Mocking Witch had driven them away.

After Ismail died, she had returned to the outskirts of her town with the purpose of finding her parents, of laughing in their faces and dealing them a lesson in life from which they'd never recover. She went home to find life had already dealt its own lesson. Her father had bashed her mother to her grave, then in the same year he himself had been beaten brain-dead during a tribe war. As was the custom of the scullion people, still half-alive, he had been cast out into the desert to be picked apart by carrion birds. Though her parents were gone, she'd seen that her sisters and brothers had taken their place and were continuing in their footsteps, the link to the next damaged generation. She had broken away from this chain. She was no longer part of it, but neither was she part of anything else. She was completely alone.

Ev'r lifted her head, sensing the outer door of the interrogation area opening. She looked up at the spyer, but the image died, concealing whoever was coming. Ev'r glanced at the table, wondering if Snack-size was watching. She guessed probably not. Just as she had known her life with Ismail was ending, she felt now her own time was up. She had no chance, but she sure as hell wasn't going down without taking them with her.

The door to her cell slid open and the human-breed guardians stood in the doorway – one Skreaf witch, one Skreaf sorcerer. Two demons glaring through the semi-glazed eyes of their hosts.

The lights in the cell flickered and dipped from the magics summoning in the room. The Skreaf thought it was coming from them, but they really didn't know who they were dealing with.

Ev'r gathered her full psychological, emotional and physical strength. She leapt from crouching to standing in an instant and released a dark curse, taught to her by the Mocking Witch. It was not Skreaf magics, but it was still powerful, at least momentarily. The curse hit both demons, driving them to the ground like a giant crushing fist. Ev'r jumped over their bodies and ran out the door. She made it into the entrance of the interrogation area and slammed into the front door, hoping to jar it open. No such luck. She stretched her bound hand painfully upwards, straining against the chains, trying to touch the release button, but it was too high for her. The curse hit her squarely in the back and flung her forward so hard her head smacked against the concrete wall. Blood trickled down her face. She staggered up and lunged behind a table on one side of the room, but Skreaf dark-words shattered it with a raw and terrible explosion. Ev'r ducked low, trying to shelter herself from the burning debris. The Skreaf closed in on her, chanting. In retaliation, she repeated her own curse blocker, but felt her strength quickly dwindling. They were laying her defenceless, and she had only one choice – self-destruction. There was a curse that would turn her into a bomb with enough power to make rubble of the entire room, along with whoever was inside it.

Ev'r stood, battered by the onslaught of dark-words but unmoving. Her lips formed the first word of the spell and her body begin to burn and shake. Blood ran down her face and neck. Her mouth tasted of hot metal. She whispered the second word and her knees started to give. The walls shivered. One more word and it was all over. Desperation to live held her tongue mute and she struggled against her own terror of the end. It was true, when Ismail had died, she had prayed for death to take her too, but now, faced with it, all she wanted was to live. Power siphoned from her as one of the Skreaf summoned a death-curse.

She had to finish her incantation. Just as she opened her mouth to begin the final word, the doors to the main area flew open. The two Skreaf spun towards the entrance as a volley of missiles sailed through the air. They struck the ground all around the witch and sorcerer. A heavy, blinding gas and the most repulsive stench rapidly drowned the room. Ev'r coughed and choked, dropping to her knees. A small hand grasped her shoulders and dragged her forward. She went with it and crawled low through the haze, past the struggling, coughing forms of the Skreaf.

Ev'r burst out of the room into the corridor, retching violently, her eyes streaming with tears. The soldier, Eli, stood beside the doors, punching in the code to relock it. Before he could, the Skreaf barged their way out. They looked from Ev'r to Eli and immediately went for their electrifiers. With unmatchable sleight of hand, Eli raised his electrifier first and shot a charge into both. They dropped dead to the ground. The Skreaf demons still alive inside them shrugged beneath their hosts' skin like convulsions. The chest of one of the guardians started to rip outwards.

'Hey!' someone screamed from down the hallway. Ev'r and Eli spun towards the voice. The other two interrogation area guardians, the giant and the Twitchbak, stood staring upon the scene.

'You killed them!' the sabre-breed snarled at Eli. 'I saw you shoot them.'

'No!' Eli said. 'Renoir, I —'

'Drop your weapons. Get down on the ground,' the guardian called Renoir shouted. He aimed his electrifier at Eli and the gargantuan soldier grabbed for his communicator and called for backup. The rip in the Skreaf guardian's chest spread.

'Run!' Ev'r barged Eli into motion, and the two of them charged back along the corridor. Electricity blasted around them. She heard Eli praying as he dashed, half-running, half-flying as fast as he could.

'In here!' he yelled, making a sharp turn and crashing through a doorway in the wall that she hadn't even seen. She found herself standing in a stairwell.

'Short cut to the roof,' Eli panted, then cried out, 'Nelly, no!'

Ev'r saw something small dart out of the soldier's pocket and scurry away down the stairs. Eli tried to chase after the creature, but a blaze of electricity from the gaining soldiers forced him back.

He flew up the stairs, Ev'r right on his heels, with the soldiers firing behind them. Ev'r struggled to sustain the speed without the extra assistance of her arms.

'Untie me!' she yelled at Eli.

'No time!' Eli gasped. He grabbed her by the chains and beat his wings hard, dragging her faster and faster up towards the roof. Bolts of electricity glanced off the steel of the stair rail beside them. They finally reached the top and burst out through the door. Ev'r followed Eli's sprinting form to a vintage-looking craft.

'That's too slow!' she shouted. 'Jump something faster.'

'Get in!' Eli yelled back, wrenching the door open. He shoved her headfirst into the passenger seat just as an electrical surge behind them blasted their neighbouring transflyer into flames. Scrambling over her into the pilot's seat, Eli started the engine and jetted them upwards while Ev'r managed to close the door with her legs. Seven or eight military transflyers lifted up immediately behind them and gave chase, their sirens blazing.

'Speed up!' Ev'r screamed.

'Hold on,' the small soldier instructed her. He gunned the engine and she felt her stomach lift into her chest. A gasp escaped her mouth. Then full throttle punched her backward into her seat. Her legs lifted over her head and she tumbled into the back of the craft, smacking against the rear window. A hoard of rubbish and machine parts half-buried her. If they had been flying an open-topped transflyer she would have been lost.

Eli navigated the craft with expert skill, flying the machine faster than Ev'r had ever gone before. They soon left the military flyers far, far behind.

'Activate military radio,' she heard Eli saying.

Soldiers' voices blared from the speakers, describing the craft they were flying. They named Eli Anklebiter as an accessory to her escape – and to the murder of the guardians. Ev'r knew the drill. Blockades would be set up everywhere and the skyways would be crawling with soldiers. They had to get somewhere safe right now and lay low.

She managed to scramble back to the passenger seat. When she looked at Eli, his chest was heaving and tears were streaming down his face.

'We have to find Silho,' he whispered. 'A witch attacked her in Moris-Isles. I have to help her.'

'Forget it. Silho's already dead,' Ev'r said. 'And we will be too if we don't find shelter. Those two guardians that you shot were —'

'Dark magicians. I know,' Eli said. 'Another one came after me in my office. I managed to get past her, and then I saw you on the screen —'

'I was going to say Skreaf,' Ev'r said.

'Skreaf?' Eli's dark eyes stretched wide in horror. 'But they're extinct.'

'They've risen,' Ev'r said. 'I saw them in the desert, now they're in the city. It's them – I know the difference.'

Eli clamped his mouth shut, but his lips still quivered. He stared straight ahead.

'Is there anywhere we can hide?' she asked.

He didn't react. He was strangling the steering wheel.

'Snack-size!' she yelled at him. 'Keep it together.'

His eyes snapped to hers.

'Is there anywhere we can go?' she repeated.

His gaze swivelled left to right in thought until he said, 'Yeah . . . there's a place. Hold on.'

Slamming on the decelerator, he swung the craft in the opposite direction with a sharp, gut-wrenching spin. He sped them to a major pipeway and dropped them straight down. Ev'r hit the windscreen and lay there helplessly, unable to prop herself up without the use of her arms. Eli flew in hyper-speed dangerously close to the roof of the tunnel above the flow of traffic. They were flying so fast that Ev'r doubted anyone would be able to see them, only feel their crafts rocked by a phantom storm. Looking up through the rear window to the light at the top of the tunnel and then down to darkness below, Ev'r couldn't help but feel that they were descending into hell itself.

16

Vagrants squabbling under the great bronze statue of King Miron II, in the centre of Elio D'An Square, quietened at a flare of white light in front of the Galleria Majora. The air shimmered and stretched and a transflyer appeared – a sleek, silverback craft with *Ory-4* inscribed on the side. Two figures emerged: a rainbow-skinned Ohini Fen with glowing nightlight bloodline marks and a human-breed dressed in black. The two stepped away from the flyer and the Fen uttered words, vanishing the craft and snatching something shimmering from the air. She placed it in her pocket and the vagrants grumbled to each other of this blasphemy performed on noble ground, where King Miron XI himself made his royal announcements.

'Hey, you!' one of the drifters raised his slurred voice to the strangers, remembering a time when he had worn the uniform of a guardian. 'You can't do that!' The Blue-Ten drug in his veins gave his words an electronic tinge. 'Hey!'

He stumbled towards them and the human-breed turned his way. The vagrant halted under unyielding black eyes, able to acknowledge and dismiss all in one stare – Copernicus Kane.

The drifter bit his lip and cursed his soggy drunken brain. He'd first met Kane back in his days on the force and knew if there was anything darker than the night itself, it was this man, just as unnatural as the father who'd spawned him. No passing of years, degree of inebriation or narcotic trance had ever faded the images scarring his memory of the day he'd seen Doctor Silvan Kane, Illusionist Extraordinaire, performing at the Rocks Amphitheatre. Even as he thought of it, the smells of animal dung, cheap booze and fire-popped corn wafted beneath his nose. He felt the masses of people jostling around him, the chill of the plastic seat on his bare legs as he took his place beside his older brother. Scullion-gypsies and carnival folk milled around, peddling their wares, trying to lure people into their rigged games of skill. He remembered the moment the chattering voices were silenced all at once as the stage curtains spread open.

Doctor Silvan Kane stood beneath a burning spotlight. His unwavering, penetrating stare swept over the crowd, seeing everybody and nobody. Somewhere into the first half of the show a stunning golden-haired girl in a shimmery outfit rolled a black box out onto the stage. The girl was showing more skin than he had ever seen or even dared to dream of, in case his mother guessed his thoughts and gave him a belting for being indecent. The lights played along the girl's body as Doctor Silvan Kane helped her into the box. It was a trick with knives. It made the crowd gasp in horror then cheer with delight when the girl emerged unscathed after the blanket was raised. But he had seen, young as he was, maybe because he was young and staring so intently, that the emerging girl, though she was the image of the other, had a mark on her ankle that the other did not. Right then, he understood that he had smelt real blood and heard real screams of agony. He knew it to be true. Echoes of those screams had driven him into the military and then, when he couldn't cope, led him to drunkenness and beyond. He could never forget.

The vagrant turned and ran, and his companions stumbled after him. Copernicus' stare followed them until their footsteps faded into silence. The commander recalled the heat signature of the vagrant, once a guardian called Pricet, a man with the unfortunate combination of a big mouth and small brain. He'd treated Copernicus like a disease and Copernicus had responded in kind. Pricet had eventually dropped away like everyone else who stood against him.

The commander's gaze lifted to survey the blackened facades of the mansions overlooking the square. These were not the modern and showy buildings of Fortitude Hill and other areas of the newly rich. These were centuries-old, hand-crafted castles, winter homes of the Ar Antarian noble-born. Curtains fluttered in one of the windows and Copernicus focused on the movement. He sensed heat from behind the fabric – someone busy minding everyone else's business, or something more sinister. There was an unusual smoky tinge to the air, usually purified here in the upper levels.

Copernicus turned back to the Galleria Majora, heart of the cultural precinct of Scorpia. Built on the bones of Scorpia's old asylum, the gothic monstrosity of archways and soaring spires reached high into the midnight sky, watched over by unblinking eyes of stone gargoyles and winged serpents. Uneasy dislike narrowed Copernicus' stare. A heavier blackness lingered around the Galleria, but not black enough to hide the marks where bars had been removed from windowsills and replaced with glass – a more civilised sort of prison.

A woman appeared at one of the Galleria's lower windows, shadows playing unpleasantly over her face, making hollow dark holes of her eyes. She stared a moment at Copernicus then slipped away. Disquiet rippled his back. Had she smiled at him or was it a snarl? He turned to Diega. She was holding the protective amulet she kept around her neck and staring at the building with similar distrust clouding her expression.

Copernicus' communicator shuddered and began to whistle again, high-pitched and loud. He grabbed it and switched it off. If anyone called him, they could leave a message.

'I've turned mine off as well,' Diega told him. 'We'll have to go back to the old system until Eli fixes them.' She avoided his eyes.

On the way to the Galleria neither of them had spoken about Jude. Diega's coping strategy of choice was denial and Copernicus was trying to restrain himself from making any conclusions until he had talked to Jude in more depth and heard the full story. He wasn't exactly buying that a clash of views was solely responsible for the attempted assassination – if that was what had really happened in the first place. He couldn't trust what Jude said anymore and that caused him more distress than he had expected. Copernicus forced his mind back to the present. They had a job to do.

He nodded and said, 'Let's go.'

They moved up the great stone steps and walked through the entrance hall of the Galleria. They passed beneath the part-wolf, part-dragon sculpture carved into the low roof. The beast appeared to be breaking out of the stone and coming for them. They entered the lobby. Since its asylum days, the interior had been refashioned all in marble with towering columns to a dome ceiling made of stained-glass murals, the images dull with no light to give them life. A strange, tar-like stench irritated Copernicus' nose, but he couldn't place the smell. His sights focused on light shining from a large open doorway at the far end of the lobby. A state guardian stood waiting for them. They headed for the light, slowing as they reached the guardian, a hulking human-breed of gorilla heritage. He didn't notice them. His expression was grim and his skin tinged the pale grey-green of sickened fear. The man's giant hands trembled as he crossed himself and murmured a prayer to the ancestors of his bloodline. Copernicus cleared his throat and the officer flinched.

'Commander Kane.' He saluted.

'You were first on scene?' Copernicus asked him.

'Yes, sir,' the guardian replied and his eyes shifted from their faces to the darkness behind them.

'Who made the emergency call?' Diega asked.

'An assistant of Vice-Standard U. He was working late on an upper level and when he came down to leave, he found . . .' The guardian's voice faltered. 'They're in there. It's not a pretty picture.'

'Thanks for the assessment,' Diega snapped and pushed past him into the chamber named, by the plaque above the door, *The Hanging Room*.

The Fen took one glance around the chamber and snarled, 'Great – a psycho with a sense of humour. Just what we need.'

Copernicus looked over the deceased – twelve figures hanging from ropes tied to supporting beams in the centre of the gallery. Painted portraits lining the chamber walls looked upon the scene with what Copernicus thought was an edge of horror in their fixed stares, but he conceded he might be seeing a reflection of his own unease. It was, as the guardian had suggested, not a pretty picture, though he might have used stronger words himself – *hell on earth.*

Copernicus walked among the dead, not touching, just observing, seeing what would be clearly obvious to anyone who had spent as much time with corpses as he had – that hanging was not the cause of death. Each of the bodies was burned at the extremities and orifices, with limbs curled up and inwards, almost foetal. Each had severe head injuries, tongues chewed off, eyeballs exploded and feet broken. The air hung foul with burnt hair and flesh, pungent urine and another scent that made Copernicus shiver – something that reminded him of his childhood. Studying the corpses, his mind turned to Christy Shawe and he shook his head. The other crime scenes might have passed, at a push, as gang attacks but this . . . he knew Shawe well and the gangster definitely wasn't into torture; he was too ill-tempered and impatient for that. All the kills Shawe had committed were the same – shootings with a high-voltage electrifier, over in moments and always in the context of the gang wars. Copernicus' thoughts returned to what Eli had said about Shawe not being involved and doubts clouded his confidence. Maybe he had allowed his personal grievance against Shawe to colour his judgement – yet Shawe, while not educated, was highly cunning and street smart. It wouldn't be beyond the Gangland king to change his patterns to throw them off his track. The question was, why would he attack the Galleria?

Copernicus leaned closer to one of the corpses and saw the burnt husk of a security badge pinned to his chest. He looked around. All the dead were wearing them. He studied the pattern of blood and matter on the floor. They had definitely died on the ground and then been strung up, which would have taken the killer some time. So it must have a purpose. Copernicus stepped back for a wider view of the scene, then turned to the wall and walked up the surface to the ceiling. He surveyed the scene from above and, forcing his eyes to focus and see the scene as a whole, he saw a definite hanging pattern – like two triangles within a square. His eyes snapped to an irregularity in the shapes. One rope had broken high up – someone had fallen. A survivor, perhaps?

Leaping down, Copernicus almost collided with a man hurrying through the chamber doors: the lead forensic investigator, B.L.

Jenkins. He was a human-breed from a hound bloodline, with heavy, fleshy bags under his eyes and a permanent scowl on his face. Jenkins puffed, out of breath. He saw Copernicus and growled a curse.

'You always have to be the first on scene, don't you, Kane?' He held up a yellow-nailed finger. 'Keep your hands off my evidence. I'm sick of telling you.'

Copernicus sidestepped him and, following a drag line of white Androt blood, ran from the Hanging Room into an adjacent chamber. Jenkins' footsteps sounded closely behind him.

In a pool of weak light, a figure lay face down, grasping the feet of a sculpture as though begging for mercy. Copernicus dropped down beside the person and carefully turned him over. The victim was an Androt man. The black barcode, bold on his neck, read 939963. His injuries were gruesome and his torn security uniform saturated with white blood, but he was still breathing and his skin was re-knitting into grey scars.

Jenkins spoke from beside Copernicus. 'I'll call the medics.'

'Diega!' Copernicus yelled. He ripped off his jacket and held it against the man's badly haemorrhaging leg. Boot steps echoed around the chamber as Diega ran in.

'Give me something to stop this,' Copernicus ordered.

The Fen pulled a coagulating syringe from her weapon belt and pressed it into Copernicus' outstretched hand. The commander applied it to the man's worst wounds and the flow of blood quickly stemmed. As he readjusted his coat under the Androt's head, he noticed a set of white bloody footprints leading from beside the victim to the chamber door. They were spaced widely as though in a run. It looked to him as though someone had found the man, run to him, seen he was an Androt and fled, leaving him to die. He guessed it was the Vice-Standard's assistant who had discovered the scene. He met Diega's eyes and saw that she was surmising the same thing. The Fen's rainbow skin flashed vibrant with anger. She squeezed the dying Androt's hand and said, 'We're here. Hold on.'

The man's eyelids flickered.

A commotion of raised voices and the echo-boom of many stomping boots sounded from the Hanging Room. Copernicus turned.

Vice-Standard U, brother of King Miron U, and Jude's alleged attacker, stormed into the chamber with an entourage of servants,
guards and red-cloaked enforcers. Copernicus regarded the silver-
skinned Ar Antarian noble with instant loathing. Since he wasn't
directly in line for the throne, the Vice-Standard didn't wear the concealing veils that the royal family did. Copernicus could see him
clearly for everything he was. The noble's clothing was spotless, hair
trimmed neatly, fingernails manicured and eyes red-rimmed and hollow as a corpse's stare.

The Vice-Standard, governor of the cultural proceedings of
Scorpia, crossed his metal arms over his chest in the exact manner
that Jude did and spoke with cold precision. 'The priceless Mazurus
Machine has been stolen from the gallery. You are to investigate this
immediately.'

'Why didn't your assistant alert the paramedics when he found
this victim still alive?' Copernicus asked the noble.

'I gave you an order,' the Vice-Standard said.

'And I asked you a question,' Copernicus replied.

'Insolence,' the noble snarled.

'In court they call it grievous indifference,' Diega said. 'Your
lackey found this man and left him to die. That's punishable by
law.'

'This man,' the Vice-Standard laughed. 'This *man* – that isn't a
man. That is a machine.'

'You're the trutting machine!' Diega cursed him.

The noble's face flushed. He ordered his people, 'Eject this *thing*.'
He pointed to Diega.

Three of his guards moved forward. Copernicus stood and they
halted, none of them willing to meet his eyes.

The commander spoke to Diega. 'Go. Search the perimeter.' She
was no use to him while she was so emotional. She opened her
mouth, then decided against speaking and left the chamber. The
medics rushed in past her. They gathered around the Androt and started treating him.

'He's the sole survivor in a multiple homicide,' Copernicus told
them. 'Make sure he lives.'

He left the man with them and walked towards the Vice-Standard, stopping just in front of him. 'Now I'm ready to investigate your machine,' he said. 'Show me where it was.'

The noble blinked. Showing him was what he had wanted to do, but having been ordered to do so, he didn't know how to act. Copernicus smiled inwardly. The Vice-Standard flicked his robes and turned. 'You'll attend to the Mazurus now,' he said, but it sounded weak and he knew it. The noble and his entourage marched out of the chamber and Copernicus followed.

As he reached the doorway, Jenkins stepped into his path and asked, 'How is he – the witness?'

Copernicus eyed him, noticing something abnormal about the way his lips had moved. Almost as though the words had been forced out. He also noted the strange use of the word *witness* instead of *survivor*. On instinct he said, 'He won't make it.'

Jenkins gave no reaction, instead he mumbled, 'Listen, I just wanted to let you know I'm grateful for the work you put into the investigations. I don't see any reason why our teams can't work in cooperation with each other.' His lips twitched strangely into a grimace-like smile. Copernicus' suspicions flared. Seven year-cycles working in close proximity and the man had never even given a hint of a smile.

'What do you want?' the commander said bluntly.

Jenkins' eyes swivelled and he lowered his voice. 'Well, I was wondering if you or any of your team found anything at the Moris-Isles crime scene.'

'Anything?' Copernicus questioned, conscious of the ring in his pocket.

'Any, let's say, items,' Jenkins said.

Copernicus felt a tugging pressure of someone trying to enter his thoughts and tightened his control over his mind. A cold sweat broke out on his back. He faked a smile and said, 'I think you're overworked, Jenkins. Why don't you take some time off and find yourself a woman. Preferably one that's still alive.'

He stepped around the investigator and Copernicus' smile was immediately gone. He felt an unnatural stare following him out of the hanging room.

The noble and his entourage led Copernicus through the Galleria to another chamber. In the centre of the room, rust and discolouration marked the large circular outline of where the sculpture had sat. Beside the empty space a hologram sign, intended for visitors to the Galleria, flashed information and a picture of the Mazurus Machine. Copernicus skimmed through the words, learning that the machine was the first astronomical telescopic magnifier, invented by Maximus T. Mazurus several eras ago. The spherical structure was made up of several thousand powerful magnifying panels on rotating hinges, allowing for multi-directional positioning of the lenses. Fundamental to the functioning of the machine was its central magnifier, a massive telescope that could be extended from the body of the machine high into the sky. According to the information, the inventor, Mazurus, had used the concept of sound to power the machine. He'd focused the magnification of the lenses onto instruments that emitted particularly intense frequency vibrations, which travelled through each of the panels, gathering force until they reached the central magnifier. The combined soundwaves blasted up the tubular body of the telescope, passing through a small circular band of special conductive metal, through the powerful lens and out into the air, creating a momentary 'supersound' through which a brief but enormous magnification of the night sky occurred. It had long since been surpassed by superior technologies, but the machine had been an important breakthrough for its time.

'Over forty years-cycles ago, when the Mazurus Machine was shipped to the Galleria Majora from the Galleria Minora, someone stole the conductive band in the core lens of the machine,' the Vice-Standard said. He stabbed a finger at the picture of the Mazurus, at the head of the central telescopic magnifier, just below the lens. 'From there.'

'Who stole it?' Copernicus asked.

'If we knew that we'd have it back, wouldn't we.' The noble gave him a disdainful stare and added, 'Your people never found it.'

'So the machine doesn't work?' Copernicus said.

'The individual panels are still powerful magnifiers, but the core telescope needs the conductive band of metal to function as it did. Nevertheless, the Mazurus is a priceless artefact of the Black Sun era,' the noble said. 'It is the largest Black Sun relic still intact.'

'Which makes it not exactly easy to pawn off,' Copernicus replied. He crouched down examining the ground. 'Or easy to carry, for that matter.' He scanned the room for any dust residue that a morpher might have left.

'All our art is protected against shape-shifting evil, if that's what you're looking for,' the Vice-Standard said.

'And yet there are no spaces here big enough for the sculpture to have passed through. Think about it. Its size must have been altered.' Copernicus refused to encourage the noble's ignorance.

'I just told you all our art is —'

'I heard you,' Copernicus cut in. 'So obviously the perpetrator is not a morpher.'

The Vice-Standard flicked back his robe. 'Who else could change the form of the inanimate?'

'A witch, perhaps,' Copernicus suggested, knowing the reaction it would provoke.

The noble's eyes stretched wide and the lizard-faced enforcers at his side glowered and hunched forward, waiting for the command to arrest him.

'How dare you!' the Vice-Standard snarled. 'His excellence, King Miron XI, has eradicated such evil from our city.'

'Just making a suggestion,' Copernicus said.

'Just do your job,' the noble demanded.

'My job is to hunt murderers. I'm only here because your machine may be a clue.'

The Vice-Standard ground his teeth, but Copernicus knew the man wouldn't have him arrested. He was a coward. The commander turned his back on the noble and searched the room for any irregularities. He spotted an unevenness in the marble floor in the centre of the vacant space where the machine had sat. Copernicus walked to it and saw someone had cut a trapdoor in the stone. He used his blade to prise up the section of marble, exposing a coffin-shaped box underneath the floor. Someone had cut out one side of the box to form an opening. A ladder led down from the opening into darkness below. A musty smell wafted up from the depth.

'That is there for maintenance personnel to access the hollow interior of the machine for cleaning purposes,' the Vice-Standard offered. 'I've been informed they stood in that box.'

The commander took the light-blaster from his weapon belt and shone it down through the trapdoor, through the open end of the wooden structure. The light skimmed piles of books.

'Written word?' he asked.

'I believe it was a library at some stage,' the noble said with uninterest.

'Where does it lead to?' Copernicus asked.

The noble blinked vivid blue eyes and said, '*I* have not been down there.'

'Of course not,' Copernicus muttered.

He tucked the torch into his belt and climbed down into the box, having to first crouch and then lie almost completely on his back before he could slide through to the ladder. As his head touched the wooden surface, the walls of the box shrank around him. Cruel laughter and distant applause echoed in his mind. Fear tightened in his chest. Copernicus forced himself to push through the open side of the box and dropped down into darkness, drawing his electrifier as he landed.

17

It was more a graveyard than a library, an abandoned place where forgotten books lay buried by dust, decaying in silence, with silhouettes of broken furniture creeping up the walls like gnarled and twisted limbs. Copernicus scanned the light-blaster through the gloom, trapping particles of dust, ghost rain, in the slivers of light. Ahead of him, on a ground made of unstable piles of books, were signs of a newly trodden path where spider webbing had been snapped and dust disturbed by footprints. The commander moved cautiously forward, careful to walk around the existing marks. He followed the long corridor until it split into two. One side led into another corridor, full of pipes, ending in stairs stretching upwards. The other side, where the footprints travelled, led to a dead-end wall. Copernicus went to the wall and examined the stonework. Crouching down, he felt cold air on his face. With a fingertip, he traced the air all the way up almost to the top of the wall. He holstered his electrifier and slid the blade from his belt. He wedged it between the stones, where he'd felt the air, and pried until a hidden door swung open, revealing a corridor lined with prison cells – remnants of the old asylum.

A solitary functioning fluoro-light lit the last cell at the end of the corridor. Copernicus made his way towards the bars. He stopped in the doorway, feeling captivity pressing in from all sides of the cell, a bare square except for a drain that dripped incessantly. Above the barred door the globe flickered, flinched, casting misshapen silhouettes over the cell's disfigured walls. They were scarred with the evidence of the damaged sanity of its previous inhabitants – scratches and marks made with blood and blunt objects, names and dates and pleas for help, final desperate hopes of being remembered. Gian was here, May, Angus, Aneka, and a thousand faded others. Something bright in the centre of the floor drew his attention. It was a pattern, an arrangement of shapes drawn in red – triangle, triangle, square. The wetness of the mark suggested it had been recently made, and what's more, the configuration was incredibly similar to the hanging pattern of the victims.

When he entered the cell for a closer examination, he saw that it definitely looked like a mark of dark magics. Sweat trickled down the side of his face. Eli had suggested a demon cult and Copernicus had accepted it as a possibility, but having solid evidence that this was true disturbed him greatly. It complicated everything. As he studied the mark, capturing it holographically in his memory, it sparked a more distant recollection. At some time in his life he must have come in contact with it, and from the vagueness of the memory he assumed it must have been a glimpse in passing many year-cycles ago, maybe even in childhood.

While trying to place exactly where and when, Copernicus took a sample of the blood used to draw the pattern, then straightened up to scan the rest of the cell. Everything appeared as it should, until he looked up at the ceiling.

The entire surface was covered with millions of tiny separate pictures, like an instantaneous and momentary snapshot of the entire city. The more he looked at it, the more he saw in it. He strained upwards for a closer look and words appeared across the whole picture, as though written in an ink only visible from certain angles – or by certain eyes. *My God, my God, why have you forsaken me?* Nerves twitched all over Copernicus' skin. These were the final words of the serial killer Englan Chrisholm, who had maintained his innocence until the end, but had been so widely and intensely hated that the state hadn't been able to keep him in any of the penitentiaries. His whereabouts were kept a secret up until his execution. Copernicus' mind flashed back to when as a kid he'd stood in the crowd for the event, familiar with pain, but a newborn to death. That day he'd learnt it had a face of its own. Not ugly, not peaceful, just nothing-ness.

He shook his head, trying to free himself from the memory, then moved swiftly from the cell, hurrying back to the ladder and up through the trapdoor to the chamber and light above. The Vice-Standard stood waiting for him, both metal fists clenched with impatience, his people milling around him. He saw Copernicus emerging and strode towards him.

'Well?' the noble demanded.

'You're right, it's been stolen,' Copernicus said, dusting off his clothes.

The Vice-Standard curled his lip. 'Do you think you're amusing? You're said to be one of the best trackers of this century, but I see what you really are – a gutter-born thug consorting with low-borns, half-breeds and criminals.'

Copernicus lowered his voice so that only the Vice-Standard could hear. 'If I did consort with criminals, I'd be in royal company, wouldn't I?'

The Vice-Standard's stare sharpened. He spoke through gritted teeth. 'Clarify the meaning of your words – immediately!'

'Put simply – for your benefit – I heard a story that twelve year-cycles ago you orchestrated an assassination attempt on Crown Prince Isaiah U. An attempt which failed.'

The Vice-Standard's composure faltered and Copernicus saw his heat signature flare with guilt.

So that part was at least true.

'Blasphemer!' the noble hissed.

'Arrest me,' Copernicus replied. 'And I'll make it known that the crown prince lives and that you tried to kill him.'

'Where is that foul half-breed product of adultery?' the Vice-Standard snarled.

'Is that why you tried to kill him? Because he's a half-breed?' Copernicus demanded.

'Where is he?' the Vice-Standard repeated.

'What is his other half?'

'Where-is-he?' The noble over-pronounced each word and glared at Copernicus with murderous fury.

'Nowhere you will ever find him,' Copernicus said.

'You'll regret protecting him,' the noble threatened.

'Send your assassins and I'll send them back to you – one piece each day.'

He sidestepped the Vice-Standard and headed for the door, barging through the centre of the entourage.

The Vice-Standard called after him, 'You – I met your father once. He was also called the greatest – what was it? – *Illusionist*. He was a drunkard, a fraud and a devil.'

The commander stopped and rounded on him. Satisfaction gleamed in the noble's blue eyes that he'd reached him, but Copernicus answered with complete control. 'Just when I'd decided once and for all that you're irretrievably witless, you go and say something so insightful.'

The entourage gasped in shock. The Vice-Standard's stare widened and Copernicus left the chamber, re-entering the Hanging Room.

The hologramographer stood capturing images of the victims. Suddenly, the shadows of the hanging bodies looked to Copernicus like dangling puppets, making him think of clowns and carnivals. A wave of sickness attacked him at the thought, and he clenched his fists in an attempt to drive it away.

Jenkins and his team were gathered around the victims, collecting samples and taking notes. When he saw Copernicus, Jenkins gave his usual scowl and barked, 'We're not done. Stay away.'

Copernicus said nothing, keeping his face expressionless. Jenkins seemed to be back to his normal self, but the commander intended to open an investigation into the forensic specialist as soon as he and Diega returned to Headquarters. He stopped at the entrance to the Hanging Room and spoke to the waiting guardian. 'Round up everyone in the building for questioning, including those on the second level.'

The guardian's face creased with confusion. 'The only people here are you, the forensics and the Vice-Standard and his people, and everyone is on the ground floor. We've already taken the Vice-Standard's assistant away for his statement.'

'There's a woman in the building. I saw her at the window,' Copernicus said.

The guardian shook his head. 'Sir, I've had the heat and ultraviolet scanners running over the entire gallery since I arrived. No one has come in or out aside from the people I just mentioned.'

Copernicus narrowed his eyes and said, 'Show me the footage.'

The guardian led him to the holo-screen set up to display the data, then proceeded to reverse the footage to its initialisation. Copernicus sped it up until he saw the heat signatures of Diega and himself arriving. At the time there was no one on the second floor of the building where he had seen the woman a few moments earlier. He studied all the heat patterns the sensor had captured over the entire time he had been there. There were none that he didn't recognise as belonging to one of the groups. That was very strange. Even wraiths and other spectral-breeds would show up. The woman had looked human-breed.

'Commander!' Diega called out from across the lobby. She ran to him, breathing heavily. 'I just checked my messages. There is something from Eli, but I can't figure out what he's saying. He sounds upset.' She replayed the message, but it was too crackly to decipher any words, just the occasional half-word that seemed distressed.

Copernicus switched on his communicator. It immediately began whining. He smacked the side of it and the whistling subsided. He also had a message from Eli, but feeling the guardian watching them, he decided to exit the building before replaying it.

Outside, Eli's voice burst out above the background noise.

'Boss! Boss! Come in – are you there? Diega – are you there? Silho, their machines are off, but I'm coming for you right now. I'll find you. I'll— Oh no!'

There was a whistle and a clank, which Copernicus guessed was the communicator dropping to the ground. Then Brabel's frantic screams broke through the static buzz.

'Eli! Eli, answer!'

'Silho!' Jude's voice cut in. 'I'm here, not far from you. I'm under attack as well. Look at your locator. Can you see me?' Copernicus heard the distinct cracking *zap* of an electrifier discharging and a distant screech. Silho breathed heavily into her communicator. She called out, 'I see you!'

'Keep running towards me,' Jude yelled. Copernicus heard him fire again, then the soldier moaned and his communicator dropped out, leaving only the sounds of Silho running and gasping. They heard her cry out and then the dull thud of someone getting punched. Silho kept going, and a man yelled an abusive word behind her, then gurgled as though his throat had been cut mid-sentence. Silho's footsteps stopped abruptly. She uttered something that sounded like *please*, then gave a chilling scream. The sound was cut short and the breath hacked out from her as though she'd fallen over and hit the ground hard. The message blurred with static. They heard the bashing clunk of falling rocks, then the line went dead.

With a thudding heart, Copernicus checked the locator screen of his communicator and saw that Eli was still at Headquarters, or at least his communicator was. Silho was stationary in Moris-Isles and Jude's positioner had completely vanished.

He turned to Diega and she was also staring at the screen, her skin pale almost to grey. She raised her eyes to him and there was no need for words. Snatching the silver coin out of her pocket, she threw it up into the air and called '*Xpel*!' The *Ory-4* stretched into form beside them and they leapt into the transflyer. Diega summoned all of her electrosmith skills and sent the craft shooting towards Moris-Isles.

18

When Eli was growing up, he had burned with embarrassment every time his gran'pa had started in on his Armageddon theory. He would talk about it anywhere and everywhere – in the shopping centre, at the park, in the temple, at weddings, at funerals, at birthday parties, if anyone visited him, if he visited anyone, over the fence to his neighbours and, when they stopped listening, in the garden to the trees themselves. He was even kicked off his senior Oblong Throwing team because his endless theorising was disturbing the old ladies. One nearly had heart failure because he'd scared her so much. Grampy went on and on and on. Even when Eli and his gran'ma were sitting watching the holo-screen, with the volume turned up full blast, pointedly paying no attention, there would be this quiet voice in the background talking unceasingly about bomb shelters and long-life foods. He was like white noise. He was a sub-liminal message. He was obsessed. Literally the man had only two loves in life, his hat collection and thinking the world as they knew it was going to be obliterated by a massive weapon attack, and that the only people to survive would be people like him, who had the good sense to build a bomb shelter. Techs like Eli knew that if the most advanced weaponry of Scorpia was unleashed on itself, it would take more than a sunken concrete room and a few timber boards to escape the utter destruction, but gran'pa didn't listen to this mumbo jumbo. Upon his deathbed, his last words to Eli were – *Take my hat collection ... and build a bomb shelter ... promise me* – before he groaned and was gone. Eli had taken the hat collection, but for many years he had resisted building a shelter. He thought he could escape it, but finally the haunting of the old man's last words drove him to comply. He built a bomb shelter beneath a derelict house he bought for next to nothing in an industrial suburb called Tarpits. It was his shameful secret. Yet as he landed the *Summer Holiday* outside the ruined house, he wished he hadn't made so much fun of his gran'pa.

He checked his rear-vision mirror, but the street was deserted. It was only during break times at the factories that he'd ever seen anyone in the area. He steered the craft into the hangar beside the house and activated the chameleon function of the flyer that made it and its passengers blend in with its surroundings and vanish completely. Eli sat for a moment, still gripping the wheel, his knuckles pure white. Taking a few deep, calming breaths, he managed to pull his hands away, then turned to the lunatic fugitive sitting beside him and said, 'Hi.'

'Untie me,' Ev'r demanded.

Eli shook his head.

'I said, untie me!' Ev'r snarled through gritted teeth.

'No,' Eli refused, although he felt like fainting. 'You're still a prisoner of the state and I'm still a soldier.'

Ev'r laughed unpleasantly, cracking the dried blood on her face. 'You sure about that?'

Eli could see she'd taken a severe bashing. One of her eyes was swollen almost shut and her neck was puffy and discoloured. Her jawline was also strangely distended and he noticed she was having some difficulty swallowing.

'You're hurt,' he said. 'I have medical supplies underneath the house.'

'Trutt your medical supplies,' she snarled.

Ignoring her, Eli took the diamond hanging from his rear-vision mirror. He pushed the chain over his head, and it clinked against the protective amulet he was already wearing.

Ev'r sneered, 'That won't help you.'

'You sure about that?' Eli threw her words right back at her. He popped open his door and climbed out of the craft. Flexing his tired and aching wings, he walked around to the passenger side and let Ev'r out. She struggled to move on a badly damaged leg, both trousers and skin shredded. Her eyes shifted around the hangar and Eli could see she was calculating her chances of escape. In a blur of motion, he drew his stunner and aimed it at her.

'I don't want to do it, but I will,' he warned.

She growled some words, then coughed violently.

'Through here,' he instructed her, gesturing with the weapon.

They climbed through a hole in the wall into the interior of the house wreck. Every door was ripped off its hinges, every window broken. Glass crunched under their boots and the floorboards groaned weakly. The damp timber had given way in many places, leaving jagged and dangerous holes. The smell of mould tainted the air and black grime from the factory chimneys coated everything.

Eli led them to the centre of what was once the kitchen of the house. It had a small window looking out over the jungle backyard. Walking to the broken-down stove, Eli looked into the reflective steel over the heating plates. His face-recognition system activated and a holo-screen appeared above the stove elements. Punching in his security code, he waited a second before a trapdoor slid open in the centre of the floor, revealing a flight of narrow stairs winding downwards.

'You first,' Eli said to Ev'r.

She grudgingly stepped down onto the stairs. He followed her, re-activating the security. The trapdoor sealed shut above them and the shelter lights flickered on.

Ev'r reached the base of the stairs and stopped to gaze around. When giving in to building the shelter, Eli had decided if it had to be done, it was going to be done properly, so he had installed all that was necessary to live underground for several lifetimes. The result was a large open space struggling somewhere between comfortable home and technology laboratory. It was his second workshop, where he came to work away from Headquarters. The shelter was vast and, he'd thought in the past, impressive. He felt little pride now as he stepped around Ev'r and walked to his workbench. He stood staring at the wall. He put his hand in his pocket and found it empty.

'I left her,' he finally whispered.

'Who?' Ev'r asked behind him.

'Nelly.'

'Who?' she repeated.

'My . . . my pet otter. She jumped out of my pocket. There was nothing I could do.' Tears swelled in his eyes and he blinked savagely to keep them back.

'You're crying over an otter?' Ev'r laughed at him. 'And you call yourself a soldier.'

A rare streak of anger burned through Eli and he rounded on the fugitive. 'I could have left you to die, you know, I didn't have to help you. I could have just saved myself and gone to help Silho. She might be dead because of me and because of you. You can laugh, but I think you're heartless.'

'You're right,' Ev'r said. 'I am.' She stepped under the light, her bound form momentarily just a lean silhouette, then she reappeared much closer to him.

'Didn't you ever have a pet, even as a child?' Eli asked her.

'I didn't have *food* as a child. The animals were worked or eaten,' she said.

'That's sad,' Eli said. 'I feel sorry for you.'

'You should feel sorry for yourself.'

Eli heard the threat behind her words. Before Ev'r could even blink, he moved swiftly, grabbing an extra length of chain from his workbench and lassoing her as well as the chair behind her, pulling hard and knocking her into the seat. He wrapped the rest of the slack around her body and fastened it at the back of the chair.

'Comfy?' he asked.

Again she growled and coughed. It was a deep and unhealthy sound.

Eli left Ev'r chained to the seat and went into his medical room. He retrieved the ingredients for the medicine he'd designed for her at Headquarters and mixed them. When he came back out into the main area, Ev'r was slumped in the chair, sagging forward, as though she'd passed out. As he approached her she raised her head, looking up at him in her predatory way through her fringe of white-blonde hair. Her eyes appeared to have changed colour to a very dark green, and the skin around her fingertips was stained black. Intrigued, but not about to ask questions knowing he'd get no real answers, he stabbed the needle into the muscle of her shoulder and she jolted and cursed. Leaving Ev'r in the chair, he went to his workbench and activated the shelter computer system.

'I dropped my communicator back at Headquarters, but I should be able to use this older prototype to tap into the commander's line from here,' he said, talking more to himself than to her.

'Good for you, Snack-size,' Ev'r muttered. 'Tell that gadfly I said hi.'

Eli sat down. His gran'ma had always said action was the antidote to despair. He didn't know how true that was, but he thought if he stopped too long to consider how he was feeling, he might break down altogether. If it was as Ev'r had said and the Skreaf order had been resurrected, things were about to get very bad very fast.

He picked up one of the prototypes of the newest communicator system he had designed. The machine was similar to the final version except that it didn't have the locator screen. He ran a lead between the machine and the computer system and typed in some codes. Without a doubt the Regiment would have tapped his line, so he conducted a line-scrambling method commonly called a *hedge*. While adjusting the system settings, Eli caught a whiff of himself and almost retched. His clothes, his skin, his hair and wings all stank like skunk gas. He felt he could say without reservations that the trial of the new bombs had been a success, but that didn't make bearing the foul odour any easier.

Once the hedge was complete, he activated the communicator and said, 'Call the commander.' Immediately he heard the clunk of his system locking on to another line.

'Boss? Is that you?' he tried.

Static hissed and a high-pitched squeal shrieked in his ear. Copernicus' voice was only just audible around the sound. 'Eli?'

Tears sprang to his eyes. He felt like a lost child hearing his father's voice.

165

'It's me,' he squeaked and wiped his eyes with the back of his hand.

'Are we secure?' Copernicus asked.

'Yes, Commander. I ran a hedge.'

'Eli – I heard on the system. They're saying you killed two fellow soldiers and have absconded with Keets. They're marking you a state traitor. They'll kill you on sight.'

'They weren't soldiers,' Eli stammered in a rush to explain. 'They were witches. Ev'r says they were Skreaf.'

The static whispered and Eli held his breath. He expected the commander to say this was madness.

'She may be right,' Copernicus said instead. His voice waned, the screaming of the system drowning him out. Eli heard the commander hitting the machine and the interference lessened slightly.

'Boss, Silho's in trouble. I tried to go and help her, but then everything broke down at Headquarters.'

'I know. I heard your message. We're almost at Moris-Isles now. Eli . . .' the commander paused. 'Jude was attacked there as well.'

A shudder ran through Eli's body and he said, 'Is he . . . okay?'

'I don't know.'

'Why are the Skreaf attacking us?' Eli asked.

'I don't know that either,' the commander admitted, 'but I will find out. Eli, at the Galleria there was a major attack – someone stole the Mazurus Machine. It may be connected to the —'

The line crackled and panic seized Eli's throat. He stood up, knocking his chair to the ground behind him.

'Boss!'

'Are you somewhere safe?' The commander's voice came faintly.

'Yes, boss.'

'Then stay put.' His words were faint. 'We'll find the others and then we'll find you. We're close to Silho's signal now. Listen, whatever happens, do not free Ev'r Keets. Do not trust her for one second. Don't —'

The line broke away.

'Boss!' Eli desperately punched in codes trying to reconnect. 'Commander!'

'He's gone, Snack-size,' Ev'r said without emotion, behind him. 'He's probably heading into a trap – and you people are supposed to be elite.'

'What do you mean, a trap?' Eli turned to her.

'What do you think? The witches obviously want you trackers down, so they're picking you off one by one. Silho and the Ar Antarian are dust, so it'll be Kane and fairy-girl next.'

'Don't say that!' Eli cried, tears bubbling out of his eyes. 'They're my friends!'

Ev'r snorted and fixed him with her dead calm stare. 'Wake up. Copernicus Kane doesn't have friends. He has servants. Do you think he would waste a second with you if you didn't do his work and kiss his arse?'

'That's not true.' Eli's heart thudded, the words stinging like a slap to his face.

'It is,' Ev'r went on. She grimaced at some internal pain. 'There is no such thing as a *friend*. Look at what happened at your headquarters. One second you're everyone's best friend, and the next they're trying to kill you. They turned on you without a second thought. They never cared about you. You were just another face in their day and another way of making themselves feel better. There is no such thing as friends or loyalty or any of that trutt. There's only one sure thing in this life – death.'

Eli fled into his storeroom. He sank down in a corner of the dark place, wrapped his wings around himself and sobbed in despair.

19

Half-dead and bruised blind in one eye, Silho took in her surroundings through the thin fog of a waking dream. Phantom forms and their shadowing shapes drifted around in the mist. An echo of a word reached her consciousness – *Omarian.* A cold draft sent a tremor through her body and a pinching sting in her arm began, growing until it eclipsed every other sense. Conjoined clarity and pain rushed through her. Silho lifted her head. Copernicus Kane crouched at her side holding a syringe in one gloved hand, the needle red with blood. Disorientated, Silho grabbed for the knife in her weapon belt and lunged at him. Copernicus easily dodged it and Diega kicked the blade out of her hand then kicked her in the chest. The Fen lifted her foot for a third time and Copernicus ordered, 'Enough!'

Diega backed away and Silho used the wall to stand. She felt along the boards, seeing with her fingertips, and staggered towards the door to escape. Her brain throbbed as though it were a crushed lump in one corner of her skull. The attack had been devastating to her system and breathing was excruciating.

Before she could reach the exit, Copernicus grabbed her arms and pressed her down to her knees. Her struggle was brief and insignificant. She fell sideways and he caught her, half-cradling her. He touched her forehead with a cool hand. Without his jacket, she could see down the length of his bare arms, the skin marked with the satiny blue, purple and black diamond pattern of the viper bloodline.

Before her eyes, the colours rippled and flowed as though the mark was the body of a serpent, gliding across his skin to the back of his hand where something had been cut out of the flesh, leaving a scarred dent and a hint of what it had been – the purple XXX insignia of his Illusionist father.

Silho scrunched her eyes shut as throbbing pain blistered her thoughts. Copernicus laid her down on the ground and she grasped at his shirt, dragging him closer to her, desperate for the comfort. She felt his cool breath on her face. He was speaking, but she couldn't hear his words. Her hands slipped from his shirt and she curled up into a foetal position, clutching her knees to her chest. Copernicus moved around her and she felt more stinging in her arm as he injected her with healing agents. Slowly the pain stabilised and her senses cleared. She heard muffled sounds of music, laughter and clinking glasses, smelt fresh sawdust and noticed huge glass flagons of Araki and kegs of ale stacked around the dimly lit room. Silho managed to sit up. Copernicus stood close by, leaning against a barrel, his arms crossed over his chest. His dark eyes bored into her and he spoke with dangerous calm.

'I clearly remember telling you to go home. Next thing we're dragging you out of the ground in Moris-Isles. You disobeyed my orders. Explain yourself. Explain to me what happened.'

Silho swallowed and cringed at the pain of her raw and swollen throat. She touched her neck and found the skin burning hot and badly scratched.

'I wanted to fix my mistake,' she whispered.

'Why are we wasting time with this gadfly?' Diega burst out from behind the commander. 'We should be back at the Galleria interrogating the Vice-Standard, forcing him to tell us where they've taken Jude. He's behind this, I know it.' Stepping around the commander, she was suddenly in Silho's face. 'And maybe you're in on it too – maybe you're a palace spy. Tell me where they've taken him. Tell me!' Diega grabbed Silho by the front of her shirt and shook her. Silho's head knocked back against a barrel and memories of the Skreaf attack, disjointed like images in a shattered mirror, flooded her mind. Panicked, she blinked into light-form vision and drew strength from the Fen's body-lights into her hands. She rose from the ground and struck Diega with so much force the Fen slammed back into Copernicus and the commander almost fell. Both of them stood staring at her, Diega's eyes wide with shock, Copernicus' expression intense but unreadable.

Trembling, Silho folded back to the ground and held her aching neck. Stinging tears trickled down her face. 'Something bad is happening,' she whispered hoarsely.

After a pause, Copernicus stepped closer. He knelt down at her side and spoke quietly, even gently. 'Tell me everything that happened. Start at the beginning.'

Silho swallowed and tried to order her memories. 'I went back to the crime scene to get the samples. I know I disobeyed, but I thought . . . I just . . . A woman was there, but she was . . .' Silho hesitated.

'She was what?' he prompted.

'A Skreaf witch.'

He narrowed his black eyes and Silho forced herself to keep going. 'I saw the demon inside her. She had a Wraith trapped. She drew on its face in blood – a triangle within a triangle within a square. Then she was trying to summon someone. I heard the name *Morsmalus*. The Skreaf was asking its help to find something – I think she said *the key*. She was going to kill the Wraith, so I electrified her and she attacked me. She cursed me and I couldn't do anything. The Wraith fought her . . . I . . . I . . . ran – Eli . . . Jude . . . he was lying on the ground in the alley and they were all around him . . . They . . .'

'Who are *they*?' Copernicus asked.

'The Skreaf . . . They tried to curse me, but something grabbed my leg and I fell . . . I fell . . . I . . .' Words failed her and Silho looked helplessly at the ground.

Diega glared at her, incredulous. The Fen's lips snarled and she said, 'There is no such thing as Skreaf.' She took something from her pocket and rattled it. 'She's taken too many of these.' She read from the label. 'Ethalam and Equinox. This is medication for delusions and hallucinations.'

Silho realised with a rush of shame and panic that they were her pills. 'Give them to me!' She snatched upwards even though Diega was out of reach.

Diega stepped back even further and taunted her, 'What's the matter? You seeing something else now? *Eizenef ore.*' She changed the bottle into a rock and threw it across the room. Silho cried out and scrambled for it, but Copernicus' words stopped her mid-motion.

'Brabel's telling the truth,' he said.

Diega's expression faltered. 'But . . .'

'Diega.' He said her name, and his tone said everything else.

Diega paled, shaking her head. 'Can't be. The Skreaf were destroyed way before our time.'

'Two of the victims at the first crime scene and one at the second were hollowed out,' Copernicus said. 'Their insides missing and the wounds cauterised. No insects had touched these bodies, as though they were contaminated.'

'Because demons had ripped out of them,' Diega murmured. She backed away until she hit a barrel and fell into a sitting position.

Silho said nothing. It matched the fragments of her vision. Two of the six dead at the first crime scene had been Skreaf, who first tortured the other four and were then killed by the Wraith – or at least the demons' host bodies were. Silho felt eyes on her back and glanced at the walls of the room searching for the grey-skinned spectral. She remembered the Wraith saying *Omarian.* The word had no meaning to her, but for some reason felt familiar.

'At the scene we just attended, the corpses were strung up in a pattern – the same as Brabel described,' Copernicus continued. 'Two triangles within a square, and I found a similar mark in an old prison area below the main floors of the Galleria.' Copernicus glanced at Silho, at the pictures on her neck and chest, and she saw him turning a thought over in his mind. 'And that smell – I couldn't place it then, but I realise now that it was Skreaf magics. I've smelt it before, when I was younger. Now the demons have Jude.'

'It's her fault.' Diega stabbed a finger at Silho. 'He was trying to save her and got caught up.'

The commander rejected the idea. 'In his message he said he was already under attack before he contacted Silho. She ran to him, not him to her. The Skreaf went after Eli and Ev'r Keets as well, at Headquarters. We were all targeted.'

'We have to find him.' Diega stood up. 'The attack wasn't long ago. They couldn't have gone that far.'

Copernicus shook his head. 'They travel through the Murk – like Keets. They can go very far, very fast.'

'I saw them dissipating,' Silho confirmed. 'They had other people as well . . . a boy . . .'

Diega ignored her. 'Then we go to Keets and force her to take us into the Murk. Make her lead us to them.'

'She won't,' Copernicus said. 'But if we go out in the open, I think the Skreaf will come to us.'

'Why?' Diega asked.

'We have something they want.' Copernicus reached into his pocket and brought out the ring. 'And they want it badly enough to have possessed Jenkins at the Galleria and made him question me for it.' Copernicus realised now that this was what had happened. 'They're desperate.'

'The ring came from the crime scene,' Silho said. 'The witch was back there searching for something – she said *the key*, but maybe the ring is the key.'

Copernicus nodded. 'This ring belonged to Stacy Shawe, Christy Shawe's brother. He's now missing.'

'One of the other prisoners they had was a red-haired boy,' Silho told him. 'He had Galley bloodline marks.'

Copernicus pushed the ring back into his pocket. 'First we get Eli. Then we find a safe place to stash the ring. Then we start tracking Jude.'

Before any of them could make a move, the door to the storeroom smashed open and Christy Shawe stood, a giant silhouette, in front of the light. He stepped forward with Jude's spider robot, SevenM, hanging lifeless in one hand and a multi-headed electrifier in the other. Beams of light singled out all three trackers and the gangster king fixed them with bloodshot eyes.

'My turn to ask the questions,' he snarled.

20

The sky bled acid rain and jagged lines of multi-forked electricity surged from above, exploding whatever they hit, lighting up the wasteland town in strobing flashes. Ruinous charcoal buildings swayed on stilts over bunkers and burrows in the mud. Dysfunctional transflyers and machinery lay scattered, half buried, decaying where they had fallen. Everything was filthy and broken, existing one step from complete collapse.

Copernicus surveyed the desolation through the dirt-smeared window of the partially submerged craft, *The Sovereign 2*. It was a royal ship that had been hijacked some years ago, now converted into a hidden room. Christy Shawe stood beside the window, alternating between drags of his cigarette and swigs from a silver flask. The gangster murmured something to himself, running a hand over his shaved head, his knuckles red with Copernicus' blood. The commander blinked to keep focus. His face was swollen and discoloured and the bindings around his wrists and ankles gnawed at his flesh. The rope was some kind of unfamiliar plant vine that constricted tighter the more he moved.

Diega and Silho sat in similarly bound states. Diega was staring at SevenM. The arachnid robot lay in a heap on the floor, frozen, which meant either Jude was dead or too far away to connect with it. Shawe's men, Greenway Galleys, human-breeds of rhinoceros descent, stood all around the room. Copernicus recognised their faces, once childhood friends, now watching him with bitter hatred. He had betrayed them, but Shawe had betrayed him first and he had reacted then in the only way he'd known how.

Shawe stubbed out his cigarette on the windowsill and reeled towards them, heavily drunk. He cracked his knuckles and stopped right in front of Copernicus.

'One last time,' he said. 'Where is he?'

Copernicus sighed and braced himself for the next onslaught.

'We don't have him!' Diega shouted at Shawe. 'How many times do we have to tell you? The Skreaf have taken him – same as they've taken one of ours. The longer you keep us here the less chance we have of finding them alive!'

Shawe gave a crazed laugh, sour-sweet Araki heavy on his breath. 'The Skreaf.' He shook his head and laughed louder, then his eyes snapped back to fury and he smashed Copernicus across the face, mashing the flesh of his cheek into the sharp viperous fangs behind his blunt front teeth.

'Where is he?' Shawe bellowed.

Copernicus spat out a mouthful of blood and venom. It had been a long time since he'd used his venom and its bitter taste brought images to his mind of a terrible past when he'd been helpless and trapped. He considered trying to reason with Shawe, but there really was no point. He was too drunk and ignorantly stubborn to change the path of his thoughts. He was convinced they'd taken Stacy, more son to him than younger brother.

From Shawe's drunken ranting, Copernicus had gathered that Shawe had given his brother the original family ring, handed down from their father, and had worn a replica himself. Now Shawe wore both rings, original and copy, on his middle finger. Copernicus studied the metal bands inscribed with the Galley rhinoceros, and though his mind was hazy from the punishment, he still struggled to figure out why the Skreaf would want the ring. Brabel had said it could be a key – but to open what?

Shawe's fist drew back and rushed forward, snapping Copernicus' head sideways. Copernicus spat and Shawe grabbed him by the front of his shirt and shouted, 'Final chance - where is he?'

Copernicus blinked stinging eyes. When he didn't reply, Shawe's jaw tightened. He growled, 'You brought this on yourself.' He turned to his men and said, 'Take off his hands – finger by finger.'

Shawe moved back to the window, looking out to the storm, confirming to Copernicus that the gangster hadn't changed. He still hated torture, but unfortunately he wasn't beyond ordering it. One of the Galleys drew a hatchet and stomped towards Copernicus. The commander spat venom into his face and the man shrieked and stumbled away, his skin sizzling. Four of the gangsters lunged at Copernicus and fists smashed him from all angles. Sounds became distant, but he managed to hold onto consciousness. The blood from his wounds greased his hands and he began to work them free. As the attack continued, Silho started to cry out for them to stop. She fought violently with her binds, rocking the chair, half-choking herself before Copernicus heard the clatter of the chair crashing to the ground. Her voice rose again, this time with an unnatural calmness, which made Copernicus' attackers pause.

'I see two men. I hear their words. They're making a deal – *100 green for 10,000 gold*. One is a gangster dressed in black, a Jada at his side, the other is Christy Shawe. The man leaves and Shawe speaks to someone through his communicator – he says he's leaving, follow him. Now I see a man. He has Galley bloodline marks and a tattoo of a mermaid on his chest. He's kissing a woman. She's naked. He whispers her name, *Angeline . . .*'

'Angeline?' Copernicus heard one of Shawe's men repeat. 'What does she look like?'

Silho spoke again. 'She has pale skin and red hair, caught up in a silver angel brooch.'

'Oi!' the man yelled. He rounded on another Galley and, grabbing him by the shirt, ripped it open, exposing the mermaid tattoo on his skin. 'Did you touch my woman?'

'No, I did not!' the other shouted back. 'Get your hands off!'

The two men wrestled for a moment, then started to brawl.

'Break it up!' Shawe's voice shook the room and everyone froze. The gangster boss moved over to where Silho's chair lay on the ground.

'You saw the past. What are you – a witch?' Shawe growled at her.

Silho shook her head.

He seized her and lifted both her and the chair upright.

'What are you?' Shawe demanded again. When she didn't respond, he said, 'I'll see for myself then.'

He grabbed a switchblade from his pocket and flicked it open. He cut off Silho's jacket and hacked into the bandages around one of her arms. Silho struggled, but couldn't stop him. Shawe ripped away the binds and stepped back. Copernicus stared at her bloodline marks – they were not the marks of Ivory Condor and Nightcat that her personnel file stated they would be. They were firebird dragons and flame. The flame was, in itself, a rarity, very few people claiming the Pyron heritage – one of those the late Commander Oren Harvey. As for the firebird, no one living in Scorpia had this mark, and only one person dead – Englan Chrisholm.

Copernicus' mind sped through the possibilities. He knew Chrisholm had a daughter, but she perished in a fire in the detention block where she was held after her father's arrest. Oscuri Trackers had found the body. Oren Harvey herself had identified it after she'd gone in to try to save the child . . . *and maybe she did save her . . .* Copernicus shook his head. He couldn't believe it. He glanced at Diega. The Fen was staring, stunned.

Shawe stepped back a few more paces, his face creased with confusion, hand hovering over the electrifier in a holster at his side.

Silho raised her head and whispered, 'He was innocent.'

A twisting electrical current burst through the darkness right beside the sunken room. It exploded into a nearby building, crumbling the foundations. Above the screech and shatter of collapsing steel and glass rose a terrible wailing scream.

Silho gasped and Copernicus' skin chilled. He focused his senses outside of the room and felt a mass of body-heat gathering on all sides.

'The Skreaf,' he said. 'They're here.' He looked up at Shawe. 'They want the ring. You have to hide it.'

Shawe's face set into grim resolve and he turned towards the door.

'Don't be stupid,' Copernicus warned. 'They're demons and you're drunk.'

Shawe ignored him, stomped to the door then flung it open. Storm winds, heavy with the stink of dark-words, gusted into the room.

'Shawe!' Copernicus called, but the gangster stepped out into the acid rain and all his men rushed to follow. The door slammed shut behind them.

After a second of silence the screaming began.

Copernicus and Diega struggled against their binds. 'Trutt,' the Fen grunted, the vines pulling tighter and tighter around her limbs and body. 'They're living plants, I can't morph them.'

Copernicus managed to get one hand, slippery with blood, free. The vines whipped back and forth, trying to re-curl around his wrist, but he grabbed the squirming end of the plant and bit into it, injecting venom. The vine shrivelled to a dry stick and Copernicus smashed free. He freed Diega in the same way and the Fen ran to the opposite side of the room to get their weapon belts and SevenM. Something heavy crashed into the roof of the makeshift room and Diega ran back to Copernicus, keeping close to the ground. Copernicus fastened his belt around his waist. He looked up sharply at movement beside him and saw a grey-faced Wraith with long black claws watching him from inside the wall.

The door burst open.

Christy Shawe staggered in, dragging one of his men, both of them soaked in blood. A curse hit them from behind and they collapsed to the ground writhing, convulsing, burning from the inside out. Copernicus armed his electrifier and sent a blast out into the darkness of the storm. Diega darted forward and slammed the door shut. She morphed a table into a thick plank and wedged it against the door handle to hold it closed.

Shawe's man twitched, groaned and died, but Shawe's body relaxed and he lay stunned with his eyes wide open, chest rising and falling slowly. Copernicus checked Shawe's hand. He still wore both rings, but his whole limb was badly burnt. Only the unusual thickness of his skin had kept him from being killed. Copernicus dragged off the metal bands and pocketed them.

'They're everywhere,' Shawe said. 'Devils . . . my boys . . .'

Shouting, screams and explosions continued outside and the door began to shake. Something struck it hard. It dented inward and started to open. Copernicus sprang up and slammed his body against the steel to hold it shut.

'We can get out through the window,' Diega said, and aimed her electrifier to break the glass.

'No!' Copernicus yelled. 'It'll let them in.'

'Any better ideas!'

'This was a craft,' he reminded her.

For a moment she didn't understand, then her eyes cleared and she cursed herself. She concentrated and sparks crackled from her skull, travelling along her hair. The whole room trembled as she used her electrosmith skills to try to get *The Sovereign 2* airborne.

'Something's blocking me!' Diega gasped.

'Fight it,' Copernicus ordered.

Diega clenched her fists and shook from the pressure of the invisible battle. The craft rose slowly from the mud. It hovered and strained, as though anchored to the ground. Diega held it there for several moments, then the flyer lurched and crashed back down. Diega collapsed, blood spilling from her nose.

The fall threw Copernicus to the ground, but he leapt back up immediately. The steel of the door contorted and the commander leaned all his strength against it. He heard the chanting outside. It echoed in his mind and he struggled to breathe. He felt as though he was back in the box with his Illusionist father hacking into it from the outside, wondering if this would be the time when the magician sawed straight through him, as he always threatened he would. He heard the applause and smelt the floral perfume of the pretty assistant. She'd hanged herself shortly after. At least that's what he'd been told. Words surfaced from the depth of his consciousness, but he closed his eyes, refusing to hear them, refusing to remember. His boots slipped backward as dark magics pushed the door in. He couldn't hold it any longer.

The bulk of Christy Shawe slammed into the door, firmly pushing it back into place, but soon the pressure began to rebuild and it became clear to Copernicus that even the two of them wouldn't be able to keep it shut. He looked back at Diega. She lay on the ground, murmuring listlessly. The grey Wraith stood over her.

'Get away from her!' he snarled at the spectral-breed.

She ignored him and knelt beside Diega. The Wraith whispered a Cos enchant, a call to nature, and the craft shuddered. The mud beneath it gathered into a funnel and lifted them up, away from the ground and away from the Skreaf curses. The pressure on the door withdrew and Diega recovered consciousness. The Fen rolled onto her knees and caught control of the craft. It jolted, then started to glide just above the ground, picking up speed the further they flew from the Skreaf.

Copernicus left Shawe kneeling at the door and moved to a porthole in the stern. He looked out into the storm-blackened night and saw hundreds of blotches of red body-heat flying through the sky behind them. The Skreaf, riding the wind, were quickly gaining. Curses grasped at the craft, trying to slow it, dragging it back, shunting the flyer to one side and then the other.

'Diega – get this ship moving,' he ordered. 'They're right behind us.'

'Doing my best,' Diega returned through gritted teeth. 'What's our destination?'

'The city.'

'No chance!' Diega said, already shaking from the dark magics depleting her strength. 'The closest option is Outpost 109. It has a nuclear bunker.'

'Then take us there,' he said.

'I'll —' Diega started, then groaned and fell to one knee at the controls.

Copernicus turned to go to her side and came face to face with the Wraith. She drifted around him to the porthole window. Her body took on the colour and sheen of the steel, and then she vanished into it. He looked through the window and saw her shape drop from the craft and glide downwards. Moments later, mud tidal waves rose out of the ground, swallowing the oncoming Skreaf. Some were dragged down; others smashed through the mud and kept coming.

Diega managed to stand and drove them forward, speeding, weaving through the storm haze. Silho still sat strapped in the chair and Shawe crouched on the ground, trying to bandage his injured hand with fabric from his shirt.

Copernicus went to Silho and drew his knife. Silho looked up at him, her eyes fearful, but he only grabbed her binds and cut her loose. The vines whipped around and he kicked them into one corner. He then dragged Silho to the stern portholes and put an electrifier into her hands. He used the glass-cutter from his weapon belt and cut a hole just big enough for the muzzle of her gun to fit through.

'Shoot,' he ordered and Silho nodded.

Copernicus moved to the window beside her and repeated the actions for his weapon. Christy Shawe joined them. He punched a porthole and completely shattered it. Copernicus cursed as glass flew inward and ripped at his face.

The three of them began blasting. Shawe fired madly and wildly, but Brabel was a dead-on shot, taking out every witch she aimed for. Copernicus focused his attention on the centre – on the leading witch. She kept vanishing and reappearing, diving in and out of the Murk, impossible to hit. Copernicus could feel the influence of her curses that were trying to force him to turn the weapon on himself. Even with the storm and distance diluting her strength, she was incredibly powerful. Resisting took all of Copernicus' mental and physical strength. He looked back at Diega and shouted, 'Diega – how far?'

She glanced over her shoulder at him and Copernicus saw the haze clearing from the front window of the craft. The solid wall of an Outpost tower appeared just ahead of them. He shouted and Diega spun back around. Cursing, she slammed the craft vertical, flying upwards along the wall. The sudden shift of direction threw everyone else to the back of the ship with everything in the room crashing down on them. Copernicus struggled to kick the chairs and tables away. He heard Diega cry out. The craft hit the top of the tower and jolted violently. With the shriek of ripping steel, one side of the ship tore away, taking Shawe with it. The wind screamed around them and gravity caught up, dragging both parts of the craft down the tower tunnel in a nightmare rush.

The narrowing sides of the entry to the lower bunkers slowed their descent. Sparks flew as the sides of the craft scraped rock. Copernicus braced himself for the impact. As they hit, he crashed upwards against the roof, then smashed back down to the floor.

Pain lanced his side but he managed to leap to his feet. Fighting through pieces of the wreck, he ran to the controls at the front of the bunker and typed in his authority override code to engage the lock-down system. Red warning lights flashed. Copernicus looked into the darkness above, searching for signs of the witches. He could hear their distant screams. He saw that the second piece of the craft containing Christy Shawe had crashed onto a ledge above them.

One by one, the floors closed over between the levels of the tower, shutting out the Skreaf and separating Shawe. The final level clamped closed and the building groaned as it settled. The commander leaned against the dusty bench of the control system and breathed out.

Part Two

21

The resurrection of light at dawn moved Eli from mourning to morning. He stood above the shelter in the middle of his house wreck and watched the new day's suns wash rainbow colours across the grey sky of the industry-choked level. He clenched his communicator in one hand and lifted it to his mouth.

'Call the commander,' he tried again, speaking clearly and loudly into the receiver.

Again his system reached out to connect, but was, as every time before, immediately booted off, as though something was blocking the line. Eli knew it was not a technological block, which meant it was a magical barrier, and the only conclusion he could rationally devise was that the Skreaf were either still hunting his team or had already captured them. The dull blurring of his disconnected communicator suggested the latter, but he refused to believe it. He couldn't. Instead he listened to the faint whisper of hope that said they had escaped and that he had to help them before it was too late. He was the only one left who knew the truth.

Biting his lip to stop it quivering, he hurried back down the stairs into the shelter where Ev'r sat, still chained to the chair, her head down, an occasional shiver rippling her back. It was an understatement to say she was unwell. Eli had given her every kind of painkiller and antibiotic potion he could think of, on top of the slowing elixir, but nothing was helping. He knew she couldn't be telling him the whole truth of her illness, but he didn't have the

185

time to run tests. He had to find a lead to the others before all the tracks went cold.

'I'm going,' he said, gathering up various items from his work-benches – body-heat blockers, system scramblers, an electrifier, a blade, an extra skunk bomb and his computer pack. He clipped his communicator onto his weapon belt. 'But I won't be back – I mean – *I will* be back.'

Ev'r lifted her head and stared up at him from beneath her lashes in her beast-like way. 'LET ME GO.'

'I told you no, Keets. I'm not as weak as you think I am. And just because you've never had any friends doesn't mean they don't exist.'

He pulled an electro-proof vest over his head and hid it beneath his jacket. It helped to conceal his wings. And as for his face, he stood in front of the mirror and gulped down the potion he'd mixed earlier. The sharp triangularity of his features morphed and shifted. His chin and nose rounded, his ears and eyes shrank. He didn't exactly look like a different person – more like a badly swollen version of himself, which was hopefully enough to stop anyone recognising him.

Ev'r gave a humourless laugh from her prison chair. 'You look even more ridiculous than you usually do. You would have done better dressing up as a girl. You already look like one anyway.'

Eli deflected the cutting remark. 'And you look like a man, so I guess we're the perfect match.'

He marched past her up the stairs as she yelled abuse at his back. The shelter trapdoor snapped open then shut, silencing her fury.

Eli left the *Summer Holiday* in chameleon mode. It gave him the ability to fly unseen and undetected along the skyways, bypassing the military checkpoints backing up traffic in all directions. There was a disadvantage to it, though. People couldn't see him, so they weren't stopping for him. They were pulling out in front of him, swerving dangerously close beside and behind him. He sat on the edge of his seat and tried to look in all directions at once. The sad clanking of Nelly's empty carry cage wrenched at his heart. He hoped his poor little friend had found a corner to hide in, away from crushing boots and cruel hands. She would be so scared without him.

Eli navigated the craft towards Eastend, Moris-Isles, where he had last seen the green dot representing Silho. The commander had said Jude was also attacked there, and that he and Diega were going to find them. This was where their trail ended and it was the logical place for him to start.

He managed to fly in right behind a lumbering public transporter craft and rode directly in its wake. It led him into the Isles, where he veered off and flew low along several backstreets until his navigator beeped their arrival at the approximate destination. Since he had lost his new communicator with the locator function at Headquarters, he could only go on memory of where Silho had been, though his memory rarely let him down.

Eli brought the transflyer down to the ground. He checked no one was in front or behind him, then opened the door and jumped out. Shrugging deeper inside his jacket, he pushed his hands into his pockets. Eli moved towards the alley mouth, trying to walk with the casual swagger of a person who knew that they were the baddest on the street, but when he caught sight of his reflection in the window of one of the buildings enclosing the alley, he saw it was more like the uptight hobble of someone desperately seeking a toilet.

He came out onto the main thoroughfare heading to and from Mortimer Road Marketplace. He stood for a moment watching people pass – refugees, scullion-gypsies, outlaws and illegals. Here in the underside everyone was hiding something, so the appearance of a puffy-faced imp in an oversized jacket didn't draw so much as a glance. Eli found his eyes following the pockets of passers-by and his hands tingled. They longed to explore what he was seeing – to take, to steal. His nervousness tested his therapy-achieved control, but he managed to hold himself in check. He joined the relentless flow of buyers and sellers, hagglers and stealers, and began retracing the steps Silho had run the night before.

Elbows jostled him from side to side and the scents of rotting garbage, heavy body odour and gypsy incense mingled unpleasantly under his nose. Women leaned out of buildings, beating carpets on windowsills, raining dust down on the crowd. It made Eli sneeze. Scullion children played and laughed, shoving their way through, under and around everyone. They poked grubby hands into Eli's face and demanded payment. He sidestepped them, not lifting his eyes. A streetwalker standing in a doorway singled him out and hissed a price and proposition of what it would buy.

'Yes,' Eli said, then mentally kicked himself and said, 'No, I meant to say *no*, sorry.'

She gestured rudely and called into the dingy hallway behind her, summoning someone Eli knew would be very large, very ugly and not very sympathetic to an imp with speech impediments. He scurried faster and vanished into the crowd.

Finally he reached the place where Silho had turned off the main street into a back alley. He tried to take the same turn and stopped short. State guardians had cordoned off the street and a group of forensic investigators stood around something lying on the ground. Through a gap in the onlookers, Eli saw an arm skewed at an unusual and horrible angle.

'Move along,' a guardian Eli recognised as Harper Patterson barked at him.

He complied as quickly as he could, crossing the street and hurrying to the next alleyway. He ducked into it and peered around the wall to see if anyone was following him. It didn't appear as though anyone had recognised him.

Someone grunted behind Eli and he spun around. A human-breed man leaned on the opposite wall, drinking from a bottle of Araki. The man's scruffy, dirt-trap beard and mismatched, moth-eaten clothes screamed homelessness.

'Hey there,' Eli said, giving an awkward wave.

'Kicked me out of my home, didn't they!' The man drew back and spat fiercely onto the street.

Eli guessed at a goat-blood heritage, though the man's bushy arm hairs concealed his bloodline marks.

'Think they're so good – trutting state trutting gadflies,' the man ranted. A noxious stink of liquor seeped from his mouth and possibly his skin as well.

'Yeah.' Eli nodded along. 'Who do they think they are?'

'Damn right,' the man rumbled.

'What happened there?' Eli asked, nodding to the crime scene.

'Didn't see nothing.' The man spat and Eli dodged the spittle spray.

'Looks like someone got theirs though,' he tried again.

'Something like that.' A sneer stretched the vagrant's dirt-crusted face. 'Too bad, hey? One less stinking scullion to steal my treasures. What a damn shame.'

'Someone cut him?' Eli asked.

The man's eyes flickered up to his and they weren't as unclear as Eli expected them to be. Several decades of street cunning stared from behind them.

'I didn't see nothing – now trutt off. This is where I stand.' The man took another chug from the bottle and Eli decided not to challenge him on that.

He ducked out of the shadows back onto the main strip. Crossing the road again, he headed into another alley, intending to cut through and search for signs of Silho on the other side. Halfway down the backstreet stretch, Eli heard a scuttling of feet following him. When he glanced back he saw no one. He started again and the scuttling continued. He increased his pace and the scuttling grew faster. He broke into a run, and the sound clattered louder. Eli sprinted to the end of the alley, turned into another and flung himself behind a massive dumpster. That was when he saw a figure break around the corner.

'Stop! I'm armed,' Eli yelled, poking the end of his electrifier out from behind the metal bin.

The hooded person halted and slowly raised its arms. It had no hands, just metal hooks on the end of fleshy stumps.

'What do you want?' Eli demanded.

'I want to sell you some information,' the figure, a woman, spoke. 'I heard you talking to Rupert. You're a reporter, right? Your kind always come down here looking for something juicy. Well I've got something nice and ripe, but it will cost you.'

'How much?' Eli asked, playing along.

'Seven sovereign coins,' she said.

'I'll give you one, but only after you tell me.'

189

'Two – half before and half afterwards.'

'One and a half and you tell me everything now or I shoot you.' Eli tried to keep his words from trembling. The electrifier rattled against the side of the dumpster. The hooded woman took the sound as a sign he was serious and said, 'Fine. I was on the rooftop last night. I looked over the edge and saw a girl running through the alley. She —'

'What did she look like?' Eli interrupted. There was nothing rare or special about girls running for their lives through Moris-Isles.

'I dunno. I only saw her from above. She ran into the dead guy back there, except he was still alive, but not for long. She thumped him and kept going, and something dark ran over him and ended him real quick. I saw the girl go into Smiths Pass. It's a dead-ender and she never came back out. So she, or whatever is left of her, is still there. You'll get pictures for your story before the guardians find her.'

'Smiths Pass?' Eli repeated. 'Where is that again?'

'Down there.' She pointed a hook to the end of the alley where they stood. 'Turn left, then it's the first left. Now pay up.'

Eli withdrew a quarter-sovereign from his money pouch. He flicked it onto the ground it front of the woman and said, 'Payment rendered.' He knew enough about the underside to know no one expected to be paid the full agreed amount. It just went without saying that you were lying to each other.

'Take it and go,' he instructed.

She lowered one of her hooks and the money clanked magnetically to the steel. As she straightened up, her hood slid back off her head. A deep X-shaped scar ran from one side of her face to the other, crossing on the point of her nose, which had been half hacked away. It was the sign of a disgraced gang girl – a rat. It reminded him of the meeting he had witnessed in the Gangland – of Christy Shawe's threat against the commander. The girl hooked the fabric and pulled the hood back over her face. She backed away and Eli saw her feet were also robotic replacements, probably cut off with her hands at the same time she'd gained the X.

Eli waited until the girl had vanished from the alley and then he bolted. It was highly likely that she was running to rally a group of

friends to rob and bash him. He would only have moments to find
Smiths Pass, check it out and leave. So he dashed to the other end of
the street, ran left, then veered left again almost straightaway, only to
freeze in front of a breach in the street where a Tangelan Burrower's
tunnel had broken out of the ground. Up ahead, the walls of the
dead-ender were stained black with dark magics and splattered with
Androt blood. A cloaked figure stood in the alley, its back to Eli.
His skin prickled and his senses warned him of danger. The stranger
began to turn and Eli dropped into the Burrower's hole. He hit the
rocks and rolled several times, then scrambled into the shadows.
He stared upwards and held his breath, expecting a face to appear
above, but nothing happened. Eventually he dropped his gaze and his
eyes zeroed in on a square object partially buried in the rubble. He
reached forward and pulled it free. It was an ID wallet. It belonged
to Silho Brabel.

Eli's heart thudded louder. He studied the ground around him
and saw drag marks. The marks took him deep into the ground to a
place where the ceiling had partially caved in. Here rocks had been
pulled away, and footprints and drag patterns suggested two people
had freed a third person. Eli took out his fingerprint analyser and
checked for familiar prints – both the commander's and Diega's registered. They must have found Silho here and taken her out.

Eli looked around for alternate exits and saw another tunnel leading upwards. He took it, and eventually crawled up out of the burrow
onto a side street beside a pub called 'The Counting'. Here there
were more fingerprints around the fractured street and Eli felt a
tremor of hope. This was where the others had entered and left the
burrow. He scanned the area. It was deserted save for a few stray
people here and there, mostly bar patrons entering and exiting the
pub. This struck him as strange, since secluded backstreets like this
tended to attract gatherings of sellers selling and users using, both
groups trying to keep out of sight. So why not here?

Something nestled under the overhang of the pub roof drew his
attention. It was a security I-eye surveying the area. Eli threw himself back out of its range and grabbed the computer pack from his
weapon belt. He quickly hacked into the frequency of the camera

and a holo-image of its current footage appeared before him. He flicked backward through the captured footage to the previous night. The images blurred and cut out. Someone had scrubbed the machine's memory. Someone who didn't want to be linked with anything the I-eye had captured. Eli worked fast, splicing in repair codes and memory patches. The images he retrieved were grainy and sliced, but he clearly saw the commander and Diega pulling Silho out of the ground and carrying her towards the pub. Diega morphed away the lock on the storage shed at the back of the building, next to the icehouse, and they entered. The hologram fuzzed up and the next momentary flash of image Eli caught was Christy Shawe moving the three trackers out of the backroom at gunpoint. Eli froze the image. Shawe held SevenM in one hand.

A scratching sound alerted Eli that he wasn't alone and he looked up fearfully. He found himself gaping in disbelief. On all the ledges and surfaces above him, Androts stood silently watching. Deep scars marked their necks from where they'd hacked out their barcodes. Their expressions were not friendly. Gangs of Androts turned rogue like these lived among the other illegals and outlaws in the Matadori Desert, but, as far as Eli knew, they never entered the city. He had never seen anything like it. But he had no time to reflect – he heard a clatter of rocks from inside the burrow as though someone was climbing out after him.

'Time to fly,' he murmured. He ripped off his jacket and whirred his wings, jetting up off the ground, between the gathered Androts to the rooftop above. Leaving the side street far behind, he zipped back towards where he'd parked the *Summer Holiday*. Eli found the place, landed, and ran towards his invisible craft. Unfortunately, he mis-judged the distance to the transflyer and smashed into the side of it, knocking himself onto the ground. Gathering himself up, he quickly glanced one way and then the other, flashed open the flyer, and leapt in.

The invisibility of his craft settled his fear and he sat for a moment, trying to think around his pounding heart and heaving chest. Was it possible that the Skreaf hadn't ambushed the soldiers at all, that Christy Shawe had taken them or maybe even that Shawe was actually working with the witches? Eli didn't know the answers, but he knew what his next step had to be. He started the engine and set the navigation of his craft.

'To the Gangland,' he said.

*****

There was a saying scrawled on the entrance signposts of most imp-breed suburbs in Scorpia. *ToUp*, which crudely translated from Impish into Urigin as *Enter if you Dare*. Being of the race, Eli understood the subtle shades and subtexts of the message. There were layers of meaning – a riddle, a joke, a warning, a gibe, all of which made absolutely no sense at all to anyone who wasn't imp-breed, even if he tried to explain it, and was, therefore, widely ignored by most as gibberish. It wasn't so uncommon, inter-racial misunderstandings happened all the time, but as Eli stood staring up at the entrance to the Crook'd Town Pride territory, he highly doubted anyone of any race would misinterpret this gang's welcome signage.

A disembowelled person dangled from the end of a noose tied to one of the buildings. The rope creaked as the body swayed in a listless sort of way. The gradual movements were slightly hypnotic and wholly horrific because time kept ticking by and no uniformed soldiers appeared to analyse the scene, identify the body, hunt down the perpetrator. From an adolescence of mingling in the vicinity of gangsters, Eli understood Gangland law – you lived by the gun and died by the gun – but he'd been a soldier for so long now, he'd grown accustomed to a more regimented society. In his world, the state decided who was guilty or innocent, who should live or die. Here, the bosses decided, and state law didn't mean a fig. This land was a city within a city, a society existing of, and completely apart from, the rest of Scorpia. Truth was, no soldiers were coming to clean up this scene – ever – because no matter what bravado the Governmentals put on when they were making announcements from their safe and securely guarded high-level offices, no one in the entire city had the spine to actually enter the Gangland and confront Christy Shawe and the other bosses – except perhaps Copernicus Kane. Which was why, now, despite a clear warning of *Enter and Die*, Eli was still seriously contemplating entering this land.

'For the commander,' he whispered.

In order to get to Greenway from this part of the city he had to pass through the territory of the Crook'd Town Pride, ruled by the mighty gangster boss Caesar K-Ruz. It was a massive risk, but Eli felt that the lives of his friends might depend on his bravery, or his balls-out stupidity – whatever worked.

He gulped and stepped gingerly over the threshold onto Pride land. Crouching low, he sped from one shadow to the next, past wall after wall decorated with the gang's symbols of claws and jaws and lion faces and with their call – *prey together stay together*. His wings buzzed behind him, but he kept himself grounded. Flying would draw too much attention. He followed a straight line towards the threshold between Crook'd Town and Greenway, which led him past the territory's central square. It was hemmed in on all sides by houses, mainly yellow-and-white sandstone structures. Pride members, dressed in gold and purple, and their giant feline companions crowded the square. The men lounged around, conversing in lazy ways using gang slang and signs, taking noncommittal swipes at Spats that ventured too close.

Already among the children he saw the future leaders and followers, their games imitating life. He spotted a gathering of gang girls. The boss's cousin, Smudge, and her black panther stood dominant in the centre of the group. Smudge's dark gaze roamed over the square and Eli couldn't help but admire her beauty, a captivating mix of menace and vulnerability. Then he saw her sniff the air and decided it was time to keep moving.

Eli crept onwards, finally reaching the threshold building. He took a chance and flew to the rooftop. Crouching low behind a ledge, he used his telescopic glasses to scan the suburbs of Greenway. The streets were relatively empty, which was possibly because it was morning and most Galleys were still drooling into their pillows in a hungover daze. Or maybe because they'd all gathered to watch Christy Shawe execute the commander. Eli lowered the glasses and only then sensed the slightest hint of movement behind him. He looked over his shoulder and stared at a huge pair of boots. He followed them up and up, past bulges of muscle and rippling scars to darkly rimmed, golden lion eyes. They were locked onto him with the formidable focus of a sniper's shot. He silently counted down from forty-six to try to stop himself from fainting. The glasses clattered out of his grasp.

'Eli Anklebiter,' Caesar K-Ruz said, recognising him from childhood despite his swollen-face disguise. Caesar's lion shadow stood behind him, twitching the end of its tail. Eli thought he could feel the shadow beast's hot carnivore breath.

'Boss K-Ruz,' Eli squeaked. He wondered if it would be completely bad taste to headbutt Caesar between the legs and try to make a run for it.

'I wouldn't,' the Pride boss said, his voice quiet but threatening like distant storm thunder.

A crazed giggle escaped Eli's mouth. He gulped it back. 'I'm truly sorry for the trespass.'

'Are you now?' Caesar said.

'No,' Eli replied before he could stop himself. 'I mean *Yes* – Yes, definitely. I'm hugely sorry. I just . . . I just have this problem with talking . . .' He gathered up his glasses and clutched them to his chest.

'I remember,' the gangster said, his focus not shifting for a second. 'I remember everything about you. Why are you here?'

'I'm looking for somebody – somebodies.'

'Who?' Caesar pronounced the word, giving a glimpse of his sharp white teeth. A trickle of sweat slithered down the very centre of Eli's back between his wings at the sight of them.

'Copernicus Kane and the trackers.'

'Kane.' K-Ruz wrinkled his nose in a feline snarl.

'But I think he's actually in Greenway,' Eli confessed.

'And you thought you'd just take a short cut through my land?'

'No.' For once in his life Eli was grateful for his lying disorder. 'Certainly not – I just found myself in the situation where I had no choice but to trespass, and I meant no harm – truly and honestly. I am just – out of options.'

'Considering you're now a state traitor,' the gangster said and Eli wasn't surprised Caesar already knew. Nothing much had ever slipped by him. In that sense he was very much like Copernicus. 'Why would Kane enter Greenway?'

'I believe Christy Shawe took him and the others prisoner.'

Caesar's expression remained neutral, but his eyes darkened in a menacing way. 'How do you know?'

'I saw footage of Shawe taking them from a pub in the Isles.'

'Shawe left the city last night. He went out into the desert and hasn't returned,' Caesar said.

Fear spiked in Eli's chest.

The gangster boss sensed it. 'What is it?'

'The Skreaf witches have been resurrected,' Eli replied without considering his words.

Caesar gave a slight snarl, but he didn't seem entirely surprised – dark magics had a distinct smell.

'They've infiltrated the city. They tried to kill my boss and team-mates – and me.'

'Is that so,' Caesar said, calculating the information, weighing it up, spreading it out, fitting it into the overall picture. Unlike Christy Shawe, he was a man of agonising patience and unwavering self-control. He was a strategist – timing was everything. He was also undoubtedly the greatest hunter in the city and Eli sensed now that he'd said way too much. He'd left himself with nothing to bargain with.

Caesar appeared momentarily distracted by something to one side of them. Eli managed to stand and was disconcerted to see he only just reached the centre of Caesar's chest. His entire width was smaller than the top of one of his legs.

Caesar looked back at him and said, without a shift in the stillness of his voice, 'I cannot allow someone to just wander onto my land, spy on my people and then go. You know the penalty for trespass.'

Eli swallowed around the clot of fear in his throat. 'Death.'

Caesar nodded. 'You knew and you still tried to help your companions. I admire your bravery. It'll serve you well in the afterlife.' The gangster pulled a blade out of his belt. Eli stepped back, his thoughts spinning wildly. He knew Caesar didn't revel in violence, but he didn't shrink away from it either. Caesar grabbed Eli by the front of his shirt and lifted him into the air.

'Wait!' Eli squealed, kicking his legs. 'I can help you.'

Caesar eyed him. 'Help me? How?'

Eli took a deep breath and a massive leap of chance. 'You said you remembered me, so you'd remember I'm good with inventions of all kinds. I can make a cure for you.'

'For what?'

'For love sickness,' Eli said. 'For Smudge, so she doesn't love you like that anymore, so she can move on.'

Even as he uttered the last word, Eli cringed, expecting the blade to slash out across his throat, but Caesar just stared at him for several long moments. Finally he spoke. 'You can do that?'

'Yes,' Eli said, unsure himself if it was the truth or a lie. 'But first I have to stop the witches, otherwise there won't be any point, because we'll all be dead anyway. Afterwards, I'll make the potion.'

'Swear to me,' Caesar demanded.

'I swear to you.'

Caesar drew him closer, right in front of his face so that Eli was staring directly into the gangster's eyes.

'If you are lying to me or do not deliver . . .' He didn't finish the threat. He didn't need to. Caesar took a step back and hurled Eli over the edge of the building.

Eli's wings burst into a blur of movement and he flew back the way he'd come without pausing for a whisker of a second. He passed the gruesome threshold leading into Crook'd Town, swooped low between two buildings, and crashed out into the suburb of Sweepington. He skidded into a gutter and sat there gasping. A shadow fell over him and he gazed up at the reptilian face of a palace enforcer.

'You, imp-breed, get in line.' It jabbed a scythe-blade pitchfork in his direction, then gestured to the gathering of pedestrians waiting at a roadblock several metres from where he sat. A group of red-cloaked enforcers and uniformed state guardians were scanning each person as they passed through. Eli's pulse sped back up. His transflyer stood on the other side of the roadblock and there was no way to turn back now without appearing suspicious.

He nodded and gathered himself up. He dusted off his clothes and walked to join the end of the line. Pushing one hand into his jacket pocket, he activated the body-heat blocker stashed inside. When it came to his turn, an enforcer grabbed his shoulder with a rough, scaly hand and ran the scanner over his body. The blocker distorted the heat signature and stopped the enforcers matching it against the profile they had displayed on a holo-screen beside the roadblock. Eli glanced over and saw his own name, face and statistics. He was well and truly 'Wanted'. He gulped and the palace guards glared at him with beady black eyes. They shoved him through the roadblock and he started to move away in relief when his face began twitching uncontrollably. He grabbed at his chin and felt the skin rippling. He was changing back.

Eli tried to walk faster, but tripped over, the body-heat blocker clattering out of his pocket. He looked back. The soldiers and enforcers had stopped scanning. One of them yelled out, recognising him.

Eli scrambled to his feet and ran headlong through the maze-like cobblestone streets of Sweepington. Originally built as an underground sewer system, the streets had, in more recent times, been uncovered and transformed into the walking paths of the now ultra-chic, laughably expensive suburb. Eli wasn't convinced. He didn't care how much the real estate cost, the place still smelt like dung. Footsteps pounded behind him, but being a slight and lithe imp-breed meant he was made for the constant sharp twists and bends and tiny, narrow alleys.

His wings whirred and he sped ahead, soon leaving the enforcers crashing behind him, but he didn't stop there, he didn't even slow, knowing the enforcers wouldn't be so easily put off. Once they caught the scent of someone with their extra-sensitive glands, they never lost the trail. Eli reached into his pocket and clutched the spherical form of a skunk bomb.

'Take a whiff of this,' he said. He threw the bomb over his shoulder and sped up to maximum speed, barely escaping the foul explosion. With immense satisfaction he heard the enforcers begin to wheeze, their steps slowing, staggering, then turning back and fleeing in the opposite direction. It brought a weary smile to his face. He skipped to a stop in a particularly narrow avenue and leaned against the wall, panting.

No sooner had he stopped than a tremor ran through the ground beneath his feet and he started back, thinking that the enforcers were going to burst up out of the ground – but they didn't, and everything fell still.

'Must have been a mini-quake,' he whispered to himself. He gave a nervous giggle and slapped a hand over his mouth to stifle it. How was it possible that he was still in one piece? He turned in the direction of his waiting transflyer and found himself staring into the skull-like face of a Death. He opened his mouth and screamed so loudly no sound actually came out – just a whistle of air exhaled at super-fast speed. The face vanished into the shadows and left Eli gasping. His legs took off before his mind registered he was running, and he didn't stop praying until the *Summer Holiday* was zipping through the sky back towards his shelter.

22

Silho lay on her back watching a sky full of dying stars that flashed and flared, blazed and burst, to be swallowed by the darkness and reborn again. Her unconscious mind cavorted. It unearthed old graves so that memories and feelings scrambled out and staggered about, unsure of their place in the broken terrain of her thoughts. They were the real her and threw into sharp contrast what she had become.

Silho reached a gloved hand towards the swirling sky. She tried to sit up but hit a steel bar lying just above her chest and slumped back down. Pain sharpened her thoughts and she remembered. *They know.* She'd spent so long thinking about this moment, but her imaginings had never taken her here. She didn't know what to do, how to feel. Instinctively, she reached into her pocket and grasped for her medication, the black pills that gifted her control over her abilities and over her emotions, but her pocket was empty. The pills were gone, left in the back room of the pub where Diega had thrown them. Panic hit and sent prickling spirals twisting through her body. Suddenly she was aware of each bead of sweat welling up and overflowing on her skin. The slight tremor of her hands grew to a shake. Her temperature flashed from hot to cold and back again. She squeezed her eyes shut against the visions above her. There was no ignoring these signs. They were the first of the physical symptoms of withdrawal from the drugs and a prelude to disaster.

Several times during childhood, through carelessness or stubbornness, she had let the medication wear off – always with the same disturbing consequences. Somewhere between the first sweats and the later nausea, the draw to use her skills and access the memories of the walls became unbearable, a pain far beyond starvation or thirst. Her resistance fell to pieces – to ashes – and blew away in the wind. Even if, somehow, she could have resisted her own need, the walls themselves worked against her. They called to her mind, growing from one whispering voice to a shouting million, gradually drowning her reality. She couldn't hide from them, she couldn't stop them; not without her medicine. Silho knew she had to escape this place and get back to the city before she lost control. She had to move now.

'*Get up*,' Silho whispered to herself.

She sucked in a deep breath and blinked her eyes open. The dancing creations above her were gone. Now she saw the dying stars were flashing lights embedded in a low concrete ceiling. With each flare, the bunker room took shape around her, its outdated tech and dusty benches, the aged boxes and bags stacked around the walls. A bitter, stinging smoke spiralled out from the crashed craft strewn all around her. Silho held her breath and listened for movement. All she could hear was the slow whirr of the engines running down. She manoeuvred out from underneath the wreckage and stood up. Instantly, she froze, sensing movement behind her, but before she could even think about escape, Copernicus Kane seized her and pinned her hands behind her back.

He forced her out of the steel rubble into the centre of the room where Diega stood watching them. In the one-tone flashes of light, Diega's rainbow skin appeared red and her bloodline marks glowed like hot metal. The Fen rushed at Silho and struck her across the face. Silho staggered back. Diega lunged at her again, but the commander intervened, releasing Silho to restrain Diega. She thrashed violently, but couldn't break his grip.

'Let me go!' she screamed.

'Not until you're in control,' the commander said.

'You're going to have to kill me,' Diega snarled. 'Either me or her.'

Copernicus grabbed the magnetic restraints off his weapon belt and cuffed Diega's hands. He kicked her legs from underneath her and pressed down on her back with one boot, holding her down. He snared Silho with his dark eyes that left nowhere to hide.

'I'm going to ask you some questions,' he said, 'and you're going to answer them. Whether you answer them truthfully will determine whether you live or die. Do you understand me?'

Silho nodded.

'Are you the child of convicted serial killer Englan Chrisholm?'

Silho stared at the ground. She remembered her father teaching her to paint. His gentle, encouraging words whispered in her thoughts. It was one of the only clear memories of him she had left.

'I'm the daughter of the artist Englan Chrisholm,' she said. The confession sent shivers through her body that she couldn't control.

'You were reported dead. Tell me how you survived.'

'Oren Harvey saved me from the fire.'

'Why?' Copernicus asked.

'She was my mother.'

'She herself told you this?' he said.

Silho nodded, the ever-present images of her escape from the prison flashing in her mind. The commander's voice snapped her back to attention.

'Commander Harvey vanished after that fire. Where is she?' Copernicus demanded.

Silho paused then said, 'She's dead.' The word seemed to echo around the underground chamber.

The commander took a moment to process the information before continuing. 'Tell me about your skills. Tell me everything you can do.'

Silho breathed in deeply. She clenched and unclenched her gloved hands. 'I can touch a surface and see what's happened in the past directly in front of it, and I can see people as light-forms. I can see where they are weakest and strongest and I can take from their strength to build my own.'

'Can you take all their strength and kill them?' he asked.

'No,' Silho said. 'Only some, otherwise I set alight.'

'Oren Harvey was a Pyron – you don't have her skill?'

Silho shook her head. 'I'm not a firelighter. I'm not resistant to the flame.'

'That's all?' Copernicus asked.

'That's everything.' She held his stare.

The commander reached down and dragged Diega, still struggling and screaming, to her feet. He pulled her around to face him.

'She's told the truth as she believes it.'

'I don't care!' the Fen yelled.

'Then do you care about Jude?' Copernicus turned Diega towards the wreckage of the craft, where SevenM lay lifeless among the scattered debris. 'With Brabel's skills we may actually have a chance of tracking the witches and finding him. Without them, I'm not sure.'

'My sister was murdered!' Diega said. 'You want me to just forget about that?'

'No, but Brabel didn't kill her.'

'How do you know that?' Diega challenged.

'I know a murderer when I see one,' Copernicus replied. 'And so do you. Silho was six year-cycles old when it happened.'

'I told you,' Diega said. 'I don't care. I don't care about anything. I want her dead!'

The commander held Diega closer and forced her to look into his eyes. 'Do you trust me?' he asked.

She stared back at him defiantly.

'I said do you trust me?' He raised his voice.

'Yes. Yes I trust you!' she shouted back.

'Then listen to me. She was a child. Just like you were. Just like your sister was. She did not kill anyone.'

For several moments Diega's fury remained, but then she looked away from him and finally stopped struggling.

After some time she spoke, her voice calmer, 'Let me go.'

'Are you in control?' Copernicus asked.

She looked back into his eyes. 'Let me go.'

The commander nodded and slowly unlocked her restraints.

She shoved away from him and turned to Silho. 'You're dead. Now or later. It doesn't matter.'

'Diega,' the commander warned.

She glared at him, then went to gather up SevenM. Using her jacket as a sling, she tied the arachnid robot to her body.

'I'm giving you a chance here,' Copernicus said to Silho. 'If you slip up, if I see you trying to hide anything, I will kill you. Do you understand me?'

The commander's face was bruised and swollen from Shawe's beating, but Silho saw in his eyes that he meant every word. She nodded.

The commander walked to the bunker's control panel. 'Their tech is ancient,' he said. 'We'll have to go higher to get reception on our communicators.'

He headed to the elevator that travelled between the lowest room and the next section of the tower.

Silho forced herself to move, following Diega and Copernicus into the elevator, while the Fen stared at her with dagger-like eyes. They reached the next level and the elevator door opened. Just as they stepped out, Silho caught movement to their left. She turned to see Christy Shawe crouching beside the dead body of his gang-mate. The gangster king's eyes found the commander's. Shawe crossed himself three times in the human-breed gesture to send his friend's soul to his ancestors in Paradise, then, in a sudden rush of movement, Shawe and Copernicus both drew their weapons. The commander got a lock on Shawe's head before the gangster had even lifted his arm. Shawe spat on the floor between them.

'Throw down your weapon,' Copernicus instructed.

Shawe held his position and Diega armed her electrifier and aimed it at the gangster's chest. 'He said stand down.'

Shawe gave a humourless and dangerous laugh. 'Who would have thought,' he said to Copernicus, 'that you'd be desperate enough to have *this one* as your right hand. Don't you remember what she was like in the day? Girl bedded more gangsters than I can even name. What did I call her? Something about —'

'Shut it,' Diega warned. 'What do you know about me? You're just a pisshead thug with an over-inflated ego.'

'Why don't you go and sit down, sweetheart?' Shawe mocked her. 'And let me deal with your boss here.'

'You couldn't deal with him if you had a whole army at your back,' Diega said.

Shawe gave his crooked smile. 'Really?' He glanced at the commander and shook his head. 'Keeping secrets, are we?'

'Shut your mouth, Shawe,' Copernicus warned.

'What's wrong? Are you embarrassed?' Shawe mocked him. 'Why don't you tell your lady friend here about who you really are? Tell her how you wouldn't even be alive if it wasn't for me.'

'*Fsx,*' Diega swore at Shawe in Fenlen.

'Tell her!' he demanded. 'Or I will.'

'What does it matter now?' the commander maintained his cold control, but Silho could see he was tense.

Shawe snorted and regarded him with disgust. 'Pissweak you are, just like when I first saw you – scrawny, stuttering, tripping over your own feet.'

'So what?' the commander said. 'I was a kid.'

'You were a circus monkey,' Shawe spat, 'performing for candy.'

'What's your point?' Diega snapped. 'Everyone knows his father was an Illusionist.'

'Ah, but he wasn't,' Shawe said. 'The father was a fake, but your boss here was the real thing, only he was too scared to do anything about it. I'd let him put on little shows for me and the boys and we'd give him food – our scraps.'

'Enough,' the commander growled, but Shawe kept going, speaking faster and louder.

'One night I turned up at the circus and heard that some of the scullion carnies had seen us and ratted him out to the doctor – told him what his son could really do. I tracked down Silvan Kane. He was finishing up burying something in the ground. When he left, I dug it up and there was your boss – buried alive.'

Silho found herself staring at the commander's face for a reaction, but he was completely closed. She felt sickened by what he'd suffered.

After a brief pause Diega said, 'That's your big news, Shawe? His father was a lunatic who tried to kill him? It's sad, but it doesn't change anything.'

The gangster scowled with annoyance. 'I saved his neck! I let him run with me. I hid him. I always had his back, even though my own dad almost killed me for associating with an outsider. We were brothers. Then he went and sold us out to the state. Got many of us locked up, some of us killed, including my dad.' He spoke to Copernicus. 'You're a backstabbing, squealing dog traitor. I should have left you to rot.' Shawe armed his electrifier. 'Tell me where my brother is – now!'

The commander armed his weapon as well, keeping it trained on Shawe's head. The two men stared each other down, neither moving a muscle.

Silho saw worry grow in Diega's expression as she looked between them, and she realised there was an actual possibility they were going to open fire on each other. The commander hadn't shown his feelings, but obviously Shawe had shaken him.

'We already told you, Shawe, the Skreaf have him.' Diega spoke quickly. 'We don't know where, but I do know that Copernicus is your only chance of finding him, so if you care about your brother like you say you do – just lower your weapon.'

For several moments nothing changed, but then Shawe's hands hesitated and he let his aim relax. When the commander finally reciprocated, Silho exhaled relief.

'The witches have him.' Shawe repeated. 'Because of the ring? I don't understand. Why would they want it?'

'We don't know,' Diega said.

Shawe glared at her and Silho could see thoughts formulating in the green of his hard stare. 'You said they'd taken one of yours as well?'

She nodded.

'And you're going after him?'

'Of course.'

'Then I'm coming with you.'

'Like hell,' Diega said.

Before any more could be said, the commander's communicator beeped with reception. He dragged it off his belt and tapped in a number.

'What are you doing?' Shawe demanded.

Silho heard the line connect and a female voice say, 'High Commander Levis Kline's office.'

'This is Commander Kane. I need to speak with High Commander Kline,' Copernicus responded.

'The High Commander is occupied at present. Can I take a message and —' The girl cut out and a man with an aged, gravelly voice spoke up. 'Kane, this is Kline. What's your status?'

'My team was attacked by Skreaf witches. The sect has been resurrected,' Copernicus paused for a response and when the High Commander spoke again, Silho noticed no change at all to his flat tone.

'Who have you told about this?'

'No one as yet,' Copernicus said. 'We're in the Matadori – Outpost 109. We need a recon unit to come as soon as possible.'

'I'll dispatch one immediately,' Kline said.

The commander's communicator began to whistle and he said, 'End trans—'

'Kane,' Kline cut in. 'I have your report in front of me regarding a ring you found at a Moris-Isles crime scene. Do you have this object on you now?'

The commander frowned, then he disconnected the call.

'What is it?' Diega asked.

'We have to get out of here now,' Copernicus said. He moved past Christy Shawe to a second elevator behind him.

'Why?' Shawe asked.

'I never wrote a report on the ring. The Regiment is compromised.'

'What a shock,' Shawe snorted. 'And, by the way, great work telling him exactly where we are.'

The commander seemed to ignore the gangster's taunt, but hit the elevator button with more force than necessary. The door began to part, then ground to a halt.

'They're shutting us in,' the commander said and Silho's skin chilled.

'The stairway.' Diega pointed to the emergency exit.

Copernicus grabbed the handle and found it locked.

'Move,' Shawe commanded. He rammed his shoulder against the steel. It buckled and broke open.

Copernicus led the group at a run up so many flights of steps that Silho lost count. Finally, with burning muscles, they reached ground level and burst out into the desert. The first shards of light from the rising suns had pierced the dawn-grey darkness. Silho stepped onto the sand and an overwhelming urge to touch the ground swept over her. She clenched her gloved hands and pushed back the feeling, trying to keep calm, silently reassuring herself that she would make it back to the city in time. The alternative of losing control in front of the commander and the others was unthinkable.

The team ran away from the outpost tower to a clump of sand dunes in the distance. They dived behind the dunes just as the dull roar of military fighterflyers sent a tremor through the ground. Silho covered her ears as the flyers landed beside the outpost and several troupes of soldiers disembarked and stormed the tower.

'Death squads,' Diega spat.

Copernicus nodded grimly. 'We have to get moving. They'll widen their search once they find we're not there. Do you have the *Ory-4*?'

'Shawe's men took everything from my pockets.' She cast the gangster a loathing glare.

'Then we're on foot,' Copernicus said.

'Not likely,' Shawe said. 'We'll be lost in seconds.'

Copernicus took the nav-tech device off his belt and studied the compass face. He frowned and tapped the machine. The directional readout was swinging wildly from one point to another.

'You'll need something much stronger this far out,' Shawe said. 'We'll have to nick one of their jets.' He nodded to the flyers.

'Not possible,' Copernicus responded. 'They're covered with sensors and traps. It'd be suicide.'

'Unlike wandering endlessly through the trutting Matadori Desert?' Shawe demanded.

Silho swallowed her rising anxiety and forced herself to speak. 'I think I can get us back to the city.'

'No one asked you,' Diega snarled.

'How?' The commander turned to her, his expression guarded.

'I grew up in the Matadori. I was taught to read the sand.'

'By who?'

'My carer – an ex-tracker called Hammersmith.'

Copernicus raised an eyebrow. Hammersmith, Oren Harvey's mentor, had been notorious in his time and left behind a reputation of the mixed variety.

'And you know where to go?' he asked.

'If we head that way,' Silho pointed southward, 'we should reach the town of Tracy before the midday burn. We may be able to find something that flies there, but we have to go now to outrun the heat.' The suns were already spreading firelight across the vast desert.

'Then we're moving,' Copernicus said.

'I'm not following her.' Diega crossed her arms.

'So stay here and die,' Copernicus said. 'I'll let Jude know what happened. Brabel – take the lead.'

Keeping low behind the dunes, Silho started heading in the direction of Tracy. Without warning, a voice whispered in her mind, making her steps stumble and vision waver. Panic assailed her with the realisation that she had less time than she'd thought. Determined to overcome, she clenched her hands and pushed herself forward. The boots of the others, including Diega, fell into step behind her.

23

Ev'r could have blamed the creature she was becoming for her desperation to live. It would have been easy to claim that it had stopped her from finishing the enchant that would have ended her, but Ev'r didn't believe in that kind of self-sparing weakness – always looking for something else or someone else to blame – when the real problem was staring straight out of the mirror. *She*, her own worst enemy, had stopped the enchant. *She* had been unable to do what was necessary, and now she doubted that she ever would, even when turning was inevitable. No matter how much she denied her blood heritage, *survival at all costs* ran through her veins. Scullions were always the last ones standing.

The pressure of the changes made her body convulse and strain against the chains. Her jaw distended more, ripping the skin under her chin, and the black stain on her fingertips spread to halfway along her hands. The slowing potion Eli had given her was losing potency, so there were only two choices now: get out, get back to the desert, find the O'Tenery Asylum, retrieve the witch's cure-all and hope like hell that it worked . . . or force Snack-size to kill her. She snorted. Really, there was only one choice – she was getting out no matter what. Threatening Eli hadn't worked, but she had a fair idea of what would reach him.

A mechanical whirr above her and light footsteps on the stairs signalled Eli's return. When he appeared, he was back to his normal pointy shape. She could see from his dragging wings and blinking eyes that he was exhausted and still emotionally raw. *Perfect.*

'Find anything?' she asked.

He slumped down at his desk and spoke, his voice lower and slower than usual. 'I went to Moris-Isles and found out that Christy Shawe has captured the commander, Diega and Silho and then I went to the Gangland and discovered that Shawe went into the desert last night and hasn't come back and then . . .'

While he was speaking, Ev'r began blinking, accessing the extra tear ducts that all scullions were born with. She squeezed against them with her facial muscles until tears streamed from her eyes. Then she began to sob. Eli paused and she could feel him watching. She leaned forward in her chair, making her shoulders tremble. The sobs sounded so real, she almost surprised herself. Eli's chair scraped back and he approached her, stopping just out of kicking range.

'Are you okay?' Eli asked. 'Ev'r?'

'No,' she whispered. 'I don't want to die like this. I know I seem cruel, but I'm not, it's just the way I've had to be to protect myself. You don't understand what it's like to be different, for everyone to look at you as though you're a freak. I've tried to fit in and be normal, but I can't. All my life people have beaten me, spat on me and called me names. I've had no choice but to become this monster you see. I had a pet – a cat – I fed it in secret, I loved it, but my father found out and broke its neck. I never had a chance to love anything. You don't understand. I'm sick now, very sick, I'm in pain. I'm dying and I want to change. I don't want to be like this anymore!' She kept crying and eventually felt a small hand slide onto her shoulder.

'It's alright,' Eli comforted her. 'Everything will be okay. I'm going to help you. I'll give you something for the pain and I'll help you change.'

'It's just my arms,' she snuffled. 'See how my hands are turning black? It's because the circulation is cut off. It hurts so bad. I know you can't untie me. I wouldn't untie me either, but maybe you can inject my hands with a numbing agent so I can't feel them dying.'

211

'I'll loosen the chains right now,' Eli said. 'I'm so sorry, I didn't realise how tight I'd tied them. I feel terrible.'

He crouched behind her and she heard some rattling, then the chains went slack around her arms. Her hand was free in a blink of a second; with lightning speed she spun in the chair and grabbed Eli by the throat. He gasped, shock bulging his eyes. Ev'r dragged her other arm free and stood, keeping her tight grasp on the struggling imp-breed. She shook the chains down her body and stepped out of them, then dragged Eli by the neck to the workbench, where she grabbed up a length of plain rope. He feebly resisted as she bound his hands, tied the end of the rope into a noose and pushed it over his head so that if he struggled he'd choke himself. Satisfied that he couldn't escape, Ev'r shoved him to the ground. He stared up at her with his big dark eyes full of hurt and sorrow, brimming with tears.

'I believed you,' he whispered.

'Well, you should have listened to Kane,' Ev'r said, collecting weapons off his workbench and shoving them into her belt and pockets. They were a poor substitute for her own tools and she felt completely naked without her blade, Morsus Ictus, but it would have to do.

Eli tried to stand, but she kicked him hard. He cried out and collapsed. She searched through his pockets for the starter flash to his transflyer. Her arms and hands shook from being tied for so long.

'As I said to you, Snack-size, trust is the blindfold of the ignorant,' she said. 'By the way, how does it feel to be tied up? Not so great, is it?' She found the flash and pushed it into her pocket. She shoved him back against the bench, took more rope and bound him to a leg of the table. He struggled and gagged as the noose tightened around his neck. The green diamond pendant chain slipped out from his shirt. Ev'r glanced at it and laughed. 'So much for that.'

'Where will you go?' Eli murmured, half passing out.

'Away,' Ev'r replied. 'As away as I can get before the storm breaks. Maybe even the Brine.'

Eli groaned.

'Don't worry, I'm sure you'll asphyxiate before you die of dehydration. It's not such a bad way to go,' she mocked, remembering how the soldiers had stood around her feeling so important, telling her to choose how she wanted die – good or bad. They were fools. There was no such thing as good dying.

Straightening, she stepped back from the slumped little figure and turned, ready to take off. But before she could take a single step, something hit her hard from the left and knocked her to the ground. She rolled as she landed and leapt to her feet to face her attacker. A Death, the most rare and dangerous of the spectral-breeds, stood before her, cloaked in swirling shadows, colourless skin stretched over a skull face, eyes like black pits. It bared sharply pointed, blood-stained teeth and snarled. The beast in Ev'r growled back, but she controlled it. She hissed a curse at the Death that glanced off the creature. It moaned, but didn't flee. It stepped towards her. She lunged at Eli, cut the ropes tying him to the bench and pulled him up in front of her as a shield. If the Death charged her, she could throw the imp-breed at it and run while it consumed him. Ev'r backed her way to the stairs with Eli squirming and choking in her arms. He clunked against each step as she dragged him to the trapdoor above. The Death followed closely, gnashing his teeth, but didn't attack.

'Opening code,' she growled at Eli, shaking him.

He whispered the code and she punched it into the holo-screen. The trapdoor opened and she pushed him up through the hole and jumped out. Eli started whimpering about shutting the trapdoor, but she ignored him, leaving it ajar. With Eli slung over her shoulder, she ran to the hangar beside the house. She flashed the transflyer open and felt over the invisible craft for the passenger side door. Finding it, she threw the imp-breed in, then ran around to the pilot side. A group of men were standing on the street in front of the house, smoking cigarettes and drinking cans of beer. They glanced at her as she climbed into the craft. One of them pointed. She gunned the engine and smashed through the hangar roof, lifting the craft up and into the sky – into freedom.

24

The Matadori Desert was like death in a way. It took both king and servant and set them even. No riches could appease it, no intelligence could outsmart it, no speed could outrun it. Copernicus had trained himself to withstand all kinds of pain and deprivation, but the burning, insidious nothingness of the desert reduced him to desperation so quickly he felt as weak as a child. The basic need for water threatened to overwhelm all his experience and control, so when Tracy appeared on the horizon, a ramshackle shanty town spewed out across the sand, he couldn't help but feel a burst of relief.

Tracy was a poorer version of the towns Copernicus had seen closer to the city gates. The larger villages were ruled by a dominant scullion clan, but Tracy appeared open to anyone who was crazy or desperate enough to live so far from Scorpia. It bulged at the seams with the outcasts of the outcast – the worst criminal outlaws, the most deranged addicts, flocks of the diseased and the lowest of the scullion low. Everyone looked old and used, even the children. They loitered around the tent-houses and poked through the mountains of rubbish that encircled the settlement. People spat and shat and pissed wherever, whenever, and the stink of the place was beyond any word Copernicus knew in any of the languages he spoke.

The commander shoved his way through the directionless crowds, ignoring the beggars and the self-confessed mystics offering to bless his money. The four of them stayed close, their hoods pulled low over their faces. This far from civilisation they would be in serious danger if anyone recognised them as military. Diega and Shawe lagged, struggling against the ferocious heat, but Silho kept up the same punishing pace with which she'd guided them through the desert, and Copernicus stayed at her side. Despite everything, Copernicus couldn't help but be impressed by her skill. She'd found their path by reading sand that to Copernicus' eyes had all appeared exactly the same colour and consistency.

Looking at Brabel, knowing the truth of her heritage, he realised why she had seemed familiar to him. She had Oren Harvey's eyes, and evidently her formidable strength as well, but he saw that something was distressing her. Every now and then she grimaced with a pain that she tried to hide and her heat signature pulsed and flared brilliant before she managed to stabilise it. He could see that the struggle to control whatever was affecting her was becoming more and more difficult. He kept his hand close to his weapon. No matter how gifted the girl was, if she suddenly lost her mind in any kind of violent way, he *would* take her out.

Shawe coughed and Copernicus' attention shifted to the gangster. Back at the tower Shawe had spoken some truths, but not the type that set people free – more like the ugly truth that hurts. Copernicus' truth was that he did have genuine Illusionist skill, which he'd inherited from his mother's side, but he had never, to this day, wanted it. The second truth was that he and Shawe had been the best of friends until the fight that had made them enemies. Now what they had fought about was meaningless to him, but at the time it – *she* – had meant everything.

Copernicus slowed his pace so that Diega caught up. 'Go find something that flies. We'll get water. Watch your back,' he ordered.

The Fen nodded and separated from the group.

Copernicus followed Silho to the trade centre of the town, to a vendor selling casks of water obviously stolen from the city. Silho started towards the tent shop, but then halted. She cringed and gripped her stomach. Copernicus stopped beside her.

215

'What's wrong?' he asked.

Silho straightened up with effort and answered breathlessly, as though she had been winded, 'Nothing . . . it's just the heat.'

'Brabel,' Copernicus said, keeping his voice low so that Shawe wouldn't hear. 'Do you remember me saying if I saw you trying to hide anything I would kill you? Did you think I was joking?'

Silho's eyes flashed fear. 'I'm not hiding anything.'

Copernicus studied her face. She had lived in the shadows for so long that lying was completely natural to her. He found it fascinating – and highly aggravating. 'I can *see* that you are,' he said.

'If you can see it then I'm not hiding.' Her expression took on a defiant edge and Copernicus again saw Oren Harvey glaring back at him. Few people he'd met had the spine to argue with him. Most couldn't even make eye contact. She didn't break his stare.

'You have three seconds,' he told her.

Silho swallowed and he could see her thinking over the options, or maybe calculating how much she would have to tell him.

'One second, Brabel.'

'I need medicine,' Silho finally said.

'For what?'

'My skills . . . for seeing . . .'

'Those pills – Ethalam and Equinox.' He remembered from the pub. 'What happens without them?'

'I can't control my skills.'

'Meaning what?' Copernicus asked. His thoughts automatically brought up images of her father, Englan Chrisholm, and all the children he had murdered.

Silho flinched as she read his expression. 'I can't stop myself from touching the walls, and even if I could, eventually I hear and see things without touching anything. It just happens.'

'How long do you have?'

'I don't know. It's getting worse. There are so many buildings here.' She looked around them and Copernicus noticed her pupils were dilating then shrinking rapidly, and her hands trembled. He thought quickly. He had some heavy anaesthetics on him. If her control failed he could give her a shot and knock her out, but then who would guide them the rest of the way to the city? He decided it was better not to give her that as an option.

'You're just going to have to keep it together,' he told her. 'We're a long way from a chemist.'

'I know,' she murmured.

'So do what you have to do,' Copernicus said.

'I will,' she replied.

He narrowed his eyes at her sharp tone and she clenched her jaw and looked away. He stepped around her and headed for the water vendor.

'A cask,' he told the man at the counter, a skinny scullion with a pinched face and constantly darting eyes.

The scullion stared them out, trying to see their faces beneath the hoods. He sniffed suspiciously and curled his lip. 'These are not for sale.'

'Then why does your sign say they are?' Copernicus pointed to the writing scrawled in scullion script on a board hanging at the front of the tent.

'Sign's wrong,' the man said and the commander saw one of his hands stray under the counter, most likely to grab a concealed weapon. Christy Shawe shoved in beside Copernicus. The gangster dropped his hood and the man gaped. Even in the lost places of hell people recognised Christy Shawe – and were afraid.

Shawe rested his fists on the counter with a clunk and said, 'Two casks.'

The scullion moved as though he'd been prompted by electricity. He dragged two water containers to the counter and grunted, 'Five sovereigns.'

Shawe didn't move a muscle. He just stared down at the man.

The scullion's face twitched and he added rapidly, 'But for you, no charge.'

Shawe gave the seller a disgusted look and spat on the ground. He shouldered both casks and headed for the nearest shady alley.

Cracking open one cask, Shawe began guzzling from it, tipping water all over his sun-scorched face and body. Copernicus opened the other. He offered it to Brabel, who was leaning against the wall opposite to him with her head down. When she didn't take the water Copernicus called, 'Brabel!'

Silho looked up and he saw a helpless, almost pleading look in her eyes. She shook her head once – not a refusal to the water but a silent message: *I can't.* Her legs gave way and she hit the dirt, and immediately began clawing at the ground. Her gloved hands sank up to the wrists, as though the solid dirt was mud. Her eyes started shifting left to right so fast her pupils became a blur, and an unintelligible stream of words babbled from her mouth. Copernicus grabbed Silho and tried to lift her up, but her hands were stuck in the ground and getting sucked further and further in with incredible force. Shawe saw the struggle and latched onto her legs. Together they wrenched her free.

Copernicus rolled her onto her back and Silho lay in a stunned state. The whites of her eyes were blood red and tears flowed down her cheeks.

He dropped to his knees beside her and shook her. 'Brabel! Can you hear me?'

She gave no response. He grabbed her wrist and checked her pulse. It was way too fast.

'What's wrong with her?' Shawe demanded, leaning down for a closer look, dripping water and sweat all over them.

'She doesn't have her medication,' the commander said.

'So give her some of mine.' Shawe slid the silver flask of Araki out of his pocket. 'First some for me,' he took a noisy swing of the potent alcohol, 'then some for her.' He offered Copernicus the flask, but he pushed it away. Silho needed to control her mind, not lose it further. He thought for a moment then asked Shawe in a lowered voice, 'Have you got your mints?'

'Why? Are you going to kiss her better?' Shawe mocked. 'You'll need more than a few mints to get rid of the stink in your mouth.'

'Have you or not?' Copernicus ignored the gibe.

Shawe checked his pockets and drew out a crumpled packet of Barkers Mints; Copernicus had never known him to be without them. The commander took one. He was thinking that if they could make Silho believe she'd taken her medication, it might help her, except that her pills were black. He looked past Shawe to the alley mouth, scanning for Diega.

'What?' Shawe asked, glancing over his shoulder.

'It needs to be another colour,' Copernicus said. 'Diega can morph it.'

'Why don't you just do your marble trick?' Shawe said, leaning against the wall. 'That one where the colour keeps changing.'

Words stirred in Copernicus' mind, but he refused to hear them. 'I can't,' he lied.

'Yeah you can,' Shawe argued. His eyes searched Copernicus' face, then the gangster gave a slow smile of realisation. 'You're scared!' he bellowed. Scullions passing at the entrance to the alley stopped to stare at them.

'Of what?' Copernicus demanded.

'Who knows,' Shawe said. 'Who cares! Either way, the great United Regiment Commander Copernicus Kane is *afraid* of performing a little trick.'

Copernicus felt a strong urge to smash Shawe right in the mouth, but before he could react in any way he sensed the vibration of Diega's footfalls nearing them. He stood up and whistled as she appeared on the street in front of the alley. When she joined them, she held up a silver coin.

'Speed-drift platform,' she said. 'Complete junk, but it will do.' She saw Silho lying on the ground and just shook her head as if to say *I knew it.*

'Her pills,' Copernicus said, giving the Fen a dark look.

'What about them?' she said, glaring back.

Suddenly Silho's body flipped over and she grasped at the ground again. Copernicus managed to catch one of her hands, but the other pushed into the dirt. She began convulsing and gasping as though she was choking. Copernicus struggled to drag her free and Shawe stepped in again to help. This time even when her hand was out of the ground they had to restrain her thrashing body and flailing arms.

'Cuff her!' Copernicus instructed Diega. The Fen dragged the restraints off her belt and slammed them around Silho's wrists, fastening them with unnecessary brutality. Copernicus sensed a stirring of heat beside him and turned as the Skilsy Wraith who had helped them escape the witches stepped out of the wall. Both Diega and Shawe drew their electrifiers.

'Don't move!' Diega ordered.

The Wraith ignored her and crouched down beside Silho. Copernicus smelt the spectral-breed's earthy scent like damp forest foliage. A shimmery, web-like bloodline mark crisscrossed the skin of her reedy arms. She reached clawed hands towards Silho but before she could touch her, Copernicus dragged Silho back, not knowing the Wraith's intentions. He had never seen a spectral-breed so close before. The twin cities of the spectrals, the Memlirlands and the Skilsy Shadelands, had fallen to an unknown darkness when he was a child. The people had scattered, many fleeing to Scorpia in terrified flocks, but they had always kept to themselves, contact with outside races rare and strange.

The Wraith leaned in again, unperturbed by the weapons pointed at her face. She whispered some words and laid her hands on Silho's head. Silho's convulsions stopped and she slumped, unmoving, in Copernicus' arms. He passed her back, still cuffed, to Shawe and stood up. The Wraith mirrored his movements.

He met her enigmatic grey eyes and demanded, 'Who are you?'

The Wraith's stare flicked past him to Silho.

Copernicus rested his hand on the whip-like binding band on his belt, used to restrain dissipaters. 'I said – who are you?' he repeated.

She returned her gaze to him and whispered with a voice Copernicus would have described as sinister, 'Raine.'

'Why are you following us?' Copernicus asked.

When again the Wraith didn't reply, he drew the binding band. 'I really don't like repeating myself,' he said.

The pale Wraith inhaled sharply. Her eyes swivelled left to right, then rolled back. Her body shivered and her head and shoulders collapsed in towards her stomach and out of her back, resettling into the form and features of a horned, red-eyed he-Wraith. Copernicus knew Skilsy Wraiths were born with both genders in one body and separated into two forms later in life, but knowing it and seeing it were two different matters. He took an involuntary step back and heard

Shawe curse. The he-Wraith towered over all of them. Raine's moth-wing cloak barely reached his knees, stretching threadbare across the lean muscles of his shoulders and chest. He spoke with a deep voice unlike Raine's hiss.

'I am Amateus. We are following you because we share a common enemy and now a common hope.'

'The Skreaf,' Copernicus said.

Amateus nodded. 'They have enslaved many of our people. Raine and I made a vow to stop them.' The red of his eyes flickered like flames. 'But up until now all our efforts have been in vain. Skreaf demons are ever-living, immortal but for one weakness, and their weakness is known only by Omarians – a rare people born in another realm, with the firebird-dragon bloodline mark.' He looked to Silho draped over Shawe's arms. 'When her father was framed by the Skreaf and executed, we believed we'd lost the last Omarian and our only hope of defeating the Skreaf, but then we found her . . . she found us.'

Copernicus took in the words. 'The Skreaf framed Englan Chrisholm?'

'He was hunting their leader, the High Skreaf, Bellum. He didn't realise she was also hunting him,' Amateus said.

'He's lying,' Diega hissed.

'He's telling the truth.' Copernicus saw it in the Wraith's eyes and his body-heat.

'If Chrisholm wasn't crazy then who butchered all those kids?' Shawe asked and Diega bit her lip.

'Bellum,' Amateus spat the word out of his mouth like something rotten. 'She is the worst evil and she is truly powerful.'

Copernicus' mind returned to the cell he'd found beneath the Galleria where Chrisholm was imprisoned until his execution. He saw the pictures on the ceiling and the words *My God, My God why have you forsaken me?* scrawled across them. His memories flicked back even further to the execution itself, to the raised stage where the soldiers had dragged Chrisholm, shouting his innocence. He and Shawe and some of the other guys, teenagers at the time, had hidden under this stage afterwards to avoid the guardians. He remembered looking up and seeing a mark etched in the wood beneath where Chrisholm had died – one triangle within another within a square.

Copernicus jolted from his memories, a coldness sinking through his body. 'What are the Skreaf planning?' he asked Amateus.

'They are trying to raise their master, the Morsmalus. He is the pain-maker, the creator of dark-words, imprisoned long ago in the Envirious Realm by warriors made anonymous through time. He was sealed in by their sacrifice of their own lives.'

'How will they raise him?' Diega asked.

'There is a prophecy among our people: *By the blood that sealed it, shall the hell realm be reopened,*' Amateus said. 'We believe this to mean they must spill the blood from the line of the original warriors over the seal and couple it with a curse of terrible power. The Skreaf have acquired a machine to help them, but it is missing an essential piece.'

'The key,' Copernicus said, taking the rings from his pocket and showing the he-Wraith.

Amateus nodded.

'How do we stop them?' the commander asked.

'Silho. Only Silho can answer that and only she will be able to do it,' Amateus told them, 'but she is untrained and only half-Omarian. She has dulled her senses with chemicals for so long that the extent of her ability is unclear. She must take full control of her own mind if she is to have any hope at all. Raine believes in her strength, but I fear for her life against Bellum. Just the High Witch alone is more powerful than you can imagine and she's raised a legion of demons to fight with her. Silho will need help. She needs your guidance to focus her skills.' The he-Wraith looked specifically at Copernicus and the commander understood he was talking about something beyond military training. Illusionist magics centred on mental focus and the alignment of body with mind. Uneasiness twisted inside him and the scars on his hands where he'd cut out his family insignia started to itch. Shawe's words echoed in his thoughts . . . *the great Commander Copernicus Kane is afraid* . . . He felt a pang of disgusted self-loathing. He *was* afraid. Doctor Silvan Kane, his Illusionist father, had been dead for more than twenty year-cycles and he was still terrified of the man.

'Wait,' he said, his mind continuing to calculate. 'It's just on fifteen year-cycles since Chrisholm's execution, so why has it taken the Skreaf so long to strike after supposedly destroying the last person who might stand against them?'

'The High Skreaf has used this time to raise her army and to formulate her plan to free the Morsmalus,' Amateus explained. 'It is not a simple matter, and to the ever-living fifteen year-cycles feels no more than a day.'

'But why the act?' Copernicus continued to interrogate him. 'Why would Bellum go to the trouble of framing Chrisholm when she could have just killed him outright?'

'Cruelty. Revenge. We also believe she wanted to use his love for his child to bend him to their will,' the he-Wraith said.

'Why? What did they want from him?'

'We do not know exactly, but we are searching for answers,' Amateus said.

'Enough chit-chat!' Shawe broke in. 'What about my brother? The ring belongs to him.'

The he-Wraith blinked his red eyes. 'If he is alive, they would have taken him with the other slaves to the seal of the Envirious Realm. We do not know where this is.'

'How can I find it then? Where do I start?' Shawe asked.

'Find the man you know as Jude. He is connected. If the Morsmalus is raised, we will all suffer, we will all die. Our world will be no more.'

The he-Wraith sucked in a sharp breath and his head and torso collapsed backwards, folding into itself and wrapping back around as Raine. She stepped into the wall and vanished. Diega cursed and Shawe thudded a fist into one hand. Copernicus drank from the cask of water, thinking on the Wraith's words. *Jude is connected – how?*

The sensation of a familiar body-heat pattern moving through the shanty town intercepted his thoughts. It left almost no vibration in its wake and it wasn't alone.

Copernicus dropped the water and grabbed Silho out of Shawe's grasp.

'What's wrong?' Diega asked.

'Caesar K-Ruz and the Pride are here. They must have heard about Shawe's men. They're hunting you,' he said to Shawe.

Shawe swore and looked over his shoulder. Copernicus had never known the gangster to run from any fight, but one man against an entire gang wasn't a fight – it was an execution.

Carrying Silho in his arms, the commander led the others at a run out of the alley towards the outskirts of town. He sensed the heat signature of K-Ruz and his Pride upping their speed, fanning out into an arrowhead kill formation.

As soon as they reached the last line of shacks, Copernicus ordered Diega, 'Launch now!'

She flicked the coin into the air and morphed it back to the speed-drift platform. She leapt on and used her electrosmith skills to power the dead engine. The others clambered up behind her and they swooped away from Tracy. Copernicus lowered Silho to the platform. At that moment he felt K-Ruz right behind them, then right above them as the gangster sprang from the roof of the last house. He tackled both Copernicus and Shawe off the moving platform. The three of them crashed into the sand and scrambled to their feet. Caesar was swift, but Copernicus had the edge, pulling out his gun before the gangster could strike. Copernicus pressed the weapon into Caesar's forehead as all the members of the Pride and their feline companions appeared from behind the line of buildings around them. Shawe drew his electrifier and scanned it over the gangsters. Diega swooped back around and zoomed in behind them. As she took aim with her weapon, the Wraith materialised up from the sand onto the platform, where she crouched protectively beside Silho. None of the gangsters moved a muscle. They knew what Copernicus could do.

'This doesn't involve you, Kane,' Caesar said. His voice held the mellifluous Crook'd Town accent and was deceptively soft.

'So we should get back on the platform and go on our merry way?' Copernicus said. Everyone there knew full well the whole team would be gunned down the second he took his aim off Caesar – just for the insult.

The Pride boss narrowed his golden eyes in a calculating leonine smile. 'Give yourself up,' he told Shawe. 'You know the law.'

'Kiss my arse,' Shawe responded, arming his electrifier.

'Hold,' Copernicus cautioned him. 'You drop him and we're dead.'

Shawe glared hatred at K-Ruz, but managed to keep his control.

'Back up to the speed-drift,' Copernicus instructed Shawe. The commander maintained his aim at Caesar's head while the two of them inched back to the platform. Diega lowered it for them to step on, then lifted it again once they had reached it.

The commander raised his voice so all the gangsters could hear. 'This is a long-range sniper shot. Make a move while we're still in sight and your boss is dead.'

'I'll remember this,' Caesar said, his voice low.

'I hope so,' Copernicus replied. 'Might save your life in the future.'

The gangster boss gave a snarling smile, a predatory glint in his eyes.

Diega revved the engine and sped them away.

When they had lost sight of the town and the Pride, Shawe cursed and slammed his fist against the metal of the platform so hard that it nearly tipped them.

'As soon as I get back to the city I'm rallying up whoever is left of the boys and we'll take out that yellow-eyed gadfly!'

'Your call,' Copernicus replied.

After a moment, Shawe's expression sobered. 'But what about Stacy?'

'What about him?'

Shawe opened his mouth to speak then snapped it shut. Realisation sparked in his eyes. He was the only one left alive who cared enough to fight the witches for his brother and if he went back to Greenway and faced K-Ruz, he was dead – only the sheer numbers of the Galleys had kept the Pride back all this time. So it was a choice between his brother's life and his Gangland title and reputation, his land, his people, his whole life up until this point.

Shawe's shoulders sank as he decided. King Christy Shawe had fallen. He took the silver flask from his pocket and gulped down the Araki. It was a day of ugly truths.

'Where are we going?' Diega called back to them.

Copernicus took Silho's shoulder and shook her lightly. Her eye-lids flickered and opened.

'Brabel, are you with us?' he asked her.

She blinked red-raw eyes and leaned weakly against his arm. The skin around the cuffs locking her wrists together in front of her was bruised purple and black. Copernicus loosened the restraints, but left them in place.

'Brabel,' he prompted her, 'we have to get back to the city.'

When she didn't respond, he leaned in closer to her and said, 'I wouldn't have thought you'd give up so easily.'

Her body tensed. After a moment she whispered, 'Left.'

'Veer left,' Copernicus instructed Diega.

'Left takes us back out to the desert,' the Fen replied.

'Diega, left!' he commanded.

The Fen soldier gave him a sour look, but followed the direction, steering the speed-drift platform around.

In the far distance, the dark line of the city appeared on the horizon. Soon they would be back within Scorpia's shadow, where an enemy of unknown power lay in wait. Copernicus closed his eyes. He didn't believe in religion, in faith or Paradise, but if he had, he would have prayed.

25

Eli staggered across the sand, squinting watering eyes, exhaling fire through stuck lips, his mouth too dry to swallow. Burning wind, like waves of flames, flicked up whips of sand that flayed his baking skin. Blisters had risen on his exposed hands, and the blood from where the rope was cutting into his flesh had dried to a hard crust. Ev'r had flown the *Summer Holiday* until it ran out of fuel, then she'd taken the noose from his neck and fastened it around his body and wings. Now she dragged him by one end of the rope through the terrible infinity of the Matadori Desert. Ahead, Ev'r paused for a moment. She shielded her eyes and looked out through the heat-rippled air to the yellow-orange desert stretching endlessly around them. Cracks in the parched earth gasped for water, the land eternally punished by two low blue suns, which rose on separate sides of the sky in the morning and slowly moved closer together until, at midday, they merged for one unbearable hour. It was close to this hour now and Eli, soaking in his own sweat and exhausted after trudging the whole long night and half the day without rest, wasn't sure how much more he could take. The ragged black silhouettes of corpse birds circling in the sky above them was not an encouraging sign.

'Keets!' he called to her, his voice a mere croak. 'We need to find shelter. Please. We need water.'

Ev'r yanked on the rope and forced him forward. Once during the night, he had fallen and she'd just dragged him until he'd managed to scramble up. She showed no mercy, no remorse and no sign of stopping anytime soon. She marched ahead, unaffected by the temperature or by his pleas, her movements almost beast-like. She lumbered. Her shoulders jerked, and she occasionally growled.

Eli realised now there was something seriously wrong with Keets. What it was he wasn't sure, but it looked almost as though she was fighting some kind of possession. He wondered, with a sense of growing horror, if she'd let herself be filled with a Skreaf demon. Eli couldn't stop cursing himself for being so stupid. The commander had said not to trust her for a second. Now he understood why.

The rope jerked his hands painfully and he stumbled forward, kicking up sand under his boots. His green diamond pendant bounced on his chest. From somewhere behind him, he thought he heard a sound like the swish of fabric. He looked back. An endless sea of yellow nothingness shimmered through waves of heat. As he faced the front, the sound came again. He thought it might just be an imagining, a mirage of sound, but Keets disproved that idea by glancing over her shoulder in the direction of the noise. Her eyes, now more black than dark green, swept across the sand, looking for the Death that stalked them.

Eli considered the ghostly beast. When it had first appeared to him in Sweepington he had been sure it was a Death, but now, after seeing it in his shelter, he wasn't so certain. It definitely looked like one, but it didn't really act like one. It had seemed almost – afraid. Keets obviously hadn't noticed this. He knew her fear of the Death was the only reason she still kept him with her.

Eli felt the rope go slack and saw Keets had stopped again. This time she was crouching on the ground. She lifted a handful of sand and let the grains slip back through her fingers.

'Here,' he heard her murmur.

'Keets,' Eli approached her.

Her head whipped around and she spoke in a snarl that wasn't her own voice. 'Keep back.'

He recoiled. She threw the end of the rope at him and it smacked him in the face, then dropped to the sand.

Ev'r stood, hugged her arms around herself and jumped. Her body dissipated to a grey vapour that was sucked down into the ground. Eli raced to the place where she had vanished, fighting to wrench his hands free from the bindings. There was no sign of her.

Eli took in his surroundings. He could just make out the Boundary Wall in the far blurry distance. His thoughts turned to the commander and the others lost in the same hostile vastness and he imagined seeing them on the horizon.

A lunatic howl echoed through the desert silence.

An answer came from the other side of where Eli stood. Close – too close. Desert freaks were closing in. Eli stumbled in a circle, not knowing what to do. He would never be able to outrun them. He could definitely outfly them, but his wings were bound tightly to his back. He struggled violently with the bindings. 'Ev'r!' he yelled. 'Please come back! Please!'

Light shimmered off an object just ahead of him and Eli ran towards it. It was a piece of jagged glass lying in the sand. He tried to use the sharp edge of it to saw away the ropes, but it wasn't working. Then an awful rotting odour permeated the air and, with trepidation, Eli looked up. He was completely surrounded by a band of desert mutants, atrocities caused by interbreeding and leakages of dark magics into the atmosphere. They stared with sunken eyes, drool dribbling from their exposed jaws and teeth. One of them cackled. Eli's wings buzzed frantically but couldn't lift him and he couldn't get a grasp of the electrifier in his weapon belt. All he could do was stumble around, staring at them.

'Keets!' he cried and the mutants mocked his terror, all calling out their distorted versions of the name and pretending to sob. Being mocked by the monsters who were about to eat him alive was almost more than he could take.

'Back off! I'm not a soldier – I mean – *I am* a soldier!' he yelled. They screeched and cackled harder.

The ground beside Eli quaked and the sand caved in then exploded out as Ev'r burst from the ground. She was clenching something in one fist and staggering, shuddering, shaking her head like an animal with water in its ears or like someone exhausted fighting to stay awake.

'Keets?' Eli whispered.

Her eyes cleared slightly. She drew one of Eli's blades from her belt and fixed the mutants with her bloodshot stare. No one was laughing now.

Eli sensed a disturbance in the atmosphere around him. He gasped as the air above their heads ripped open like a sheet. Mist filtered out and solidified into the form of three Skreaf witches. Eli dived to one side, crashing into the sand, as both the Skreaf and Ev'r released dark-curses at each other. A stray curse struck a mutant and set him alight. He ran screaming towards the Skreaf. They cursed again and exploded him. The mutants bellowed and howled as they all charged in. Boots stomped Eli's back, pressing him into the sand and knocking the breath out of his lungs. He slithered, trying to escape, but clawed hands grabbed at him and flung him over onto his back. A mutant grabbed his neck and tried to bite his face. He fought, kicking and trying to hold them back with his bound hands. Another mutant joined in and held Eli's legs. He struggled desperately, expecting at any moment to feel the searing pain of a ragged-tooth bite.

The mutants' howling ended abruptly. Something behind Eli picked them up and threw them. They crashed into the ground several metres from where Eli lay. They didn't move again. Eli managed to sit. More mutants rushed in at him, but skidded to a stop and backed away. He couldn't understand why, until he looked up and saw the Death standing over him, the folds of its shadow cloak coiling around its body and arms. No one dared to come near it. Eli stared at the terrible creature. It appeared to be doing some kind of little dance, two steps towards him, two steps back, three steps forward, four steps back. It wavered in indecision.

Not far from Eli, Ev'r fought savagely against both mutant and Skreaf. She stabbed, cursed, kicked and punched, one hand still clasped around whatever she'd found under the sand. Eli saw she was trying to protect it from the blows pelting her body. She was struggling. Sweat-diluted blood streamed down her face. Two of the Skreaf grabbed her and pinned her to the ground. The third stood over her. Its low, monotone chanting chilled Eli to his soul. They were killing her gradually and luxuriating in her suffering. On instinct, Eli sprang to his feet and charged them. He had no weapon, no shield, no clue what he was doing – except that whatever it was, it was happening now and fast. He managed to lift his bound hands far enough to rip the green diamond from the chain around his neck. He held it up and screamed the first thing he thought of.

'Stop!'

He threw the diamond at them.

To his utter shock, all three Skreaf shrieked, the screaming mouths of the demons inside them stretching their skin. In a smoke-reeking bang of dark magics, they dissipated into mist and vanished back into the rip in the air before it sealed over.

'Keets!' Eli grabbed her arm and helped her stagger to her feet. Liquid dripped from one of her hands. Whatever she had been holding had broken. The mutants, who had paused their attack for several seconds, now started back in. Ev'r deflected a swinging club and kicked another one in the face, smashing its jaw.

'Grab on!' she yelled at Eli, holding out her hand.

He obeyed and seized her whole arm. There was only a moment to notice the unusual scaly feel to her skin, then the most excruciating pain he had ever experienced exploded through his entire body. He was falling out of control through a blur of grey, speeding down and down and down, screaming, until he was suddenly hurtled back into real time and slammed into the sand.

Eli lay unconscious, for what felt to him like a second but could have been a day, before he jolted to clarity. He scrambled up and managed to manoeuvre the light-blaster out of his weapon belt. Lifting his tied hands as high as he could, he shone the beam through the darkness and saw they'd landed in a giant Skither tunnel under the sand. He strained his ears for any slithering sounds, and when he heard none, he scanned the light around him. The beam picked up the shadow form of Ev'r, kneeling close by with her back to him. A blackness had spread all over her patchwork skin, blotting out her tattoos and scars and everything that was her. Now he recognised the scale forming over the darkness – the red-tipped shiny black armour of a Ravien.

Eli stared, incapable of words or sounds. He'd only heard of a few ancient cases where people had been infected by the beasts, and in every story the person had turned to Ravien almost straightaway, but Ev'r had held it back for who knew how long – until now. Her body heaved. Eli crept towards her on numb and shaking legs. He trod a wide path out of arm's reach and stopped in front of her. She knelt with her head down and eyes closed. Pieces of a broken vial lay in one open palm. Blood dripped from her mouth and lips from where she had tried to drink from the shattered glass.

'Ev'r,' Eli whispered.

Her eyelids flicked open and she stared at him with eyes almost completely turned to liquid darkness. She slid the blade from her belt and Eli backed away, but Ev'r held it up to her own throat and positioned the point just above her jugular.

'No!' Eli rushed at her and grabbed her hands as best he could, fighting to drag the knife away. 'Don't do it! I can help you!'

'No one can help me!' Ev'r said, the sound alternating between her own voice and an alien snarl. She threw him off, but he quickly found his feet and shone the torchlight on her. He saw the darkness of her skin receding.

'Look!' Eli yelled. 'Your skin is changing back.'

Ev'r lowered the blade and examined her arms. The scales had vanished and the blackness was shrinking back down towards her fingers. It stopped on the very tips, leaving a small dark patch, like blood dried black under the skin.

'It's only reversed it,' Ev'r said, her tone dull. 'It hasn't cured it. I couldn't get enough from the broken pieces.' Her fingers clenched around the knife handle.

Eli stepped in quickly. 'Then I'll analyse the glass. I'll figure out what was in the potion and I'll re-create it. I'll help you – I promise.'

Ev'r stared up at him, distrust narrowing her green eyes. 'Why would you help me?'

'Because you're going to help me,' Eli said. 'You need a cure. I need to save my friends.'

'Did it look as though I can fight the Skreaf?' she asked.

'We don't necessarily need to fight them. We just need to try to figure out what their plans are so that we can find the commander and the others and stop the witches together.'

She snorted. 'You think it will be that easy, do you?'

'Well what are the options? Kill yourself? Turn into a Ravien?' Eli said. 'Do you really want that?'

Ev'r considered it and finally shook her head.

'So, okay,' Eli said. 'I help you, you help me. First step is we have to get back to Scorpia, back to the shelter. I'll start analysing the potion and you can start compiling what we already know about the Skreaf. Okay? . . . Ev'r?'

She wasn't listening to him. She was staring over his shoulder instead. He turned around slowly. The Death stood right behind him, its fangs bared.

The creature lunged. Eli gasped and shut his eyes. Air gusted past him as the Death leapt over his head. Eli spun around. Ev'r slashed her blade at the creature, but the Death smacked her to one side and kept running. He vanished around a bend in the tunnel and soon they heard snarling and ripping cloth.

'Untie me!' Eli said. Ev'r hesitated then sliced through the ropes binding his hands and body. He shook himself free and they both ran towards the sounds. The closer they came to it, the stronger the meaty stink of decay grew. They turned a corner and halted. Eli pressed a hand over his nose. The tunnel ended in a hollowed-out lair where the gigantic coiled form of a Skither lay lifeless, its grey tongue protruding from its mouth. Beside the beast's head was a pile of human-breed corpses. Eli could see the marks in the sand where the Skither had dragged in its victims. They moved cautiously closer to the corpses. Suddenly, the Death reared up from behind the pile, its mouth bloody. It staggered towards them, spitting out chunks of dead flesh. It held out its hands and it noticed the gore dripping from them. Its sunken eyes stretched wide and Eli saw clear horror. The Death reeled and collapsed onto the ground.

Eli stepped towards it, but Ev'r grabbed his arm and dragged him back. 'Don't you learn from your mistakes?'

She went first and from a reasonable distance, extended her foot and nudged the Death. It retched and vomited violently, then collapsed again.

'He's sick,' Eli said, squatting down beside it, shining the light over its body and face.

'Really,' Ev'r replied wryly.

'Look,' Eli said, noticing how the creature's waxy, colourless skin blended with its shadow cloak. He leaned closer and saw an extremely faint bloodline mark – the triangular pattern of a Midnight Man, mixed with something else. Eli squinted. It was the green and brown scales of a non-venomous human-breed snake line.

'Wow!' Eli said, his fingertips tingling with the excitement of discovery. 'I've never seen anything like this. All the cross-bred Midnight Men the government executed were mixes with other spectral-breeds – none of them were outside of the race. Human-breed and spectral-breed are completely incompatible. How would it even happen without the human-breed getting killed?'

'Artificial insemination – experimentation,' Ev'r said. 'You think babies are only made after people fall in love and get married, do you?'

'No,' Eli mumbled, though he had been imagining how the scene would look when a pleasant-faced human-breed girl brought a bloodthirsty, feral Midnight Man home to meet her parents. He examined the man more closely, noting his gaunt face and protruding cheekbones, his stick-thin arms.

'He's starving,' he said. 'He can't feed properly.'

'What do you expect from a mix like that?' Ev'r replied.

'Well he must be able to eat something; he's survived this long.'

'It's because of the metamorphosis,' Ev'r said.

'I don't understand.' Eli shook his head.

'Look at him – all that skin drooping around his face and neck. That's the way the Midnight Men are before they mature. Before their changing time, they can get away with eating any kind of meat, but when they come of age, they have a day when they have to feast properly on the near-dead – then they change, but if they don't feast they die. It's a protective function of the species – only the strong survive. I would have thought someone like yourself, professing to be intelligent, would already know all this,' Ev'r said with a sneer.

'I never claimed to know everything about spectral-breeds,' Eli said. His eyes returned to the prone man. 'I don't think he wants to eat the dead or near-dead. Did you see his face when he saw the blood? He was horrified.'

'Sounds like his problem,' Ev'r said.

'He's part human-breed, though.' Eli spoke his thoughts aloud. 'I wonder if the whole devouring near-death thing could be diverted somehow. Maybe he doesn't have to eat dead flesh. It doesn't look like it agrees with him anyway.'

'A vegetarian Midnight Man?' Ev'r raised one eyebrow. 'I don't think so.'

'Maybe we should take him with us and try to help him.'

'Hell no,' Ev'r spat. 'You want to escape the authorities, find a cure for a Ravien-bite, defeat the Skreaf *and* drag an illegal, dying cross-breed along for the ride. What's wrong with you?'

The man's eyelids flipped open. He stared at them and his mouth gaped open in a silent scream. His skin blended into the shadows of his cloak and he vanished completely. Eli saw the shadows stirring as the man ran through them, out of the chamber and out of sight.

'Problem solved,' Ev'r said. 'Look at this bunch.' She nodded to the pile of corpses. 'They're all Galleys.'

Eli stood and shuffled nearer to the bodies, shining the light onto them, over their horn-shaped Galley bloodline marks and green clothes. Ev'r was right. They were Shawe's men. Eli recognised the dead staring face of Shawe's cousin, Malcolm, and a chill spread over his skin. His heart thudded faster. Copernicus, Diega and Silho were last seen being captured by Shawe – who had left the city and never returned.

'Are they here?' he squeaked, more to himself than Ev'r. He ignored the smell and started searching through the bodies. Each had dark stains all over their skin.

'Dark magics,' Ev'r said beside him. 'Death-curses.'

'Skreaf?' Eli whispered.

'Probably. The magics were strong enough to kill the Skither when it fed on the corpses.' She pointed to something sticking out of the giant monster's mouth. What Eli had thought was the creature's tongue was actually someone's arm. He gagged.

He voiced his fears to Ev'r. 'Maybe Copernicus and the others are here – dead.'

'Hopefully,' she said.

Eli blinked back tears and then his logic kicked in. 'I'll run a test.' He took the scanner from his pocket and set it to body shape. He keyed in the approximate dimensions of his boss and teammates, then ran the scanner across the pile of dead and over the Skither in case it had already swallowed them. The machine beeped – no matches.

'I don't think they're here,' Eli said, almost not daring to hope. He looked over all the dead bodies – at least half or maybe more of the Galley gang members must have been there.

'We should bury them,' he said. 'It's the human-breed way. They'd want that.'

'I hate to be the one to break the news to you, Snack-size,' Ev'r said. 'But corpses don't *want* anything, and we have to get out of here before the demons find us again. We've wasted enough time as it is.'

'Let me at least cross them into the afterlife, then,' Eli said.

'Cross them?' Ev'r sneered. 'Since when were you human-breed?'

'Never, obviously, but *they're* human-breed so it's the right thing to do.' Eli stood in front of the bodies and crossed himself three times in the human-breed way.

'Go to the ancestors,' he said, not knowing what else to say. Something shimmering beside the corpses caught his attention and he bent down to examine it. He lifted up Diega's silver coin, the *Ory-4* in its morphed state. As he stared at the coin a possible sequence of actions played in his mind.

'Shawe must have captured the commander, Diega and Silho. Then the witches attacked and killed the Galleys, and somehow the others escaped into the desert. Otherwise they'd be here. We need to search for them.'

Ev'r shook her head. 'Do you know how vast the Matadori is?'

'Very vast?' Eli took a guess. 'But I have equipment —'

'Which doesn't work out here. Besides there're no guarantees they are here, maybe the Skreaf took them. Either way, do you actually think the witches are going to wait for you to regroup with your little friends before they strike?'

Eli had to shake his head.

'Then let's go.' She held out her hand.

'No, no, no,' he said. 'I'm not going back into the Murk. Do you know how much that hurts?'

'We can travel the hidden path and it will take us seconds to get to the city or we can walk and it'll take us weeks. What would you prefer?'

Eli took her outstretched hand.

'You have to want to sink in otherwise it won't work,' she told him. 'No one unwilling can be dragged into the Murk, except through dark magics.'

'I want to,' Eli whispered.

'Sure you do,' Ev'r mocked.

Eli gritted his teeth as the ground gave way beneath his feet.

26

Silho sat slumped on the speed-drift platform, staring up at the monolithic wall encircling Scorpia. Above the impassable black stone fortress, the upper levels of the city reached high into the sky, stretching up to Paradise and falling so far short. Silho heard voices from the wall calling her, dragging her in. Flashes of their memories intersected her thoughts. Her hands strained against the restraints and her skin froze, then instantly began to boil. Her heart began pounding frantically, then almost stopped. She trembled all over and gasped with stomach cramps that contracted all her muscles, making her double over with pain. She felt like smashing her head against the platform to knock herself out.

The only thing that stopped her was the Wraith, Raine. The strange spectral-breed whispered constant reassurances beside Silho's ear. Her voice was so soft and cool that it could have been just a breeze, except Silho knew full well there was no such thing as a gentle breeze in the Matadori. She shivered despite the heat and her restraints clanked together. The handcuffs binding her hands brought up a hazy memory of her father being dragged out of their house by soldiers. He'd been cuffed just as she was now . . . *When her father was framed by the Skreaf and executed, we believed we'd lost the last Omarian* . . . The truth spoken by the he-Wraith continued to reach her battered mind in degrees, spreading ripples of shock through her body. She had always believed her father was innocent, but hearing it from someone else . . . It removed all the whispers of doubt that had plagued her in the mid-dark when she'd lain wide awake chasing sleep. A second of unanchored euphoria fought through the pain, but almost instantly faded into hollowness because she was still here and he was still gone and there was so much left unsaid and so many questions unanswered.

Silho returned her gaze to the wall and saw the commander walking back towards them. He had left her and the others waiting on the hover platform while he'd gone on foot to the Scorpian Gates to investigate the line-up of people stretching from the only official entry to Scorpia far back into the desert. When he was close enough to be heard, the commander shook his head. 'Palace enforcers and Regiment soldiers are double-scanning everyone. They're scoping for us. We have to find another way in.' He stepped onto the platform.

'What about the access tunnels into the Gangland?' Shawe said from beside Silho, the taint of Araki heavy on his breath.

'No good,' Copernicus replied. 'We need to get as close to the underside as we can, preferably inside Moris-Isles itself.'

Shawe scratched his chin and the others sat silent in thought. Finally the gangster said, 'There is a way directly into the Isles, but you're not going to like it.'

'Tell me,' Copernicus said.

'The Brown River. The main sewer line. It runs through the whole city.'

Diega cursed under her breath.

'If that's the only way then we'll have to use it,' Copernicus said.

Shawe gave a rumbling laugh and rubbed his bloodshot eyes. 'The man who sweeps his room seventeen times a day and bleaches his underpants thinks he can handle swimming in other people's —'

'I can do whatever is necessary,' Copernicus cut in. 'Can you?'

'You know it.'

'Then sober up.'

Shawe took a defiant swig from his flask, but then pocketed it.

'Around the wall – that way,' he said to Diega and pointed east. 'I'll tell you when to stop.'

Diega glared at him, refusing to take his orders.

'Do it, Diega,' Copernicus instructed.

'Yes, do it Diega,' Shawe echoed with a smug smile.

'Shut it,' the commander snapped at the gangster.

'Why is he still with us?' Diega demanded.

'Because you need me,' Shawe said.

Diega gave a nasty laugh. 'Like a hole in the head – like a rash that won't quit.'

'You'd know all about that,' the gangster bit back.

'Copernicus – seriously, it's me or him,' Diega said.

'I agree,' Shawe said.

'How about I shoot you both,' Copernicus said, drawing his electrifier and pointing it at one and then the other. 'We're facing a demon army without any backup. I need soldiers, not squabbling children. You're just slowing me down.'

'She started it,' Shawe said.

'Not another word, Shawe,' Copernicus warned him, his voice dangerous. 'Diega, fly.'

The gangster muttered something. Diega gritted her teeth and drove the platform eastward around the great wall.

Shawe called out when they reached a row of large circular metal hatches embedded in the black rock of the wall.

'The centre one,' Shawe told them.

Diega set the platform down and the others stepped off. Silho felt Raine's silky hands helping her to sit up. As soon as she did, the world spun around her and the call of the voices in the wall grew louder. The Wraith's words did nothing to help her now.

Copernicus turned to them, his eyes seeing beyond the surface, analysing the situation. He approached Silho, taking a syringe full of a green liquid out of his weapon belt.

Raine stood up in front of Silho. She hissed, 'She needs to stay awake. She needs to overcome the sickness.'

'What my soldier needs is my business,' the commander told her. 'Move.'

The red eyes of the he-Wraith flashed behind the grey of Raine's stare. The sky above them darkened, but Copernicus didn't back off. He sidestepped Raine and crouched down beside Silho. He spoke

240

and his words cut clearly through the babble inside her head. His voice was even comforting.

'This will help you for now. We'll figure out something more permanent once we find shelter.'

'Thank you,' Silho managed to whisper and meant every letter of the words.

He held one of her arms and pressed the needle into the skin. He pushed down on the plunger, but the liquid didn't budge. The transparent plastic of the syringe fogged over. The substance inside was frozen. Copernicus looked up at Raine.

'Thaw it – *now.*'

The Wraith shook her head, the silver strands of her dark hair shimmering. 'I can see. You are motivated by your own fear of the past, not by her pain. We will not allow you to compromise Silho's progress.'

The commander's fury surfaced like a sudden deadly storm, but vanished again immediately as he regained control. When he spoke his voice was flat, devoid of emotion.

'You're right. I am afraid. I'm afraid of what I'm seeing inside my soldier. I'm afraid that her pain will grow until her mind is gone and her heart stops. I'm afraid that the blind fanaticism of the spectral-breed standing before me will prevent me from administering the aid that she needs before it's too late. And I'm afraid that afterwards there will be nothing much left of the spectral-breed once I'm finished with her.'

'She's far stronger than you think,' Raine responded. Her eyes shifted rapidly as though the he-Wraith was trying to take over their form.

'Your other half doubts her,' Copernicus said. 'So you're divided against yourself. You're confused and I'm supposed to trust your judgement over my own?'

'You can trust that we'd die for Silho, for her cause,' Raine said. 'She needs to overcome her physical pain. She needs your help – but not in this way. You have to teach her. Only you can. How long she suffers is up to you.'

'Are we doing this or what?' Shawe called back to them from where he and Diega stood beside the wall.

'I'm holding you responsible for whatever happens to Silho after this,' Copernicus said to the Wraith.

'My thoughts spoken,' Raine countered.

Copernicus gave her a dark look. He lifted Silho in one arm, carrying her so that her face pressed against his shoulder. Inside her mind she was screaming at Raine to let him help her, but she couldn't make a sound.

The commander stopped beside Diega and nodded to her. She tightened the sling tying SevenM to her body and said, '*Dimenef traml.*' The hatch shrank down, exposing a gaping black hole in the wall.

The evil stench that blasted out forced everyone to step back. Diega gagged.

Shawe wafted the air towards Copernicus' face and said, 'Smell that aroma . . . it's a million times worse down there. Sure you can handle it?'

'Follow me in,' Copernicus responded. He carried Silho to the hole, climbed through and dropped some distance into the pipe below. They splattered down in knee-high filth. The all-consuming stink hit them so hard that Silho's senses cleared a bit. The commander swore and she heard Shawe laughing at them from above. Copernicus took the light-blaster from his belt and shone it upwards, catching Diega dropping down. Shawe followed straight after, spraying everyone with muck. Diega snarled a string of curses in her native language.

'Did I get you?' Shawe laughed. 'My apologies.'

Copernicus directed the beam of light into the gangster's face, forcing Shawe to look away. He then turned and headed down the pipe.

The water level rose steadily the further in they went, and soon they were swimming. Copernicus and Diega dragged Silho through. The voices she heard down here were softer, but they whispered darker things, haunting her mind. Shawe started singing an off-key Galley tune. Silho kept her mouth shut and tried to breathe as little as possible, until something huge and slippery eeled around her legs. She gasped, sucking in some of the filth and gagging it back up. Blinking into light-form vision, she stared down into the murky waters. The body-lights of something massive were circling underneath them.

'What's that?' Diega said, as it touched her as well.

'Probably just a Spitting Myban,' Shawe said from behind them. 'Harmless – except in mating season.'

'What happens in mating season?' Diega asked, anticipating bad news from the smug look on Shawe's face.

'They spit out live offspring that burrow into the skin of whoever they come across. The little ones feed on body fluids until they're big enough to break out.'

'When is mating season?' Diega said.

'Who knows?' Shawe replied with a grin in his voice.

Silho heard the Wraith hiss a Cos enchant, '*Sapphire.*'

Whatever the creature was, it dived away until Silho lost sight of its body-lights.

'Left!' Shawe bellowed. 'The second ladder.'

They followed his directions and found a rust-eaten ladder leading up to another sealed-off hatch. Diega tried to morph it, but this one didn't change.

'Must have something living growing on it,' she said. 'We'll have to clean it.'

'Out of the way, sunshine.' Shawe palmed her aside and climbed the ladder. It creaked and groaned, straining under his weight. He pressed against the porthole with one hand and it broke upwards. The gangster hauled himself out of the hole and reached his hands back down. Copernicus lifted Silho into the gangster's rough grasp and he dragged her up onto a backstreet in Moris-Isles. He leaned her against a wall and straightened to eye the few passers-by. They rushed past.

A sudden onslaught of voices and images filled Silho's mind. The force of the attack sent her sprawling onto her side. The mental pain of the visions was starting to overcome the physical pain of the drug withdrawal. The skin of her face and head felt too tight for the bones. From somewhere among the lost voices in the walls, Silho heard Jude calling to her – *I'm under attack as well. Look at your locator. Can you see me?*

Shawe pulled Silho upright and studied her with sharp green eyes. 'Girl, you don't look so good,' the gangster murmured. 'How about a smoke?' He took out his packet of cigarettes, but it was drenched with sewer water. 'Maybe not,' he said and threw them into the gutter. He took out his flask instead and put it up to her lips. The fumes alone made her head snap back.

'I said no, Shawe,' Copernicus said as he and Diega emerged from the porthole in the footpath.

'Then what? She needs something.'

Copernicus glanced around them. He slipped a syringe out of his belt. Immediately the plastic fogged over again as the substance froze. Raine stepped up out of the ground beside Silho. She and the commander exchanged loaded looks.

Shawe glanced from one of them to the other and asked, 'So what are we doing here?'

'We have to go to the place where the Skreaf took Jude and try to find a lead,' the commander said.

'Follow me,' Raine hissed. 'I'll take you.'

'Will you,' Copernicus said dryly. He took the dissipater restraint off his belt and wrapped it around his wrist ready for use. 'Just in case.'

Raine regarded him with ambivalence. She turned and drifted away down the street. Copernicus lifted Silho and the ground blurred beneath her as the commander's soundless steps moved through Moris-Isles.

Raine took the team through the underside suburb, bringing them to the street to where Silho had fled the night before. She recognised the Burrower hole through which Raine had dragged her to save her life. Beyond that was the place where the witches had surrounded Jude. The walls of the alleyway were blackened and sprayed with white machine-breed blood. There was a sticky pool of it on the ground.

The team entered the alley. Copernicus studied the blood-spatter pattern and the blackness of the walls. He set Silho down on the ground and took a Grenyen Glass light, designed to detect the presence of magics, from his weapon belt and shone it on the stain. Everyone jolted. The black was not a simple stain. It was a mass of overlapping Skreaf symbols, the triangle within a triangle within a square. Demon faces, an echo of the magics that had created the stain, pushed out of the blackness and snarled at them. Diega stumbled back and struck her ankle against something hard buried in the garbage strewn on the ground. She bent over and dragged out Jude's communicator. The internals were completely burnt out and obliterated. Copernicus took it from her and examined it before handing it back. Diega's face set into a stony expression.

'They've left no tracks,' the commander said. He glanced at the Wraith. 'Do you know where they took the prisoners?'

Raine shook her head. 'We've told you everything we know.'

Silho looked at the pool of drying white blood and a blinding flood of flowing colour drowned her senses. Distorted sounds first shrieked then bellowed, booming in her ears, shaking her skull. Several clear images fought through the confusion. She saw Jude being struck by a curse and falling. White blood sprayed from an injury to his neck. The witches gathered around him and she heard some words – *now . . . go . . . take him . . . the holding . . . this one . . .*

She resurfaced to Copernicus shaking her. She could hear a gurgling, choking sound and it was several moments before she realised it was coming from her. With intense effort, she managed to tell them what she had seen and heard.

'Jude was bleeding white blood?' Diega said at the end. 'That's not possible. She must be wrong.'

'Maybe not,' Copernicus said and Diega gave him a questioning look.

Shawe spoke up. 'The holding? You think that means one of the minimum-security pens?'

'We know the witches have infiltrated the military, so it's a possibility,' the commander said.

'So there's how many,' Shawe said, 'five, right? Sydnoble, Castlereagh, Penright, Darby and Firestone. Which one is it?'

Copernicus shook his head, then his attention snapped towards something beyond the alley.

'Don't linger,' Raine hissed. 'We're not alone.' She stepped into the wall and vanished.

Copernicus dragged Silho up and threw her over his shoulder.

The team moved out of the street, heading for the main drag of Mortimer Road.

'We need to find a place to lie low until dark,' Copernicus said, looking behind them after every few metres. 'Somewhere well hidden.'

'What about a pub cellar or that ammunition hold in Cleary?' Diega suggested.

'Too public – too out in the open,' Copernicus replied. He turned to Shawe. 'Do you remember that decommissioned research lab under the river in Nureyev where we used to go as kids? Do you know if it's still standing?'

Shawe shrugged. 'Maybe. It's worth a look. Easiest way there is through the water pipes.'

'Fastest way is to boost a craft and fly,' Diega said.

'What about skyblocks?' the gangster asked.

'I can sense them. We'll find ways around,' Copernicus said. 'We have to keep a low profile and move fast.'

The group turned a corner and hit Prospera Street, the longest stretch of grindhouses and strip joints in the city. The buildings here were fashioned around different themes. Flashing neon lights in every blackened window made promises to passers-by of what they'd find inside. Half-naked women, men and all kinds in between loitered around in groups.

'There,' Diega said, pointing to a shiny silver transflyer with the name of *EnvyMe* parked in front of one of the grindhouses. The craft had a stretched centre and illegal blinder lights at the front and sides. 'It's seriously modified. It's got the speed we'll need if we're made.'

Two burly thugs dressed in matching black stood at the door of the building in front of the craft.

'I'll distract them,' Copernicus said. 'Diega, get the craft. We'll all meet up at —' He stopped as Shawe broke off from the group and charged the men. He punched one and then the other, dropping them both instantly. The gangster turned back to the team and a third man

246

who had been hidden by the doorway lunged out and stabbed a knife into Shawe's back. The blade ripped through the gangster's jacket and shirt, hit his skin and snapped in half. Shawe turned and the man's face twisted with terror as he saw who it was. Shawe slammed the thug headfirst into a wall and he slumped to the ground, where he stayed.

'Go,' Copernicus said to Diega. She ran out and the commander followed, carrying Silho. Diega fried the craft's security system with a device from her weapon belt and they leapt in. The Fen gripped the steering hook and brought the engines roaring to life. The craft lifted into the air as more thugs spilled out of the brothel. The hyper-speed function kicked in and Diega sped the transflyer straight upwards. The force pinned everyone to their seats. Copernicus glanced at Shawe sitting beside Silho in the back seat.

'What?' the gangster said.

'Low profile,' Copernicus reminded him. 'The last thing we need is K-Ruz finding our tracks.'

Shawe snorted. 'Let him come.'

Silho blinked and time skipped. She fought through to awareness as Diega landed the craft in a side street in the suburb of Nureyev.

27

The Catadral Mercy stood as one of the oldest churches in Scorpia, one of only three from the Neothessalonic Era to have survived the gorgon attack in the year-cycle of the Thorn. Its steepled roof and belltower cast a far-stretching shadow across the Asher River, which passed along one side of the church. The choppy brown waters of Scorpia's main river rushed through most levels of the city through interconnected pipeways and waterfalls. Silho, draped over Shawe's arm, smelt the river scent of sediment sludge as the team approached the front of the Catadral.

She blinked to adjust her eyes to the soft candlelight as they entered and felt Shawe shiver at the drop in temperature. His footsteps echoed on the uneven stone floor, marked with the tombs of the great and mostly forgotten. Immense columns reached up to the ceiling where the famous painting, *Creo Paradisum*, had been born and painstakingly restored. Silho glanced up at the artwork and instantly regretted it. There was so much history in the picture that it felt like being plugged into electricity. She tore her eyes away, focusing on the few random human-breeds kneeling at the front of the church.

Shawe paused to cross himself three times then followed Copernicus to a shadowy corner of the great building hidden by a pair of confession boxes. The commander indicated to Diega to keep watch for witnesses and knelt down beside the wall. He slid his blade behind one of the stones and pried until it loosened and he was able to drag it out. The stone was a fraction of the thickness it appeared to be, a mere façade to hide the opening into the tunnel behind it, which was barely big enough for them to slither inside.

Copernicus and Diega entered and Shawe pushed Silho in after them. Hands grasped her, dragging her through to the end of the tunnel where it dropped down to a pipe below. Here the air tasted stale and metallic and Silho heard the sounds of rushing water all around them. Copernicus grabbed her up and moved the team through the pipe.

Their boots splashed through ankle-high water until the commander stopped at a metal hatch with a heavily rusted opening circle. Shawe took the levers and heaved. The metal screeched, unwilling, but it stood no chance against the gangster's strength. He turned the circle until they heard the clank of a lock shunting open. Shawe lifted the hatch and Copernicus dropped down with Silho. He sat her on the ground and flicked on the lights of the abandoned underwater research facility. Boxes lined the walls where dirt-frosted windows looked out into the river. Shawe and Diega's boots thudded down near Silho.

Shawe looked around. 'Been a while,' he grunted. He and Copernicus locked eyes, then both looked away.

Silho turned towards a window and peered, with stinging eyes, through a cleared patch of glass. She looked down on one of the underwater suburbs of the city, inhabited by the human-breeds of aquatic bloodlines. Rock and coral houses crowded the river base and the streets teemed with water dwellers going about their daily lives. Some rode seahorses, others darted here and there on flat flying-carpet stingrays or giant anaconda eels. Those who lived here had built up resistance to the corrosive pollutants of the Asher River.

Silho heard fewer voices down here, but now they were yelling and the visions were lasting longer and longer. She shook her head, trying to clear a space in her mind to think. She spotted SevenM lying on a table nearby where Diega had put him. The robot's eyes were dull. The commander started rummaging through boxes, pulling out tech equipment and handing it to Diega.

'What are you doing?' Shawe asked them.

'We have to set up a hedging device to stop the military from tracking us when we ring out,' Copernicus told him.

'Ring out to who?'

'Eli,' Copernicus said.

Shawe snorted. 'What are we calling that little insect for?'

Copernicus' back stiffened. Diega glared at Shawe and said, 'We're calling *Eli* because he's brilliant. He might have information that will save your brother. But if you'd rather, we can wait for someone taller to come up with the answers.'

Shawe held up his hands. 'Keep your shirt on. I didn't mean to offend your boyfriend.'

Diega mumbled something that sounded like *imbecile* and turned back to putting the tech together.

Silho swallowed as nausea swelled inside her throat. She closed her eyes and willed herself not to be sick in front of everyone. A soft hand closed around her arm and she felt herself propelled silently off the ground and carried away from the others. She opened her eyes to see Raine's face above her.

The spectral-breed carried her through a hallway made of glass into a second room with bunk beds built into the wall. She turned left into a large, open industrial bathroom, made for researchers returning from underwater treks to wash off their suits before getting undressed. The scent of bleach and other heavy chemicals still lingered in the stuffy air. Raine crossed the bathroom to the toilet cubicles and lowered Silho onto the cold tiles. The restraints clanked together as Silho doubled over, retching.

Afterwards she tried to lean her head against the cubicle wall, but she jolted back, seeing a stranger's face staring at her from the toilet piping. The face, filthy and haggard, registered shock, which deepened as Silho realised it was her own reflection. She turned away from the disturbing sight and saw Raine standing in front of one of the bathroom mirrors on the other side of the room. Instead of her own reflection, the image of the he-Wraith, Amateus, looked back at her. Inside the mirror he moved independently of Raine's movement and spoke to her, though his voice was mute to Silho's hearing. Raine replied in the language of the Skilsy Wraiths, which to Silho's ears sounded like a collection of *shhh* and *ssss* sounds. Raine lifted her hands and touched them to the mirror. The two Wraiths, male and female of the same person, stared at each other with unmistakable adoration.

Silho lowered her head, the sickness building again inside her. She focused on the bloodline marks showing through her ripped sleeves. The red of the flame and green of the dragon scales shimmered in the weak light. The colours brought faded memories to her mind of her father's works of art. In her mind he stood in front of a blank canvas, his eyes already seeing the image that he would paint. This memory, like every other of her childhood, was shadowed with the darkness of his terrible death. *She* – that woman, that demon witch – had not just killed him, she'd murdered his name and everything good that he had been.

Silho's eyes burned with tears. How could there still be tears after she'd cried so much for so long? When would it stop? She slid down and rested her head on the tiles. The Wraith appeared at the cubicle door, watching Silho with sad, almost bewildered eyes.

'Did you know my father?' Silho whispered.

'We knew of him,' Raine answered.

'Did you know the Skreaf were hunting him before they framed him?'

The Wraith pressed her pale lips together. She searched for the right words before she spoke. 'We are forbidden by our law to associate with those outside our kind, or to interfere in their matters. After your father's death, Amateus and I made the choice to fight the Skreaf – regardless of the consequences.' Her words faded in and out in Silho's mind.

'What consequences?' she managed to ask.

'Our people believe that everything happens as it is intended. To fight against fate is an insult to the gods. This merits the severest punishments. We can never return to our kind. We will never be separated into two bodies.'

'You want that?' Silho said.

A complexity of emotions stirred the shapeless torment of the Wraith's haunted eyes. They settled somewhere between desperate hope and utter despair.

251

'We are always together, but always apart – until we are released.'

Silho took in the words, processing the extent of the Wraith's sacrifice.

'Look in my pocket,' she whispered.

Raine crouched down beside her on the grimy bathroom floor. She reached into Silho's jacket and drew out the oval compact mirror Eli had given her on her first day as a tracker. The Wraith stared into it and the red eyes of Amateus looked back at her. She stroked a finger over the mirror.

'Keep it,' Silho said.

The door squeaked open and Diega entered the bathroom. She moved around the room, scouring the corners and behind the toilet doors. Raine rolled into the floor and vanished as the Fen turned their way.

Diega spotted Silho and said, 'There you are.' She approached the cubicle. 'What are you doing sneaking off like that?'

Silho cringed as the sickness boiled again inside her. The anger faded from Diega's eyes. She stood watching Silho for some time. When she finally spoke her voice was softer than usual. It sounded like beautiful, sorrowful music.

'You know, when someone dies there are a lot of empty spaces – their room, their chair at the table. They are sacred places and you can't fill them – ever.'

Silho nodded. She knew all about empty places.

Diega's face contorted as though she was going to cry, but the tears didn't come. Her voice hardened. 'The witch has to pay – but only you can end her.' She stepped closer to Silho. 'You have to find out how, right now. No more lies and hiding. No more games. You have to get control. If I were you, there is nothing in the universe I wouldn't do to get retribution. Do you understand? Here, get up. Now. Move.' She grabbed Silho's arm and tried to drag her to her feet. Silho gasped, struggling to find her balance.

The commander appeared silently behind Diega. He took Silho out of Diega's grasp and sat her down on a crate beside the toilets. He fixed his dark stare on the Fen. 'Go monitor the system.'

'I don't want to monitor the system,' Diega said. 'We shouldn't be hiding down here. We should be out there, hunting these hags, finding Jude.'

'We will be, when the time is right,' Copernicus said.

'Which is when?' she demanded.

'When I say it is,' Copernicus replied. He nodded to the bathroom door. 'Go.'

Diega's angry eyes retorted, but she obeyed and left them alone.

The commander turned to Silho. His eyes moved along her arms, studying her bloodline marks. He narrowed his stare.

'Your pictures have changed – extended,' he said, leaning in closer. 'Did you notice?'

Silho shook her head, but his words made her think of her fight with Bellum in Moris-Isles. After drawing power from the witch's body-lights, she had coughed up sparks. That had never happened before. Her pictures had been tingling and itching ever since, but the sensations had faded into the more consuming pain of the drug withdrawals.

'Bellum,' Silho whispered. 'I felt something change when we fought.'

Copernicus thought for a moment then said, 'The pictures may be related to the Skreaf – or to the skill you need to fight them. That must be your light-form vision.'

'I can't kill anyone with light-form,' Silho said.

'I know – you can only draw a small amount of strength, but maybe if you can gain better control over your mind you might be able to take more power before you ignite. Maybe enough to be lethal.'

Dizziness forced Silho to lean back. Sharp images from the wall sliced through her thoughts. She saw a much younger Christy Shawe and Copernicus sitting in the bathroom smoking illegal Estle Thistle. Purple smoke curled above them and their laughter echoed around the empty room. More people walked into the vision: researchers in underwater suits washing off under the showerheads, a maintenance crew testing the glass walls, a couple kissing in secret. The picture grew increasingly crowded as memory-people from times long past appeared. Silho heard the commander's voice calling her from a distance.

'Brabel, can you hear me? Say these words: *Claude animus meus.*'

Her numb lips mumbled over the words and the visions and sounds suddenly vanished. Silho had a moment of feeling as though she was falling through a silent void. With the distraction of the mental interference gone, the nausea amplified. She bent over, trying to breathe slowly until the sickness lessened. As it did, Silho became aware that the commander was kneeling in front of the crate where she sat. He was holding her. Silho could see along the pattern of his viper bloodline marks. His colours pleased her eyes and the coolness of his touch soothed the perpetual heat of her skin. Silho looked up at his face, into his midnight black eyes, and saw in them a lifetime of experiences that others only had in their nightmares. He had gone into the darkest places and seen the worst atrocities created by the most demented minds. He had gone in to save, but had paid a personal cost. He had been touched by the evil. There was no way to avoid it. So he had become what she saw – the villainous hero, admired and hated, revered and feared, closely followed and widely avoided because no one could understand the way he thought, and that made people uncomfortable. But she understood. She saw he was dangerous, even disturbed, but that was what she found so magnetic. Everyone Silho had loved in her life had had that same look – Oren Harvey, Hammersmith, Ismail and Ev'r – and now she realised, so had her father.

The commander watched her with caution and asked, 'Has it worked?'

Silho nodded, but then another vision flashed behind her eyes. 'But it's coming back.' She hated hearing the panic in her voice.

'Say the words again,' the commander instructed. 'In your mind.'

Silho obeyed and the hallucination vanished.

'What is it? What does it mean?' she asked.

Copernicus sat back, his eyes moving in thought. Finally he spoke. 'It means *close my mind.* It's an Illusionist enchant. They use it to centre themselves, to shut their thoughts away from outside influences and distractions – like other people's voices, other sounds, their surroundings, even their own physical needs. Keep repeating it.'

Silho silently spoke the words again with the same clearing effect. 'How long will it last?' she asked.

'Illusionist magics aren't just tricks – they're a way of thought,' Copernicus said the words carefully as though he wasn't comfortable with them. 'People without natural Illusionist skill need to practise the magics and build up strength with time. If you continue to repeat the words, they will become imprinted on your mind. They will create new pathways in your brain, the way exercise creates new muscles in your body. Eventually you won't need to actively say the words. Think of it as if you're building a wall around your mind – every time you say the words is one brick of the wall. Do you understand what I'm saying?'

Silho nodded, then asked, 'You have ... natural Illusionist skills?'

Copernicus' body tensed. The scars on his face stretched tight. Silho lowered her eyes and saw his fists were clenched, making the scars on the back of his hands stand out white.

'I'm sorry. It's not my business,' she said.

After several moments of silence, the commander said, 'I made these scars before I realised that just cutting the memory out of my skin couldn't get rid of it from where it mattered the most.' He lifted his hand, touching the side of his head. 'You and I have something in common.'

Silho saw a shift in the blackness of his eyes, a hint of feelings he usually kept hidden beneath cold control.

'You remind me ...' Silho tried to tell him what she had been thinking earlier, but realised after she'd started to speak that it might not be such a good idea.

'I remind you of what?' the commander prompted.

Silho thought fast and couldn't come up with anything to say that didn't sound bad – *of my mother, of my father, of Ev'r Keets.* 'Of everyone I knew.' She finally settled on that, though it still sounded strange, even to her.

Copernicus narrowed his eyes, but then his expression relaxed and he nodded. Silho wondered what he'd made of her words, but didn't want to ask and he didn't explain.

She heard a click as Copernicus unlocked her restraints and slid them over her gloved hands. Silho shivered.

'Are you sure?' she asked, the panic speaking again.

'I am,' Copernicus said. 'Are you?'

Silho considered the question. Most of her physical symptoms had passed except for the lingering nausea. When she repeated the enchant she was able to control both her need to access the walls and their voices calling to her, but as soon as she wasn't thinking of the words the sensations returned, so her mind was in a constant state of struggle, like the ocean against the sand. She couldn't imagine being able to sustain the control without her drugs, but according to Raine it was the only option if she was to have any chance against the Skreaf – to stop them from destroying their world. She was the only one who could. Exhaustion pressed heavily on her shoulders.

'You're tired,' the commander said. He stood up. 'Take power from me.'

Silho looked up at him and it was a moment before she comprehended what he was saying. 'No, no,' she said as soon as she did. 'I can't. I'm alright.'

'I'm not asking, Brabel. I need you regenerated. There's no time for natural recovery.'

'But what about you?' she asked.

'I'm fine. Do it – now,' he insisted.

Silho stood reluctantly. She swapped to light-form vision and saw the commander as a figure of brilliant lights, a fortress of strength. The only dimmer spots were around his mouth, but even they she wouldn't have considered a weakness. She'd never seen anyone with lights like that. Obeying his order, she raised her hand and took as much of his strength as she could. It didn't deplete him at all. She broke off and blinked back to normal sight, feeling renewed.

'Better?' he asked.

'Yes.'

The door handle rattled and Diega called from behind the locked door, 'The hedge has halted.'

The commander cursed softly. 'Keep repeating the enchant. I'll be back in a second.' He crossed to the door and pulled it open. He glared at the wall as he left. Raine's face appeared for a second in the place where he'd looked, then sank back into the plaster.

Silho breathed in deeply and sat back down on the crate. She wrapped her arms around herself and lowered her head, repeating the words he'd taught her in her mind, pushing back the visions, building the wall against their force.

Time slipped past silently until the sound of stomping footsteps roused her. Christy Shawe pushed into the bathroom. Without noticing her, he headed straight for the row of urinals and unzipped his pants. Silho shifted uncomfortably on her crate and decided to try to make a silent exit. She stood and crept for the door, but her boots caught on an exposed pipe. She tripped and fell hard on her hands and knees. A blaze of images shot through her mind and she screamed, unable to disconnect, unable to breathe. Big hands, rough and scarred, pulled her over onto her back and she stared up at Shawe's face.

'You right?' he asked her.

She managed a nod.

'If you wanted to take a peek, love, all you needed to do was ask.' The gangster king grinned.

Copernicus and Diega burst into the room with their electrifiers drawn. They looked from Shawe holding up his pants with one hand to Silho lying on the ground, half underneath him.

The commander's eyes darkened. He armed his weapon and brought it up to Shawe's chest.

'She fell.' The gangster stood and backed away from Silho. 'I was helping her up.'

Copernicus set his finger on the trigger.

'Truthspoken!' Shawe said. 'You know me.'

'Yes, I do,' Copernicus replied, his voice as dark as his eyes.

Shawe's face flashed surprise then reddened. He held up a finger. 'No – no way. You know the way that went down. She came to me!'

Diega narrowed her eyes. 'Who came to you?'

'No one.' Copernicus held his aim.

'His girl,' Shawe said. 'And I wasn't the only one. She was all over the place. He knows that.'

'What are you saying?' Diega asked. 'You cheated with his girl-friend?'

'I didn't know she was his *girlfriend.*'

'You said you two were like brothers, but you didn't know she was his girlfriend?' Diega challenged him.

'I was drunk!' The red of Shawe's face deepened. 'And she was there. He sold me out for a woman!'

'He sold you out for a woman?' Diega said. 'How about you be-trayed him first – *for the same woman.* But it's not your fault, right Shawe? You're just the poor defenceless victim.'

'Well, what about you,' Shawe returned. 'I can see how it is. You're supposed to be with that Jude, but you really want this guy.' He nodded to Copernicus. 'You probably hope your boyfriend's dead so you can move right on.'

'You shut it!' Diega yelled at him, her colours blazing the bright-est Silho had seen them.

'Bullseye.' Shawe laughed at her.

The gangster and Diega drew their weapons on each other at the same time, both taking aim, with Silho stuck between them. Raine stepped out of the wall and hissed a Cos enchant. The showerheads beside Shawe and Diega burst on, spraying them with water. Over their swearing, Silho heard the tech device they'd rigged up to run the hedge give out a series of beeps. The commander ducked in and dragged Silho up. He helped her out to the main chamber and went to check the hedge. Silho saw his face was rigidly controlled as al-ways, despite what Shawe had said. The others followed, drenched, still cursing at each other and at Raine.

'It's finished,' the commander told Diega. He disconnected his communicator and dialled into it.

The line hooked and a voice, both tentative and hopeful, answered, 'Hello?'

28

Her name grew ill-fitting. She wore it uncomfortably for a time, if only because the echo of Ismail's voice still lingered on the words, but the change was inevitable. She wasn't the same person anymore. She had no home to return to; she had no future to reach for, so she wandered from one desert outlaw town to another, stealing what she needed to stay alive, and only barely that. If let alone, she left alone, but if attacked, she struck back without mercy. She destroyed. There were men along the way, many faceless no ones. She felt nothing for any of them. It was just biology, a raw and ugly grappling, a momentary escape. As deceptive as any of the quick fixes. It washed through her and out, leaving her emptier than ever. People drifted across her life without making any difference, until in the town of Tinder she met treasure hunter Marshall 'Spartan' McHenry, with his long white hair and ice-blue eyes that saw straight to the heart of everything. He'd made every difference.

Ev'r stepped out of the Murk into real time and faced Eli and his big, hopeful stare.

'It's all gone. There's nothing left but ashes.'

The imp-breed soldier cursed. He turned away from her and peeked around the corner of their hiding place, back down to where his shelter had been. Coils of thick black smoke rose from the spot. It joined the industrial pollution hanging like storm clouds in the sky. The United Regiment had gone overkill, as they always did, reducing the wrecked house and underground bunker to nothing more than a rubble-filled crater. Keets knew that if she had shut the trap-door the shelter most likely would have survived the attack. If Eli was thinking this as well, he didn't say it.

'I hope that bunker didn't take you long to build,' she said, knowing it was a cruel dig.

He blinked and said, resigned, 'No, not long – just my whole life.'

'So what now?' she asked, hating that she had to ask him that question, hating that her weakness, her fear of death, now tied her to this person. The smashed vial had deleted her final hope and she could already feel the beast re-building inside her.

Eli had promised to help her. The hope was as slender as spider's thread, but if anyone could produce a cure for her condition, she knew it would be this one. He had a shimmer of undiscovered greatness about him, somewhere underneath the bumbling, stammering imp exterior.

'Well,' he said. 'All my equipment is gone, all my supplies – pretty much everything I own. We have nowhere to hide. We have nowhere to work, and there are soldiers everywhere hunting us down —'

'I already know the bad news,' Ev'r cut in. 'Now tell me the good.'

'The good news?' Eli said. 'They don't understand how we think.'

'So?'

'So no one will be expecting us to return to Headquarters, but for me it's the only option that makes any sense.'

'How does walking back into the military centre of Scorpia make any sense?' Ev'r demanded.

'Most soldiers will be out in teams looking for us. We can slip in undetected.'

'Not through the Murk, we can't,' Ev'r said. 'Your Headquarters' walls are insulated with a blocker. Believe me, I know.'

'I didn't mean the Murk.'

'Then how?'

'I designed the security system for the newer parts of the building and I know all the hidden pathways in the walls. That's my world. I can get us in,' Eli said.

'It's risky.' Ev'r considered it.

'And suddenly the legendary treasure hunter, Ev'r Keets, is afraid of risk.'

The corners of her mouth twitched upwards at this unexpected jab. 'Fine, let's do it.'

She held out her hand and Eli grasped her arm without a word. He set his jaw, and even though she didn't like him, she had to admire his nerve. Without the proper training, travelling through the Murk was agony. He'd taken the pain without making a sound.

Day had started to give in to night and the buildings threw long shadows over the streets. The lantern lights flickered on, one by one, as they caught the sense of darkness. Ev'r followed Snack-size along the back wall of a building neighbouring the military Headquarters. The imp-breed paused, looking out over an open stretch of trans-flyer parking lot. He darted out to the first craft. She followed and they weaved their way to the back of Headquarters. Eli moved with stealth, scurrying along the wall to a set of stairs leading up into the building. He hid in a damp-smelling space beneath the stairs and Ev'r pushed in beside him, crouching on a multitude of discarded cigarette butts.

They heard the door above them screech open and Eli gasped. Ev'r held her breath. Boots clomped down the stairs in front of them – boots and big canine paws. Eli squeezed further back into the darkness. The soldier and his dog stepped off the last step and headed out into the parking lot. The man paused to light a cigarette. He unclipped the dog's leash and let it free. Another soldier appeared from around the corner and came up to the man. They spoke in sign language as the dog checked the transflyers, sniffing at each one, moving with highly trained confidence. Ev'r watched the animal carefully and saw it pause, pick up their scent and run towards them. She drew her blade, but Eli grabbed her arm and shook his head. The big shaggy beast pushed its head under the stairs and stared at them. It didn't bark or snarl as she had expected, as the guardian dogs usually did. It just stared at them with knowing yellow eyes.

'KC,' Eli whispered. 'Please, buddy. Let me go. We're innocent.'

The dog cocked its head, and Ev'r swore it was considering what he'd said. It gave a little moaning whimper, backed out and ran to check the other craft, carrying on as though it had never seen them. Soon the man finished his conversation, stubbed out his cigarette and called the dog to his side. They went back up the stairs, the animal snuffling at the gaps all the way to the top. Eli exhaled and Ev'r nudged him.

'I'm calling you Dogman from now on,' she said.

'Anything's better than Snack-size,' he replied with a shaky grin.

He led her out from beneath the stairs, along the building, until they reached a grate. Eli took a systems scanner out of his pocket and moved it over the grate, making visible the hidden security bars and a holo-screen keypad. He typed in the override code, then removed the clasps of the grate and pulled it away. He nodded to her and she crawled in, the tunnel scraping against her sides. Eli followed her, replacing the grate behind them.

'Keep going,' he whispered, then pinched her on the backside.

'Do that again and I'll kill you,' she said.

He sniggered in a decidedly impish way.

Eli's office was a wreck – tables upended, machinery shattered and scattered, written word ripped up and discarded. Everything was everywhere and Ev'r felt the slightest tinge of pity for the imp as she watched him sift through the wreckage of his precious things, trying to hide the fact that he was searching for his pet.

'They must have been looking for something,' he said.

He paused over a piece of equipment and lifted it up. A red light flashed on the side of the machine. He activated the message and a holo-screen opened. Words spread across the screen.

'It's the metals report I was waiting on,' he said. 'The scan of Christy Shawe's ring that the commander found in Moris-Isles. Not really sure what it means.'

'Give it here.' Ev'r snatched it from his hands and read through the words. 'It's saying the ring was made of meterodoro, extinct gold, which means it's old – very old – probably from the Black Sun era.'

'The Galleys wouldn't have been around during that time, would they?'

Ev'r snorted. 'No, nowhere close.'

'But the ring belonged to Christy Shawe's father. It had the Galley insignia on it.'

'Obviously it belonged to someone else first and Ironfist stole it and stamped it with his mark. The man was a thief at best.' Ev'r thought about where it could have come from, and the answer came to her. 'The Mazurus Machine.'

'What?' Eli said, the words obviously triggering some kind of meaning for him.

'The Mazurus – it's an ancient telescopic device. When it was shipped from the Galleria Minora to the Galleria Majora after the building restorations about forty or forty-five year-cycles ago, a piece of it was stolen. The focusing core – the apex of its functioning.'

'The ring?' Eli raised an eyebrow.

She nodded. 'I'd say either Ironfist thieved it himself or took it from the person who did.'

'Ev'r, the Mazurus Machine itself was stolen from the Galleria the night we were all attacked. Commander Kane went to investigate.'

Ev'r's mind turned over the information like puzzle pieces to slot into place. 'So the Skreaf took the Mazurus, but they also need the ring to make it work,' she said. 'Explains why they attacked Shawe.'

'But what would the Skreaf want with an outdated telescope?' Eli asked.

She shook her head. 'I don't know.'

'Well, we have to find out. I know a rare written word dealer who could have some information on the Skreaf.' He saw something on the ground and snatched it up.

'It's my communicator,' he said. He turned the machine over to look at a screen on the back of it. 'This is the locator. No one's on the map except for me.'

Ev'r saw his eyes mist over for a moment, but then he controlled himself. He picked up another locator screen and connected it with the communicator from the shelter that he already had clipped to his belt. He adjusted the settings.

'Here.' He handed it to her. 'It's an older prototype, but it still has the same kinds of functions. I've overridden the fingertip recognition, but remember, don't try to dismantle it or it'll explode.'

'Great,' she said, taking the machine. It lit up under her touch and she saw another grey spot appear on the locator lens beside Eli's mark.

'That's you,' he said. 'Now if we get separated we can find each other.' The little imp-breed tapped the screen.

'Planning on ditching me, are you?' Ev'r said darkly.

'Why would I give you the locator if I wanted to ditch you?' Eli asked. 'Really, don't be so paranoid.' He glanced at the holo-screen he'd set up to monitor the hallway and said, 'I think it's time to go.'

Ev'r turned. The screen showed a soldier just down the hall from where they were, opening each door in turn and checking inside the rooms.

'So much for hiding out here,' she said.

'Don't worry,' Eli said, stuffing as much as he could into a bag and slinging it over his shoulder. 'There's somewhere else here we can go where no one will find us. Follow me.'

He dashed out of the room and led her down the corridor in the opposite direction from where the soldier was approaching. Eli cut through a hidden door in the wall. It took them into a stairwell. The imp-breed paused and looked around the shadows of the steps.

'Nelly?' he called softly.

He scanned the area then turned away, heading up the stairs. Ev'r saw a little furry face emerging timidly from a crack in the wall. She snapped down and grabbed up the little creature – Eli's pet otter. She stuffed it into her jacket pocket and zipped it up all but a fraction so it could still breathe, but couldn't squirm. It would be a good bargaining tool when Snack-size turned on her.

Ev'r ran after him up many flights of stairs until he opened another concealed door. He looked left and right and then slipped out, leading her onto a much higher level of the building. The hall was silent, but Keets noticed Eli continuing to click a piece of machinery in one hand, blanking out the security spyers embedded in the walls and ceiling. They headed along the corridor until they came to a set of double doors. Eli pushed them open and they entered into a portrait-lined hall. Ev'r glanced at the painted faces as they passed. She recognised a few and made the connection.

'Oscuri commanders.'

Eli murmured a response without taking much notice. They reached the end of the corridor and Eli knelt down in front of the security holo-screen. He started hacking the system, his forehead creased in concentration. Ev'r looked over the final few paintings hanging on the wall. The last pictured commander, the last Oscuri leader before Kane, was Sammael Sy, and before him, Oren Harvey. The famed commander stared down at Ev'r with hardened, formidable eyes and Ev'r thought, not for the first time, that Harvey would have been a worthy opponent, maybe even a friend if their life-paths had matched up. Harvey had been an oddity, a radical, a revolutionary at heart, fighting the system from the inside. She was the first ever female Oscuri commander and the struggle of that showed in the hard lines of her face. And yet, as one damaged woman looking at another, Ev'r saw she was beautiful – perfect in imperfections. Her daughter was growing to look exactly like her.

'She looks like her,' Ev'r said aloud.

'Who?' Eli asked.

'Silho.'

'Yeah,' he said, distracted. 'Someone's been trying to break in, the system's all jiggered, but I'm almost there. Okay – we're good.'

He stood and the security lasers ran up and down his body. The system's voice said, 'Welcome, Commander Kane.'

'You wish,' Ev'r said. 'I bet you have little fantasies about being him – don't you, Snack-size?'

'I do not,' Eli said, but his face flushed into bright red splotches.

Ev'r laughed at him.

The doors slid open in front of them and they entered Kane's living quarters. Ev'r stared around the walls at all his weapons. Her heartbeats quickened. Some of his pieces were priceless. Her eyes zeroed in on one blade.

'*Solace*,' she breathed. She rushed to the knife, but didn't raise a hand to touch it. 'Oren Harvey's blade. How the hell did a hack like

Kane get *this*?' she asked, her eyes exploring every inch of the famous knife.

'He's not a hack,' Eli said. 'How can you judge him when you don't know him?'

'Easily,' she said, still studying the weapon. 'Is it hot in here?'

'Not as hot as when you dragged me through the desert.' Eli gave her a look.

'What can I say?' Ev'r said.

'Sorry is always a good start.'

She snorted. 'Don't believe in the word.'

Eli went to the large, black desk placed in one corner of the open living space. Ev'r noticed he chose not to sit in the chair, as though it were sacred or something. While his back was turned she took a cloth from her jacket, wrapped it around Harvey's blade and pushed it into her pocket.

Eli activated Kane's system and three holograms flickered up – Silho Brabel in the centre, with Englan Chrisholm and Oren Harvey on either side.

'Looks like the commander was running a face match,' Eli said examining the systems' records.

Ev'r nodded, mildly impressed. 'Kane's a complete gadfly but he's sharp, I'll give him that. She didn't stand a chance.'

'What are you talking about?' Eli looked up.

'Silho Brabel is the daughter of Englan Chrisholm and Oren Harvey.'

Eli laughed. 'No she's not. She's an orphan. Her parents died when she was young.'

'Exactly.'

'But . . .' She could see through his eyes, his mind wrestling with the facts, trying to figure it out. He looked back at the holograms and the matching points that the system was listing.

'This is not good,' he said. 'If the commander finds out . . . I mean, Diega's sister and . . . it's not going to be good for Silho.'

'She thought her father was innocent,' Ev'r said.

'How do you know?'

'I met her in the desert when she was a kid. She was living with an ex-Oscuri Tracker from the generation before Harvey's – a guy by the name of Hammersmith. Burnt-out old Blue-Ten junkie.'

'And Silho told you?' Eli asked, staring at her wide-eyed.

'In a way,' Ev'r said, remembering the moment, how Ismail had read Silho's mind the way he had read all people. He had been highly skilled. He had been many things.

Scratching sounds came from outside the apartment door. Eli erased the pictures and shut down the system. He grabbed a device from his pocket and swept it over the floor. The sounds from outside continued, growing louder and more insistent.

'What are you doing?' Ev'r hissed. 'We have to get out of here.'

'There will be a trapdoor somewhere in this room. I just have to . . . Here it is.' He pointed inside a diagnostic chamber that led off the main area. 'Come in here.'

He ushered her in and shut the door, then activated the holo-screen inside the room and swiftly punched in a series of codes. Ev'r didn't even bother trying to follow the speed of his hands. She stumbled as the floor shifted beneath their feet, gradually sliding down like an elevator.

'The boss's secret laboratory,' Eli whispered.

'If it was a secret, how did you know about it?' she asked.

'I didn't.'

'Then how did you know there was one?'

'Because I know him.' Eli glanced at her. The floor shuddered to a stop and he pushed opened the door. They stepped out into a large underground workshop. Ev'r looked around the space. It was extremely tidy and organised in the way she'd expect the workshop of someone as anal and controlling as Kane to be, but a terrible stench was stifling the air.

Eli rushed over to a cluster of smoking equipment, turning off switches and removing objects. Ev'r came to stand beside him, waving the smoke away from her face.

'He left it running. I guess he thought he would be back sooner,' Eli said sadly.

'What was it?' she asked surveying the burnt-out machinery and vials.

'I think it was his flesh and blood experiment,' Eli said, looking at a holo-screen set up beside the equipment. 'It was something he wanted my help with – producing synthetic flesh and blood that had real properties.'

'Why – was Kane secretly a Midnight Man?' Ev'r smirked.

Eli stared up at her, his eyes stretching wide. 'The man in the desert, the cross-breed, maybe this is for him. Maybe the commander was helping him. He must have seen me with Copernicus. Why else would he have followed us?'

'Because we were about to die and that's what Midnight Men do,' Ev'r said though she thought the other explanation was a possibility, aside from the 'Kane helping someone' part. Kane never did anything unless it would benefit him. She voiced this thought but Eli shook his head vehemently.

'That's not true. You don't know him.'

'I know him better than you think,' she said.

'What do you mean?' Eli asked.

'I knew him when he ran with Christy Shawe. He likes antique weapons – and so do I – so we made an acquaintance.' She lifted her eyebrows and Eli nodded, understanding.

'Then you knew him as a lover, probably as a rival, but not as a friend.'

'How many times do I have to tell you?' Ev'r sat down on a chair beside the workbench. 'There is no such thing as friends.'

'Then what are we?' Eli asked her.

'A means to an ends,' Ev'r replied. 'That's all.'

'We'll see,' Eli said. He touched the holo-screen beside the spoiled experiment and scrolled through the information.

'Look! I was right. There's a hologram of him!' he said.

Ev'r stood up, noticing a growing heaviness in her limbs and discomfort in her jaw. She hid her unease and went to look at the image of the man they'd mistaken as a Death.

'The commander has notes on him,' Eli said. 'His name is Luther Birman. He first appeared to the commander at his father's carnival when they were both still kids.' Eli read directly from the notes. 'Luther is voiceless like all Midnight Men, but like a human-breed he wants to communicate. He has to eat meat, but he cannot kill. He does not want to. He has a conscience and he feels pity. The opposing needs of his body make him constantly ill. He is always hungry and never satisfied. Luther is desperately lonely and unable to connect with anyone – neither Midnight Men nor human-breed will accept him and he lives in constant danger of discovery by the state. Luther has explained in written word that as he draws closer to the metamorphosis, he grows sicker. He needs to feed on the near-dead, but cannot morally do so. He said he would rather die than kill. An alternative to the flesh and blood of the dying must be found to feed him. His time is limited.'

'I know how he feels,' Ev'r said then cursed herself. It sounded so weak.

'Do you have the broken vial?' Eli asked. 'I'll start analysing it now.'

Ev'r took out the cloth with the jagged pieces of glass and un-wrapped them. The imp set them up inside the compound-assessor on a parallel bench.

'I'll set it for deep analysis 7,' he said. 'It'll have to be exact. Any idea what could have been in there – just to give us a jump on it?'

Ev'r shook her head. If the Mocking Witch had produced it, it could be absolutely anything. She watched Eli precisely lining up the glass inside the machine to get the best possible reading. His actions tested her distrust and scepticism.

'You're really going to try to find a cure?' she said.

'I promised you I would.' He said it so simply and she could hear he believed it. 'But the devil will be in the details,' Eli added, still manoeuvring the glass.

No the devil is in me, she thought. 'And if it doesn't work?'

'Then I'll buy you a nice cage.' He gave her a slightly evil grin.

He started the machine and straightened up. He gazed at the vials of blood encased behind glass along one wall of the laboratory.

'There's something I'm missing,' Eli said. 'There was Androt blood at the place where the Skreaf attacked Silho and Jude. One of the crime scenes we attended just before everything happened involved a missing Androt, presumed dead – and while I was in

Moris-Isles I saw a renegade bunch of Androts hanging around. Perhaps the machine-breeds are somehow part of the witch's plan.' He turned to Ev'r and asked, 'Can you go into the system and do a search for case notes 1618? Run it through search code 24 – that'll hedge it, so no one can see us in the system.'

Ev'r walked over to the computer and keyed in the passcode. Holograms and compiled information flashed up on a holo-screen. She flicked through, looking over the scenes of obvious dark magics attacks – bodies where the demons had burst out of their hosts. One of the victims lay in a pool of mixed human-breed and Androt blood.

'Flick over to the next picture,' Eli said, coming to stand beside her.

She did and saw a hologram of four Androts in serving uniforms.

'The man,' Eli pointed to one of the machine-breeds. 'His name is Kry – he's the one who went missing from the second scene. Can you run another search for any updates on his status?'

Ev'r ran the check and while the system was searching, she studied the face of the Androt man. There was something about his grey eyes that didn't sit right with her, the way they didn't smile even though his mouth did – their fixed stony stare.

The computer returned a search summary and Eli said, 'That's very strange.' Kry's status as *missing* had been changed to *dangerous fugitive* and *state traitor*. Ev'r touched a link under his name that took them to a report regarding machine-breeds in the city. It included an order from top military officials that Androts were to be rounded up, without warrants or reason, and taken to a holding facility at Castlereagh for questioning regarding a suspected plot against the king.

'I don't understand,' Eli said. 'It doesn't make sense. Randomly arresting Androts without proper evidence is unlawful. How could this be?'

'The Skreaf are inside the military,' Ev'r said. 'You must be right. They need the Androts for some reason, and in particular they need this guy.' She flicked back to the image of Kry.

'Why?' Eli asked.

Ev'r shrugged. The imp-breed went back to the other bench and began mixing some kind of formula as he thought through what they'd discovered. Ev'r's stomach grumbled, reminding her it was almost three days since they had last eaten anything. She said to Eli, 'Do you think Kane has any food down here?'

'I can't imagine the boss would ever eat where he worked, but I put some things into that bag.' He nodded to the backpack he'd brought from his own laboratory.

Ev'r snatched at the rucksack and dragged out packets of dried chips and a few cans of juice. As she was shoving the food into her mouth, she noticed Eli was deliberately not looking and took that to mean he was also starving hungry, but was being chivalrous and letting her eat everything. It almost made her smile. He was so very naively hopeful and unshakeably pleasant that it was laughable. She'd never met anyone like him before.

She ripped the packets more and spread them out between them.

'Don't be shy,' she said. 'Or there'll be nothing left. Where I grew up you ate fast or not at all.'

'I can do fast,' Eli said and grabbed up a handful in a flash of movement.

'You are fast, I'll give you that,' she said.

'You know, these taste great with tomato sauce,' he said with his mouth full. He went to a set of cupboards above the parallel work-bench and opened them, digging through the contents. 'Hey!' he called. 'Look what I found.'

Eli dragged out Ev'r's own bag. She lunged at it and snatched it away. Ripping open the zips, she checked her equipment. Anything liquid had been removed, but everything else was exactly as she had left it. To her, these objects felt like home. She grabbed her blade and clenched it in her hand. It buzzed and hummed against her skin, and the little otter kicked again inside her pocket, trying to free itself to get to Eli. A strange feeling niggled inside her gut. What was it? She looked at Eli. He had gone back to working on his formula.

'I'm just whipping up a new slowing potion for you,' he said. 'It'll keep the symptoms back until we can come up with a cure.'

The feeling gnawed again and she recognised it – guilt. Its appearance startled her. She hadn't felt guilty in longer than she could remember. The feeling was more unpleasant than pain.

Ev'r unzipped her pocket, grabbed out the otter and shoved it under the bench.

'Hey, Snack-size, I think I saw something moving under the table,' she said.

Eli glanced under and his face stretched into the biggest and most joyful grin she had ever seen. It was a truly disturbingly wide smile.

'Nelly!'

He pounced on his otter and lifted her up. She licked his face with a pink darting tongue. He laughed and hugged her close against him.

'I can't believe it! You found her!' Eli threw an arm around Ev'r before she could stop him. She pulled away, but found part of her wanted to stay in the embrace. It had been so long since anyone had touched her except in violence or lust, she'd forgotten how warm it could feel.

When his excitement settled, Eli put the otter on the bench with a dish of water and some fish treats from his pocket, then finished mixing the elixir. Still grinning, he handed Ev'r a full syringe of it for her to dose herself.

They both jolted as Eli's communicator buzzed. He checked the signal and said, 'Unknown.' He pressed the answer key. 'Hello?'

'Eli.' Ev'r recognised Kane's voice, sharp and cold like a frozen blade.

'Boss!' The imp-breed's eyes welled up with tears. 'Are you alright? Are the others okay? Where are you?'

'We're back in Scorpia and we're all fine except for Jude,' Kane responded. 'He's been captured by the Skreaf. Eli, I'm running a hedge on old tech so we don't have long. Do you have anything on the witches?'

'Yes,' Eli said quickly. 'We believe the ring you asked me to analyse is a missing part of the Mazurus Machine, which the Skreaf stole from the Galleria, but we don't know why they'd want an ancient telescope.'

After a brief pause, Kane said, 'We think they're trying to raise their master, the Morsmalus. We have a prophecy that indicates they need the blood from the line of the warriors who first imprisoned him and a powerful curse. It could be that they think they can use the Mazurus to magnify their curses.'

Ev'r thought it made sense, but kept quiet. She'd rather have her tongue cut out than be heard agreeing with Kane.

'We also thought the Androts might be involved somehow,' Eli said. 'We found a Regiment order to round them all up and take them to the Castlereagh Holding for questioning.'

'The holding?' Copernicus repeated, the significance of the words not clear to Eli.

The communicator gave a warning beep that the hedge was running out.

'And we also discovered that the Androt Kry's status has been changed from missing to fugitive traitor,' Eli added.

'The Skreaf must want him,' Kane said. 'We have to get to him first, but more importantly we have to find where they've taken the Mazurus, which will be where they're planning to raise their master. Eli, there was a survivor from the Galleria attack. He was taken to Scorpia State Hospital. We have to talk to him – see if he knows anything.'

'I'm on it,' Eli said.

'Be careful. He may be under surveillance.'

'Ev'r and I will manage.'

'Keets?' Copernicus' voice darkened and Ev'r smiled. 'Watch her, Eli. Don't turn your back.'

The communicator beeped for the second time.

'Boss, just one other thing,' Eli rushed. 'Your friend Luther appeared to us. He needs help.'

'Help him if you can, but he can't be a priority,' Kane replied, and it sounded as though it affected him to say that. 'The rest of us will track Jude.'

'Where will we meet afterwards?' Eli asked.

'I think it's better to stay separate. If something happens to us, you'll have to carry on.'

273

'Now that I have your frequency, I'll run a hedge and call you back when it's ready,' Eli said. 'Boss, I —'

They heard the third and final warning beep and the communicators automatically disconnected.

Eli's wings drooped and Ev'r studied him. She held the Morsus Ictus behind her back.

'Now that you know your friends are alive, you don't need me to help you,' she said.

'Of course I still need you,' he said. 'And you still need me. Nothing's changed.'

Ev'r didn't reply, but gradually pushed her blade back into its sheath.

'I think we should try to talk to the survivor now.' Eli eyed the compound-assessor processing the witch's cure-all. 'It'll be running for a while yet. I can get the results remotely through my communicator.'

He began moving around the room, replenishing the stores of his weapon belt from Kane's stock. His hand strayed to his neck, feeling for the chain and pendant that he'd lost in the desert.

'Why do you think the Skreaf reacted like they did to the diamond?' he asked Ev'r.

'Skreaf magics are based on symbols,' she responded.

'And the diamond means good and they mean evil,' Eli said.

Ev'r shook her head. 'Any symbol can be used for good or evil depending on who is using it. It's not what the symbol *is* – it's what it can *be* in your hands. They intended harm – *you* intended help and your intention behind that particular symbol was stronger than theirs. It's a fundamental of magics.'

'Do you think,' he asked in a lowered voice, 'that their intention to destroy us will be stronger than our will to survive?'

'I don't know,' Ev'r said truthfully. She had tried to use her scullion skills to look into the future, but all she had seen was an all-consuming darkness. Their paths were unset, their fate unwritten.

She dragged her backpack onto her shoulders and said, 'No rest for the wicked.'

29

Copernicus laid his weapon belt out on the table and checked his guns one by one. Bringing a gun to a battle of dark magics was like bringing a spoon to a nuclear war, but he checked them anyway. It was a necessary distraction. During the last few days he'd felt as though his secrets were a bunch of joined scarves being extracted with an excruciating gradual unravelling out of a magician's hat. Now it was known: he had a heart and it had been broken, he had trusted and been betrayed, had thought he knew someone and been wrong, had dreamed of a future with a girl who wasn't dreaming of him. He wasn't the first person in history and he wouldn't be the last, but it still felt so shameful, perhaps because he had spent so long building up his image as a person who couldn't be hurt, someone not afflicted by the same needs and drives, hopes and fears as everyone else. All the pride and fury of the younger man he'd been, just seventeen year-cycles at the time, had driven him to a revenge he now regretted. In hindsight he saw the girl hadn't been worth that kind of vengeance, but hindsight was one of those ultimately useless things, like sympathy without any offer of help.

He understood why he had fallen for her. She had been the first person – the only person – to tell him that she loved him. She'd been a good liar, or maybe not; maybe he had just wanted to believe someone could love him, even though his mother had left him as a baby and his father had hated him enough to want him dead.

Regardless, he knew he couldn't change the past. All he could do was control his actions in the present, and now, with the cover of darkness, extended by the noctus-renium spreading across the city, their objective was to find Jude, alive or dead and, in doing so, hopefully not just recover a member of the team, but advance their knowledge of the enemy. Copernicus hated flying blindly from moment to moment and, as it stood, all they had on the Skreaf was conjecture and prophecy. They needed some solid facts.

He secured his weapon belt around his waist and turned to the others. After their communication with Eli, he'd ordered everyone to shower off their foul sewerage taint. Then they'd searched the facility and found both clothing and several packets of dry provisions. So now they were slightly less ravenous and significantly cleaner, but the mood was still black. Diega paced the room, arming and disarming her electrifier in a compulsive way. Shawe sat on a crate, swivelling his blade in one hand. Raine drifted in and out of the shadows staring into a hand mirror and Silho stood at one of the windows. The vibration of her thoughts was a steady constant pattern as she repeated the enchant he had taught her over and over in her mind. She sensed his eyes and glanced back at him. He held her stare, needing to know if Shawe's latest tell-all had changed her opinion of him. She met his eyes with the same searching gaze as before. Now he realised he'd been wrong thinking she looked like her mother. Oren Harvey's eyes had been hard and pitiless. Brabel's eyes were far softer. They told him she understood what it was like to make mistakes and she could forgive.

He found himself studying the way her hair curled at the ends, the uptilt of her eyes, the shapes and curves of her body. Uncomfortable, he looked away. He'd seen as soon as they'd met that she had a natural allure about her, something quite different from anyone else he'd ever seen, but it had been just a fact. Now it was a feeling – one he didn't want.

He adjusted his weapon belt. Diega stopped pacing and gave him a dark look. Fens sensed hormonal changes in the opposite sex. Copernicus' discomfort deepened. He cleared his throat and the others looked up at him.

'It's time to move out,' he said. 'As you know our target destination is the Castlereagh Holding, which I believe may be where the Skreaf have Jude. We won't know what security measures we're facing until we get there. I want to emphasise, at this point, the utmost importance of maintaining focus on our objective. Uncontrolled outbursts and irrational reactions will not only jeopardise the mission and our lives, but the survival of our whole world. This is far bigger than any one of us.' He directed his words at Diega and Shawe. He seriously doubted either would pay the slightest attention to it, but at least it was said.

'You know this is probably a trap,' Shawe said. 'Why else would they have your man out in the open where they know you can find him?'

'I've considered it and you're probably right, but we're out of options and time,' Copernicus replied. 'You can stand aside if you want – wait until we have a fixed location on your brother.'

Shawe shook his head. 'I'm in.'

'Final checks, then,' Copernicus said. He took out the rings, bounced them jingling in one hand, then slipped them back inside his jacket. He didn't like going in with them on him, but he couldn't leave them behind either. They were too important. As long as they had the rings, they could stall the Skreaf's plan, which gave them longer to figure out how to destroy them. The others stood watching him.

'Diega, go lead. Have the transflyer ready,' he instructed.

The Fen nodded. She jumped up the ladder and pushed out through the hatch.

Copernicus and the others followed her, moving silently through the pipes back up into the church. Once everyone was out, Copernicus replaced the tile and glanced around at the Catadral. The flickering flames from millions of tiny candles lit the great building. It was empty save for one human-breed. She stood at the front, singing before a statue of the Great God. Her voice rose, echoing, haunting. Copernicus saw Silho staring up at the painted ceiling of the church. She was clenching and unclenching her fists and her heat signature flared around her head and hands as she struggled for control. She was stronger than before, but still far from stable. He had grave doubts that the five minutes of training he'd given her would be enough to get her through going back out into the city, but they had little choice now. Silho's fate and their world's survival were inescapably intertwined. Copernicus could only hope that the power he'd glimpsed in her would surface and overcome. Silho managed to drag her eyes downward. She shook her head once as though to clear her mind then headed towards the front entrance of the Catadral, where Diega had morphed the stolen transflyer *EnvyMe* back to shape and had it hovering, waiting. Copernicus moved to follow her. Before he reached the entrance, Shawe stepped out in front of him, blocking his path. Copernicus tried to sidestep him, but the gangster grabbed his jacket and held tight.

'I want a word,' Shawe said.

'We don't have time.'

'Tough,' he spat. 'I need to say ... We can't change what happened back then and I don't see any point in crying and moaning about it now – but I shouldn't have done what I did with Marley.'

Copernicus felt a knife twist in his back at the mention of her name.

'I regret it,' the gangster continued with difficulty, an apology as uncommon and uncomfortable for Shawe as giving birth to a beer keg.

Copernicus swallowed slowly. Because of him, Shawe's father was dead.

'Your father —' Copernicus began.

'Trutt that old sod,' Shawe cut him off. 'He ran out into open fire and got the end he wanted. I couldn't care less. He didn't give me a damn thing except bruises. But Stacy . . .' He cleared his throat. 'My point is, I can't make up for what I did, and you can't change what you did, but I'm asking you now – for the mates we used to be. If I die, find my brother, just . . . find him.' Shawe's hands slipped off Copernicus' jacket and the two stepped apart. Diega revved the engines of the transflyer and they both hurried towards the craft.

Copernicus paused just before he left the church. He drew his blade and studied the worn ebony pearl handle. All his life he'd been denying what he was – what he could do. When his father had found out that Copernicus had true Illusionist skill, he'd tried to kill him in a jealous rage – but now Silvan Kane was dead *and he can't hurt me anymore.* As soon as the thought entered his mind he felt stupid, having to reassure himself the way he had every night as a child after Shawe had helped him escape. He'd survived the memories by pushing them away, by distracting himself first with his life in the gangs and then with his job, all the while understanding that one day he would have to face up to everything that happened if he ever wanted to really escape. That day was still to come – but not today. Today was just about surviving. If they survived then he would worry about emotional cleansing.

Breathing in deeply, he held his blade to the snake pattern of his arm. The weapon vanished into his skin. They were going into combat blind, and if it was a trap, he wanted to have a few counter-tricks of his own.

Copernicus ran the last few steps to the entrance of the Catadral and climbed into the waiting craft.

'Take us up,' he said to Diega.

She lifted the flyer up to roof level beside the Catadral belltower. The commander sent out his senses. He found a concentration of body-heat signatures he recognised as United Regiment soldiers all along the major skyway between their level and Level 420, where the Castlereagh Holding was located.

'We'll have to take the backroads,' he told the Fen.

She veered the craft to the right and took off.

They were forced to take several more detours to avoid subsequent skyblocks and their path took them to the outskirts of the Gangland. A massive cloud of smoke hung over Greenway and fires still glowed inside many buildings. Shawe said nothing. He just stared down at his fallen kingdom, his home, flames reflecting in the green of his eyes.

Beyond the Greenway breakwall, a storm had gathered over the Matadori. Electricity ripped through heavy black-green clouds. A savage wind whipped acid rain towards the city. The closer the team flew to the holding, the more skyblocks appeared. Soon there were no flight options left and they had to land and go on foot.

Copernicus led the team through the backstreet shadows of Castlereagh until they reached the outer perimeter fence of the prison. They crouched beneath a sign that warned trespassers would be shot on sight. A fine spatter of rain began to fall and a steamy scent rose from the concrete.

Copernicus pulled his hood over his head and studied the holding security. Squadrons of state soldiers patrolled the area between the outer perimeter fence and the inner fence that penned in a cluster of square concrete buildings. The soldiers moved in a crisscross formation to minimise unguarded ground and blind spots. Rain hit the inner fence and sparked away from the electrified razor wire. Guard towers stood on either side of the entrance gate, both with spotlights roving over the prison facility. A military surveillance craft made continual droning fly-bys over the Holding buildings. The security was beyond intense, and that was just the measures they could see. Who knew what traps and tricks the witches had laid? The only way in that Copernicus could see was to distract the soldiers and guards long enough for them to break into the building. He hated the messiness of a smash and grab, but his personal preferences were irrelevant.

Diega squeezed his arm and he glanced at her. SevenM, strapped to Diega's chest, had started to twitch. The robot's red eyes flickered on and off. It meant Jude was alive and near. Copernicus reached his senses towards the buildings and felt an unusual drag of air, as though he were pushing through a net of magics. He glimpsed Jude's heat signature inside the largest of the buildings and pulled back immediately. It was possible the witches had already sensed him. They had to make their move. He turned to Diega.

'Have you ever tried to control a craft without having physical contact with it?' he asked his soldier.

The Fen shook her head. 'Not sure it's possible, but I can try.'

'Then try,' Copernicus said. 'We need that sky patroller brought down into one of the guard towers. And Raine,' he addressed the spectral-breed standing in the wall beside them. 'Can you use your magics to call up the water out of the ground and down from the sprinkler system inside all the buildings? We need as much water as possible to cover us.'

The Wraith gave a silent nod.

Copernicus saw the flyer making another pass over the buildings and said, 'Diega, now.'

The Fen scrunched her eyes shut and gathered her electrosmith strength. Her hair sparked and the lights around the perimeter fence began to blow one after another as the force of her skill intensified. Copernicus and the others watched the military flyer start to struggle. Its tail lagged down and its engines roared to maximum capacity as the pilots fought to keep control. The flyer started to spin, slowly at first, then faster and faster. With the strength of her mind, Diega brought the distressed craft down into the right-hand guard tower, crashing the structure to the ground with an explosion of metal and fire. Panic erupted, alarms screamed, lights flashed and squads of soldiers ran towards the crash site. The spotlight of the left tower remained focused on the debris of its twin.

'Now!' Copernicus said. He grabbed the metal-cutter blade from his belt and slashed a hole in the perimeter fence. The team dashed across the concrete as the ground ruptured all around them and powerful jets of water exploded into the air, concealing their body-heat.

They reached the inner electrified fence. Copernicus cut the razor wire, his hands protected by his electro-proof gloves. They went through one by one, careful not to touch the sharp, zapping sides. The commander led them along the side of the main building, to-wards an entry door where two guards, wearing anti-stunning electro-proof armour, held their posts. Diega fired a sleeper dart into the exposed neck of each guard and they fell instantly, silently. She morphed the locks on the side door and they entered the building.

Water gushed from the overhead sprinkler system and the alarm sirens blared. The building lights had failed, leaving only a blue glow from backup generator globes. As soon as they were inside the building, SevenM's eyes flared. The arachnid robot dragged himself out of the sling and, jumping down, took off. The team followed him, keeping to the sides of the corridor. Soldiers ran past them, distracted, unseeing. SevenM led them through the facility, bringing them to the prison area. Two heavily armed guards stood on either side of the cell block door.

They were huge: three-eyed gargantuan special-ops commandos. Shawe charged towards them. One of the soldiers got a shot off, but it didn't breach the gangster's skin. He hit them front-on and took both of them down, grappling with them on the ground.

Copernicus hurdled over them and smashed through the door into the prison area. He paused. Thousands of Androts – men, women and children – packed the prison cells with standing room only. They gripped the bars and stared at him with fear. He nodded to Diega. She ran to the control panel beside the door and fried the central locking system. All of the barred doors slid open and the Androts poured out. Over the top of the surging masses Copernicus spotted the shimmer of red lights. Jude stepped into sight at the other end of the corridor, with SevenM riding his shoulder. The soldier moved unsteadily, gripping the bars to support himself.

Copernicus cut through the crowd with Diega and Silho right behind him. When he was within reach, he grasped Jude's metal arm and the Ar Antarian jolted. His silver skin was a sickly pale grey and he had a deep cut in his neck, spilling white Androt blood all over his clothes. The wound revealed a faint half-caste Androt barcode reading 939994, which had been hidden by fake skin. The numbers immediately brought to Copernicus' mind the barcode of the Androt Kry, who had been missing from Fortitude Hill. It was 939993. This coding match meant Kry and Jude were half-brothers.

Copernicus felt a ripple of surprise. He'd known from his interrogation of the Vice-Standard that Jude was a half-breed of some kind, and had suspected, since they'd discovered the white blood in Moris-Isles, that he was part Androt. Now he knew for sure why the Vice-Standard had tried to kill Jude. He and the rest of the king's people would never have allowed a machine-breed to take the throne. And it didn't feel coincidental that Jude and Kry were related and that the witches had targeted both of them. It suggested to Copernicus that the Skreaf needed someone from their bloodline, but for what purpose?

Diega hugged onto Jude and Shawe crashed into both of them. He grabbed the injured soldier by the front of his shirt and shouted over the noise of the alarms and escaping Androts, 'Where's my brother?'

Jude just stared at him, his electric blue eyes glowing in the muted light.

Raine appeared in the wall just ahead of them and hissed, 'They're coming. She's here – Bellum.'

As she spoke the words, Copernicus felt the awful prickling sensation of the High Skreaf's presence. Diega snarled and Shawe armed his electrifier. Both of them turned to face the door where they'd entered.

'No time!' Copernicus said, shoving them all towards the back of the prison area. Jude stumbled and Diega grabbed his arm to support him.

They found a door and joined the stream of escapees running through the back corridors towards the building's exit. They soon hit an assemblage of guards blocking their path. The guards opened fire and Androt civilians fell screaming all around them. Shawe ran out in front of the team, electricity glancing off his skin. Diega morphed everything she could see into weapons, which Raine, using Cos magics, turned into projectiles. Those guards who managed to dodge the missiles Silho hit hand to hand. She drew from their body-lights and smashed them backwards. Copernicus ran upside-down along the ceiling, gunning down whoever was left standing. The guards tried to target him, but were disorientated by his position. A shot struck him at waist level, snapping the locking gauge of his weapon belt. It crashed to the ground, but he didn't stop to retrieve it. They finally hit the exit door and burst out of the building.

The fury of the storm had broken over the city. Booms of thunder trembled the ground and explosions of electricity struck rooftops and transflyers in mid-flight, obliterating whatever they touched. A brutal wind drove rain into their faces and gigantic hailstones dropped like ice bombs from the sky. Through the confusion of running people, Copernicus spotted the hole where they had entered. Diega staggered under Jude's weight. Copernicus grabbed the Ar Antarian's other arm and the two of them dragged him towards the fence and through the hole. Shawe and Silho ran right behind them, but before they could pass through, the fence's backup security kicked in, replacing the cut-out section with a virtual fence that would carve them into pieces if they tried to jump through.

'Keep going, we'll find another way!' Shawe yelled. He took off with Silho in the opposite direction.

Copernicus cursed, but they had to keep running as electricity zapped all around them and the spotlight of the guard tower swung their way. He and Diega fled with Jude across the stretch towards the perimeter fence. They crashed through where they had entered and didn't stop. It was unsafe for Diega to launch the transflyer until they were clear of the guard tower's gun range.

They ran through the backstreets, taking corner after corner until one turn brought them to a sudden stop. Two cloaked Skreaf witches stood blocking their path. Diega reeled back and she and Jude toppled onto the road. Copernicus instinctively grabbed at his weapon belt, but it was gone. He snatched the knife he'd hidden in his arm and slashed at the witches while they were still forming their curses. They both fell. One was hurt but started to regenerate straightaway, the other he'd mortally injured. The demon ripped out of the dead host body and discarded the skin like a wet coat.

Copernicus didn't pause to a have a good look at the sinewy demon dripping mucus and blood. He grabbed Jude and Diega and hauled them at a sprint up the side of a nearby building all the way to the roof.

'Diega, launch now!' he yelled over the scream of the storm. The rain had turned to acid and bit at their faces. The Fen dragged the silver coin out of her pocket and morphed it back into its original transflyer form. In a sudden rush of movement, Jude grabbed Copernicus' blade from the commander's hand. He backed away from them and held it up to his own neck.

'It's my blood they need. It's my blood . . . I can't let them get it. This is the only way. I'm sorry,' he said, the tip of the knife drilling into his flesh.

Copernicus detected the vibration of the demons climbing up the side of the building after them. With no time to reason, he struck out and grabbed Jude's arm. He spun the Ar Antarian around and pinned his arms behind his back. Diega snapped restraints around his metal wrists. Copernicus dragged open the transflyer door and threw Jude onto the backseat. SevenM scuttled in with him and Copernicus slammed the door shut. In a momentary pause of storm sound, he heard a scream echoing into the night. He recognised the voice.

'It's Shawe,' he said to Diega. 'I have to find Brabel. Go back to the hide. We'll meet you there. Don't release Jude until I'm back.'

Diega panted, dripping wet, her skin a pale grey.

'Go!' He pushed her.

She scrambled into the flyer and took off, dodging blasts of electricity from the sky. Copernicus ran across the building and leapt from that rooftop onto the next. He headed towards the screams, sensing the net of a trap closing in all around him.

30

Eli stumbled out of the Murk and into a room at the Scorpia State Hospital. He tripped on a bed leg and fell flat on his face on the cold floor. Ev'r's boots thudded down beside his head and she dragged him up.

'You have serious problems, don't you?' she said unhelpfully.

'Yes, and I'm not alone.'

A shadow appeared at the frosted glass panel in the door and they both dropped behind the bed. The door handle rattled and the hinges creaked open. Eli peeped around the metal bedframe and saw two uniformed guardians standing in the doorway. Their faces were vaguely familiar, as though he might have seen them in the corridors once or twice. They scanned the room, waited there a moment then backed out, closing the door behind them. Eli sighed in relief. The sheets near his nose smelt of bleach and were coarse to the touch. Machines peeped and bleeped above them, the robotic monitoring systems positioned in a circle around the bed like concerned relatives.

Eli stood up and gazed at the survivor of the Galleria attack. He felt a jolt of surprise to see a young Androt man lying still, his eyes restfully closed. A black stain, identical to the darkness on the dead Galleys' faces, spread over the pale skin of the Androt's cheek and down to his neck, smudging the tips of his barcode numbers – 939963. Newly formed grey scars covered his chest and arms. A more serious wound on his shoulder was still healing, tendons, muscles, flesh and skin re-knitting as they watched.

'He was the only one of thirteen victims to survive,' Eli whispered.

'Not surprising,' Ev'r said. 'He's a machine-breed. They have a high resistance to magics.'

'I didn't know that.' Eli watched the slow rise and fall of the man's chest.

'Not many people do,' Ev'r said. 'See that mark?' She traced the black on the man's face. 'That's a death-curse. He was hit close, too. These other marks are torture scars.'

'How do you know?' Eli asked.

She glanced at him then lifted up the front of her shirt. The same type of thin straight scars crisscrossed her stomach and sides to her back. 'You learn dark magics through what witches call *corporal application*.' She dropped her shirt. 'Basically they torture you until you pick up enough to fight back. They must have needed information from this guy – otherwise they wouldn't have wasted the energy.'

Ev'r's eyes darted to the door as more shadows appeared and passed. 'We may as well go,' she said. 'He's fried.'

Eli touched a hand to the man's arm, the skin cold beneath his fingertips. 'Keep well,' he said.

The Androt's eyelids flipped open. He stared at them, terrified. 'Please don't leave me,' he whispered. 'The witches are here. They're just outside the door.'

Eli helped the Androt man, Lao, sit up in the bed.

'I've been too scared to show anyone I'm conscious,' Lao said. 'The soldiers guarding me are some of the witches who attacked the Galleria.'

'How do you know if you haven't opened your eyes?' Ev'r asked.

'Beak6.' He pointed to the little parrot robot sitting on the side table. She appeared to be deactivated, but when he named her, she blinked and red lights fired up behind her eyes. The lights reminded Eli of SevenM. 'I can see with her eyes.'

'What happened at the Galleria?' Ev'r asked.

The man gulped. He shivered as he remembered. 'They came in. They . . . they were asking me things . . .'

'What were they asking you?'

The Androt bit his lip.

'Do you want our help or not?' Ev'r demanded.

'They wanted information about someone.'

'Who?' Ev'r asked.

'I can't say.'

'Let's go,' Ev'r said to Eli. 'We're wasting our time.'

'Wait!' Lao said. 'They wanted to know about Kry.'

'Kry,' Eli repeated, his nerves jumping. 'Kry – who works at Fortitude Hill?'

'Yes,' Lao whispered. 'Did they find him? I didn't give them anything. I swear I didn't. Is he . . . okay?'

'We don't know. We never found a body, and the military is now reporting him as a threat.'

'Then I have to find him. I have to warn him,' Lao said.

'What did they want from him?' Ev'r asked.

'I don't know. They were chanting – something about blood.'

Ev'r gripped the bed frame and almost doubled over. Eli saw that the black on her fingertips had started to spread again along her fingers and hands.

'Time to go,' he said to Lao. 'Do you need any of this equipment?'

'Just my medicine.' He pointed to the bottle of pills on the bedside table. 'It's for my allergy.'

Eli grabbed the bottle and noticed the medication was the same one that he took for his allergies, except his tooth refill was in liquid form. A thought sprouted in his mind.

'You wouldn't be a cross-breed by any chance, would you?' he asked.

The man's eyebrows lifted. It wasn't a question that was usually asked so directly, if at all. 'Yes I am, actually,' he replied. 'My father was part human-breed.' He pulled back the covers and manoeuvred himself out of bed. Beak6 flapped to his shoulder.

Eli turned to Ev'r. 'I think I know how to help Luther.'

'Who?' Ev'r asked. She clutched at a pain in her stomach.

'The Midnight Man cross-breed. I don't think it's just the metamorphosis that's making him sick; I think it might also be an allergy that's stopping him taking in nutrients. Allergies appear to be common for mixed people. I know several others in the same situation. I hadn't made the link before, but maybe Luther's allergies are just flaring up now that he's reaching maturity, like a delayed effect because of the way a Midnight Man's body changes at the time of metamorphosis. Maybe if I treated his allergy, he wouldn't need to eat the near-dead to change and survive. Maybe he just needs to —'

The door to the room swung open and a nurse stood in the doorway, holding a tray of medication. She looked from Eli to Ev'r to Lao, then dropped the tray with a clattering crash and screamed. Eli screamed as well. Ev'r grabbed him and the Androt by the wrist and sank them into the Murk.

Eli plummeted through the uncertain space behind space. He could hear Lao yelling in agony. Eli found it didn't hurt him as much as it had the first time, but it was still painful and disorientating. It was like one of his recurring nightmares where he was running away from something bad, but could never quite focus his eyes.

Colour suddenly ripped into the grey and the three of them sprawled out onto the concrete in the middle of the largest shopping level in the city. It was packed with people enjoying the all-night sales in honour of the noctus-renium. Shoppers cried out and scattered in all directions. Some froze to stare at them. A pleasant upbeat tune jingled in the background. Eli scrambled to his feet and pushed the Androt and Ev'r into a side street. He checked Nelly in his pocket and felt that she was alright – sleeping soundly.

'Quick.' Ev'r grimaced and clutched at her stomach. 'The Skreaf were in the Murk. They're onto us.'

Lao moaned in fear and held his injured arm.

Not far from where they had dropped out, the two guardians from the hospital appeared from around a corner and began scoping for them with body-form sensors.

'You two keep going. I'll try to lead them away,' Eli said.

'No,' Ev'r argued. 'We stay together.'

'You're both sick!' Eli said. 'I can fly. Just go. I'll find you!'

Eli darted out from the side street and the military sensors instantly locked onto him. The guardians spun in his direction. Eli ripped off his shirt, buzzed his wings and took off. He kept to the packed shopping strip, jumping off people's shoulders and scrambling through the crowd, using them as a shield. The guardians struggled to keep up, nowhere near as fast as he was and unable to discharge their electrifiers or to use their dark-words with so many witnesses around. He raced past the centre of the open mall, past a stage of performing dancers. Someone yelled behind him and the sound was answered by more shouting and frightened screams.

Eli glanced over his shoulder. Gangsters from the Crook'd Town Pride had spread out behind him, and all around them shoppers were fleeing as fast as they could go. The Pride's feline companions roared and flexed dagger claws. The guardians chasing Eli were forced to stop and question the gangsters. Eli, sure that Ev'r and Lao would have had time to disappear, took the opportunity to vanish as well. Whirring his wings, he flew upwards, above the lamp lights lining the strip and further into the sky. He flew parallel with an enormous, many-storeyed transflyer parking centre. He ducked through onto one of the higher levels and dropped down behind the wheels of the closest craft. As he was pulling his shirt back on, he heard approaching voices. Peering from his hiding place towards the sound, he saw that two human-breed women, laden with shopping bags of all colours, were heading to their craft. Their voices echoed in the quiet of the parking lot and he picked up on their conversation.

'They just came and dragged him out of the house. They didn't even explain why. They just said he was being detained by the state. Camilla was devastated. That Androt had been with them for years. I think it's wrong.'

The other woman, with the long neck and pursed lips of a goose-blood human-breed, cast a nervous look around the parking lot and said, 'Let's talk more inside the craft.'

They disappeared behind a row of transflyers and left Eli to consider their words. They supported his theory that the witches were using the United Regiment to hunt Kry. Eli realised that in locating Kry's cousin, they now actually had a chance of finding Kry himself before the Skreaf did.

He grabbed his communicator and checked Ev'r's location. She was moving through a lower level of the city. The machine buzzed and displayed a message that the results from the elements analysis had been sent from the laboratory's system. He glanced around for witnesses then opened the communicator's holo-screen to read the outcomes. The ingredients of the potion that Ev'r needed flashed up. Eli stared, reading through the list with growing disbelief. All the ingredients were either impossible to come by without spending a lifetime searching for them, or were completely extinct. There was zero chance he would be able to re-create the potion in time to save Ev'r.

His communicator buzzed with an incoming call and he saw it was the woman herself. He breathed in deeply and answered, 'Ev'r.'

'You clear?' she asked.

'Yes – are you?' he replied.

'Far as I can tell.' Her voice gasped at the end of the sentence and Eli winced. The slowing elixir he had given her wasn't having as much effect as last time.

'Where are you going?' he asked her.

'The Androt says he knows a place to lie low. He thinks Kry will be there.'

'Perfect,' Eli said. 'Ev'r, you have to convince Kry to come with us so that we can protect him.'

She grunted agreement. 'Did you get the lab results?'

'Yes,' Eli said and cringed. He had been trying to lie and say no.

'And?'

'It's all good, I'll be able to get the potion together,' he said in a falsely positive tone.

'Then it better be soon because . . .' She didn't finish and she didn't need to – the growl behind her voice was enough. Eli gulped.

'Keep your communicator with you. I'll find you,' he said.

She disconnected.

'What am I going to do?' Eli whispered, holding his head in one hand. He had to find an alternative cure for Ev'r, but before that he needed to find out where the Skreaf had taken the Mazurus Machine. He stretched out his aching legs, his closed eyes prickling with tiredness. The ground shuddered underneath him as another mini-quake shook the city. It spurred him to keep moving. He dragged himself up and spoke to Nelly, who was peeping out of his pocket.

'Plan B – on all accounts.'

She chattered nervously and Eli said, 'I know. I wish we didn't have to either, but we're running out of options.'

He gave her some fish treats to calm her then clipped his communicator back in place and stepped out from behind the transflyer.

Caesar K-Ruz crouched on the railing of the parking level just ahead of him. His nocturnal eyes glowed in the darkness and his shadow beast stalked along the wall beside him.

'Where is he?' Caesar demanded.

'Who?' Eli squeaked.

'Shawe.'

'I don't know.' Eli shook his head.

'He's with Kane. Have you had any contact?'

'No – I mean *yes*, but we didn't discuss locations or Shawe.'

'Call your boss and get a location – now,' Caesar ordered.

'I can't. I have to wait for the hedge we're running between our systems to complete, otherwise the Regiment will pick up on the signal.'

'How long?'

'I'm not sure – there's been some damage to the machines and a lot of interference. They're definitely targeting the commander's lines. It could be some time —'

'Then we'll wait – together,' Caesar said, settling down on the railing.

'I can't wait,' Eli said, panic stirring nerves in his wings. 'The Skreaf are taking over. I have to keep working.'

'You'll wait,' the Pride boss responded. It wasn't a request.

Eli stepped from one foot to the other, gnawing on his lip with frustration. Obviously if his main focus was on killing Shawe and taking over the Gangland, Caesar hadn't comprehended exactly how dire their situation was and how much worse it could become.

'Instead of killing Shawe, can't you just banish him like the olden-day kings used to – just declare him gone and take over his rule?' Eli suggested.

'No. Shawe must die. It is Gangland law.'

'So change the law.' Eli's voice rose slightly, his urgency overcoming his fear of the gangster.

'Who am I to do that?' Caesar said.

'The warlord Damesai said, *rules are set by the powerful and re-written by the great*,' Eli said, thinking quickly. 'I don't know whether you realise this, but you are great. Everyone looks up to you, even your rivals, and it's not because of your religious adherence to the law – it's because you're different. If I were you, I would make changes. I would let Shawe live just as an example of what I could do.'

'Let him live?' Caesar growled. 'Impossible.'

'Is it?' Eli said. 'Why? Did you ever think that maybe even the gangsters are tired of the bloodshed? Why do you think everyone wants to unite?'

The glow of Caesar's eyes flared. 'How do you know that?'

'I know things like you know things.' Eli deflected the question. 'And something else I know is that our whole existence is about to crumble if we don't stop the Skreaf. They're going to raise their master, the Morsmalus.'

Caesar took this in. 'How?'

'I'm not exactly sure, but they have a machine they stole from the Galleria and we know they're hunting for an Androt named Kry.'

'Kry,' Caesar's voice registered recognition.

'You know him?' Eli said.

'He's the leader of the Androt uprising.'

'The Androts are uprising?' Eli asked with no small degree of shock.

'Kry is a maniac,' Caesar said.

'Well, Ev'r Keets has gone to talk to him now. Hopefully she will be able to reason in a way he understands.'

'The blind leading the blind,' Caesar snarled. 'You said this creature Morsmalus could destroy us?'

'To put it nicely.'

Caesar studied Eli for a long moment. His expression remained cool, but a storm raged in his eyes.

'Then I'll get Kry,' the gangster finally offered. 'You find Shawe – and I haven't forgotten our deal.'

Caesar stood up and leapt from the parking level. Eli ran to the edge and saw the gangster boss landing comfortably on an awning far below. He jumped down onto the street and vanished from sight.

'Time to fly,' Eli whispered to Nelly. He vaulted over the railing and took off into the dark sky.

*****

The beaded curtains swish-clink-clanked as Eli pushed them aside and entered the basement shop. He blinked through the haze of musk incense mingling with the sweet smoke of illegal fungi. Particles of matter danced beneath the faded globes hanging from the low ceiling. He moved into the entrance of the shop, laid out like a waiting room with a few tattered chairs along both walls. The wooden floor was scratched and scuffed, the polish long gone.

He stopped at the front desk and knocked on it. A reply sounded somewhere past the black sheet hanging behind the desk, obscuring the innards of the shop. Tapping footsteps made their way towards him, gradually growing louder until a face pushed out of the blackness. Purple eyes fixed on Eli and his old Greer friend, Swifty, gave a clearly wicked, sharp-toothed grin.

'Please tell me that's not how I look when I smile,' Eli said.

'Eli!' Swifty rushed out and smothered him in hugs and kisses.

'Okay, okay.' Eli untangled himself.

'Haven't seen you in ages, man,' Swifty said, speaking in Impish. His eyes roamed over Eli's jacket, sizing up the pockets. 'What? You're too good for your peoples now you're a big-shot military soldier?'

'You heard, then, did you?' Eli said, realising the United Regiment must have released his profile to the media to aid in hunting him. 'How much does silence cost?'

'*Lai Lai*, Eli man . . . you think so little of me. I know I'm not tall but I'm not that small, you catch me?'

'How much?' Eli repeated, patiently. Being imp-breed, especially half-Greer, half-Glee, made him well aware of the general weaknesses of his race. They were addicted to causing havoc and couldn't keep a secret to save themselves, but he hoped money would be enough at least to buy him some time.

Swifty stroked the little purple beard on his chin and said, 'What's coin between brothers, Eli?'

'Swift – how much?'

The Greer rolled his eyes. 'You're no fun anymore. Must be the Glee in you.'

'Low blow,' Eli said. He pulled a fat coin bag from his pocket and handed it to his friend. 'That's all I have. Frisk me if you doubt it, but trust me on this – the only result you'll get from calling the Regiment is a smashed-up shop and jail time for all the contraband you've got here. They won't give you a cent of any reward. You know I'm right.'

Swift took the coin bag with light-speed stealth and shoved it into his pocket. 'Speaking of contraband . . .' He flashed his grin.

'No,' Eli said.

'I have Blue-Ten, I have Estle Thistle, I have red, orange *and* pink fungi.' He raised his eyebrows. 'We could set up a few rounds – just like old times.'

'I just gave you all my coin,' Eli said. 'How do you think I'm going to pay for it?'

Swifty considered it for a moment. He took a sovereign out of his pocket and gave it to Eli. He said with a grin, 'Now you can pay.'

Eli slapped the coin back into Swifty's hand and said, 'No. I want to see Mr Bellbeater.'

'Books?' Swifty yawned. 'You bore the life out of me, man, you're no fun at all. Fine though, come through.'

He led Eli behind the counter and through the black sheet. Swifty made a few gestures in the darkness and a chain appeared in the air. He dragged down on it and the dusty floor peeled back to expose a set of stairs.

'All yours, man,' Swifty said.

Eli headed down the steps, grasping the rickety rail and blinking his eyes to adjust to the darkness. He reached the last step and stopped, breathing in the dry, musty scent of old papers. The room was crowded with bookcases stuffed to bursting with written word of all shapes and sizes. Eli spotted an ancient, crooked-back Greer, Mr Beatlebee Bellbeater, sitting at the back of the room at a low desk reading from a book by candlelight.

As he stepped down off the last step Mr Bellbeater spoke.

'Eli Anklebiter,' the old man said without turning, his voice very high and quavering. 'Enter.'

Eli walked over to the man and stood beside him. The Greer looked up under bushy purple eyebrows, his glasses perched on the end of an extremely crooked nose.

'How is your gran'ma?' Mr Bellbeater started the conversation the same way he always did.

'Fine,' Eli gave the standard answer.

'You never visit her – how do you know she's fine?'

'I don't visit her because she always tells me what's wrong with me.'

'What's wrong with that?' Beatlebee squeaked. 'She's your gran'ma – it's her right to point out all your many faults. You should be grateful. Your gran'ma is a fine woman – a very fine woman if you know what I mean.' The old imp winked and gave a gap-toothed grin.

'Ewww.' Eli recoiled at the horrendous images of Mr Bellbeater and his gran'ma that popped into his head.

'Did you kill those soldiers, Eli?' Bellbeater's face snapped instantly to seriousness.

'No,' he said.

'Pity,' the old Greer turned back to his book, 'that you have to lie to me. Must be the Glee in you.'

Eli sighed. 'They weren't really soldiers. They were Skreaf.'

Mr Bellbeater raised his eyes, searching for a lie in Eli's face, but finding only truth. 'Well then, the apocalypse is on us,' he said matter-of-factly. 'And there is no point trying to fight it. It is already written in the future history, the present past. It has and will happen – no matter what you do.'

'I don't happen to share that belief,' Eli said.

'No you don't. I hear you've abandoned all your beliefs.'

'No, just the ones fabricated by people.'

'Their faith led them, boy.'

'And my faith leads me!' Eli yelled, reaching a point of sheer exhaustion. 'Why don't you just help me? Can't you see I'm trying to save our world?'

The ancient Greer stared at him for several moments, eyes wide behind his thick glasses. Then, with effort and grunting, he slid off his chair and hobbled, leaning on a knobbly walking stick, to one of the bookcases. He tapped the shelf with the stick and a book shot out. With incredible agility, he leapt up and snatched the book down. He blew a storm of dust off its front cover and handed it to Eli. Eli read the title: '*Bellbeater's Complete Encyclopaedia of Dark Magical Sects* by Beatlebee Bellbeater.' He glanced at the old man. 'You wrote this?'

'Of course I wrote it,' he snapped. 'You didn't think I got this old doing nothing, did you?' The ancient Greer put his hand over the cover of the book and said, 'Knowledge is power, Eli.'

'Only if you use it,' Eli replied. He slipped the book into his jacket. 'And I need something on the Ravien.'

Bellbeater's eyebrows shot up. 'What kind of something?'

'Anything – information about the way they live, what's in their poison . . . how to stop someone from turning after being bitten.'

Mr Bellbeater shook his head. 'Once bitten, nothing stops a person from turning.'

'Do you have any information or not?' Eli asked.

The old Greer hobbled back to the shelves. muttering to himself. He produced another book and handed it over.

'That's everything I have on them, which isn't much.'

'I have no money to pay for these,' Eli admitted.

'And you have no time either – the soldiers are above us,' Bellbeater said, as dust rained down on their heads.

'Trutt!' Eli cursed. 'Swifty ratted. What's wrong with you people?'

'Go down the corridor into the bathroom and climb through the window, take the fire escape up to the street,' Bellbeater instructed.

'Come with me. They're not soldiers, they're Skreaf. They'll kill you!'

'I can take care of myself, thank you very much,' the old Greer said indignantly. 'Unlike my useless, brain-dead great-great-great grandson, who I can hear clearly needs my help.' Mr Bellbeater's big ears twitched. He shuffled for the stairs, muttering.

Eli took off in the opposite direction. He ran down the corridor and barged through the door into the bathroom. There he wrenched up the window frame, stubborn with dampness and age, and dragged himself through onto the subterranean fire escape. He clutched the books to his chest with one arm and used the other to climb up the rails. They took him up through a hole in the side street beside the building. Eli ducked low in the shadows as United Regiment soldiers swarmed the front of the shop. How many of them were Skreaf he couldn't tell – maybe even all of them. It was a terrible thought. He took off running, unsure if the Skreaf were behind him or if his imagination was supplying the sound of pounding boots. Whirring his wings, he lifted up into the air, flying until he recognised the open space and grand mansions of Elio D'An Square, home of the Galleria Majora. He dived down above the giant domed building and landed on one of the ledges, where he squatted down beside a gargoyle hoping to blend in. The lantern lights surrounding the square cut eerie shapes in the darkness. Eli held his breath and surveyed the square and the air for any twitch of movement, but didn't see anything. Boots marching in unison sounded directly beneath him and he gazed down at the entrance landing of the Galleria. A group of red-cloaked enforcers were patrolling the area. He shrank further into the shadows and whispered a prayer not to be seen or smelt. His stomach rumbled deeply and he grabbed at his skin and pinched hard. Now was not the right time to get gas. When the tapping boots headed in the opposite direction and faded Eli released a shaky breath.

He lowered the heavy books onto the ledge and Bellbeater's encyclopaedia of dark magics flipped open by itself to the chapter on the Skreaf demons. Eli gulped and stared, nerves prickling along his skin. Nelly slipped out of his pocket and scurried up his arm. She peeked over his shoulder and chattered in his ear. He forced himself to lean forward and read.

The Skreaf is the most ancient and unarguably dangerous of the dark sects. Members of the sect allow their bodies to be inhabited by Skreaf demons, who gain control over their actions and thoughts. The Skreaf pay homage to a mythical figure, the Morsmalus, who was imprisoned in the Envirious Realm by a band of brother warriors – believed to be *machine-breeds* . . .

Eli felt a murmur of surprise inside him. He re-read the line to make sure he was seeing it correctly, then continued.

Their resistance to the dark magics of the Skreaf gave them victory over the demon-god. Though the Morsmalus had been banished, his followers continued to haunt Aquais, trying many times to resurrect their leader. In order to rid the land of the ever-living demons, the machine-breed warriors summoned from their sister realm, Omar Montanya, Skreaf hunters known as Omarians. Only the male of this race was equipped with skill to fight the Skreaf, and the demons' one weakness was their secret alone. Though the Omarian numbers were few, their skills were powerful and they spread out into the land, culling the Skreaf.

Eli flipped the page and stared at the picture of a great dragon exhaling a blast of fire.

But even they could not destroy all the demons, who will never rest until they have succeeded in freeing their banished god from his prison. It is believed that portholes can be forged into the gateway land that lies between our realm and the Envirious Realm where the Morsmalus is imprisoned. This gateway land is known as Woulghast. It is a miscreation fallen from the afterlife, a grey hell-land where pain was first discovered and let loose on mortality like a disease without a cure. It is a place of fears where nightmares come to life.

Memories filled Eli's mind of childhood horror stories of a place with blacked-out canvases, gateways into lands of nothing, where people could enter but never escape. He shivered and continued reading.

> To pass through the gateway land one must survive a number of challenges. Firstly, the Carnival of the Damned and then the three chambers of the sorcerer Megotenor – the chamber of dead dreams, the chamber of hate and the chamber of lust. If one makes it through these tests alive they will find the sealed entrance to the Envirious Realm.

The book snapped shut. Eli tried to prise it open again, and when he finally succeeded, the pages were blank. He lifted the book up to his face. The encyclopaedia squirmed, stretched and morphed into a crow. The black bird pecked him on the nose, flapped free and flew away. Nelly scolded it in her squeaky chattering voice from her place on his shoulder. Eli held his nose and stared at the vanishing shadow.

'Well, now we know where they are – but not how to get there,' he said. He had never heard of any portholes leading out of their realm, nor of how to make them.

He grabbed the other book, fearing it might grow feet and scurry away as well. When it didn't flip open by itself, he searched the index for mention of the Ravien and found the page number. There was little more than a paragraph on the strange race, the information possible to be summarised in one sentence. Their poison was derived from the plants they ingested, and was stored in glands in their mouths, and if a person from another race was bitten by a Ravien, there was no hope whatsoever in the entire universe of preventing that person from changing into a Ravien. Eli chose to pay attention only to the first part of the sentence: *plant-derived.*

'If it's plant-derived, then maybe it can be plant-cured,' he said to Nelly. She sat up on her back legs and tilted her head to one side. 'What is the strongest medicinal plant in Aquais? The Venus Lily, right? So we need to find a Lily.' The only problem with that was there was only one place the Lily was believed to grow – Venus, the lowest level of the city, the place Commander Oren Harvey had entered and returned from so traumatised that she was unable to speak of it for all her living days.

'There's no other option,' Eli said as Nelly eyed him accusingly. 'We promised we'd help Ev'r. We can't leave her to die – or worse, change.'

He knew he had to concentrate on their fight against the Skreaf, but his heart told him that Ev'r was an important part of that fight. The commander had always said he needed to believe in himself. Eli checked Ev'r's location on his communicator. The location spot was holding stable. Hopefully she was managing to reason with Kry. The hedge he was running in-system between his and the commander's communicators was still processing, so he decided to leave a message in the lines that the commander could play back when the hedge had cleared. It might be his only chance. Shaking the idea away, he entered the number Copernicus had used earlier and left a detailed message of everything that had happened and everything he had read. Then he said goodbye and disconnected. Eli found himself shaking, with tears streaming down his face. Nelly burrowed back into his pocket and he sniffed.

'Keep it together,' he whispered to himself. He just felt so tired. His arms and legs were lead. His eyes closed for a moment. Something tapped his shoulder and he gasped and toppled off the ledge. He buzzed his wings and spun in the air. The Midnight Man cross-breed, Luther, stood on the ledge, his face even more hollow and emaciated than before. He looked fearsome, but he was wringing his hands and Eli saw how scared the strange man really was. Eli fluttered towards him. Luther shuddered and vanished into shadows.

'Luther, I know you're Copernicus' friend. I want to help you,' Eli whispered into the darkness, unsure if he was still there and listening. 'I think I know how, but first I have to go to Venus. Then I'll be back. I promise. Find me and I'll help you.' He wasn't sure if Luther had heard, but he couldn't stop to search for him. With time running out all around him, he had to stick with his plan – hot-wire a transflyer, point it straight down, and fly into an unknown hell.

Eli leapt off the building and took off, not sensing the shadow shape of the Midnight Man following him.

31

An earthquake tremor dredged Silho from deep unconsciousness. She found herself splayed on her stomach in the middle of a muddy construction site. Just the skeleton of the building stood, providing no shelter from the storm. Rain pelted her back and each flash of electricity was blinding. With effort, she lifted her head. Her dripping hair hung in her eyes and she tasted the sour metal of blood streaming down her face from a cut in her forehead. She re-membered running through the building site with Shawe. She saw herself tripping. Silho's breath caught in her throat as a tortured scream strangled the air close to where she lay. Her skin prickled and she struggled to her feet, staggering. The scream came again and she drew her electrifier and moved towards the sound, picking her way over scattered offcuts and forgotten tools. At the front of the building site she hid behind a pile of stone bricks.

Ahead of her, Shawe lay slumped against a partially constructed wall. The High Skreaf, Bellum, stood over him, torturing him with curses that convulsed his whole body. Silho witnessed Shawe, with his eyes squeezed shut, drag one of the rings out of his pocket and give it to the witch. Bellum clenched the metal band in her fist. Her lips twitched into a smug smile and the demon leered through her eyes. She began drawing the shadows for a death-curse to finish Shawe. Silho repeated the Illusionist enchant and all the sounds inside her mind and outside around her silenced, except for the rhythmic thud of her heart. She stepped out from her hiding place and called to the witch.

'Bellum.'

The High Witch turned. She regarded Silho with her cadaverous stare.

'Well, my dear, it seems I underestimated your father,' she finally said, her voice sly and whispery. 'He led me to believe your mother died as you were born. It was wise of him to keep Oren Harvey a secret – very wise – and yet . . .' Bellum stepped closer, 'it didn't save them, did it?'

'No, but it saved me,' Silho said. 'Stay back!'

Bellum took another step forward, and Silho could smell the rank stench of her rotting scent and see the demon moving behind her skin. She avoided the Skreaf's horrible gaze.

'Your father . . . he cried a lot in that cell before his execution,' Bellum continued.

'My father was strong. He never cried.'

'He did when I told him what we were going to do to you if he didn't cooperate with us.' Bloodlust gleamed in the witch's eyes.

'He would never have helped you,' Silho said.

'All of our planning would have been for nothing if it hadn't been for your father,' Bellum told her. 'From his prison cell, he painted a porthole into the realm where our master awaits his freedom. When he had finished, I told him you were already dead. He knew it was true. The look on his face . . . I'll never forget it.' The witch gave a cruel grin and Silho struggled to contain her hatred. It filled every space of her body and mind and made it impossible for her even to remember the words of the enchant. She turned the full force of the hatred on Bellum.

'My father showed you what he wanted you to see so that I could escape. You didn't kill him, he sacrificed himself so that I could live, so that I could stop you.'

Bellum's face twitched and the demon growled through her mouth, 'You talk too much, just like your father.'

'And I can kill you, just like he could,' Silho said.

'Let's see it then!' Bellum screamed, her hair twisting into snakes.

Silho snarled and blinked into light-form. She raised her gloved hands and power surged from Bellum's body-lights into her. Silho trembled from the build-up. Her hands burned then ignited into flames, forcing her to cut the connection. As she did, she saw a flash in her mind of her Pyron mother walking unharmed through the fire in the detention centre the night she'd saved her. Silho shook off her melting gloves and Bellum shrieked a curse and launched herself forward. She hit Silho across the face and grabbed her by the neck, lifting her into the air. Silho coughed up a spray of sparks and gasped. She kneed the witch hard, but Bellum's grip only tightened. The witch summoned her terrible power and a death-curse formed on her maggot lips. Silho's body froze rigid. Behind Bellum, the red-eyed he-Wraith, Amateus, appeared in a flash of electricity. He used a Cos enchant to lift a discarded steel post and ram it into Bellum's back. The Skreaf dropped Silho and turned on him. She hit him with the death-curse meant for Silho. It threw him backward and out of sight and his terrible, agonised scream faded to silence.

'Not this time,' Bellum croaked, turning back to Silho. 'No one can save you now.'

Copernicus lunged out of the shadows. He stabbed a blade through the witch's chest and spat venom into her eyes. She screeched horribly, ripping at her face. While she was reeling, Shawe stepped up with a plank of wood. He swung it like a club and sent her flying. The darkness formed a net to catch her. Silho's breath shunted out as the commander grabbed her up and threw her over his shoulder. She clutched his shirt as he sprinted through the dark streets. Shawe crashed behind them and Bellum walked the wind right at their heels, her cloak whipping around her. Curses ricocheted off buildings, crumbling their bricks, bringing them crashing to the ground. Copernicus swerved to avoid the falling giants. The dying memories of the collapsing walls yelled to Silho. She fought against the ravenous desire to reach out to them, trying to take back control of her mind. Copernicus halted suddenly and dropped down behind a parked transflyer. He dragged Shawe in beside them and snarled, 'Don't move a muscle.'

The commander closed his eyes and mouthed some words. Bellum appeared before them and Silho froze. She held her breath. The witch looked one way and then the other and flew straight past them.

Copernicus exhaled deeply and Silho whispered, 'What happened?'

'An illusion,' he said. 'We've got to get back to the hide.'

He grabbed Silho's bare hand and she flinched. The skin was scorched and blistering.

'It didn't work,' she said. 'I can't . . . think.'

'Say the words, Brabel,' he instructed. '*Claude animus meus.* Keep saying them.'

Silho focused on the sound of his voice and found her control.

Shawe staggered up and moved unsteadily beside them. 'What's the plan to get back to Nureyev?' he asked.

'The river,' Copernicus said. 'It cuts through Castlereagh several blocks up.'

'You want to swim down forty levels?' Shawe said. 'We'll never make it.'

'Would you rather stay here?' Copernicus said.

A distant wailing Skreaf curse ended their conversation. Copernicus supported Silho and the three of them broke into a run, soon coming to the T. Sypher Bridge that crossed over the Asher River on that level. Silho stood beside the commander, staring down into the roaring black rapids.

'How will we know when we're close to the hide?' Shawe yelled.

'I'll know!' Copernicus shouted back.

'You – halt!' a voice rang out.

Silho jolted and spun around. A squad of soldiers had turned a street corner and spotted them. Copernicus grabbed her hand and dragged her over the edge of the bridge as the soldiers opened fire, crumbling the place where they had stood. Silho felt the terrible, helpless rush of falling, then they were smashing down into the river.

The current caught them and flew them downstream. Silho struggled to keep her face above the surface, choking and coughing, the water stinging her eyes. Copernicus pulled her onto his back and she clung to his shoulders. The water swept them through Castlereagh and its adjoining suburbs to the pipeway waterfall connecting the level with the one below it. They crashed over the edge and plummeted down the terrible drop. The water pummelled them, trying to trap them below its deadly surface. They made it up to the air and the river dragged them onwards. Silho completely lost track of time and distance, her muscles burning and then falling numb. Finally she heard the commander yell, 'Dive!'

Silho sucked in a deep breath and Copernicus hauled her under. She pushed her body beyond its limit, using every last ounce of energy and strength to cut through the current down to stiller waters below. There, she stared around with blurred vision, and heard a clunk and a grinding sound. Hands pushed her through a hole and she dropped into a pipeway filling fast with gushing water. She panted and clung to the sides of the pipe. The others dragged themsleves in and Shawe sealed the hatch above them. They trod water, their ragged breathing echoing in the darkness. After a moment, Silho heard Shawe take in a deep breath and dive under. He resurfaced soon afterwards and the water level receded until they touched down on the metal base of the pipe. Silho saw where Shawe had opened another hatch, which led out. The gangster and Copernicus clambered through, but Silho paused to look back the way they'd come. They were bruised, broken and exhausted, but the fact they were still alive after facing Bellum – it seemed almost too easy to believe. Fear whispered soft sinister words in her ears.

'Brabel,' the commander called for her.

She turned away and dragged herself after the others.

32

S he couldn't see for the suffocating smoke, or breathe for the sul-
phuric flames burning all the oxygen out of the air. She crawled,
digging her nails into the ash-covered dirt and dragged herself forward. Zakiah was lost somewhere in this burning hell.

'My baby.' It was a scream that only managed to come out as a
whisper.

Everywhere strange men with bloodline marks of big, winged
lizard-like beasts fought the demons that had kept her people imprisoned for their whole existence. Before her disbelieving eyes
these men were reducing the ever-living Skreaf to ash, then exhaling
fire from their mouths. Through the veil of smoke she saw him, her
little boy, just ahead of her – standing, crying, one hand in his mouth,
the other clutching at his own shirt. A winged shadow appeared in
the sky above her baby. It plummeted down towards the infant. She
ran.

Ev'r jolted upright, violent coughs racking her body. She gasped
and hacked until she managed to clear her lungs. Once she could
breathe, she took her hands away from her mouth and saw they
were black with soot. It reminded her of what she had just seen
in her vision of the past – the way to destroy the Skreaf lay in
Silho's bloodline. She staggered to her feet and a shattering pain shot
through her body. Ice-cold agony seared in her jaw, the pain bending her double. Though her mouth hung open, she couldn't make a
sound. Eventually, the torture subsided and she was able to straight-

en, feeling the light-headed euphoria that comes after the passing of severe pain, but she knew it would be back.

Ev'r rapidly processed her surroundings, trying to orientate herself. The last thing she remembered was the Androt survivor, Lao, saying they were almost at the hideout. Where she stood now was a functional space, devoid of any personal touches or comforts. There was a chair tucked under a table, a computer system and a plain bed mat lying flat and straight in one corner. No effort had been made to break the concrete monotony of the floor and walls. Ev'r scanned the room and her senses spoke to her. This area represented the deliberate and focused deprivation of someone who wanted nothing – perhaps even drew strength from it – and that was unusual. She moved towards the desk and rummaged through the hard files that were stacked alphabetically beside the computer system. It was a collection of works by the philosophers, sociologists and psychic analysts considered to be the greatest of the era, among them Axis, Pelterbelt and Neridium. They were heavy intellectual works that few people read and, of them, even fewer understood. Once she had started into a Neridium manuscript about the continuum of life patterns and had emerged several hours later with a dry mouth and a jumbled mind. Whoever owned this room, the person who thrived on nothing, also thrived on knowing – to the point of self-torture.

'Activate,' she said to the computer system and it sparked to life, displaying files on a holo-screen. She selected a file entitled *Writing – my*, and opened one of the file's many documents, one named *Always be*. Writing flashed up on the screen.

She whispered the words, 'He said, let it be Music Man, play a song for me; Let it roll Music Man, rock and roll for me. Stay a while Music Man, stay and laugh for me; Always be; Never go; Never end the show; It must go on; Endless, seamless, streams of dreams; It seems the seams are splitting without you here; He said I fear myself without you here; I hear you laughing, humming, saying something, singing something, something for me; Forever be, Music Man, play a song for me . . .'

Ev'r caught movement out of the corner of her eye and turned towards it.

An Androt man stood in the doorway, his arms crossed over his chest, his face still, his expression unreadable.

'Obviously no one taught you the rudeness of rifling through other people's personal effects.' He pronounced his words precisely. His voice was the kind that carried with little effort, the kind that gave authority to unproven words and made others believe. The Androt man looked Ev'r up and down, and she heard, loud and clear, the meaning between his well-spoken words. She was an ignorant, ill-bred scullion who wasn't worth the air she breathed. Straightening up to her full height, she looked him directly in the eyes.

'This poetry – it's very good. I can see influences of the theobaldist and the neo-classical movements in its choice of rhyme and rhythm. Whoever wrote it knows their stuff. So who did write it? *Obviously* it wasn't you.' She looked him up and down and said with her eyes – *because you're just a slave, machine-breed*. And he heard her – loud and clear.

He took the counterattack with a perfunctory nod of his head and entered the room. He stepped deliberately, moving in a wide circle around her, sizing her up. While he studied her, she studied him back. He was muscular and heavy-limbed. And extremely attractive. She would have liked to add the disclaimer *for a machine-breed*, but that would have been a lie. He was attractive without limits, and in a dangerous sort of way, the way that couldn't be pinpointed exactly to one feature or another as it was a combination of everything. In the kind of way that would instantly disarm people and make them want to like him. But she wasn't fooled so easily.

He stopped moving, squared up to her and said, 'The great Ev'r Keets. I'm honoured.'

She dipped her head to him now and replied, 'The deliberately anonymous Kry. I'm on to you.'

He clenched his teeth hard, but again took the hit with the slightest of nods. In the moment of his movement, Keets saw a flash of his Androt barcode below the collar of his shirt – 939993. Androts were not permitted to wear shirts with collars. She added *defiant* to the list of his characteristics she was mentally compiling.

'You and your imp-breed partner are on the United Regiment's most wanted list. Your friend has been connected to murders all over the city now,' Kry said.

'I'd rather be hunted by the Regiment than by Skreaf demons,' she said. 'How did you escape Fortitude Hill after losing so much blood?'

'I'm no stranger to injury.' His hand twitched towards his chest and she assumed his shirt was hiding a wad of bandages and partially healed wounds.

'Obviously,' she gestured around the room, 'you're against the system, so why were you serving at that house in suburbia and not out in the Matadori with your outlaw brothers – cutting your barcode out of your neck and plotting an impossible uprising?'

The Androt swallowed slowly and she knew she'd hit a spot.

'Of all my so-called brothers who have left the city, how many of them have made one inch of difference? None. The problem is here. So I've stayed here. And as for my barcode,' he gestured to his numbers, 'this is my family heritage. This is who I am. Why would I ever be ashamed of that? Would you cut out your bloodline mark?'

'Yes,' Ev'r replied, rapping her knuckles on the gold bands covering her scullion marks. 'In a second, if I thought they wouldn't just grow back. And if I could somehow rearrange time and fate and be born as any other race, I would.'

'Well then, that's where we differ,' Kry said, fixing his deep grey eyes on her. 'I would never want to be anything but an Androt. I am proud of who I am and what my people are.'

'Good for you,' Ev'r said dryly.

'Did you know,' he said, stepping closer to her, 'that there was a time in history when machine-breeds ruled the world and it was the human-breeds that were our slaves?'

'Is that so,' Ev'r said with feigned uninterest. In truth, she had studied this time in depth. Treasure hunting and knowledge of history were a married couple. In a test to see how much he knew, she asked, 'So what happened to them?'

'The same thing that always happens – revolution and war.'

'Why?' she asked.

'Inequality, poverty, desperation – so few were so rich and so many so poor. Something had to eventually give. It always does. The machine-breeds of that time were as foolish as the Ar Antarians of our time, but a time of change is coming again,' Kry said, clenching one fist.

'You've got that right,' Ev'r said. 'The Skreaf have risen and they're all over the city. Pretty soon, if history holds any truth in the present, we'll be in the midst of a demon war we can't win.'

'Demon war,' Kry snorted. 'A few random dregs of dark magics and you're preaching takeover. It's not the Skreaf who are going to rise up.'

'Let me guess, it's the Androts – led by you.' Ev'r sneered, but inside she was checking off his personality traits – charismatic, educated, very intelligent, obsessively self-driven, revolutionary and fanatical. Just the right mix for the leader of a major civil war, someone who could save the Androts from their slavery and degradation – but then who would save them from him? However, it would never get to that. The Androts would eventually fall to the Skreaf just like everyone else.

'Open your eyes,' Ev'r said, 'and see what's really happening around you.'

'They are open,' Kry responded, 'all six of them.' His steady gaze lifted to the ceiling and Ev'r looked up. A scorpion-shaped robot was staring down at her with four red eyes. 'And I know exactly what is happening.'

'Right.' Ev'r saw he couldn't be reasoned with. 'Good luck with that.'

She walked to the door and out into a large, concrete basement-like area. From all directions Androts crowded in on her, herding her into the centre of the room and barricading her exit. She studied them. The barcodes of some were still intact, others had been cut out – and every face was set in rage. These were a people right on the edge of complete abandonment, of all-out revolution. They were blood-hungry, but if they messed with her they would get more than they bargained for. She rolled her head from one side to the other and felt a growl building inside her. Kry stood at the door of his room watching the monster crowd he'd created flexing its muscles. His scorpion robot sat beside him on the wall.

'Stop! Leave her alone!' Lao, the survivor, pushed through the Androts, shoving back those who were pressing in too close. His own bird robot, Beak6, perched on his shoulder.

'Kry, she's a friendly,' he appealed to his cousin, whose expressionless gaze didn't waver.

'Zale is back!' someone yelled out and there was a general murmuring and shuffling as the crowd parted to allow two Androts to help a third, who was limping badly, to cut through the centre of the room to Kry. Ev'r saw the newcomer had been shot in the leg with an electrifier. His melted skin was struggling to reconnect and seal over the open wound, which was weeping white blood. He stood in front of Kry and Ev'r had to admire the strength of the machine-breeds. Kry nodded and the man spoke.

'There was a break-in at the Castlereagh Holding. All the Androts who tried to escape were executed. The United Regiment has now issued a public order that all Androts are to report to Military Headquarters by sunrise; those who don't will be tracked down and charged with treason.'

A vein in Kry's neck twitched, but his mouth remained a straight line.

'Good,' he said, then addressed the mass of Androts. 'Our time of hiding is over. Alert everyone. The plan is going ahead.'

The crowd stirred, excitement buzzing in the air.

'No!' Lao called out to Kry. 'The Skreaf are out there looking for you. They're instigating this round-up of our people to get to you. If you leave here, they will capture you. I saw what they can do. They tortured me! Why won't you believe me?'

Kry ignored him, speaking in a low voice to several of the Androts standing closest to him.

'You should listen to your cousin,' Ev'r said. 'You go out there and the Skreaf will have you in seconds. Your race is resistant to their curses, but even you can't stand against them forever. If you come with me, we may be able to protect you.'

'No witnesses,' Kry said to his men. His gaze shifted momentarily to Ev'r's and she saw this decision was purely strategic.

312

The Androts stomped towards her and she sneered, 'You think so, do you?'

And with that she sank into the Murk and vanished from the room.

Ev'r travelled for a few long, reaching steps, but found she was unable to maintain it, feeling out of control in the spiralling grey. She sensed an uninhabited area around her and stepped back out into reality. Instantly, she doubled over with agony and fell to one side, where she rolled one way and then the other, clutching her chest and stomach, containing her scream to an extended moan behind gritted teeth. The pain eventually lessened, but only slightly. Her whole body was throbbing and she could smell the Ravien's raw stench in her nose. Blood trickled down the skin of her throat from the rips in the flesh made by her distending jaw. She grasped at the alley wall beside her and tried to stand but couldn't, so she slumped to the ground and stayed there, gazing with misting sight out into the street.

It was almost mid-dark and a group of people were strolling down the footpath, their pace the slower, more subdued rate of people heading home after some hours of partying. A young couple dropped out from the main crowd and stopped under a lantern light. They hugged each other and kissed. The man stroked a hand lovingly through the girl's hair. Ev'r felt hatred for them, and she felt sorrow for them, and above everything else she felt so very tired, as though she'd lived a thousand lifetimes all in one. With a shaking hand, she drew the Morsus Ictus out of its sheath. She grasped her old friend in one hand, but she couldn't manage to raise it to her neck. Her arms were completely black. Tears trickled from the corners of her eyes and her vision blurred. The heavy heartbeats of the beast she was becoming thudded in her ears. It was too late now. There would be no redemption.

33

Copernicus took stock of his team. The Wraith was missing in action, presumably dead. Shawe had collapsed to the ground. Silho sat hunched in one corner with her head resting against the wall, her arms and hands burned red and blistered. She'd set alight without making any dent whatsoever in Bellum's strength. Diega appeared controlled, but he knew her too well to believe it. The closer Diega was to falling apart the less emotion she showed, and right now she was completely blank. She avoided looking at Jude, who stood, still handcuffed, on the other side of the room. His expression was calm, but in an unsettling way. Copernicus had seen it before in suicides. It was the serenity of a decision made.

Of all of them, Jude required his immediate attention. Copernicus decided not to sugarcoat it.

'There is no point killing yourself to stop the Skreaf,' he told the Ar Antarian.

Jude lifted his chin. SevenM glared at him from his perch on Jude's shoulder.

'You see your barcode there?' Copernicus indicated Jude's neck.

Jude shrugged as though trying to cover it, but the cuffs kept his hands behind his back. He hesitated then answered, his voice desolate. 'What about it?'

'It reads 939994. The Androt missing from the Fortitude Hill crime scene had the barcode 939993. Do you know what that means?'

Jude's expression shifted from consideration to confusion to shock and then dismay. 'My brother . . .'

'Half-brother,' Copernicus corrected. 'According to Eli, Kry is still alive, but the witches are hunting him as well. It's obviously your family bloodline that they need for their plans, but if you kill yourself, they can still get to him. Do you see why it would be a pointless sacrifice? We need you – alive – to fight them.' He paused for the words to sink in. 'Do you understand?'

Jude lowered his head. Finally he nodded and said, 'I understand.'

Copernicus unlocked his cuffs and the Ar Antarian flexed his metal hands. 'I thought it was the only way.' He met Copernicus' eyes then looked away.

The commander could see that Jude was a good man, a brave man, searching for the right path, but he was also disturbed and displaced, unpredictable because he didn't even know himself. He would need to be watched – closely.

Copernicus glanced at Diega. She shook her head and walked to one of the porthole windows to look out. She'd expected to save Jude from the Skreaf, not from himself. It was the sort of thing that was difficult not to take personally.

Copernicus went next to Silho. He crouched down beside her and took one of her arms in his hand. The limb had turned black, but as he touched it, the black came off onto his fingers like soot and he saw that underneath the skin had healed. Before he could comment on it, Silho whispered, 'Commander, Bellum has one of the rings.'

Copernicus grabbed at the pocket where he'd stored the metal bands and found it empty. Nerves spiralled through his stomach.

'How?' he demanded.

Silho looked past him to where Shawe lay on the ground. Copernicus cursed. Shawe must have lifted them from him during their conversation at the church. He moved over to the gangster and booted him in the side. Shawe stirred. He wiped his mouth and looked up at Copernicus.

'This can't be Paradise,' he groaned.

'Far from it,' Copernicus replied, barely containing his fury.

315

Shawe sat up and took his flask from his pocket. He put it to his lips, but Copernicus kicked it out of his hands. Shawe shot to his feet and shouted into Copernicus' face.

'What's your problem?'

'You stole the rings from me and lost one to the Skreaf.'

'What?' Diega rounded on them.

Jude pressed his hand over his eyes.

Shawe's anger subsided and he gave a guilty sideways glance. 'I took back what was mine. I thought I could keep them safe. The witch got into my head. I couldn't stop myself.' He slid the remaining ring out of his pocket. 'She only got the one.'

'Oh – well that's alright then,' Diega said mockingly.

'Which one?' Copernicus asked. 'Original or fake?'

Shawe held the band up to his eyes. 'I don't know,' he finally admitted.

'How can you not know? They're your trutting rings!' Diega yelled, her colours flashing brilliantly.

'Back off, sunshine,' Shawe shouted back. 'I had the second one made to be an exact replica.'

'Give it to me,' Copernicus ordered.

Shawe held back. 'It's all I have of Stacy.'

'And it's all you'll ever have of him if we don't stop the witches.'

The gangster reluctantly pressed the ring into Copernicus' palm. 'How are we going to do that?' he asked, sinking down onto one of the crates.

'We find the place where they've taken the Mazurus Machine. We go in and destroy it. It's a temporary fix, but it'll buy us time.' He glanced at Silho. 'Eli is working on a location now. We can call him once the hedge is up. Until then we stay low.'

'I'm not waiting,' Shawe disagreed. 'I'm going back out there. There's no point sitting here.'

'He's right – for once,' Diega said. 'We're wasting time here.'

Jude gave a hollow laugh. 'You two really have no idea what we're facing, do you?'

A heavy silence filled the room and everyone slipped into their own thoughts. Copernicus went to the table and checked the tech they'd set up to re-run the blocking hedge into his communicator. Its regeneration was almost halfway. He looked at his chronograph and saw that the device was melting, and the skin on his wrist had puffed out into welts. They extended up his arms in an angry red pattern. It was a reaction to the acid waters of the Asher.

'Anyone else affected by the water?' he asked the group.

Shawe shrugged and an arm fell off his jacket. Diega and Jude checked themselves. They'd also been dunked when Diega had crashed the craft into the river to escape the storm. A clump of Diega's hair fell out in her hands. Her eyes widened.

'Hit the showers again – now!' he ordered the team.

Shawe dragged open the main faucet and the shower heads, embedded into the walls around the open bathing area, spluttered and sprayed out jets of water. It was cold and brownish, but at least fresher than the river swill. Everyone dispersed into different corners to undress. Jude went to stand close to Diega. She didn't look at him, but she didn't turn away either. Copernicus chose a spot along the same wall as Shawe. Shedding his clothes, he stepped under the shower jet and scrubbed at his skin, washing out the pollutants. He saw Silho in the reflection of the tap and paused. She was smaller and more fragile than he had first thought. Now he understood why the Wraith had said he feared for her life against Bellum. The witch was impossibly strong and she'd knocked down all of Silho's defences with only a few words. It was clear to Copernicus that just teaching Silho the enchant was not enough. At this early stage of her learning, the magics would fade as soon as Silho's focus failed. He needed to help her understand what got to her – where her emotional weaknesses lay and why.

While he was thinking, Shawe shuffled closer to him and grunted, 'Not bad.' He nodded to Silho.

Copernicus shot him a look of disgust. 'We're on the verge of annihilation and you think I'm checking her out? Are you really that stupid?'

'Don't get crazy,' Shawe said. 'I know what's what. I'm just saying, she's easy on the eye and I know exactly what type of girl you go for. If you remember, I was the one who dragged your scrawny, pitiful self into your very first grindhouse and paid up well for you to have an hour with a fine-looking girl, although, as I recall, you didn't need anywhere near that time.' Shawe grinned, flashing his crooked, stained teeth.

Copernicus glanced over his shoulder to see if the others had heard. Luckily, everyone was preoccupied with their own thoughts. He rubbed his face, trying to re-banish images of that unfortunate first encounter. Shawe stood watching him.

'What do you want?' he asked, assuming Shawe's real reason for making conversation was not just to drag him down memory lane again.

'What are the chances Stacy is still alive?' The gangster's tone turned to seriousness.

Copernicus thought there was no chance at all, but he said, 'He has as good a chance as anyone.'

'So you think he's dead, then.'

'I really don't know,' Copernicus replied.

'It's been over a week now,' Shawe said. Deeply buried emotions surfaced in his expression, twisting his face in unrecognisable ways. 'Why him? Why my little brother?'

'Everyone who dies is something to someone,' Copernicus said. 'Even the people you've killed.'

Shawe glanced up sharply. 'Don't you remember how we grew up? Dad put a gun in my hand and told me to shoot or get shot. Maybe I still deserve to go to hell, but I raised Stacy differently. He's never hurt anyone. He's innocent. So why the trutt didn't the witches take me and leave him? How is this fair?'

'It's not,' Copernicus said, and his memory took him back through the year-cycles of his career, through year-cycles full of innocent dead and grief-stricken loved ones searching for meaning in the madness, searching for revenge, for peace, absolution, something, anything. There was a reason he'd grown so cold.

'You have a far better chance of finding Stacy than he would have of finding you,' he told Shawe.

'And you think that's the Great God's way of trying to even out this life?' Shawe asked in a low voice.

'I think it's just a fact,' Copernicus replied. He stepped out of the water stream and went back into the other room where they'd left the boxes of clothes. They were badly creased and musty and some of the shirts smelt faintly of other people's body odour, but the only other option was nudity – not exactly suitable for going into battle. He found some more trousers that fit and was still searching for an acceptable shirt when Shawe, Jude and SevenM entered the room. Shawe started rummaging through the clothes, dragging on shirts that ripped as soon as he bent his arms and flexed his muscles.

'You'd better get in while there's still something left in one piece,' Copernicus commented to Jude, who stood staring at the piles of clothing.

The Ar Antarian turned his vivid blue eyes to Copernicus and said, 'I'm the Crown Prince and my mother was an Androt slave.' He gulped and blinked rapidly as though he couldn't believe he'd just said it aloud. Copernicus understood Jude needed to have this conversation.

'You are whoever you want to be,' the commander replied.

'What I am is both Ar Antarian and machine-breed, but I can't be both.'

'Why not?' Copernicus challenged him. 'Because that's what other people believe? I've always known you to think for yourself, to think logically and deeply and form your own opinions. That's one of the reasons why I recruited you.'

'Would you have dismissed me,' Jude asked, 'for lying to you about being the prince, if all this hadn't happened?'

Copernicus considered the words then replied, 'No.'

'Why not?'

'Because I also think for myself. Your race doesn't change the way I see you. However, your honesty does. If you're upfront with me from here on, then you'll always have a place with the trackers – whatever happens.'

Jude's eyes misted and he looked away. After a moment he cleared his throat. 'I have a brother. I don't even know my own family.'

Copernicus thought of the scars on his own body and mind and said, 'Sometimes that's not such a bad thing.'

319

Jude lowered his head. 'I know.'

'Come on.' Shawe walked past them and slapped Jude on the shoulder. 'Cheer up, Your Highness. Who do you think you're with – a bunch of nobles or something? I'm gutter-born, your girl's a fairy-breed, Kane's as strange as they come and that one,' he nodded at Silho as she emerged from the bathing room, 'you don't even want to know.'

Jude stared at Silho's bloodline marks as she grabbed up some clothes and disappeared into the adjoining bunk room. Copernicus noticed she had a freely bleeding wound on her back.

Jude shook his head, perplexed. 'I don't recognise Silho's marks.'

'Shawe will explain,' Copernicus said, temporarily abandoning his search for a shirt. 'I have to dress her wound.'

'Sure you do,' the gangster said and lifted his eyebrows in a quick up-and-down suggestion.

'Diega, come with me,' Copernicus said, and the Fen walked over to join them.

'The more the merrier,' Shawe said, finally finding a shirt that fitted.

34

Eli hit the ground with a jarring thud. He rolled over, groaning, as the tangled vines above him slithered fast, closing off where he'd crashed through. The twisting creepers formed a low ceiling across the land, lit only by glowing cabbage-shaped plants that drooped from the vines.

The rash stupidity of his mission struck Eli hard. He'd left the transflyer, and, with great anxiety, Nelly, several levels higher and fought his way down to Venus, the very lowest level of Scorpia, knowing only that the lily grew here *somewhere*.

He forced himself to stand and survey his surrounds. Everywhere plants lay shrivelled and dying. The sight sent a chill shivering through him. Something slithered beside his foot and Eli scrambled back. Just ahead of him, one of the plants was changing from withered brown to bright yellow-green. It thickened, strained, and heaved up its huge, bulbous head. Spikes curved around its mouth, which opened wide, revealing a mucousy, off-yellow interior. The giant pod plunged a tentacle-like vine into the ground and pumped blue fluid into the dirt – chemical communication. Eli watched with fascination as colour spread rapidly through the garden as other pods and plants awoke.

One of the pods, Eli noticed, was a darker green. Suddenly something moved inside it, pushing and struggling. The shape of a screaming face pressed against its fleshy side. Eli gasped. The pod was digesting something – alive. Eli rushed to the huge plant and tried to wrench its mouth-spines apart. He punched and kicked it. He threw himself at it and, finally, he drew his blade and stabbed it. The pod gave a terrible whistling screech as fluid gushed from the wound. A flora-breed with a pink face and yellow petal hair pushed out through the gore, gasping and stretching for the light. The pod raised its needle-vine to strike. Eli severed it, and the plant gave a final shriek, then shrivelled back to brown.

From the silence came the swish of leaves.

Eli looked up and the breath caught in his throat. All around the garden, drooling pods were closing in on him with lurching, rocking steps. Before he could run, sinewy vines whipped out from all angles to wrap around him. He tried to hack them back, but they kept coming. The largest of the pods dragged him, struggling, towards its gaping mouth. Eli stared into the foul orifice and saw what looked like a child wrapped in a membranous sack. He strained back, kicking the pod in the face as it snapped at him.

A loud cracking sound reverberated through the air.

The tentacles instantly recoiled, dumping Eli on the ground where he lay panting. The flora-breed he'd saved peeked out at him from behind a huge mushroom. She extended a hand to him, but before he could take it, a thinner, sticky vine shot out and re-bound Eli's arms to his sides. It drained his strength until he could barely move. He dropped his blade as the vine yanked him up.

A group of spindly, long-armed figures now surrounded him. Thick moss covered their skin and nutrient-sapping vines grew out of their bodies like extra limbs. Eli had seen pictures of them before. They were Droso Mossmen – the most bloodthirsty of the plant-breeds. Eli inwardly cursed.

'Please listen . . .' he began and the Mossmen reared back, their eyes bulging, gleaming with a violet light.

They spoke to each other rapidly in Drosish, a language that sounded like forest noises. One released a cyclonic howl, revealing pieces of plant and animal flesh caught in its snaggle of barbed-wire teeth. Eli groaned as the vines constricted tighter around him. The Mossmen turned abruptly and dragged him away.

With each step the Mossmen took their feet meshed with the ground, soaking up sustenance. Eli tried to mark a mental map as they forced him through Venus to a clearing. There, a mass of savage plant-breeds surrounded him. They ripped off his weapon belt and emptied his pockets. When he tried again to reason with them, a creepy cackle rang out from somewhere behind them. Eli turned to look into the devious face of the tallest Droso there. He leered, with one sneaky purple eye stretched larger than the other. Strands of leaf hair hung down his back, and a crown of golden flowers grew out of his head. He spoke in Urigin with a high lisping plant-breed accent, his words dripping sarcasm.

'Look at our special guest. What an unexpected honour for us lowly beings.'

The gathered Mossmen erupted into laughter that sounded like boots crunching on dry leaves. One stepped to their leader's side and whispered something. The leader's eyes darkened and he stalked towards Eli. The moss skin of his face slid upwards, exposing a slimy skull-like face underneath.

He hissed with rotting breath, 'You dare to violate a Bearer.'

'A Bearer?' Eli stuttered, then remembered the child he'd seen inside the pod – a baby Droso. Terror sunk through him.

'Never mind.' The Mossman's unstable leader calmed as quickly as he'd angered. 'I, Loki, governor of the Droso Mossmen, will make you pay the price . . . but slowly, so slowly.' Eli shrank back and the plant-breeds laughed in cruel anticipation. 'But first,' Loki raised a spindly finger, 'the test of mind.'

Eli almost cried with relief. They weren't going to rip him apart on the spot. They were going to follow plant-breed custom and give him a chance to redeem his life.

Loki's eyes swivelled, then brightened. He sniggered, rubbing his hands together.

'Listen carefully, dimbulb,' he said to Eli, 'this is your clue. Our kind is solitary and jealous, and we will punish those who forsake us for another. What are we? You can answer only once and when you get it wrong, you will die – slowly.'

'And when I answer correctly you have to free me,' Eli said.

323

'But of course,' Loki simpered, then ordered, 'Take him to the Tree, for ten clicks only – beginning . . . now!'

He pointed to a large plant beside them. Nailed to it was a strange wooden chronograph with only one hand that began spinning madly. Eli's eyes widened. Beside the chronograph grew a violet and pink Venus Lily.

The Mossmen herded Eli to a giant hollowed-out tree. They forced him through the trunk to a chamber cut in the earth beneath it. A glowing cabbage-bulb hung from the ceiling. Vines sealed over the entrance and Eli's bonds unravelled and slid away. He gasped as his strength returned in a rush. Immediately, he started pacing, frantically thinking about the clue. As he neared the opposite wall, a terrible face pushed out of the dirt. Eli screamed, but then he recognised Luther and his hopes leapt high.

'Please stay! I really need your help!' he said, his words tripping over each other. 'I need to know if the Droso's governor is talking about the answer to the riddle. Can you go and see?'

Luther vanished. After what felt like year-cycles instead of seconds, he reappeared. He pointed a thin, scarred arm to the ceiling. Eli looked up at the shining plant bulb.

'What is it?' he asked.

Luther opened his mouth, but no sounds came out.

'Scratch it!' Eli said. 'In the ground.'

Using one long claw, Luther wrote a word in the dirt floor.

'Canderlight.' Eli sounded out. His eyes widened. 'Canderlight!' He had studied this light-emitting plant. It lived forever unless it was exposed to any other light. If it was, it flared for a few moments of brilliance before dying.

'It fits the clue!' Eli clapped his hands together, then his excitement plummeted. There was no way Loki was letting him go – correct answer or not.

'What am I going to do?'

Luther pointed up to the plant.

'Canderlight, I know,' Eli said. 'But how am I going to get out of here?'

Luther pointed again, more insistently, and Eli gazed up.

'Canderlight,' he dragged out the word, his mind spinning triple speed. An idea struck him. 'Luther, you're a genius.' He could use the clue against them. If he could expose the Canderlight vine to another light source, he could blind the Droso and escape.

Eli wildly searched his pockets for a lighter and found nothing. The Droso had taken everything.

Before he could think further, slapping footsteps approached. The brown vines slid back, revealing his glaring captors. Their tentacles wrapped around him and they dragged him back to Loki, who stood sneering with haughty self-assurance.

He and the others jeered for a long time before he finally said, 'Poor dullard, obviously my riddle was a little too difficult for your teensy-weensy mind.'

'Canderlight,' Eli said.

The crunching laughter instantly silenced.

It took a moment for the Droso leader to register the significance, then his expression soured. The moss skin of his face slid up.

'Evil mind-reader,' he growled. 'Evil deceiver.'

The other Mossmen howled and hissed. They closed in, gleaming purple eyes turning black, barbed-wire teeth gnashing.

'Wait!' Eli yelled desperately. He noticed his communicator lying on the ground and a thought came to him. 'I'm not a mind reader, but I have a device that does read minds. It's right there. I'll give it to you.' He nodded to the communicator.

Loki glared at him with distrust. His lips quivered, then his greed won out. He grabbed up the communicator and the machine's security system kicked in. It registered a stranger's touch and shut down.

'Just take off that bit,' Eli said nodding to the locator, which he'd need to track Ev'r. 'That makes the machine work only for me.'

Loki ripped off the locator component and dumped it on the ground with the weapon belt.

'Now just pull back that panel there and drag out a blue wire.'

Loki ripped eagerly at the system. The red security light flared. It sensed an intruder in its internals and initialised self-destruction. Eli shot a glance at the chronograph and lily, judging the distance from him to them.

Loki stared at the smoking machine. 'Broken! You lied to me,' he hissed. 'Kill him!'

'Luther, shut your eyes!' Eli yelled, seeing flames flickering inside the communicator.

He closed his own eyes as the Droso rushed him. He cringed, expecting to feel their wiry hands and vicious teeth. It didn't happen. Instead, a bright light flashed beside him as the communicator exploded. All movement paused. The Mossmen gasped. Then, as the Canderlight bulbs became aware of the light, they flared. Even behind closed lids, Eli felt his eyes burn. The Mossmen were screaming and screeching. The vines around Eli loosened and dropped away. After a few seconds of brilliance the Canderlights died, leaving absolute blackness and utter chaos.

The Mossmen howled and ran in all direction, paying no attention to Loki's shrieked orders. Eli lunged for his weapon belt and locator, then flew upwards, arms outstretched in the darkness. He thudded against the chronograph and patted around it until his fingers found the waxy petals of the Venus Lily. He plucked the flower and flew backwards, landing some way from the screaming Droso. A cold hand closed over his arm and he yelped, 'Luther, is that you?'

He took the silence to mean yes and followed as the grip led him stumbling through the writhing garden. Finally a glow appeared ahead of them, a shimmer of light beaming through a split in a huge flower stem. The yellow petal-haired flora-breed he'd saved stood beside it. She had been leading Luther through the dark. She gestured for them to pass through the stalk. Luther vanished into the shadows and Eli headed after him. He paused to say goodbye to the flora-breed. She bent down and kissed him passionately on the mouth, leaving yellow pollen dust all over his face. Eli tripped through the centre of the stem, feeling warm all over, and found Luther lay collapsed on the other side, barely breathing.

35

Silho stood at the porthole window, watching aquatic-breeds of every shape and size glide through the murky waters of the Asher. She slipped on the gloves she'd found among the boxes of clothes. Now that her truth was known, she didn't need to re-bind her arms, but she still needed to keep her hands from directly touching any surfaces.

Silho caught sight of her reflection in the window and for a moment it was Oren Harvey staring back at her through narrow olive-green eyes – somewhat lost, somewhat wary, conflicted, twisted and searching, a tangle of blonde curls hanging over her pale face. She wondered what her mother would do in her place if she were here, what her father would say if he could see her. In a way now she felt betrayed by both of them. If there was any truth in what that foul High Skreaf had said, it sounded as though her parents had separated for her sake. Or maybe Oren just left, but then had a change of heart once Silho was in trouble. Searching for answers, Silho returned again to memories of her mother saving her from the fire and the few days she'd spent with her afterwards in the desert.

Violence replayed in flashes and snatches of vivid colour, patches of silence and roars of sound – yelling, thundering explosions, clanging of metal against metal, the whispers of the dying and the hiss of the fire. She spoke in her mind to Oren . . . *We walked away. You never ran. You were Commander Oren Harvey, the genesis of defiance and a cold-blooded killer, unhinged, distorted and dis-*

turbing, your psyche wrung and shredded like old rags on a razor-
wire fence. We walked through the desert, your footsteps marked in
blood, you spoke to me, you said, '. . . war has fractured my soul,
it has stolen my name and purpose. I am an alien to myself and a
stranger in my own skin . . .'

Silho came out of her thoughts feeling, if anything, more lost.
Who were these strangers who had brought her into life? Even
after all her efforts, she still had no idea. The door slid open
behind her and she glanced back. Copernicus entered the room and
she looked away, avoiding his eyes. As always, she felt he could
see too much of everything she wanted to keep hidden. Her gaze
slipped down to his bare chest. He had a tattoo of an axe and
blade across his right pectoral. She recognised it from her academy
training. It signified membership to the highly secretive and exclusive Nuxum-Re, a fighting group whose style was based on
speed and pain resistance. A thick and jagged scar ran across from
his left shoulder, down his side and across his stomach, as though
someone had tried to cleave him in half but slipped. Smaller scars,
with equally gruesome possible origins, stretched over the form
and muscle of his stomach and chest. She felt her face flush then,
realising he would sense the change in her heat, she burned even
more. But when she dared a glance at his face, she saw no outward
indication that he had noticed.

'Your back is bleeding,' he told her. 'Take a seat and I'll bind it
for you.'

Silho moved over to one of the bunks and sat down. She saw
Diega standing in the doorway, watching her with an expression that
was not exactly dislike, but not exactly liking either.

'You look like Commander Harvey,' the Fen finally said. 'I can
see it now.'

Copernicus sat down behind Silho and pulled up her shirt so that
he could access the wound. She tensed as his cool finger brushed
against her back.

'I don't think binding will be enough to stem the flow,' he told
her. 'And I don't have any coagulating serum left. I'll have to stitch
it. Diega, hand me some threads.'

Diega took a packet from her weapon belt and walked over to give it to him. She stood beside the bunk while the commander worked on the wound.

'Did you know your mother was the first female commander in the United Regiment?' Diega asked Silho. 'She forced people to see women differently. I doubt I would have ever ended up in the military if it hadn't been for the changes she made.'

It felt strange for Diega to be making civilised conversation with her, and Silho could only assume Diega was reaching some kind of acceptance that her father was innocent.

'Why did you join?' she asked, welcoming a distraction from the pain of the stitches.

'I didn't,' Diega replied, glancing back down the glass corridor towards the other room. 'I got arrested for flying under the influence. The guardian saw I was flying an engine-less transflyer and picked me as an electrosmith. Instead of charging me, he assigned me to six months of military service. First few days I hated. After that, things changed.'

Silho remembered Eli saying that Diega's family had never recovered from her sister's death, that her parents had never taken an interest in Diega's life.

'Done,' the commander said, rolling down Silho's shirt. 'Diega, I need to talk with Brabel about her skills. Go and keep an eye on the others. Have more of the food. Close the door behind you.'

The Fen sent Copernicus a look Silho couldn't read but still left the room, shutting the door behind her with a snap. Her footsteps faded down the corridor.

Silho turned to face the commander. His eyes were clouded in thought.

'Tell me what happened out there,' he eventually said.

Silho shook her head as she remembered the fight with Bellum. 'I had control, but then she started saying things about my father and I lost it. I couldn't even remember the words. I attacked but then – the fire.'

'You were burned, but now you're fine,' Copernicus nodded to her arms.

'It mustn't have been as bad as it first looked,' Silho said.

'Either that or you've healed fast.'

'I heal at a normal speed,' Silho insisted.

The commander gave her a sceptical look but let it go. 'What exactly did the witch say?'

Silho thought of Bellum's taunts and so much anger rose inside her that she couldn't talk.

'You do understand that she was baiting you?' Copernicus asked. Silho nodded.

'Why did you let her?'

'I didn't. She said what she said and I had to react.'

'You have to be able to withstand taunts, Brabel,' the commander said. 'People should be able to say anything to you without you breaking control.'

'Usually people *could* say anything – it's just because it was her.'

'Are you sure? Because if you have unresolved feelings about anything, you —'

'There aren't any unresolved feelings,' Silho interrupted. 'Every second someone is saying something about my father. I can handle anything – just not from the witch.'

'Okay.' Copernicus nodded. 'Now I'm going to say something that may sound harsh, but I think you have to hear it. Nothing is going to bring your parents back. Not you returning to the city and becoming a soldier, not even you proving your father's innocence. You're chasing ghosts and shadows. What you have to understand is that your parents weren't just your parents, they were people who made decisions and these decisions ended up getting them killed. They decided to take the risks that made you an orphan. They decided to leave you alone in this world.'

'That's not how I see it,' Silho said, her throat tightening.

'It's clear how it is,' Copernicus replied. 'Your mother and father put their wants above your needs.'

'That's not true,' Silho argued. She massaged her forehead as the walls started talking in her mind.

'Of course it is!' The commander raised his voice. 'They loved themselves more than they loved you. They didn't care what happened to you.'

'No!' Silho leapt to her feet. 'You have no idea! Everything they did was for me!'

'Brabel – you are completely deluded,' Copernicus said. 'Just like your father.'

Silho's resistance snapped inside her. She flicked to light-form vision, drew a blast of the commander's power into her hands and lunged at him, but he was ready. He grabbed her and slammed her to the ground, pinning her arms above her head. She screamed and struggled wildly.

'Brabel. Look at me!' Copernicus spoke above her and the complete composure of his voice made her stop and open her eyes. Immediately, she saw that everything he had just said to her had been a test.

'Say the words, *claude animus meus*,' he told her, as she tried to regain control of her mind. He stood up and dragged her to her feet. Silho stood still, repeating the enchant until the voices were silenced. This time it happened much quicker than before. She sensed Copernicus studying her with his incisive eyes.

'Unresolved feelings,' he said. 'Talk about them – now.'

Silho sighed, swaying with fatigue. 'I don't know . . . I don't know what to tell you.'

That was a lie. She knew what she felt – the uncontrollable anger, inconsolable grief, unfathomable helplessness and then there was the guilt . . . that was the worst feeling and the only one she couldn't understand. Bellum had played on it and provoked her into fury. She felt guilt that she hadn't done anything to save her father and mother. She'd watched him being dragged away to his death and watched her mother vanish into the desert knowing she would never come back. Of course, the question was, *What could she have done as a child, only six year-cycles old?* and the answer was *Nothing*. So why the guilt? Unexplainable.

'I'm not going to force you to talk,' the commander said. 'I understand about . . . feelings and not wanting to talk about them. But I will say you have to think about them, because they're affecting your ability to control your skills. Do you understand?'

Silho nodded.

'I will also say that I think you *are* getting stronger – the amount of power you took from me just then was a lot more than you took from Diega in the backroom of the pub under similar circumstances of anger.'

'Maybe,' Silho said. 'And – I'm sorry.'

'Don't be,' he said. 'I said you were getting stronger, I didn't say you were stronger than me. You need to keep practising.'

'I don't feel comfortable attacking you,' Silho confessed.

'Why?' he asked, studying her.

'Because I don't.' She refused to elaborate.

He narrowed his eyes, but didn't push. 'Okay, we'll work on your other skill. It uses the same strength of mind principle. Come to the wall.'

Silho obeyed, following him to one side of the room. She stood in front of the wall and the commander stood close behind her. She could feel his cool breath on her neck.

'Hold the words in your mind, then touch the wall,' he instructed.

Although she felt reluctant to expose herself to another trance, she complied, slipping off one glove. As she reached out to the wall, Copernicus put his hands on her hips. Immediately she faltered, losing focus.

'Block me out,' he said. 'You have to block everything out.'

Silho stared at the wall and held the enchant in her mind, managing to keep control even when he wrapped his arms around her and held her against him, trying to distract her. Her fingertips pressed against the wall. A rush of information assaulted her mind and the thirst to take everything in almost overwhelmed her, but as she kept saying the words gradually the images slowed and the sounds became clear. The pictures were so sharp she could see all the fine details of the room. She saw the team before they had gone to find Jude. She observed all their actions in sequence, not the spliced and patchy images of all her earlier visions under the influence of the drugs. She also found that she didn't need to stay with just the one wall she had touched; her mind darted from surface to surface, following the team out of the research facility and into the pipeway leading to the church.

'Brabel,' she heard the commander's voice call faintly. 'Come back.'

She tried to obey, but struggled to move, feeling as though she were stuck in the image. Panicking and flailing, she shot back the way she'd come in a flash of a thousand images and sounds in one moment. Her mind snapped back to where she was and Silho found herself lying on the ground with the commander kneeling over her.

'What happened?' he asked.

She related what she had seen. 'It's never been like that,' she said.

'Good. That proves it. You are gaining more control and your skills are advancing. The training is working.' He helped her to sit up.

'I'll try again.' Silho stood, but lost balance and almost toppled over.

Copernicus clutched her arm and steadied her. The cold of his touch was soothing against her fevered skin. She reached for an aching place on her neck and grimaced at the pain.

'What is it?' he asked, lifting her hair aside to see for himself. 'There are more pictures,' he said. 'They've spread even further than last time. It must be as we thought. The pictures are somehow related to your increases in Omarian skills – with every battle with a Skreaf your skills progress.'

'But not quickly enough,' Silho said. 'I won't survive facing Bellum again. I think she killed Raine.' A pain twisted in her chest. 'I heard them scream.'

'Don't think about it,' Copernicus said. He helped her over to a bunk and sat her down. 'Just rest for a moment.'

She looked up at him, at the beautiful pattern of scars crisscrossing his face. One line touched the curve of his lips. Silho looked deeply into his eyes and felt herself drawn, helpless, into their darkness. She turned away. She didn't want him to see the truth of her feelings – the guilt, the fear that she thought she was going to die no matter what they did because that was the only fate she could see. Her mother had been fearless, but she was terrified. Whatever life she had it was hers – and she wanted to live.

She stared at her hands and the next sensation she felt, from a sleepy distance, was the commander lowering her backwards onto the bed. He spread a blanket over her and tucked in the edges around her shoulders. It was a gentle gesture that she wouldn't have expected from him. Dragging one of her arms free of the sheet, she caught hold of his hand. She held it to her face and pressed her lips against the skin. She said, her exhausted voice barely a whisper, 'Stay with me.'

She could hear him breathing just above her. He leaned down and whispered, 'Rest.'

He tucked her arm back under the covers and moved away. The mattress of the bed compressed near her feet as he sat down. She gazed along the line of the blanket and watched him through the dreamy daze of near sleep. Her eyelids closed. They flickered open at the sound of a voice. She didn't know if seconds or hours had passed, just that Shawe was now standing beside the bed.

'You didn't —' he started.

'No,' the commander cut him off.

'Gutless,' Shawe snorted. His heavy footsteps crossed the room to one of the other beds and he proceeded to lie down with a series of grunts and groans.

'I could use a drink,' Shawe said in the darkness. 'A nice, cold Araki. You remember how we used to sneak into the old man's cellar and drink all night?'

'I remember,' Copernicus replied.

'Wouldn't mind the company of a good woman either. You remember how —'

'I remember,' Copernicus cut in.

Shawe chuckled. 'You just going to sit up all night?'

'Yes.'

'Want company?'

'No. I need to think.'

Shawe yawned. 'You're still as broody as a woman. You haven't changed one bit.'

Jude and Diega's voices rose from the other room in a loud discussion.

'Oi, keep it down, will you,' Shawe bellowed out to them. 'I'm trying to get some shuteye in here.'

The sounds paused and several seconds later the gangster was snoring.

*****

Silho awoke with a nightmare haunting her mind. For a moment, she stared up at the ceiling, uncertain of where she was, but then her memory caught up with her and realisation settled heavily inside her chest. She rubbed her eyes and forced herself to sit up. Pain shot through her back. Every muscle, bone and joint in her body ached. Grimacing, she forced herself to roll out of bed. The sound of voices and the others moving around came from the next room. Silho decided to re-try her skills before joining them. *It could be the last chance I get before facing Bellum again*, she thought, then banished the idea as a terrified sickness swelled inside her.

She hobbled to the wall and slid off one glove. She repeated the enchant in her mind before reaching out and touching the cool rock wall. Images from the night before sparked instantly into clarity. She saw herself and Shawe asleep while the commander stood at the glass looking out at the underwater suburbs. She saw Shawe entering the room, herself talking to Copernicus. She jumped from that wall to the corridor and travelled along into the adjoining chamber where Diega and Jude stood close together in a distant kind of way. Diega had her back to him, her head hanging low. Jude's eyebrows were drawn together and his mouth turned downward. His eyes were sad. Silho's sight leapt up the hatch and out through the pipes. She paused there, aware of not going too far. The images shivered and she saw something up ahead. She drifted closer. A group of cloaked Skreaf crouched in the tunnel. Silho caught sight of the gnarled claw-like fingers and jagged fingernails of Bellum. The hooded High Skreaf lifted her head and stared directly into Silho's eyes.

Silho jolted back from the wall, wrenching her hand away. Sweat had broken out all over her skin and her heart smashed against her chest. She turned and found the commander standing in the doorway watching her. The still blackness of his eyes shifted instantly with unease at the look of horror on her face.

'Brabel?' he asked.

'They followed us,' Silho breathed. 'She's here.'

The sounds from the other room had fallen silent.

Copernicus turned instantly and ran down the corridor. Silho followed him. They stopped in front of the transparent sliding door that had been closed between the hall and the main room. Silho saw the three others gathered around a table. Shawe sat slumped with his head lolling to his chest. Diega had slipped in her chair, with her arms hanging down, some kind of food spilling from her fingers onto the ground. Jude was staring straight ahead, like a machine shutdown, with SevenM frozen on his shoulder. Copernicus tried to slide open the door, but it was sealed firmly shut. He bashed on the glass and rammed his shoulder against it. It didn't give at all. Silho sensed a malevolent presence and saw mist swirling around the ceiling of the chamber. The mist materialised into five Skreaf witches, Bellum among them. She fixed Silho with her droopy-lidded stare and a terrible sneer stretched her thin grey lips. The witches surrounded the table where the others sat helpless.

'Leave them alone!' Silho yelled.

Copernicus kicked and smashed against the glass, shaking the whole structure. Bellum jabbed a finger at him, muttering dark-words. The curse flew at the commander, but reflected off the glass and struck one of the other witches instead. She fell convulsing to the ground. Silho blinked to light-form vision. She held up her hands and drew from the squirming demon body-lights of Bellum and her servants. The massive drag of energy, magnified by the glass, set her hands and arms immediately alight. Silho managed to think of the enchant and while she had it in her mind, she blocked the pain and held the connection. Lights flickered in the air around the witches, but as Silho's torso caught alight, the burning agony grew too intense. Fear of the pain, of the death it would bring, forced her to break free. She dropped to the ground, spewing up flames and smacking her hands against the floor, trying to put out the fire.

The force of her power-charged strike fractured the corridor and cold water seeped through the cracks. Copernicus ripped off his jacket and threw it over her arms to smother the flames. The water level rose quickly around them. Silho looked back into the room. Bellum and two of the witches were performing some kind of incantation around the table, where they'd drawn the Skreaf symbol, the triangle within a triangle within a square, in blood. The witch who had been struck by Bellum's curse was still twitching on the ground. The forms of Shawe, Jude, Diega and the Skreaf became nebulous, shrouded by a mist that grew thicker and heavier, until it completely consumed them. The mist spiralled up through the roof and vanished, leaving the room empty. The corridor shrieked around them and fractures spread along the walls of the main chamber. The whole facility trembled.

Copernicus managed to wrench open the sliding door. He grabbed Silho and carried her into the room. Snatching up his communicator, he bolted up the ladder and out into the pipes. Silho lay shivering in his arms while he raced through the watery tunnels. Her nerves jolted at the terrible screeching explosion of the facility giving way behind them. The sounds of rushing water chased them all the way to the hidden exit into the Catadral. The commander dragged them out into the church. He ran to the front of the building and out into the air. Silho stared up at a sky without stars, a darkness without light.

337

36

'Please . . . Please . . . Please . . .' The prayer ebbed and flowed as Ev'r's consciousness swept forwards and back like the drifting, dragging tide.

'I didn't cover his grave. I couldn't put the dirt on him . . .' she breathed.

'Ev'r . . . Keets . . . Keets . . . Stay with me . . . Ev'r.'

'I couldn't,' she said.

In her mind, Ev'r lay just below the surface of a dark river. She could see shadows moving around her, through her. Her body floated suspended in motion. All was silent – *except for that woman crying.* It was a soulless, desperate sound and dragged her towards clarity.

Ev'r twitched one finger and found her hand could move. She twisted her wrist and her arm jolted into motion. Her body animated and she swam towards the edge, surfacing beside her ancestor, Leila. The dark-faced woman, with glowing yellow-wolverine eyes and serrated carnivore teeth, didn't stir. She just lay crumpled on the floor, the tortured sound rising from her mouth in an almost disembodied way. Blood had pooled around her, but she wasn't crying for herself. Ev'r reached out a watery hand and brushed her fingertips over the woman's rough skin. Leila spoke, her words divided into many unified voices, the receptacle of her people.

'The Indemeus X has risen. He is coming. All is lost. All is dust and darkness.'

Something grabbed Ev'r's leg and dragged her downward through the water at an impossible speed. She gurgled a scream. She struggled, twisted and thrashed, then crashed out onto a cold concrete floor.

Ev'r lay on her back, staring up at Eli. He stood over her, his sleeves rolled up, his eyes wild and terrified.

She found her arms, once again, pinned to her sides with the special chains. Her legs were also bound.

'Is it you, Ev'r?' Eli whispered.

'Just like old times,' she said and the words stung her raw throat.

'It worked!' Eli threw himself down on top of her and hugged and kissed her fiercely.

'Who is the Indemeus X?' Ev'r asked, her voice quavering.

Eli raised his head and looked into her face. 'I don't know, but for some reason I don't like the sound of that name.'

'Neither do I,' she said darkly.

He scrambled up and hauled her into a sitting position then proceeded to unwrap the chains from around her body. She stayed slumped, the woman's cry echoing through her mind.

'Look,' Eli lifted one of her hands and showed her that the blackness was completely gone from her fingertips, but for some reason, Ev'r felt no relief or joy.

'It was the Venus Lily,' Eli continued. 'It was a close call. When I found you, I didn't even recognise you.'

'Where are we?' Ev'r said, shivering.

Eli gave a nervous half-giggle. 'Well, I had to mix the potion somewhere and the only bowl I could think of quickly was a . . . um . . .' He shifted to one side and Ev'r realised they were in a public toilet block, sitting on a pee-stinking floor, inside a graffiti-covered cubicle. The toilet bowl was spewing out a bubbling, purple substance. Ev'r touched her wet hair and her hands came away purple.

'You dunked my head in a toilet bowl?'

Eli giggled again and coughed over it. 'It was clean – mostly. I was desperate.'

Ev'r leaned back against the cubicle door and stared up at the ceiling. An obscene, crudely drawn naked picture looked back at her. She was numb.

'We can't stay here long,' Eli said, gathering up various objects from the ground. 'Things are going crazy out there. Androts are being dragged from their houses and locked up.'

His words reminded her of what happened with the machine-breeds. She told Eli.

'Trutt,' he cursed. 'If Kry has already left his hide, then the Skreaf might already have him. We have to get going.'

He took Ev'r's arm to help her stand. She let him. He had kept his promise to her. It was the first time in her life that anyone had. When she could, she lifted her rucksack onto her back with weary arms.

Eli unlocked the cubicle and they moved out of the toilet block and onto the street. It was mostly deserted, except for a few vagrants shuffling along the footpath, sifting through the garbage piles beside the buildings.

'It must be three-quarters dark-time,' Eli said, gazing around the foggy street. 'It feels like it.' Ev'r shivered.

'Hey.' A vagrant moved towards them.

'We have no money,' Eli said. 'And we're contagious so keep away – please.'

The ragged person paid no attention and Ev'r drew her weapon as she sensed the electrical zing of magics. The vagrant's head jolted up in an unnatural, jerky way. She was an old woman, one of her eyes piercing sharp, the other completely missing from the black hole in her face. She stared at them through a lock of matted grey hair. Ev'r noticed the purple cross branded into the woman's neck.

'Darmel the Premonitionist. I haven't seen you in a while,' she said.

'But I've seen you,' Darmel croaked. She was a mildly powerful witchdoctor and seer whom Ev'r had encountered several times in the Matadori. Popular speak said Darmel had died long ago, but zombified herself into immortality with her own dark magics. Darmel ground three dice in one filthy, yellow-clawed hand. 'In my mind. You're always running, but you're never moving, and the ground is giving way under your feet.'

Ev'r gave a humourless smile, as sneaking disquiet snaked cold fingertips up and down her spine. 'Sounds like the story of my life.'

'No, it's the story of your death.' Darmel threw the dice into the air and let them fall onto the ground. Her voice became suddenly clear and her cyclopean gaze fixed onto Ev'r. 'Beware. Grim Death walks the streets tonight calling your name.'

'Yes, thanks, but you're a little bit late,' Eli cut in. 'We just fixed that problem – so thanks again, but you can leave us alone now.' Red splotches had broken out on his neck from the effort of deliberately being close to discourteous.

'The end of days is near,' Darmel crooned. 'An ever-living enemy is rising. You must spread a warning. You must prepare a means of travel and escape this land. There is no hope of survival.'

'Just an update,' Eli said, his voice shrill with frustration. 'They've already risen, they're already here and you're wasting time we could be spending trying to stop them.'

He turned and strode off down the street.

Darmel spoke in a low voice, so only Ev'r heard. 'One worse than the Skreaf hordes is coming. The Indemeus X has risen. All is lost. All is dust and darkness.' And with that Darmel vanished into the mist of the Murk and Ev'r shivered to hear the words from her vision repeated.

She turned and hurried to catch up with Eli. 'Where are you going?' she asked.

'We have to find Kry, but first I have to help Luther. I'm sure I know how. He's in a transflyer just down the road.'

Ev'r pulled up short and dragged him to a stop. 'I don't know whether you get this, but the city is almost cooked. The best thing we can do is grab a craft and head for the Brine. We may still be able to escape.'

He pulled out of her grip and said with a sternness foreign to him, 'I will not abandon Luther to die. I will not abandon my friends. I will not give up. I helped you, Ev'r Keets, and I fully expect you to keep your end of our deal and help me.'

'Who do you think you are, going around saving everybody?' Ev'r demanded. 'You need to wake up. The city is falling and you'll die along with everybody else.'

'Then I'll die,' he said without any waver of fear in his voice. 'And I would rather that than live knowing I ran away when I could have stood up and fought. I said I expected you to fulfil your end of our deal, not because I can make you do it, let's face it, I can't, but because I know – even though everyone said that you're a lost cause and that you won't change – *I know* you're better than that. I believe in your strength. You won't back down. You won't run away. You won't stop fighting. You and I are a team and you're my friend, whether you believe in friendship or not. I'm going to the chemist to get some medicine. You go to the grocery store and get some fresh, uncooked meat, then come to KJ Street. I'm depending on you.'

He turned his back and marched away and Ev'r stood staring, strange feelings stirring inside her – *you and I are a team and you are my friend* . . . She found herself moving towards the red sign of an all-night grocer.

As Ev'r reached the door, a shadow shifted in the alley beside the shop. She snatched up her blade as a figure stepped into the lamp light. Ev'r recognised the boss of the Crook'd Town Pride, Caesar K-Ruz. A twinge ran along the five-claw scar he'd given her year-cycles earlier. With one swipe, he'd sliced through her back, inches from her spine.

'Where is Anklebiter?' K-Ruz asked.

'How should I know?' Ev'r replied, keeping her blade ready.

'Give him this message,' the Pride boss demanded. 'We tried to recover the Androt leader, but the witches got to him first. There are many more of them than I believed. Our situation is grave.'

'Just catching on now, are you?' Ev'r sneered. 'You gangsters think you're invincible, but you and yours will fall with the rest of us.'

Caesar snarled and Ev'r noticed he was gripping an injury in his stomach. Blood seeped around his fingers.

'Just give him the message, Keets.'

'Where did they take the Androt?' Ev'r asked.

'The Galleria – they took him inside.'

Caesar's lion shadow circled him and, with another grimace of pain, the Pride boss stepped back into the darkness, leaving just the glow of his eyes.

Ev'r pushed open the grocery store door and entered.

37

Copernicus smashed the lock of the pub icehouse and pulled back the hatch. A gust of sub-zero air billowed out. He gritted his teeth and sent his senses inside the dimly lit freezer room, checking for heat or movement. Detecting neither, he lowered Brabel through the trap-door and jumped down beside her, his boots crunching on ice cubes.

Silho's skin all over her arms, chest and face was severely burnt. Her eyes stared open, glazed with shock. He piled ice on top of her. The bitter cold burned his hands numb in seconds. His teeth chattered and shivers ran through his body. Almost instantaneously, Silho's skin began to heal and her bloodline marks of firebird and flame grew back along her arms. This time the tiny pictures had spread even further across her neck and chest. He touched the images and pulled away. They were burning hot despite the ice.

Silho blinked, her sights clearing. She sat up, the ice cubes rolling off her. She studied her own hands and arms. 'I don't understand it,' she murmured, exhaling mist.

'You must have inherited your mother's Pyron skills,' Copernicus said.

'But I didn't – I burn and it hurts.'

'Yes, but you also heal from the burns almost immediately. You're a half-breed . . . maybe the key to killing the Skreaf isn't increasing your power so much that you don't set alight, maybe it's resisting the pain of the fire. If you resist the pain for long enough to kill them you'll regenerate.'

343

'I'm not sure I can resist,' Silho confessed. 'And even if I could, there're too many of them. How would I drain them all at the same time? My skills would need to be magnified.'

Her words triggered a thought in Copernicus' mind. 'The Mazurus Machine is a magnifier. The Skreaf are using it to strengthen their curse to free their master. Maybe we could use it against them.'

'Bellum has the others,' Silho said. She held her head in one hand. 'I couldn't stop her. I failed.'

'I was there too, Brabel,' the commander reminded her. He used his skills to access the shape of her thoughts and saw that her mind was repeating the enchant without her conscious effort. She was growing stronger at a much faster rate than he would have expected, but he doubted it would be fast enough. He had no idea what their next step should be.

Copernicus felt a vibration on his hip and took the communicator out of his pocket. The hedge had completed before they'd fled the facility and there was a message from Eli waiting in the lines.

'Play message,' he instructed the machine and he and Silho listened as Eli told them what he had discovered about the Skreaf, the Envirious Realm and the gateway land of Woulghast.

'He said that portholes can be forged from our realm into Woulghast,' Copernicus said once the message had ended. 'According to the Wraith, Omarians painted portholes between their realm and ours. Did your father ever talk about this?'

'No, but Bellum did.' Silho's face darkened. 'She said they'd forced him to paint a porthole in his cell before he was executed, that without it, their plans would be for nothing.'

'In his cell,' Copernicus repeated and his mind took him back to the night at the Galleria when he had found Englan Chrisholm's final prison. He'd seen the painting on the ceiling.

'We have to go to the Galleria,' he told Silho. 'That's where the porthole is. We have to try to pass through into the gateway land.'

Silho lowered her head. 'I don't think . . . I'm not strong enough. I can't do this.'

Copernicus recognised this confession as the first time Silho hadn't tried to hide or lie through her pain and fear.

'Tell me why you think that,' he said quietly.

'Because my mother was the greatest at everything and Bellum still killed her. I'm nothing compared to her.'

'That's not true,' Copernicus said. 'You have skills Oren Harvey never had.'

'I don't think we're going to make it,' she whispered. 'I don't deserve to.' She looked up at Copernicus with tears in her eyes. He didn't understand what she meant, but he could see what she was feeling. She felt completely alone with the odds stacked up against her like an impenetrable wall, with no way over or around. She was facing death – they both were. Realistically, Silho was right. There was no chance he could see of them coming through this alive. They were just too heavily outnumbered.

Instead of lying, Copernicus put his arms around her and pulled her close against him. 'You're not alone. I won't abandon you,' he promised. 'Whatever happens, I'll be with you.' He looked down into her eyes. Their faces were so close that their lips almost touched.

An earthquake tremor shook the tiny icehouse. The ice cubes rattled and the boards of the structure clattered together. For a moment Copernicus wondered if this was it, if they were already too late, but then the quaking subsided. He and Silho looked at each other, understanding that they had no more time.

Copernicus stood and pushed open the hatch. He hauled himself out and lifted Silho up after him. The sky was lightening to a dark grey as dawn-light fought against the blackness of night.

They moved silently through the streets of Nureyev scouting for transport. To get to the Galleria they needed to ascend over 150 levels. They found an old model transflyer parked outside an unlit house. Without Diega's skill, it took Copernicus a lot longer than he would have liked to override the security system, even though it was outdated. He hadn't boosted a craft since he was a kid. Finally the engines coughed and started. Copernicus jumped into the pilot's seat and took off.

They found most of the skyways were clear because the blocks had been removed. Neither of them said it, but they both knew this was a bad sign. The Skreaf obviously felt as though they had already won. Copernicus touched the ring in his pocket. Their only hope was that this was the original. The witches couldn't use the machine without it.

He sped them through the main tunnels until they reached their destination level. There they abandoned the craft and went on foot to the Galleria. They paused on the fringe of Elio D'An Square. Masses of palace enforcers and state guardians stood positioned around the Galleria. A group of machine-breeds worked to set up a stage at the museum's front entrance. The royal banner and flags flapped in the chill breeze. A line of soldiers in full riot gear held back a growing gathering of protestors.

'The king must be making an announcement today,' Copernicus whispered to Silho.

'Which means there'll be no way in,' she said.

Copernicus considered their options. They could find a way into the underground tunnels beneath the Galleria, but that would take time they didn't have. Their other option was to go straight through the front door, but that meant he would have to perform advanced Illusionist cloaking magics that he had never used before. He took a deep breath and made a decision.

'Follow me.'

They left the shadows and walked directly through the centre of the square, passing the bronze statue of King Miron II. He felt Silho hesitating as they neared the entrance of the Galleria, crowded with soldiers, but she didn't stop. She stayed by his side.

Copernicus held an image in his mind of how he wanted people to see them – as red-uniformed enforcers. They reached the sentinels and passed them without incident. They walked under the part-wolf, part-dragon sculpture carved into the entrance-hall ceiling and entered the grand foyer of the Galleria. Copernicus didn't pause. He led Silho towards the hanging room, which had been reopened for public viewing, and through the corridors to where the Mazurus Machine had sat. They went to the loose marble square and Copernicus used his blade to prise it up, exposing the cleaners' standing box underneath. He sent his senses down to the tunnel below, but the reading was clouded. Dark magics smothered the air. He nodded to Silho. She crawled into the box and slid through. He followed, dropping down onto the masses of abandoned written word below.

A light shone ahead of them and they inched towards it. Silho struggled to keep her footing on the unstable piles of sliding books. He gripped her arm and they made it to the place where Copernicus had found the cell block hidden behind a fake wall. The wall now stood open and the flickering fluoro light in front of the last cell lit their path. They moved towards Englan Chrisholm's final prison.

Inside the cell, they found a bench with knives and tubes had been set up for use. Copernicus' senses picked up on voices echoing behind them. A man yelled and a scuffle broke out. The vibrations grew nearer, but the haze of magics stopped Copernicus from seeing who they belonged to. He turned to Silho. She stood staring up at the ceiling of the cell, at the painting – all the tiny pictures so similar to those on her body. She whispered the words written across the artwork, '*My God, my God, why have you forsaken me?*'

A burst of light exploded from the images and engulfed them. Copernicus felt himself lifting off the ground and his last thoughts were on the trials and tests of the gateway land that Eli had spoken about. What would be waiting for them on the other side?

38

Eli entered the chemist shop, jingling the bell above the door. He kept his head down in case of military I-eyes or spyers implanted in the ceiling, and ducked swiftly into an aisle to start searching for the medications he needed. His own allergy medicine was prescribed, so he knew he wouldn't be able to find it on the shelves, but he thought a mix of extra strength, normal anti-allergy pills might be enough. He was going just on a hunch, but he hoped that treating Luther's allergy would cure his inability to retain nutrients. If not, he was out of ideas and time.

He saw one of the labels he was searching for and snatched the bottle, pushing it into his jacket. The speed of his hands covered his thievery, but clammy patches of sweat were appearing under his arms and on his back. His wings twitched irritably and Nelly kept quiet in his pocket, as though she was also holding her breath that they didn't get caught. As he reached the end of the aisle and found the second packet of pills he was looking for, he realised that he hadn't needed to be so concerned. The chemist and all the shop attendants were occupied, standing at the serving counter staring up at a holo-screen broadcasting the news. Eli pocketed the pills and peeked around the corner of the shelf to listen in.

'Violent scenes have erupted in front of Palace Sirenseron as protestors sympathetic to the machine-breed cause demand an explanation from the king regarding his order that all Androts submit themselves to the authorities or face capital charges . . .' The screen showed images of thronging masses of shouting people being pushed back from the palace gates by reptilian-faced enforcers. 'The Standard has released a statement that King Miron XI will make an announcement in Elio D'An Square at the dawning of tomorrow's day. In other news, experts believe the deep core tremors that have been shaking Scorpia for the last week now are a result of minimal earth shifts and should not be viewed as a major concern. Now, let's go to Ray for a weather update. Looks like more acid rain on the way . . .'

The shop attendants stirred and began talking among themselves and Eli took the chance to slip out of the shop. He darted to the other side of the street and ran along the footpath until he saw the sign for KJ Street up ahead. He slowed to a jog and took the corner. Ev'r stood there, holding two slabs of wrapped meat in one hand and eating a bread roll with the other.

'Here.' She fished another one from her pocket and threw it to him. 'Eat before you pass out.'

Eli caught the roll and gnawed off a chunk of bread, gulping it down as he raced to the end of the side street where he had parked the transflyer with Luther inside it.

Ev'r's boots thudded behind him. He ripped open the passenger side door. The transflyer was empty. Eli felt over the seat then climbed in, felt all over the floor, all over the pilot's side, the back seat – Luther was nowhere.

'He's gone!' Eli said, dismay dragging heavily on his heart. 'Why would he go? He was barely conscious.'

'Maybe he died and disappeared. That's what happens with Midnight Men,' Ev'r said.

Eli jumped down and said, 'Well he couldn't have gone far. We'll just look for him and —'

'Snack-size!' Ev'r interrupted. 'Listen to yourself. You want to find a semi-conscious, invisible, mute man, lying somewhere in the city, who has most likely already died and vanished. Caesar K-Ruz approached me at the grocery store. He said the Skreaf had taken Kry to the Galleria. We have to go.'

Eli's shoulders slumped and he shook his head. 'I promised

Luther. He was so scared, but he helped me.' He sank down to the ground, his mind so tired he could barely lift his head.

Across the street a dog barked at them from inside a narrow three-level house, built shoulder to shoulder with its identical neighbours. Eli looked up at the window where the pure white wolf-like creature stood staring out. Three cats were also pressed up against the glass pane, trying to scratch their way out. The scope of his stare widened and he took in a pile of uncollected hardcopy mail items at the front of the house. The lawn was overgrown.

'There's no one there,' Eli said. He forced himself to his feet.

'What are you talking about?' Ev'r asked.

'At that house. No one is there, but the animals are locked inside.'

'So?' Ev'r demanded. 'Are you delirious or something? Remember – Skreaf demons taking over the world. I think that has priority over some stray animals.'

Eli ignored her. He moved out of the alley and across to the house, where he pushed open the creaky front gate and ran up the stairs. Several pairs of feet tick-tapped on the boards behind the door as Eli drew his blade and worked at the lock.

'Trutt,' he cursed. He'd never been good at jimmying locks.

'Here, give that to me.' Ev'r grabbed the blade and shoved him out of the way. One turn from her practised fingers and the door sprang open. The big white dog and three cats dashed, meowing and woofing joyfully, from the house. They circled Ev'r who was still holding the fresh meat. She ripped off the wrapping of one packet and threw it down on the grass for them to eat. The cats attacked it immediately, but the dog only sniffed it then bounded over to a place in the yard below the window where the animals had been sitting. It sat down and bayed. Eli looked up at the windows of the houses all around them, expecting lights to go on and faces to start appearing to investigate the disturbance. He hurried over to the dog, trying to shush it. Nelly shrank down in his pocket.

'Good boy, well done, that's enough.' He encouraged the dog to be quiet.

Eli tripped over something on the ground and sprawled onto the grass. He got up onto his elbows and looked behind him. There was nothing there, but the dog was nudging something with his nose – something in the air. Eli scrambled onto his knees and crawled forward with his hand stretched out in front of him. His fingers bumped against skin, and then felt a face . . .

'Luther!' he hissed. 'Ev'r! He's here! He's here!'

She ran over and he held up his hands around the invisible body to stop her from stepping on the unconscious Midnight Man.

'Is there any meat left?' he asked her.

She held up the remaining packet.

'Can you take some out?' he asked her. He ripped open the packet of one of the medicines he had stolen and unscrewed the lid of the other. Using his blade, he crushed the pills together onto the lid.

'Meat.' He held out his hand and Ev'r pushed some of the squashy substance into his palm. He poured the medicine powder onto the portion.

'Okay,' Eli said. 'You open his mouth and I'll put it in.'

Ev'r felt over the invisible man's face and found his lips.

'Don't cut yourself on his teeth, they're sharp,' Eli warned her.

She managed to prise his jaw apart and said, 'Ready.'

Eli pushed the meat in between her hands and hooked it onto a row of ragged teeth so that Luther wouldn't choke. Ev'r pressed his mouth together in a chewing motion, mashing the medicated meat into a liquid pulp that would slide down his throat.

For several minutes nothing happened, then the prone man coughed, and as he did, he appeared, his shadow cloak swirling around him. Luther opened his eyes and Eli helped him to sit up.

'Here, eat some more,' Ev'r pushed another piece of meat into the man's mouth. Luther chewed weakly and swallowed with effort. As he swallowed, his whole body morphed – filling out, growing stronger. The sagging skin of his face stretched back to reveal darkly handsome features, nothing like the monster he'd appeared to be while he was ill. The effects didn't last though, and he changed back to his wasted state virtually straightaway.

'What was that?' Eli asked.

'Partial metamorphosis,' Ev'r said. 'Looks like the medicine is working and the meat is enough. He doesn't need to feed on the near-dead. Probably the more he eats the stronger he'll get. Here.' She handed the slumped Midnight Man the whole packet of meat she had stolen from the shop. 'Get under cover and eat. We can't stay with you anymore. Eli, let's go.'

She stood, but Eli sat for a moment beside the man who the commander had described as desperately lonely, wanting to be near people, but no one wanting him. He was too frightening – too strange. Eli noticed the animals had gathered around in a conference-like way and were watching the Midnight Man and the food resting in his lap. Eli had an idea. He took Luther's hand and placed it on the wolf dog's shaggy white head. The dog nuzzled and licked the Midnight Man's fingers. The cats pressed in, brushing against his legs. Eli noticed Ev'r was avoiding looking at the animals. Luther's lips twitched upwards and he stroked the dog's head.

'Take care of them. Their people are gone,' Eli said. 'And take these pills, one of each every day. You have allergies. That's what's making you sick. Do you understand?'

Luther nodded.

'Find me when they run out and I'll get you more. Take care,' Eli said, thinking in his mind that the possibility that the city would still be standing then and that any of them would still be alive was slim to none. A heavy knot squeezed his gut. 'We have to go.'

He pushed himself to his feet, but before he could move Luther grabbed his hand. His grasp was freezing cold. He traced letters in the air with one clawed finger. Eli watched his finger and said, 'I-R-E-P-A-Y-U. I repay you. That's not necessary.'

Luther gestured, 'I-W-I-L-L,' then, 'C-O-P-E-R-N-I-C-U-S?'

'Trying to stop the Skreaf.'

'Snack-size,' Ev'r called him from out on the street.

'I have to go. We're trying to stop them too.'

Luther nodded again. The dog nuzzled the Midnight Man's fearsome face and licked it. Luther made a movement like a shudder and Eli realised it was a silent laugh. He left the man sitting with the animals and walked with Ev'r back towards the transflyer. He glanced over at her. She was staring straight ahead.

'You weren't lying about your father killing your cat, were you?' he said.

'We have to get to the Galleria and get Kry before the witches use him,' she said, her eyes fixed forward.

They reached the transflyer and they both went for the pilot's side.

'No chance,' Ev'r said. She pushed Eli aside and climbed in. He snorted and ran around to the passenger side. He jumped up beside her and dragged the door shut. The sound triggered his memory of the news item. 'Oh no,' he said.

'What?' Ev'r glanced at him and started the engine.

'I heard in the chemist that at dawn today the king is making an announcement at Elio D'An Square. The place will be crawling with soldiers and palace enforcers and the Galleria will be closed. How are we going to get in?'

'We'll think of something,' Ev'r said. 'We have to, unless you've changed your mind about flying out to the Brine.'

Eli shook his head. 'No more running.'

'How did I know you were going to say that?' Ev'r said. She released the brake and eased the craft up into the greyness of the pre-dawn sky.

39

Silho blinked as the light around them faded. She turned to Copernicus and found herself looking at a young boy with piercing black eyes and a scarred face. Silho stared at her own hands and saw they were tiny. Her body felt strange, so light, almost as though it were floating.

'What's happened to us?' she asked.

'We're children again,' Copernicus said, his voice high and unbroken. 'This must be part of the tests.'

Silho recalled Eli's warning about the gateway land of Woulghast, but her memories dissolved as they formed until they were completely forgotten.

'Look!' She pointed ahead of them to the lights and rides of a carnival. She ran towards it and Copernicus followed.

Silho stopped in front of a carousel with horses wearing bridles and saddles all colours of the rainbow. They galloped in circles, their manes and tails flying out behind them. Other children were already travelling around and around to the merry music. Silho went forward to pass through the gates and join them, but Copernicus grabbed her hand.

'Silho, no.'

'But I want to,' she said.

She struggled against him and he shouted at her, 'Silho! Look at them!'

The urgency of his words made her stop fighting and take another look at the carousel. She now saw chains around the children's legs, fastening them to the horses. They had a vacant inward stare in their eyes and the music scratched along with the distorted, creepy twang of a music box running down.

'We have to get out of here,' Copernicus said.

'I'm scared.' Silho began to sob.

'Hold my hand,' he told her. 'We'll stay together. We won't leave each other ever.'

They grasped hands and held tightly as they walked along the path, past other rides full of children. They seemed to be laughing, but when Silho listened closely their laughter became screams, and their smiles faded to grimaces of terror. She focused on the pathway ahead, trying to ignore the candy shack with a fountain of red syrup that was really blood, the stalls selling toys cheaply for just a simple soul, and clowns whose face paint barely disguised the monsters lurking beneath. A woman materialised in front of them, cloth wrapped around her head, hoop earrings dangling from drooping lobes.

'Come children, let Madame Douval show you your future.' She beckoned with one red-nailed finger and smiled benignly. 'Come.'

Silho's focus drifted, but Copernicus squeezed her hand and she shook her head at the woman. When they were far enough away, Silho looked back to see the woman's smile stretch into a rotting snarl and a maggot wriggle out of the wart on her face.

The path finally ended at a tent with a veiled doorway. Copernicus pushed it aside and they entered a gloomy room, choked with wafting clouds of musky incense. To Silho it felt as though they had stepped into someone's sleeping mind, into a dream – or the beginning of a nightmare. She squinted through the mist and saw they were standing in front of a large mirror, with another mirror behind them reflecting their images into infinity. Something stirred ahead of them and they moved closer to their reflections, and closer still. They leaned forward, staring at the children who stood before them, the children they used to be. Silho heard the sound of someone stepping towards them through the mist, heel-toe, heel-toe, and she felt Copernicus tense beside her. A man appeared in the mirror. He had dark hair and a beard, black eyes that cut like razors. He wore a purple cloak and had the XXX insignia burned into the backs of his hands. She recognised the Illusionist – Doctor Silvan Kane.

'You,' he snarled at Copernicus.

Copernicus stared at his father, mute with terror.

'Get here now!' the Illusionist yelled.

His hand lashed out of the mirror and latched around Copernicus' throat, trying to pull him through. Silho grabbed Copernicus by the arm and her shoes dragged in the dirt beneath them.

'Leave him alone!' she screamed and her voice swapped halfway through the sentence from a child to an adult sound. 'Copernicus – fight back!'

The Illusionist made a gesture with his hand and Copernicus' arm became as slippery as if it were covered in oil. Silho could barely hang on and Copernicus was disappearing further and further inside the mirror. Through the panic, Silho could hear her inner voice repeating the enchant, the Illusionist magics, *Claude animus meus, claude animus meus. Close my mind.* A silence descended over her. She swapped to light-form vision and saw the body-lights of what was holding Copernicus. It was not a human-breed, not his father, but a shape-shifting demon. She drew strength from the demon's body-lights into one hand and used the power to wrench Copernicus back out of the mirror, but the creature clung onto his neck, refusing to release him. Silho's strength was draining quickly. Her arms were trembling, ready to give.

'Copernicus! It's not him. He's dead! Do something!' Silho screamed.

'You'll do what you're told,' the Illusionist snarled. 'Or you know what will happen to you – and the girl.'

Anger sparked in Copernicus' dark eyes and he pulled back. As he did, his body grew bigger and closer to its adult shape. He struck the mirror with all his force. It shattered, a million pieces of glass exploding out at them, a million reflections of the Illusionist. They fell to the ground and he was gone.

Copernicus doubled over, coughing and holding his throat. Behind the empty frame of the mirror, Silho saw a staircase leading downwards. She heard demon sounds coming from outside the tent door and grabbed Copernicus' arm. She led him through the open frame of the broken mirror to the top of the staircase. As they went forward onto the first step, the staircase straightened and they slipped down a steep slope. They changed fully back to their adult forms as they crash-landed.

Silho struggled to her hands and knees. Copernicus knelt beside her, staring, disconnected.

'It wasn't him,' Silho said. 'It was a demon, a shape-shifter.'

Copernicus blinked and swallowed, regaining some of his composure. 'I know.'

He rubbed a hand over his face and stood. Silho looked towards the stairs where they had fallen. The steps had vanished and they were enclosed in a cave-like chamber. The light was brighter and warmer here than in the land above. It flickered and danced over the walls, carved from intensely coloured rocks of emerald green, violet purple, ocean blue and rose pink. The shine and glitter of the stones calmed Silho's senses. She took deep breaths of the sweet air and began to drift. A clunking sound roused her mind and she saw Copernicus had fallen back down to one knee.

'I feel . . . so tired,' he breathed.

Silho's eyelids flickered and closed.

'Brabel!' The commander's yell woke her. He stumbled towards her, powerful magics numbing his limbs. He grabbed her arm and dragged her out of the chamber and into another. As they crossed the threshold, clarity rushed over her like a bucket of freezing water dumped over her head. She sat up and looked behind them. She sucked in a sharp breath. The ground of the shimmery-rock chamber was covered in decomposing corpses they had not seen. Worse than that, the walls themselves were made of bodies, bone and flesh and faces, squirming, writhing, their eyes shut. *The chamber of dead dreams.* Silho remembered Eli's warning. A glimmer bounced off the wall and into her eyes and the corpses vanished. She drifted again into dangerous contentment and sank down to the ground to sleep.

A harsh punch from Copernicus brought her around. She exploded in rage, lashing out and smacking him hard over the mouth, his weakest point. The blow pushed the flesh of his cheek into the fangs behind his teeth. He stumbled back, spitting blood and venom onto the ground. His eyes gleamed red and he rushed at her. The two locked in battle. Rage and hate coursed through their bodies. Copernicus overpowered her and threw her to the ground. He squeezed her neck with both hands. She changed to light-form vision and drew his strength into her, then ripped his hands away and shoved him back. Copernicus recovered fast and lunged again. He smacked her across the face and grabbed her head. He pulled it to one side, trying to snap her neck. Silho drew again from his bodylights and kicked him. She scrambled towards a rock, intending to use it as a weapon, but in crawling for it, she passed out of that chamber and into a third.

The rage dissolved as instantly as it had flared. She slumped facedown on the ground, the pain of her injuries erupting in an agonising surge. Copernicus charged out of the chamber after her. He grabbed her, but his grip softened immediately, his anger dissipating as Silho's had.

'We're in the three chambers,' he said, breathing heavily, confirming what Silho already suspected. 'That was hate . . . I hurt you, I'm sorry.'

'I'm sorry too,' she said. 'I'm . . .' Silho looked up into Copernicus' dark eyes and her desire for him stole her words. He reached out and stroked her face. She ran a hand up his arm over his viper bloodline marks – over the diamonds of black and purple, over the blue. His skin was cool to her touch, the perfect opposition to her heat. She turned and kissed his hand and Copernicus shivered. He dragged her to him and pressed his lips against hers, kissing her deeply. They held each other as closely as they could and kissed until their lips were numb. Nothing else mattered anymore. Silho's mind drifted blissfully until she tasted blood and faint memories disturbed her. *Who am I? Where are we?*

Copernicus caressed her and whispered, 'I love you.'

The words jolted Silho. *The chamber of lust.* She scrunched her eyes shut and used all her force to pull back from him. Her arms shook from the pressure pushing them together. Just managing to untangle from his grasp, she rolled onto her stomach, and crawled painfully, slowly, towards the chamber's threshold. Copernicus tried to hold her back, first talking to her, then holding her arms, then finally pushing her to the ground. He tore at her clothes and she reached up a trembling hand to the threshold line.

Velveteen fingers locked with hers. With a heave, they ripped her out from under Copernicus, dragging her from the chamber and into a dark tunnel. Copernicus followed her, also crossing the threshold of the third chamber. As he crossed over, he blinked, disorientated, then dropped to his knees. Silho sat up and looked back into the chamber. It was littered with bodies and skeletons of people, intertwined, trapped in the spell, loving each other to death. She shuddered and looked up at the person who'd saved them. Raine stared down at her with grey eyes that appeared now, if possible, more haunted than before.

'I thought you were dead,' Silho said.

The Wraith crouched down and took the compacted mirror Silho had given her from her moth-wing cloak. Raine held it up in front of her face and Silho saw the spectral had no reflection. Bellum's death-curse had hit the he-Wraith in Castlereagh and killed him.

'He's gone,' Raine hissed. 'My love.' Slow tears trickled down her grey face and Silho felt a terrible pang of grief for her.

'What is it?' Copernicus asked.

'Amateus,' Silho said. 'Bellum killed him.'

'He believed in his cause,' Copernicus said to Raine.

'So do I. Do you?' The Wraith asked.

'Of course,' Copernicus said.

'Follow me then. Let's kill them all or die trying.' Raine stood. She pushed the mirror back into her cloak and drifted further along the tunnel, leaving them in the shadows of her disturbing words. Copernicus helped Silho up and they stood close together. He pulled her against him and they held each other for a second longer, then separated and walked together into the darkness.

40

As the suns rose, two lines of new daylight spread across the crowded Elio D'An Square. Ev'r shoved her way through the masses of people. She could feel the air buzzing around her, all the individual thoughts becoming one crowd mind, teetering on the edge of riot. Eli paused in front of her and Ev'r pushed in beside him. His gaze was set on the giant domed Galleria Majora in front of them, completely surrounded by many layers of military defence and palace enforcers. There was no way, as far as Ev'r could see, of getting around them, and they couldn't risk sinking in through the Murk with the possibility of the Skreaf close by. The witches would sense them in a second.

Eli clenched his jaw so tightly a ridge appeared on his cheek. Ev'r noticed the upward tilt of his eyes made him look determined and wise. As she had suspected, the imp-breed had shown a strength that defied defeat. He was different, unique – as Ismail had been. Eli had done everything in his power to save her, and she had decided not to tell him the truth as she felt it now. She was just going to vanish and let him think she had run away. Then he could blame her, and not himself. The ground shook again under their feet, the contraction stronger this time, drawing murmurs from the crowd. A dog barked in the distance.

Eli glanced behind them towards the sound and his eyes widened.

'What is it?' Ev'r asked.

'I can see Caesar K-Ruz,' Eli whispered. 'And some of the other gangster bosses.'

Ev'r didn't bother to look back. The gangsters were the least of their worries.

A melodic blast of the music announced the king's arrival, immediately drowned out by the fierce roar of the crowd in a united fury at the royals. The sound only became more intense and ferocious as the grand double doors of the Galleria Majora opened and the heavily shrouded royal family, flanked on all sides by a five-man-thick wall of enforcers, shuffled out from the building and onto a stage set up in front of the museum.

Ev'r felt the earth start trembling again; this time it wasn't the shiver of a quake but the rhythmic pounding of an army stepping in time. The royal procession paused and the crowd quietened. The people craned their necks, staring in all directions, searching for the source of the marching. The sound grew nearer and more powerful until a vast army of Androts appeared at the main entrance of the square. The crowd fell to utter silence, and from this silence the Androts brought forth such a powerful sound of shouting and stomping that the crowd's roar now seemed like a whisper. It took Ev'r's breath away and sent chills shivering across her skin. Without further warning, the Androts charged the Galleria and the crowd surged to either side to get out of their way. The ground quaked and screams whipped the air.

Ev'r was swept up in the human tide and fought to free herself. Eli grabbed her arm. He buzzed his wings and dragged them above the heads of the other people. He flew them onto the roof of a nearby mansion and they watched as the Androts took the square, toppling the bronze statue of King Miron as they stampeded through. Soldiers and enforcers swarmed around the royal family and dragged them back into the Galleria. The great doors slammed shut and if the guards had any sense in their brains, Ev'r thought, they were now barricading every window and entrance into the museum. Other soldiers stayed on the landing of the Galleria, opening fire on the Androt masses. The screams of people still trying to evacuate rose in a panicked chorus. Ev'r smelt the burnt stench of dark magics in the air and saw people falling randomly in the crowd, as though struck down by an invisible opponent. Ev'r knew it was the Skreaf, hiding in the Murk, picking people off with death-curses. She felt strangely distanced from what was happening, as though she were watching a film on a holo-screen. Eli stood beside her with a grim expression, his eyes roving over the battlefield. Ev'r could almost hear his thoughts – their chances of getting into the Galleria just went from non-existent to minus that, and their time was almost up.

A more severe earthquake rocked the building they stood on. It knocked them both to the flat rooftop and they stayed there hanging onto the ledge. The heaving of the quake eventually subsided and Ev'r stared down at the war continuing below. The Androts had made a shield from the toppled stage and were sheltering behind it, firing on the soldiers still holding the Galleria entrance. She eyed the stained-glass dome on the top of the building.

'We could smash through the dome,' she said to Eli. 'But we'd have to fly there and there's no cover. We'd most likely get shot out of the sky.'

'What about the underground tunnel system that runs from the palace to the Galleria?' Eli suggested. 'There are cave-ins into the tunnel all over the Headquarters level. There's one just in front of Winston Dunn's diner.'

Ev'r nodded agreement. It was a far better idea. 'We'll have to fly to give us some distance from the Galleria, then we can go the rest of the way in the Murk. You ready?'

'Not in the slightest,' Eli admitted.

Ev'r held out her hand and he grabbed it. They jumped together off the edge of the building.

41

Copernicus and Silho followed the Wraith's ghostly form upwards through the rock tunnel. The echo of chanting voices grew louder and the tar stench of dark-words more suffocating with every step. The tunnel ended on top of a rock ledge overlooking a gigantic chamber.

Copernicus crouched low in the shadows and looked over the drop to the chamber floor far below. All hope abandoned him. A multitude of Skreaf witches and sorcerers, far more than he'd ever imagined existed, stretched out before them. Their voices rose united into one booming drone. It trembled the rock walls and raised bumps all over Copernicus' flesh. In the middle of the mass of black and grey stood a central pinnacle of rock separated from the rest of the chamber by a chasm on all sides. Heat and steam billowed from the black pit, the mist partially obscuring the hunched form of the High Skreaf, Bellum, standing on the plateau. A Skreaf symbol, triangle, triangle, square, covered the entire surface of the central platform. Bellum had rows of prisoners standing along the lines of the symbol. She was sacrificing them one by one and shoving their bodies backward into the pit.

Diega stood among them, bound and gagged. Copernicus' eyes shifted from the Fen to the Mazurus Machine perched on one edge of the plateau. The machine was an exact likeness of the hologram he had seen at the Galleria – a large spherical structure comprised of thousands of rotatable magnifying glass panels. The witches had placed the machine upside down with the trapdoor into the hollow device, usually at the base of the Mazurus, now at the top, and the telescopic core magnifier, normally pointing into the sky, now extending down into the pit – towards the seal over the Envirious Realm. From their vantage point, Copernicus couldn't see the head of the telescope, where he knew the Skreaf must have placed the ring Bellum took from Shawe. The Mazurus was vibrating slightly, making a humming sound as though warming up. Copernicus cursed under his breath, knowing that for the machine to be making such sounds the witches must have taken the original ring. He touched the shape of the replica in his pocket.

'There's Jude,' Silho whispered beside Copernicus and pointed to an altar half-hidden in the shadows of the Mazurus. The silver-skinned tracker lay bound to the rock, and pieces of SevenM's smashed body were scattered on the ground beside him.

'I can't see Shawe,' Silho said.

The Wraith hissed from the tunnel darkness behind them, 'He's chained below, further down in the pit with the other prisoners. They are to be sacrifices for the Morsmalus as he rises.'

'What else do you know?' Copernicus asked, keeping his eyes on Diega as Bellum cut her way gradually closer to his soldier.

'When I followed the Skreaf here from the holding prison, I saw them positioning the magnifying glasses of the Mazurus outwards. When Bellum slaughters the Ar Antarian and lets his blood flow into the pit, the Skreaf will unite in one curse focused through the central magnifier of the machine downward towards the Envirious Realm. That is when the seal will break and the Morsmalus will be freed.'

'Did you try to get the ring?' Copernicus asked.

'Yes,' the Wraith replied. 'It is in the very end of the machine below, near the prisoners. It is guarded by a Skreaf and locked behind a grate of steel, cursed so that I could not pass through it. To open the steel would require a great deal of physical strength.'

Immediately Copernicus thought of Shawe. After a moment's consideration, he said to Silho and the Wraith, 'This is what we're going to do. We free Shawe, then he and Raine get the ring. The witches need the magnification of their curses focused onto the seal in order to open the realm, but for our purposes we don't need the core magnifier to be functioning. We just need to get inside the machine and change the magnifying panels to face inwards on Silho instead of outwards on them. Then Silho's skill will be magnified and she can drain them.'

Silho eyed the multitude of Skreaf and doubt shadowed her face, but she still nodded in agreement to the plan.

Copernicus' thoughts went to the equipment they had seen in Englan Chrisholm's cell. He assumed that was Bellum's backup plan – to have Kry on standby in case anything went wrong with Jude. He could only hope Eli knew what was happening.

He said to Raine, 'Take us to Shawe.'

The Wraith stepped into the wall and he saw a ripple moving along the surface.

He and Silho hurried to keep up, running doubled-over along the ledge. They stayed with the shadows until they found a hole in the rock leading down into a tunnel. Copernicus lowered Silho into it then dropped down beside her. They followed the Wraith through a maze of sloping tunnels and turns leading into the ground. They finally came to an open doorway cut out of the rock. It faced the central stone pillar with the plateau far above them and the abyss far below. Copernicus looked down into the darkness. It was shifting, struggling, a distorted groaning-scream rising from its depths as the Morsmalus bellowed to be freed. Hot steam scorched Copernicus' face. The floor and walls around them shivered.

'There.' Raine pointed a thin grey arm.

Copernicus leaned out through the doorway and saw Shawe, close by, chained to the rock. His arms were wrapped in front of him and his head hung low to his chest. Sensing eyes on him, Copernicus looked up and around the walls of the pit. Hundreds of other prisoners were chained in a similar way. They were mainly spectral-breeds, with binding bands around their heads to stop them dissipating to escape. They watched him with terrified faces. Some distance above them, he could see the head of the core telescopic magnifier of the Mazurus Machine. Beside the magnifier, a Skreaf stood on a metal walkway fastened all the way around the central pillar. The witch was stepping along the walkway, searching the mist for any disturbances. When she had gone around to the other side of the pinnacle, Copernicus called out with a lowered voice, 'Shawe, wake up . . . Shawe!'

The gangster stirred and lifted his head. He blinked bleary eyes then focused on the nothingness below his feet. He cursed and pedalled his legs, dislodging rocks from all around him.

'Keep still!' Copernicus ordered and Shawe's attention snapped in their direction.

The witch reappeared above them and Copernicus ducked back into the shadows. She moved gradually around again and out of sight. Copernicus stepped out onto the wall and walked to Shawe. He grabbed the gangster's arms and said, 'Break out.'

'You won't be able to hold me,' Shawe said.

'Do it!'

Shawe inhaled deeply, then tensed his muscles and the chains buckled and broke. He dropped and Copernicus held him dangling over the black chasm. The commander walked backwards, straining to keep a grip on the gangster's massive bulk. When he reached the others, he and Silho dragged Shawe up into the tunnel. Shawe used the wall to help himself stand.

'Where are we?' he asked.

'At the gateway to the Envirious Realm,' Copernicus told him. 'The Skreaf are above us. They have the machine and Jude. I need you to break into the machine and remove the ring. Can you see the platform up there with the large black structure? That's where the band is, in the head of the core magnifier. The Wraith will show you.'

Shawe gazed upwards to the magnifier and further to the glint of the Mazurus on the plateau above. His green eyes scanned over the other trapped prisoners.

'I can't see him,' he said.

'Have you seen a red-haired boy among the prisoners?' Copernicus asked Raine.

'Yes, further down,' she said.

'Where?' Shawe demanded. He moved to the edge, looking as though he was about to jump. Copernicus grabbed his arm.

'If he's here, we'll find him, but first we have to stop the Skreaf or he's dead anyway.'

Shawe opened his mouth to argue, but even he saw it was irrefutable. A struggle of emotions twisted his face.

'What do you want me to do?' he eventually growled.

'Take this,' Copernicus pressed the replica metal band into Shawe's hand. 'Replace the original with the copy so the witches don't suspect. Buy us some time.'

'What are you going to do?' Shawe asked.

'Silho and I will go up to the top, get inside the machine and point the magnifiers inward. Silho can use her skill to destroy the Skreaf all at once.'

'How are we getting up there?' Shawe asked, nodding to the platform.

'We're climbing,' Copernicus said. 'Up the central pillar. The mist will give us some cover.' He turned to the Wraith. 'Help Shawe swap the rings, then start freeing your people. Use this, it will cut their binding bands.' He gave her his own blade.

The Wraith regarded him with her strange grey eyes, then took the blade and hid it in her moth-wing cloak.

Copernicus waited again until the Skreaf guarding the core magnifier had vanished from sight, then he leapt out over the abyss. He smashed against the surface of the central pillar and grappled with the rock. He managed to get a handhold and drag his feet underneath him. Sweat dribbled down his face and back.

'Throw Brabel to me,' he called to Shawe.

The big gangster swept Silho up, and before she could panic, hurled her over the abyss. Copernicus caught her and she grasped onto him with suffocating tightness. Her nails dug into his flesh.

'Climb onto my back,' he whispered.

She obeyed, freeing up his hands.

'Now you,' he said to Shawe.

The gangster cursed, sank low then launched himself out. Copernicus saw he was falling short and lunged forward to grab his arm. They connected and he swung Shawe up to the pillar. Shawe managed to grip the rocks and stayed there, frozen. The Wraith's face appeared beside him.

'We're heading for the top. Start climbing, don't look down,' Copernicus said to Shawe.

'Shove it up your arse,' Shawe muttered, his face blanched white. He reached out a shaky hand and hauled himself up, half an arm span at a time. Copernicus left him quickly behind. Carrying Silho on his back, he walked upwards on the rock surface with silent stealth. When they came to the steel walkway, he moved underneath it, waited for the witch to go to the opposite side, then hauled them up and over it. He spared a momentary glance for the core lens, a massive tubular structure reaching all the way to the top of the pillar where it joined with the Mazurus body, then he kept moving. Staying in the shadows of the telescope, he wound his way to the top, always keeping himself and Silho on the other side of the witch. They came to a place just below the plateau where the magnifier was connected with the rest of the machine. He reached out and opened one of the glass panels for them to enter the Mazurus.

42

Eli's gran'ma had always said that bravery was not great people doing great acts but normal people facing their fears. It was one of the many sayings she'd used to manipulate him to go to school, which he'd both feared and hated. She'd said if he didn't study and pay attention he would never amount to anything. She'd said he had a lot to prove because of his *condition*, that he had to work harder than everybody else, be stronger, be smarter, grow taller, otherwise no one would ever accept him and he would never have any friends. So the news that he had dropped out of school to become the world's greatest inventor had not gone down too well. She said she had failed. She cried the days into weeks and the guilt had almost drowned him – almost, but not quite. He wondered what she'd say to him now if she could see him tearing through a dark tunnel beneath the city streets, his face smeared with dirt and cobwebs tangling his wings. If she could see him running towards the danger instead of away like everyone else – a normal person facing his fears. He wasn't sure what her exact wording would be, but he highly doubted that 'brave' would make any appearance in the conversation.

Eli felt a very wide, half-crazed and most definitely terrified grin stretch across his face. The fact that Gran'ma would be absolutely appalled by what he was now doing made him absolutely sure he was doing the right thing for him. Sad but true.

He increased his pace and heard Ev'r stumble and curse behind him. Her blonde hair was still streaked with purple from the medicine dunking he'd given her. It kind of suited her. He felt a surge of affection for the woman. He didn't know if he would have had the courage to come this far if she hadn't been with him, at times dragging him.

A set of stairs appeared right in front of his feet. He skidded to a stop and Ev'r collided with his back.

'Sorry,' he whispered. 'My fault.'

'Really?' she said dryly, rubbing her arm.

Eli stared down the shadow-blackened steps. A rubbery burnt tinge to the air tickled his nose.

'Dark magics,' Ev'r said. 'We're close. The energy is all channelling this way.'

She pointed and Eli held up his torchlight. The shadows were flowing like black rivers down the walls on either side of the stairs.

'They're summoning for a curse – something big,' Ev'r said.

Eli swallowed back his fear. They headed down the steps and came out into a lower tunnel. The smell of burning was stronger and thicker here. It made his eyes water.

Ev'r dragged him back. 'Stay behind me.'

They crept down the hallway, keeping to the shadows. The roof shuddered above them, raining dirt down on their heads. Ev'r gave a sudden gasp and clutched at her stomach.

'Are you alright?' Eli held her shoulder.

She didn't reply, just straightened up and looked into the darkness behind them. She studied the shadows. Eli shone his torchlight back, but couldn't see anything, though small bumps rose all over his skin. He heard something like an animal whimpering, then a hissing whispering in the distance.

Ev'r drew in a sharp breath. 'Quick, run!' She grabbed his arm and they broke into a sprint, their boots pounding on the concrete floor. Eli had to use his wings to keep up with Ev'r.

They came to the end of the tunnel and saw a closed door ahead of them. The shadows were filtering through a crack beneath the door. Eli reached for the handle, but Ev'r shoved him out of the way. She snatched up a piece of rock from the ground and dropped it from above onto the handle. There was a hiss of magics and the handle turned black. Ev'r put a hand beneath her shirt and shoved open the door with the fabric as a shield for her skin.

They moved cautiously into the room. Eli stared around at a makeshift laboratory illuminated by a dull blue globe. Shelves of bottled organs and distorted creatures floating in coloured liquid lined the walls, blackened with the living stains of Skreaf magics. Operating benches were bolted down in the centre of the room. Fresh blood, purple under the blue light, had pooled on the steel of the benches and was dripping onto the floor. The hissing, scuttling noises sounded again, closer behind them. Ev'r slammed the door shut. She ripped the Morsus Ictus out of its sheath and dropped to her knees, scratching a symbol into the ground in front of the door. The lines were black and smoking as though the blade had burned the floor. Ev'r whispered some words over the symbol then stood. Sweat trickled down the sides of her face. She grabbed Eli's arm and dragged him to the opposite wall. She pressed her hands against the stones, closed her eyes and whispered more words. The stones began to glow and shiver. They slid apart, one after another, creating an opening in the wall into a pitch-black room. The door rattled behind them. Something hit it hard, and the symbol Ev'r had created sparked. Ev'r shoved Eli through the opening and he shone his torch around the room.

The beam trembled in his grasp. His lips parted and a soft sound of shock escaped him. The large room was packed full of cages with people hunched inside them, blinking up at him with eyes full of terror and despair. The captives were people of all ages and races, children and adults, Ar Antarians, Androts, human-breeds, Fens and many spectral-breeds. He recognised numerous faces from missing persons files he had seen.

Eli looked back at Ev'r. She stood facing the door. It was shaking now and the floor all around her symbols was cracking. Ev'r slid her rucksack off her back and lowered it to the ground. Something about the gesture made Eli's heart seize up.

'Ev'r, come on!' He held out his hand to her. 'Come through!'

She spoke without looking at him, her eyes fixed on the door, 'Keep going. Find Kry.'

'No! Not without you!' He pushed back through the opening and she rounded on him.

'I said, keep going!' she snarled.

Eli saw the blackness of the Ravien was back and spreading rapidly up her arms. Scales were forming around her neck and her jaw was distending as he watched. Eli stood, horrified, as Ev'r drowned in the form of the beast.

'No.' Tears stung his eyes. 'I found the cure.'

'There is no cure,' Ev'r said. Her voice trembled as she held onto the last moments of her self. 'Go. I'll hold them back for as long as I can.'

The door shuddered, about to give. The mist of the Skreaf seeped through the sides.

'I won't leave you,' he sobbed.

She reached out, took his hand in hers and whispered, 'My friend . . . I'm finished. Keep going.'

An uncontrollable and alien growl distorted her face and she shoved him back through the opening. She struggled to speak some words and the bricks closed back over, leaving Eli a final glimpse of Ev'r's eyes turning black as the Skreaf materialised behind her. A terrible scream shook the wall and Eli cried out, 'Ev'r!'

Other sobbing voices joined his in the darkness.

Eli scrambled to his feet and snatched up his torch.

'Don't leave us!' someone screamed.

He knew he didn't have time to help the captives, but couldn't bring himself to leave them all trapped. Running to the closest cage, he used his blade to prise open the lock. The prisoner, a human-breed woman, pushed out through the door.

'Give me something. I want to help,' she said to him.

He handed her a smaller knife and she worked beside him, freeing more captives, as the screaming and smashing from the laboratory room intensified. Eli cringed at every sound and cried for Ev'r. Some of the prisoners burst out of their cages, others stayed hunched inside grasping the bars. The captives helped each other to drag out the reluctant.

When enough of the prisoners were freed to help the others to escape, Eli said, 'I have to keep going. Do any of you know where the witches took an Androt by the name of Kry 939993?'

'Yes, I do.' A machine-breed stepped forward. 'Through there.' He pointed to the wall beside them. Eli ran to it and shone the torchlight over solid bricks.

'There must be a hidden door,' Eli said. 'I don't know how to access it.'

'Let me,' an Ar Antarian said. He pulled back one metal fist and smashed it into the bricks over and over again. The wall started to crumble and all the captives pressed forward, helping to pull away the bricks. The spectral-breeds among them, now able to access their skills without the binding bands around their heads, whispered Cos magics to lift the rocks and dump them against the opposite wall to reinforce it. When there was a gap big enough, Eli pushed through and almost slipped as the ground shifted under his feet. He grabbed the wall to right himself and shone the torchlight downward. He was standing on an enormous pile of books that covered the whole floor.

'Be careful – the ground is unstable,' he told the others as they climbed through behind him.

'I can hear something,' a human-breed woman with feline bloodline marks said. 'Through there.' She pointed to the wall ahead of them, where a glowing outline of red light revealed another hidden entrance. Eli could hear a faint chanting and saw the shadows were flowing in through the wall. He shivered, feeling like spiders were crawling all over his skin. He forced himself forward, trudging through the books. The prisoners behind him coughed, suffocated by the dark magics smothering the air. He turned back to them.

'You should all leave now. Go down that tunnel for as far as you can and be careful. War has broken out above us.'

He looked back to the wall and heard the shuffle and slide of books as the people moved away. Terrible feelings of aloneness and terror threatened to overwhelm him. He blinked sweat out of his eyes, lifted his blade to the stone wall and tried to prise open the door. In his mind he whispered a constant prayer to the Khaiti God – *please give me strength.*

The door refused to budge no matter how hard he shoved and pushed it. He strained, shaking from the exertion, and eventually slid to his knees, panting. He leaned his forehead against the rocks. He just couldn't do it alone. A shadow fell over him and he raised his head. Caesar K-Ruz and a mass of other bosses and gangsters had surrounded him. Some of the prisoners had also stayed back. Caesar nodded to him and Eli rose on trembling legs. Everyone pressed their hands against the bricks and he felt them shifting. The door swung open. As it did, a blast of red light and chanting voices shoved Eli back. He shielded his eyes and blinked into an area lined with old prison cells and packed with Skreaf all facing the end of the block. In the last cell, Eli saw the struggling form of the Androt Kry tied down to a bench. A Skreaf stood over him with a knife. The demon's eyes locked onto Eli and every Skreaf in the room spun his way. There was half a second of absolute silence in which Eli heard his heart thud twice, then a yell exploded behind him and he was barged aside as the gangsters and captives stormed the room. They wielded bricks and weapons, smashing into the stunned Skreaf. Chaos broke out as the witches fought back.

43

Silho clung to Copernicus' back, just below the surface of the plateau. She could hear Bellum's demon voice muttering curses above them. The sound sent shivers through her body. She strained to see above the ledge. The High Witch, cloaked and hooded, was moving among the prisoners, selecting her next victim. The chanting of the Skreaf masses had risen to a feverish pitch in anticipation. The whole chamber trembled. The witch passed close to Diega and paused. Bellum's sunken stare locked onto the Fen and the Skreaf's jagged knife blade caught the light.

Silho moved on instinct. She grabbed the edge of the plateau and dragged herself up off Copernicus' back, ignoring his urgent whispers to stop. Bellum pushed Diega to her knees and stood in front of her with the knife raised. Silho stepped out from the shadows of the Mazurus into sight and Diega's eyes widened, the colours of her skin flashing vibrant. Bellum whipped around towards Silho and hissed dark-words. Both she and Copernicus, who had climbed up after her, flew upwards then crashed down on their backs on the plateau. Their bodies strained under the crushing weight of the curse. Bellum stood over them, her face stretched tightly over the demon behind it and her mouth twisted into a ghastly grimacing snarl as the demon smiled.

'You're just in time, my dear,' she croaked.

Silho blinked into light-form and strained to lift her hands, but Bellum just cackled and said, 'You're weak. You're nothing.'

The witch snarled a curse that lifted Silho's body into the air and slammed her back down onto the rocks, again and again, until she almost blacked out. Behind Bellum, the Mazurus made a coughing sound, stopped shaking, then started up again, a louder hum rising from its centre. Two wings of magnifying lenses folded out from either side of the machine.

'Ah, our Lord, Morsmalus, has answered us and made ready the device,' Bellum said.

Silho gritted her teeth, realising Shawe must have actually removed the replica metal band from the machine and replaced it with the original, which the commander had been carrying all this time.

'It's time,' Bellum screamed to the mass of Skreaf, the call answered by a roar of demon voices. They surged closer to the edge of the abyss and started up a new chant.

Silho struggled against the debilitating curse, but was completely powerless against it. Bellum took the jagged-edge dagger from her cloak and moved towards the altar where Jude lay prone. Diega gave a muffled cry behind her gag. Silho could only watch as Bellum stopped beside the rock structure. She raised the dagger above Jude's heart, murmuring the same chanting curse as the other demons. But before she had the chance to plunge it into his flesh, Jude ripped up out of his chains and knocked the High Skreaf back with a powerful swing of his metal fist. He stood to his feet, electric blue eyes clear and blazing. He tore one of the magnifying wings off the Mazurus Machine and smashed it over his leg. He clutched the broken glass as a weapon. Bellum rose up and shrieked a curse. It hit Jude hard, and he staggered back, but recovered immediately. His half-Androt blood gave him strength against the demon words. Seeing her curses had little effect, Bellum lunged at him and they fought hand to hand.

With the High Skreaf's concentration on Jude, Silho found she could move again. She tried to sit up and a terrible pain shot through her body. Beside her, Copernicus lurched to his feet and charged at Bellum. He shoulder-barged the witch and she stumbled forward. He kicked her to the ground, but she flew straight back up and slammed him backwards with a curse. He smashed against the side of the Mazurus and slumped unconscious to the ground, red blood pooling around his head. Bellum seized Jude, digging her nails into the flesh of his shoulder. He cried out, weakening. Silho dragged herself to her hands and knees and crawled to Copernicus. Raine's face appeared in the shadows beside where the commander lay.

'Use her dark-words against her,' the Wraith hissed. She pressed the compacted mirror into Silho's hand. Silho stared at it, unsure of what Raine meant, then she saw her own reflection in the mirror, remembered what had happened in the underwater laboratory, and understood.

'Tell Diega,' she whispered to the Wraith.

Silho watched Raine vanish into the ground and reappear where the Fen stood with the other few remaining prisoners. The Wraith removed the gag from Diega's mouth and whispered in her ear. The Fen's eyes swivelled left to right as she comprehended and she nodded to Silho. Silho lifted up a chunk of rock, gathered her strength and rose to her feet. She threw it at Bellum where she stood over Jude, now lying prone on the ground. The rock smacked hard against the Skreaf's head and Bellum rounded on her.

'It's time,' Silho said.

Bellum's mouth stretched hideously wide, her eyes gleaming blood red. The witch took in a deep breath and raised her hands, shaking from the terrible power she was summoning to send at Silho. As Bellum released the death-curse, Silho opened the compact in front of herself and Diega yelled, '*Xpel!*'

The small mirror stretched back into its original size and shape of the shield Eli had designed. The force of the curse struck the mirror and was reflected back at Bellum. The witch screamed as her mirror-image was ripped and contorted, the damage spreading to Bellum herself. She stumbled back, her face melting into her hands. Her demon fought to get out of the disintegrating body. She tripped over a rock and almost toppled into the abyss, just managing to keep her balance. She teetered on the brink, using what was left of her power to hold herself there.

Screams rose from the Skreaf masses as they realised something was going badly wrong, but they hesitated, afraid to act without Bellum's instruction. Diega spoke, morphing the chains around her body, freeing herself and the other prisoners. She, Silho and Raine stepped towards the witch, past Jude who had dragged himself to Copernicus. The commander stirred and opened his eyes.

Bellum's skin started to split. The demon's hands pushed through her chest. Diega nodded to Silho and Raine and together they lifted the altar stone. They heaved it up and threw it at Bellum. It hit her chest and struck the face of her demon as it broke through. The stone rammed both Bellum and the demon over the edge and they plummeted, screaming, passing through the seal into the Envirious Realm, the dungeons of hell, where pain had a face and a name – *Morsmalus*.

As their screams faded, they were replaced by another more terrible screech. The Skreaf had broken rank and were flying through the air towards them.

'Inside the machine!' Copernicus yelled. He struggled up and kicked in one of the magnifiers. Jude grabbed the pieces of SevenM and lunged through, Diega at his heels and Silho scrambling just behind. The broken glass cut into the skin of her hands, but she barely felt it. Copernicus pushed through last.

'Turn the magnifiers inward!' he commanded and he, Diega and Jude stumbled around the spherical glass machine, turning as many panels as they could. The Skreaf gathered outside the Mazurus, rocking the machine, trying to dislodge it from the ground and push it into the abyss. Terrible moans rose from the darkness below. Silho stood frozen in the centre of the machine, staring at the hideous Skreaf faces leering in at them. She gasped in ragged breaths, feeling drowned by panic as the Mazurus pitched closer and closer to toppling off the edge.

'Silho, start now,' she heard Copernicus command. 'Think of the words.'

She tried but couldn't think around the pounding of her head. Copernicus seized her shoulders and said, 'I'm here. Look at my face. Focus.'

Silho stared into his dark eyes and started to repeat the words of the enchant, and soon, the screech of the machine and Skreaf chanting died out to silence.

Copernicus released her. She blinked into light-form vision and squinted against the glow of thousands of Skreaf body-lights stretched out before her. She lifted her hands and drew strength from their lights. With the panels of the Mazurus magnifying her skill, she drew so much power so quickly her skin immediately ignited. She focused on the words Copernicus had taught her, trying to block the pain. The fire spread from her hands to her arms and from her arms to her body as she drew more and more strength from the Skreaf, until she was fully alight. Silho looked through the wavering glow of the fire to where Copernicus, Jude and Diega huddled in one corner of the machine trying to escape the fierce heat of her body.

'Get out!' she yelled to them, smelling her own burning flesh and hair. The rocking of the structure had stopped.

Unable to withstand the heat any longer, Diega smashed a panel, and she and Jude dragged the commander out onto the plateau. Silho stood alone, trembling from the great power swelling in her body. She felt like a volcano about to erupt. She fell to her knees, unable to bear the pressure and pain. Her senses dimmed and sight and sound bled together in a blur of droning blackness. She closed her burning eyes and saw, in her mind, her mother and father walking together, hand in hand. Oren's bloodline marks of flame shimmered a brilliant scarlet-orange in the sun, with the scales of Englan's firebird dragon mark a cool green in contrast. They stopped and looked back at her, directly into her eyes and she felt them so close. She heard her mother whispering the last words she had spoken to her in the desert: *You are the daughter of Oren Harvey. You are the daughter of Englan Chrisholm. You are Silho Brabel.*

Silho's fear disintegrated. She lifted her head and exhaled a massive blast of flames out of her mouth, the power of the Skreaf masses channelling through her body and out. The glass panels of the machine exploded from the fury of the fire and Silho saw the Skreaf hordes standing frozen, trapped in a glowing light – and then, in an instant, they were gone. Silho collapsed to the ground. The rock rumbled underneath her and the machine slid backwards as the edge of the plateau gave way. From a distance, someone called her name, the voice echoing to silence as her mind slipped into darkness.

379

44

Eli threw himself to the ground of the cell block with curses flying over his head. People fell all around him as he dragged himself forward on his stomach, towards the last cell where the Skreaf held Kry. The walls shuddered and moaned in a terrible way. Boots thudded onto his back, bricks collapsed in and one of the captives crashed down in front of him. Her face was completely black from a death-curse, the features mashed into each other. He forced himself to crawl over the body, inching closer and closer to the cell, unseen because of his size.

He reached the cell and rushed to the bench where Kry fought to free himself. The witches had inserted tubes into Kry's wrists and were draining his blood into glass containers beside the table. Eli touched the Androt's arm and Kry turned his head and stared down at him. His grey eyes were glazed, his face sickly pale. With the Skreaf distracted, Eli was able to remove the drains from the Androt's arms and work on the chains binding him to the table. Kry struggled as well and together they managed to break him free. Eli helped him to sit up. The Androt's eyes widened and he pointed weakly upward to a painting on the ceiling. Gnarled Skreaf hands were reaching out of the painting and one of witches standing in the cell with them was lifting up a jar of Kry's blood.

'No!' Eli yelled. He lunged, and, with the incredible speed of his hands, knocked the jar out of the witch's grasp before the other demons could take it. It crashed to the floor and shattered, spilling white blood everywhere. Some of the blood splattered the roof painting and vanished. The witch Eli had attacked screamed in fury and grabbed him by the neck. She lifted him off the ground. He buzzed his wings, trying desperately to pull back, but couldn't prise the witch's claws off his throat. Nelly burst out of his pocket, scurried up his side and sank her sharp little teeth into the witch's skin. The demon shrieked and flung them both against the wall. Eli smashed into the bricks and crashed to the ground. He shook his head, dazed, and struggled to his knees. Nelly scrambled back into his pocket as the Skreaf and two others strode towards him, their terrible red eyes locked onto his face. Kry jumped up, already recovering, and grabbed the steel bench where he had been tied. He ripped it off the ground and smashed it down onto the witches' heads with brutal force. Two of the Skreaf turned on him, one trying to restrain him, while the other grabbed another full jar of blood. The third witch kept coming at Eli. Her face contorted horribly, the Skreaf demon pressing out from behind her skin. She lifted her hand and started a death-curse.

'No, please!' Eli cried out. He tried to leap aside, but the witch kicked him hard in the chest, shattering his ribs. She smashed his head against the ground and threw him back into the corner. He stared up at her through blood streaming down his face. She re-started the curse and Eli saw there was no escape. His body convulsed and burned inside.

Through watering eyes, Eli saw the shadows behind the Skreaf forming into a shape, a face, an animal snarl. The pure white wolf he had freed from the house sprang out of midair and smashed into the Skreaf's back. The big creature grabbed the witch by the neck and shook her. Luther materialised from the shadows in front of Eli. The Midnight Man was unrecognisable, his features now sharp and striking, his body bulky with muscle. He helped Eli to his feet. Behind Luther, Kry was struggling with two Skreaf, who were lifting him towards the grasping hands reaching down from the porthole ceiling. They started to drag him through.

'Stop them!' Eli yelled. Luther launched himself at the witches with the terrifying ferocity of a full-grown Midnight Man. His arm-span shadow spread unnaturally wide. He attacked the Skreaf, flinging them around the cell like an animal killing its prey. Eli tried to heave Kry down from the ceiling. The white wolf leapt up to help him, savaging the demon's hands. Caesar and the other bosses appeared at Eli's side and seized Kry, hauling him down. The Skreaf outside of the cell closed in on the bars, their screams becoming a droning chant. Eli blinked as the light of the porthole intensified. He felt himself being dragged upwards towards it. The walls of the cell split, and a crack ran along the floor from one side of the cell to the other.

'Luther, get the Androt out of here!' Eli yelled to the Midnight Man.

Luther snatched up Kry and tried to dissipate into the shadows, but the dark magics snared them in the cell. The demons chanted louder and louder. Eli yelled as his feet left the ground and an unstoppable force dragged them all towards the porthole. Suddenly, a brilliant white light exploded from the painting, slamming Eli's body back down to the cell floor. The demons started screeching, not with anger or triumph, but with fear. Eli lay flat on the ground with his hands over his head. The lights flared to an unbearable brightness and then zapped backward into the ceiling, leaving them in the relative darkness of the solitary, twitching fluoro light just outside the cell.

Eli blinked, two glowing orbs hung before his eyes from where the light had burned into his vision. He looked around at the wreckage of the cell block. The Skreaf were gone and ash covered everything. Survivors from the captives and the gangsters were starting to rise shakily from the ground. Eli turned to Kry. He had dragged himself up, white blood dripping from the wounds in his wrists. As Eli watched, the wounds began to close over. Caesar and his lion shadow were helping the gangsters. Luther and the wolf had vanished. They reminded him.

'Ev'r!' he cried out.

He scrambled up and used the last of his energy to run out of the cell block and stumble over the books. He pushed back into the dark room with the cages. Blue light shone through the partially destroyed opposite wall. Eli rushed to it and clambered over the bricks and into the laboratory. It was a complete wreck with nothing intact. His boots crunched on glass as he picked his way through the rubble, lifting boards and looking under rocks, searching for any sign of Ev'r.

He found his way to where the doorway had stood, now just a ragged hole in the fractured wall. As he stepped through, his boots kicked against something that rattled. He looked down. Ev'r's black blade, the Morsus Ictus, lay on the ground, and beside that, a ripped and discarded pile of clothes. Eli dropped to his knees and sifted through the rags until he felt something hard. He grabbed out an object wrapped in fabric and found it was Solace, Oren Harvey's knife.

A draught from above made Eli look up. A rift had been torn in the concrete ceiling, struck with so much raw power that a jagged outline of the form that had made it remained in the crumbling rock – something huge with wings. *Ravien.*

'No, Ev'r,' Eli breathed. He closed his eyes and his head sank forward to the ground. He didn't have the strength to lift it. He had failed her. The legendary treasure hunter Ev'r Keets, Zingara Ohavor, was gone. He felt Nelly nuzzling his cheek. He blinked and collapsed.

45

Copernicus lunged at the falling skeleton of the Mazurus Machine and grabbed hold of Silho's charcoaled form. It burned his skin, but he held tight, refusing to let her go. He lurched forward as the rock crumbled out from underneath him, and he, Silho and the Mazurus fell into the abyss. Jude's metal hand locked onto Copernicus' ankle and held him and Silho as the machine dropped from around them into the blackness below. As Jude hauled them back up onto the central pillar, the whole chamber began to quake. Rocks pelted them from above and lava spewed up from the abyss. The desperate screams of Morsmalus shook the air.

'The whole place is sinking!' Diega yelled.

The central pillar rocked, unstable, and Copernicus ordered, 'Jump across!'

With Silho in his arms, he sprinted the length of the plateau and leapt over the chasm to the other side where the Skreaf hordes had been gathered. He landed in the ash that now covered the ground, the only remnants of the demons. Diega and Jude skidded in beside him.

'Head for the wall!' he instructed and took off towards the base of the rocky cliff below where he and Silho had entered the chamber. He held Silho close to him. She was burned black and unrecognisable. It was completely unimaginable that anyone could survive such injuries, but he could feel her faint breath against his neck. He didn't allow himself to hope; he just ran. Diega and Jude stayed close, the Fen morphing falling boulders into pebbles that rained down on their heads. Behind and all around them, freed spectral-breeds drifted in the same direction, using Cos magics to divert the rock projectiles.

'Where's Shawe?' Jude yelled to Copernicus.

The commander glanced back and sent out his senses. They locked onto the gangster's body-heat. Shawe was hauling himself out of the abyss, a red-haired boy – his brother, Stacy – slung over one shoulder. The spectral-breeds drifted up and around the brothers, their magics keeping the caving roof from crushing the pair, but the spectrals were dispersing quickly and soon their protection would lift.

'Shawe!' Copernicus yelled back to him. 'Get out!'

Shawe didn't hear him, but noticed the danger and felt the ground sinking. Carrying his brother, he bolted for the closest cliff face.

The commander reached the wall and ran upwards on the quaking rocks. The ground was sinking fast below them. He forced his muscles to move to absolute overload and made it to the top. He clambered over the edge and kept moving, running along the tunnel where the Wraith had led them. He sensed Jude and Diega close behind. They passed back through the chambers, the magics now broken and ineffectual, and up the staircase into the carnival land. Everywhere deep chasms split the ground, dragging down screaming demons.

Copernicus ran towards a light up ahead. He looked over his shoulder and saw Shawe among the hordes of spectral-breeds following them. They made it to the light and leapt through the porthole. Copernicus crashed to the ground on the other side. Diega and Jude landed beside him. Shawe smashed down on top of him. The spectral-breeds rushed through in a flood of flowing bodies. They vanished into the walls and ceiling.

All of a sudden the flow stopped as the porthole closed on the other side. Copernicus stared up at the ceiling of Chrisholm's cell. The concrete was blank, the painting gone. He looked around at the prison block, a disaster zone covered in ash and blood and bodies. Silho shivered in his arms. Jude dragged off his cloak and laid it over her. The Ar Antarian's eyes misted over.

'He's not waking up,' Shawe muttered beside them. He cradled his younger brother in his arms. The boy's face was a disturbing pale grey.

'We have to get them help, now,' Copernicus said. He stood and carried Silho from the prison area. As he reached the open door, he registered voices up ahead and followed the sound through the crumbling walls of two wrecked rooms to where a group of people, of all different races, stood gathered around someone lying on the ground. Copernicus shouldered through the small crowd and found Eli struggling to sit up. The commander crouched down and gripped Eli's shoulder. Eli stared at him in confusion at first then threw his arms around Copernicus and hugged tight.

'I couldn't save her,' Eli whispered. 'She's gone.' Copernicus saw the imp-breed was clutching two blades, Solace and the Morsus Ictus.

'Eli,' Copernicus said to him. 'Silho needs help.'

Eli raised his head and the commander nodded to the cloak covering Silho. Eli peeked under it and horror widened his eyes.

'She may still be able to regenerate,' Copernicus said. 'But we have to get her out of here.'

Eli nodded and staggered to his feet. The gathered crowd stepped back to give him room. He grabbed an object out of the rubble and hauled it onto his back. Copernicus recognised Ev'r Keets' backpack.

'There's a way out through there.' Eli pointed then hesitated. He stared at something behind Copernicus. The commander turned.

Jude and Kry stood face-to-face. Other Androt survivors clustered around them. The brothers studied each other for several long moments before Kry said, 'I always sensed you were out there. Did you?'

Jude considered the words. 'Something was missing.'

'Come with us,' Kry said.

'To where?' Jude asked.

'To war.'

'I've just been to war.' Jude clutched the pieces of SevenM against his chest.

'Not *a* war,' Kry said, '*the* war, for our people. You can help us. You've lived with the enemy. You know their secrets, their weaknesses. You would be a great asset. We'll destroy everyone that has oppressed us.'

Jude narrowed his vivid blue eyes. 'I don't want to destroy anyone. I want to help our people more than anything, but in peaceful ways.'

Kry's enthusiasm turned to a sneer. 'You're a soldier. There is nothing peaceful about you. Obviously you're confused, but I can help you.' He held out his hand. 'Come to where you belong.'

Jude glanced at Diega standing beside him, then at Copernicus and Eli. 'I am where I belong.'

Kry's grey eyes hardened to stone. 'Then you're dead to me,' he said. He spoke to the Androts around them. 'It's our time.'

He turned and headed down the tunnel. The majority of Androts followed him. Some did not. Everyone moved to get out of their way. The shadows stirred in their wake and Caesar K-Ruz stepped into the light. He glanced at Kry's retreating form, then back to the gathered group. His glowing golden eyes locked onto Shawe. Copernicus cursed silently. He was completely unarmed and carrying Silho. He wouldn't be able to move fast enough before Caesar got a shot off. He looked to Diega, but she shook her head. Neither she nor Jude held any weapons. Copernicus spoke an enchant, vanishing himself and Silho from Caesar's sight. It was the only thing he could do. The Pride boss stepped closer, his focus not diverting from Shawe. Shawe held his brother against him and watched Caesar move towards them. There was nowhere for him to run. Caesar drew his electrifier and aimed it at his rival. Shawe lifted his head, waiting for the shot. He didn't bother begging for his brother's life. He knew Caesar too well. A shadow crossed K-Ruz's face. Copernicus noticed his gaze flickering towards Eli. He hesitated, then, to Copernicus' genuine shock, lowered the weapon and turned away. He headed along the tunnel, stalking after Kry. Shawe stared at the vanishing figure in disbelief.

A powerful tremor shook the tunnel, almost knocking them to the ground.

'The whole Galleria's going.' Diega stared up at the cracks spreading across the ceiling.

'This way,' Eli urged. He led the team and the survivors up into a tunnel, towards a distant light.

46

Eli knew it wasn't exactly luxury accommodation, with no lighting, no heating, no running water – no chance to work in peace without the couple in the apartment above either screaming obscenities at each other or bringing a dust storm of ceiling plaster down with the neverending squeaky thud of bedsprings. Still it wasn't *that* bad. It was, so far, safe, he had all his equipment at hand, Nelly had plenty of free-range cockroaches to hunt and crunch on and Eli was sure the smell of the place was improving with time. And best of all, the team was together, a bit cramped, but they were surviving – and that was the word of the day – *survival*. It really said something when the safest place in the city was a decrepit bordello-slash-boarding house in the centre of Moris-Isles.

In the aftermath of the Skreaf attack, King Miron XI had vanished. No one knew if he was alive or dead, only that he was gone. The Standard and the United Regiment had also fallen, their lines of command going down like dominoes, owing to the large number of governmentals, officials and soldiers who were either Skreaf, being possessed by them or in their pocket.

What followed was a rush to fill the power void. A war between the two main contenders erupted – machine-breeds against the gangs, Kry 939993 versus Caesar K-Ruz. Eli knew Kry's original plan was to have the machine-breeds against everyone else, but the Androt leader had been so occupied trying to keep Caesar from ripping out his throat that he hadn't really progressed that far. While the

two sides were throwing everything they had at each other, everyone else was just trying not to get killed – not such an easy feat with
the daily deluge of bombs and with both sides recruiting by force
anyone they thought might be useful to their cause. At this stage
of the fighting, Eli's bets were on Caesar K-Ruz, due to the simple
fact that, unlike Kry, he wasn't crazy. He was just as fanatical and
fixated on his overall plan of gang rule, but within the plan he was
flexible and changing, constantly shifting the shape of his attacks.
The Androt leader's rigid logic patterns struggled to predict Caesar's
moves. Despite all the technology at his fingertips, Kry failed on a
daily basis to hunt down the gangland boss. Kry had made the fatal
war error of not knowing his enemy, while Caesar had stepped into his time, gathering increasing support from inside and outside the
gangs. Now he was known as the King, not King of the Gangland or
King Caesar K-Ruz, just *the King* – as if he were the first and only
of all time.

Of course the minor distraction of leading a war hadn't faded
Caesar's memory of Eli's promised elixir of anti-love. To Eli's relief, he had been able to deliver – effectively halting Smudge's
affection for Caesar, without turning it to hate. Eli had questioned
the morality of tinkering with someone else's primal biological wir-
ing, but as the commander had pointed out, it wasn't as though he'd
had much choice. Breaking a promise to the King was tantamount
to suicide these days. So Caesar had collected, been impressed and
been hunting Eli ever since to acquire his skills for the gangs. The
payment for such services would be *not getting killed – at least not
by the gangsters*. Not really an exciting offer. So far the tracker team
had managed to evade K-Ruz, though Eli suspected it wasn't their
ingenious hiding places that kept Caesar back as much as the fact
that Copernicus was watching over them. Eli sensed that Caesar was
apprehensive about pushing the commander – he still wasn't sure he
could defeat him.

While the fighting continued, what was left of the soldiers of the
United Regiment had formed a new coalition known as the United
Resistance. Their position in the war was still a little fuzzy, since
they didn't want to back either side. From what he'd heard, the gen-

eral consensus was to let Kry and Caesar fight it out, and then to block whoever won from taking control. Exactly how they'd do this was still a contentious issue. Apparently there had been a lot of heated, passionate discussions on the topic, all of which were completely pointless.

The fact was that a new era was dawning, not based on a passing of time, but on a changing of events. Scorpia was shifting: to what was uncertain, but it would definitely never be the same again – which was why the commander and the team had made the decision not to join the United Resistance. They had agreed that they would remain trackers, but now they answered only to themselves. And since becoming his own boss, Eli hadn't had a break from work.

He rubbed his blurry eyes and stared at the hologram in front of him full of formulae. There were so many figures and numbers – endless possibilities – but only one answer to the question that plagued his mind. Over time imp-breeds had been called many things – tricksters, pranksters, eavesdroppers and stealers, annoyers, liars, flyers and players, cheaters, meddlers, mess-makers and risk-takers and the list could go on. One sour old scholar with his britches in a twist had long ago scripted the now infamous line – *And what can be said for Imp-breeds? These fickle, silly twitterbrains flitter about like overgrown mosquitoes, giving nothing and taking everything that isn't nailed down!* Given that this was the pigeonhole into which his kind had been stuffed, Eli found it, for want of a better word, amusing, that over the last three day-cycles he had been told that he was being obsessive on at least five separate occasions by five different people – luckily no one whose opinion mattered to him in the least – but what did this mean? Was he living proof of his race's gradual evolution from *fickle* to *fanatic* or could it be that the dusty old scholar had seen it all wrong and misjudged an entire race based on an unfortunately annoying and transient few?

Eli smiled. It wasn't a trick question. He wasn't some new breed of imp-breed. He was just himself – warts and all, obsessions and all, though he didn't see his ongoing determination to save his friend as an obsession as such. He didn't think about it all day and every night – just most of the all day and every night. It was a thin line,

391

he knew that, but who could give him an honest answer to the question of when it was the right time to abandon all hope? No one he'd spoken to so far. At least no one who was intelligent enough to understand that the more they knew the less they knew. The universe was miraculous and inside it miracles happened – like finding Ev'r Keets and restoring her from Ravien to human-breed. He'd given a promise to a friend that he didn't intend to break, even with bombs exploding all around him and close and distant electro-fire zapping in his ears, even though his otter, Nelly, had angrily gnawed a hole in his pocket and now had her sharp little teeth imbedded in the soft flesh of his upper thigh. He dragged her out and held her up to his face.

'What is it?' he asked.

Nelly looked longingly at the window.

'We can't go out. You know that,' he said. Her whiskers drooped and he felt guilty and added, 'But soon.'

He sighed and lowered his little friend onto his desk. Words he had scripted by hand onto a sheet of paper caught his attention – *Who is the Indemeus X?* It was something Ev'r had asked him when he'd revived her with the Venus Lily potion. It was a question that had replayed every night in his dreams. So far he'd found no clues to the answer.

Eli's security system sparked up and he turned to the hologram footage of the I-eyes monitoring the hallways. Silho was back. She and the rest of the team had gone out to replenish their supplies and, as always, for security reasons, they had taken separate routes back to the hide – and, as always, Silho had returned first. No one could deny Brabel's skills. Eli knew there were other people who could invent like him, morph like Diega, think like Jude and sense like the commander – but there was no one anywhere that could match Silho. She was unique, an original, and was only growing stronger and faster as time progressed.

Silho was a born leader like her mother, though it was clear to Eli that Silho Brabel would never lead – at least not while she stayed with the trackers. A saying Oren Harvey herself had once quoted in one of her famous speeches always played in Eli's mind when he thought of Silho. Oren had said that women could never win the battle of the sexes because they kept sleeping with the enemy. Silho would never take the title of commander while Copernicus owned it.

The locking mechanism of the door clanked and clinked open and Silho stepped in. She smiled at Eli, shook off her jacket and dumped it on her mattress on the floor. Silho's pictures had now spread completely over the skin of her chest and neck and around to her back, where the image of a firebird dragon was imprinted in shimmering colour. During her time of healing, Silho had confided in Eli that when she had been burning in the Mazurus, she had seen her parents, looked into their eyes and felt as though they were right there with her. Eli knew Silho was still searching for answers and only finding new questions, but now there was a certainty to her steps. She came and sat beside Eli and handed him a brown paper bag. He looked inside and saw the chemicals he'd asked her to find for his tests.

'Perfect,' he said. 'Exactly what I didn't need – *I mean* – what I needed.'

He gave an apologetic grin and Silho said, 'Any closer?'

'I'm not sure,' Eli confessed. 'Every time I think it's a breakthrough something fails.'

Silho nodded and the two sat in silence. If Eli wanted a laugh or an argument he spent time with Diega, for deep philosophical discussions he went to Jude, for black and white logic or for direction it was Copernicus, but to just sit in a comfortable silence and be, Silho was the one. He had also found in her an ally to his plans to revive Ev'r Keets. The others understood it was something he needed to do, but saw no real purpose in it. Only Silho had known a different side to the treasure hunter. He noticed she was watching the blank walls, her eyes moving over the white as though she were reading something.

'What do you see?' he asked.

She glanced his way, hesitated, then replied, 'Colours.'

'Why don't you try painting?' Eli asked.

She gave a small smile that didn't reach her eyes and shook her head.

'Anything salvageable at your apartment?' he asked.

'Not without an excavator,' Silho replied. 'Whole neighbour-hood's been flattened.'

'I'm sorry,' Eli said.

Silho shrugged. 'How's your grandmother?'

Eli sighed. 'It'd take more than a bomb to —'

The security alarm buzzed and Eli turned to the screen. Diega had beaten the commander back this time. They watched the Fen walk down the hallway. She opened the apartment door and entered the room, giving Silho a perfunctory nod and flashing a dazzling smile at Eli. She placed the bag she was carrying onto the table and opened it up. Weapons and tech spilled out onto the tabletop. Eli moved to inspect the new pieces. Some of them were complex weapons he'd never seen before.

'Where did you get them?' he said.

'An Androt stash,' Diega replied.

'Where?' Silho asked.

'It was completely unguarded,' Diega continued, turning her back on Silho. 'Bad sign for the machine-breeds.'

'You know, this is Kry's work,' Eli said examining the more elab-orate designs. 'He has a great mind.'

'For a complete psycho,' Diega added.

The door rattled and Jude entered with SevenM riding his shoulder. The Ar Antarian greeted Eli warmly, but avoided looking at either Diega or Silho. After the end of the witch war, Eli had barely been able to keep up with the shifting hormones of his team. Jude and Diega had attempted a reunion, but it had fizzled. Evidently there was such a thing as too much *stuff* happening to a relationship for it to survive. Yet as their love shattered on the rocks, the com-mander and Silho had started an unspoken *something*. A *something* that had managed to strengthen and deepen, despite the fact that the team all slept head to toe in the same tiny room and went pretty much everywhere as a group. Copernicus and Silho had a connection and Eli, being the romantic he was, liked to think of it as love. At the same time, Diega had made no secret about wanting to get back with the commander and it was painfully obvious that Jude held an in-terest for Silho. So it was more of a love square than a love triangle and it made for some seriously awkward cringing moments – loud silences, pointed conversations, longing glances, death stares. Eli told himself it was a good thing no one was interested in him, but he never managed to completely convince himself. He still felt it would be nice if for once love could be more for him than just a spectator sport. He held onto hope.

Jude dropped his backpack on the table with a heavy clunk. He opened the bag and lifted out a stack of written word books. 'I found these among the Galleria wreckage,' he told Eli. 'Thought you'd be interested.'

'You thought right!' Eli scooped up the books and held them against his chest.

'Great,' Diega said. 'At least we'll have something to feed the fire.'

Jude drew out another bag from his jacket and said, 'Medical supplies.' He shot Diega a look.

'Guns,' Diega pointed to her bag. 'To stop us from needing medicine.'

'The commander not back?' Jude asked Eli.

'He's here. He's invisible,' Diega muttered and went to look out the window. Jude narrowed his blue eyes. Eli's stomach grumbled and he gave an uncomfortable giggle.

Their surveillance system bleeped and the commander opened the door. He was carrying several packages. Eli's mouth watered as the smell of hot food hit his nostrils. They'd been eating everything out of cans for more months than he cared to count – the novelty of that had worn off right after the very first bite. The commander locked eyes with Silho, then placed the packages on the table. Eli sprang forward and ripped open the paper bags, inspecting the food. Everyone sat down to eat. These days no one needed a written invitation.

'Where did you find it?' Eli muttered with his mouth full.

'A few places have reopened in Southtown,' Copernicus replied.

Eli smiled. The adaptability of people to survive and continue even in the harshest of war zones never failed to surprise and impress him.

'How's it looking out there?' he asked.

395

'Quiet. Something must have changed overnight. No one's talking yet,' the commander said and the others nodded in agreement.

'How's Shawe?' Silho asked.

After they defeated the witches, Shawe had gathered up the survivors of his people and gone underground. His brother, Stacy, had remained ill for a long time, but the latest word said his health was slowly improving. Copernicus had gone to see the gangster for information.

'The same,' Copernicus replied and Eli took that to mean loud, proud, stinky and fierce.

'Did anyone see Luther?' he asked.

Everyone shook their head. The Midnight Man had survived his metamorphosis, but he still kept to himself. Usually the only sign that he was around was a glimpsing of the white wolf running through the shadows.

'And there's still no word on Raine,' Silho put in.

Diega sighed and said, 'How many times do you have to be told – the Wraith is dead. You're wasting time and resources. Even he thinks so.' She gestured to the commander.

Copernicus leaned back in his chair and said, 'What *I think* is that she's gone to find her soulmate, wherever death has taken him. I'd do the same.'

Diega snorted and rolled her eyes.

The security alarm rang out and the team jumped to their feet with a clattering of chairs, drawing their weapons in readiness. Eli tried to draw his, but ended up pulling Nelly out of his pocket instead. She chattered indignantly and he stuffed her back in, hoping no one had noticed. The others spread out to the different corners of the room to take aim and the commander moved to a place beside the door. He looked to Eli, who was glued to the hologram footage of the hallway, waiting for whoever had triggered the alarm to appear. Much to Eli's relief, he saw a tall Fen soldier turn the corner.

'It's just Santana,' he told the team. They relaxed their positions and holstered their weapons.

Copernicus opened the door to let the rainbow-skinned sniper commander in. Santana saluted the commander as he always had.

After Eli and the others were marked as state traitors, the Regiment had imprisoned Santana for refusing to follow orders against them. He was now one of the main leaders of the United Resistance. He nodded to each of the team in turn then spoke.

'I came to tell you that the war is over. Kry has been defeated and the Androts are surrendering. Caesar K-Ruz has called a meeting. He's willing to hear from the different factions on their views of the future of the city.'

'Sure it's not a trap?' Diega asked.

'We believe it's genuine,' Santana replied. 'And we won't be going in unarmed.' His focus shifted back to the commander. 'We need the trackers there. I need your guidance. Will you come?'

Copernicus considered it then said, 'Give us a moment.'

Santana started back down the corridor, but paused to add, 'There's another thing – there was a murder in one of our refugee camps. It's brutal and it doesn't make any sense to me. Would you and the team take a look after the meeting?'

Copernicus agreed, but Eli noticed the commander narrow his eyes in an uneasy way. The team gathered up their weapons and equipment. Jude lagged, distracted by thoughts.

'Alright?' the commander asked him.

The Ar Antarian nodded. 'Kry made his choices. He wanted war. I'm just thinking, what will happen to the machine-breeds now? To the innocent? They've been enslaved for so long and now this . . .'

'They're going to need help and support, a strong voice to speak for them,' the commander said. 'This is the beginning of a new society, a new order. There is opportunity for change.'

'Who will ever trust them after this war? Who will pity them?' Jude asked.

'You will. I will. They will.' He nodded to the rest of the team. He handed Jude an electrifier and the Ar Antarian took it.

The commander left the apartment and the others followed. Eli was the last. He dashed around the room in an excited frenzy, stuffing random odds and ends into his belt and bag, until he forced himself to stop. He checked Nelly was snuggled safely in his pocket and went to the open doorway. There he paused to look back at his work desk, back to the possibilities, the chances – the hidden solution waiting to be discovered.

'I'll find you,' he whispered.

He closed the door behind him and ran to catch up with the team.

Acknowledgements

All my love to my husband, George, for his belief, encouragement and support, and to the lights of my life – my boys, Josef and Daniel and niece, Charlotte.With love and deepest gratitude to my family – Mum, Dad, Berto and Emma, and Milena, Voislav, Igor and Alex.

Infinite gratitude to my incredible agent, Sophie Hamley, the person who has made all the difference. Words cannot express.

More thanks than I can ever say to all at Momentum Books, most especially to Joel Naoum and Mark Harding for their creative vision and support. Enormous gratitude to my amazing editors, Alexandra Nahlous and Sarah Hazelton.

For reading early drafts and for their continual encouragement, my heartfelt thanks and love to two wonderful friends, Claire Byrnes and Karla Johnston.

Eternal gratitude to my first mentors Judith Lukin-Amundsen, Hilary Beaton, Althea Halliday and Miss Dawn. Your words are indelibly printed in my mind.

And finally to the writers who have drawn me into their worlds and inspired me to dream beyond the walls of reality. I am indebted forever.

www.ingramcontent.com/pod-product-compliance
Lightning Source LLC
Chambersburg PA
CBHW020507020726
47493CB00001B/215